A
PORTRAIT
OF LOYALTY

Books by Roseanna M. White

LADIES OF THE MANOR

The Lost Heiress
The Reluctant Duchess
A Lady Unrivaled

SHADOWS OVER ENGLAND

A Name Unknown
A Song Unheard
An Hour Unspent

THE CODEBREAKERS

The Number of Love
On Wings of Devotion
A Portrait of Loyalty

THE CODEBREAKERS • 3

A PORTRAIT OF LOYALTY

ROSEANNA M. WHITE

BETHANYHOUSE

a division of Baker Publishing Group
Minneapolis, Minnesota

Published by Bethany House Publishers
11400 Hampshire Avenue South
Bloomington, Minnesota 55438
www.bethanyhouse.com

Bethany House Publishers is a division of
Baker Publishing Group, Grand Rapids, Michigan

Printed in the United States of America

ISBN 978-0-7642-3183-4

Scripture quotations are from the King James Version of the Bible.

This is a work of historical reconstruction; the appearances of certain historical figures are therefore inevitable. All other characters, however, are
products of the author's imagination, and any resemblance to actual persons,
living or dead, is coincidental.

Cover design by LOOK Design Studio
Cover photography by Mike Habermann Photography, LLC

Author is represented by The Steve Laube Agency.

20   21   22   23   24   25   26   7   6   5   4   3   2   1

Plead my cause, O LORD, with them that
     strive with me: fight against them that
     fight against me.
Take hold of shield and buckler, and stand up
     for mine help.
Draw out also the spear, and stop the way
     against them that persecute me: say unto
     my soul, I am thy salvation.

                                   —Psalm 35:1–3

Prologue

He could see it all so clearly. As the renewed rocking of the train lulled his fellow passengers to sleep, Zivon Marin watched the pattern of their movements. The shrug of one shoulder, the stretch of two different legs, the shifting of heads. One's cough jerked another from the edge of slumber, the jerking causing a repositioning of someone else. Cause and effect. Ripples. Patterns that played out with such consistency he could predict who would fall asleep first and who last.

The door at the end of the car opened, both the wind and Evgeni blustering in. Pulling tired eyes open. Igniting French grumbles.

Zivon's hand fisted around the ruby ring he wore—would always wear—on his right ring finger. This was what he could never anticipate with accuracy. The sudden interference to the pattern. His brother entering a train car . . . Lenin uniting those disorganized Bolsheviks.

The bullet to Alyona's head.

Zivon's eyes slammed shut. No rest came with closed eyes,

not for him. Every time he blinked too long, he saw her again. Crumpled on his doorstep. A warning. An accusation.

"Are you going to let me in or keep those long legs of yours blocking my path?" Out of the politeness Matushka had drilled into them both, Evgeni spoke in French.

With his eyes closed, Zivon heard more clearly what had been needling him in his brother's voice for weeks. He'd first called it resentment—Evgeni hadn't wanted to flee Russia. It had also reminded him of petulance—his little brother had never been one to let Zivon take the lead without arguing, no matter how many times he'd proven his decisions wise.

But there was something else in his voice Zivon hadn't detected before. Perhaps it was new. Or perhaps it had only now worked its way through the fog of his devastation.

It didn't sound like resentment or petulance. It sounded like . . . satisfaction.

Slowly, Zivon opened his eyes and looked at his brother. He tried to see him not as Evgeni—his brother for whom he'd do anything, sacrifice anything, whom he hadn't been able to imagine leaving home without—but as just another person obeying his own patterns.

The angle of his head—cocky. The gleam in his eyes—knowing. The way he moved—more energized than he ought to be at midnight in third class on a train taking him ever farther away from the home he hadn't wanted to leave.

The hand hovering too near the pocket of his trench coat.

Zivon moved his legs out of the way. "You were gone a long time, Zhenya."

Evgeni chuckled. "I wasn't quite eager to fold myself back into this sardine can."

Joviality that masked . . . something. He didn't know what. And didn't want to waste time dissecting it. He had to remain focused. Get to Paris, find a room for a few days, get messages to the codebreaking divisions of the French and British governments. One or the other would hire him. They *had* to. It was Russia's best hope.

Evgeni settled back in his seat with a grunt, reaching for the bag stuffed under his seat. Zivon narrowed his eyes as his brother opened it, unable to think why he'd find it necessary to get his satchel out *now*.

Another grunt, and Evgeni shoved the bag at him. That, at least, was easy to understand. He'd pulled out Zivon's bag, not his own. There, right on top, was the photo album he hadn't let out of arm's reach in weeks. Sentimentality, everyone would think. They'd be partly right.

He rested a hand on the smooth leather cover, stared at it, through it, without really thinking about either the photos within or the encrypted message he'd stored behind the portrait of Batya and Matushka. He was still watching his brother.

Watching as Evgeni, humming as though all was right with the world, settled his own bag in his lap. Watching as he drew from his pocket the identification papers he'd managed to procure for them—with false names. Watching as he slid the passport into the bag.

But not just the passport. The edge of another paper peeked out.

Fast as a snake, Zivon shot out his arm and grabbed the bag's strap before Evgeni could shove it down to the floor again. Slow as a tiger's crouch, he lifted his eyes to his brother's.

They didn't look alike. Not really. But they had the same eyes. Batya's eyes. And Evgeni's burned now with the same temper that had made their father a noted fist-fighter . . . but an officer who never advanced as far as he should have in the Imperial Army. His brother growled, "What are you doing, Zivon?"

He switched his words to Russian. "What are *you* doing, Zhenya? Where were you when the train stopped to take on water?"

It couldn't be anything big. Anything important. Perhaps he'd found a girl to charm—he always did. It couldn't be anything *real*.

But Zivon was keenly aware of that encrypted message under his own hand. Of the knowledge that somewhere in this region, German officers were rumbling about mutiny. And somewhere, a Prussian soldier sympathetic to the Bolsheviks had told Lenin about them.

Evgeni snorted a laugh in that way he always did when he was trying to put Zivon off the scent of something. He opened his mouth.

But no words came out. Or if they did, they were lost under the sudden screeching of metal on metal.

The floor beneath them bucked. The car pitched. The soft snores from two seats behind them turned to screams. His own joined them. Screams to God. Screams for his brother. Screams of pain.

Then darkness swallowed the train whole.

1

Lilian Blackwell held her breath and inched along the wall, praying with every footfall that Mama wouldn't look up. That the hurried explanation she'd offered the housekeeper would suffice. That she'd be able to slip out the door without the need for any more lies to slip past her lips. She put a hand over the camera in her pocket to keep it from banging against her leg—Mama had ears as sensitive as a rabbit's—and prepared for the most dangerous part of her escape: darting past the open drawing room doorway.

As she edged a little closer, she caught her sister's gaze inside the room. Ivy, blue eyes twinkling, pressed her lips against a smile and turned to their mother. "So, who's coming for dinner tonight, Mama? Officers, gentlemen, or both?"

Bless her. Lily waited until her mother dipped her brush into her oils and began to answer, then dashed by. She made it two whole steps past the door too. Then, "Lily! Is that you?"

Blast. Lily let the pumps she'd been carrying drop to the floor and slid her feet into them before moving to the door. Not *through* it, though. She didn't have much time. "Yes, Mama."

Her mother looked away from her painting with a smile as bright as the spring sunshine, though it froze and her brows arched when she saw Lily's uniform, complete with kerchief pinned over her hair. "I thought you weren't working today, my love. That you and Ivy had both taken the morning off."

She wasn't. Not at the hospital, at least. But she'd known she might be stopped, so the uniform had seemed like her best option. Especially given the note that had arrived an hour ago. "I wasn't, but Ara just sent word that they're shorthanded and asked if I could come in."

Those were, in fact, the words on the note that she'd left resting on the entryway table for her mother to find later. But Arabelle Denler, her friend and newly reinstated matron of their ward at Charing Cross Hospital, hadn't been the one to pen them.

Mama sighed. "I suppose since Ivy will be leaving soon for her appointment, I shouldn't bemoan the interruption to your time together. So long as you're home at a reasonable hour, of course. Don't forget we have guests tonight."

As they did at least twice a week. Lily darted a glance at her little sister and found Ivy grinning at the magazine she held. "I won't forget."

"And invite Miss Denler and her fiancé to dine with us soon. The week after next, perhaps?"

"I will." When she actually *saw* Ara. Though there was, she supposed, the possibility that she'd run into said fiancé today. She edged backward a step. "Well, I don't want to distract you, Mama. I know you're hoping to finish the central figure today while the light's right. You'd better make the most of it before Ivy needs to keep her appointment."

The mere mention of the painting underway urged her mother's gaze back to the canvas, as it usually did. "Mm."

Ivy's eyes went wide at whatever she'd just seen in her magazine, and she flipped the page a bit too quickly. Quickly enough that it garnered their mother's attention and made the lazy pug sleeping in the sunshine open one eyelid.

"What is it?"

"Nothing." Poor, sweet Ivy. A flush stole into her cheeks, giving her away. Lily might be the one who inherited Euphemia Blackwell's strawberry-blond hair, but Ivy, despite sharing their father's brown locks, had a redhead's propensity to blush.

Mama lifted one red-gold brow and held out her hand.

With a gusty sigh, Ivy flipped the page back to the one she'd clearly wanted to avoid talking about and held it up rather than relinquishing it to their mother's paint-stained fingertips.

Lily didn't need to look to know what it would be. Not given that particular frown on Mama's face. "More propaganda." She said it as though it were a curse word—odd, since Daddy could say the same word with fondness. Lily edged back another step.

Ivy put the magazine down. "I think it's rather brave of those artists to go to the front and try to find something beautiful in a war so utterly wretched."

"No, Ivy." Mama turned back to her canvas, leaning close to paint a highlight onto the beautiful young woman she was bringing to life with her paints—the one fashioned to look like the beautiful young woman sitting on the couch for her now, decked out in Grecian robes that would have been comical in any other house. "What it is, is dishonest. And disgraceful. The Crown has made a mockery of both the war effort *and* art by asking artists to produce work like that."

Lily clenched her teeth and pivoted on her heel before the all-too-familiar argument could really unwind. It was one of her mother's favorite topics these days, and the threads of her arguments never ceased to tangle Lily up.

"Lilian."

Double blast. There was never any escape from these snarls. She paused, hand over her pocket, but didn't fully turn again. "Yes, Mama?"

"I see you have your camera with you. Enjoy the day, of course, but *do* keep an eye on the time, my love. I mean it."

Ivy chuckled and leaned back on the chaise as her painted counterpart was doing. "Now, Mama. She's only been late for dinner two of the last six times we had guests."

Lily stuck out her tongue at her sister, earning a fuller laugh, and then rushed away with a final farewell before her mother could come up with anything else to detain her. It wasn't as though she was habitually late in general. But it was difficult to motivate herself to get home in time for yet another tiresome dinner party populated by the most boring young men left in London.

She let herself out the door and hurried down the front steps, aiming her feet south toward St. James' Park, through which she would walk to get to Whitehall. First, though, she paused to pull off the kerchief and stuff it into her handbag. That thing was the worst part about being in the Voluntary Aid Detachment and serving at the hospital.

A motorcar puttered somewhere behind her. A few well-dressed women in an open carriage clopped toward her. Lily drew a long breath of spring air into her lungs and slid her eyes closed for a second. Two. Just enough to push it all down yet again. To call up the reasons she did what she did.

Brakes squealed, pulling her eyes open in time to see the door of the automobile push out, revealing a uniform in naval blue behind the steering wheel. "Get in. And hurry up, will you? I've been driving in circles for ten minutes already, and the admiral needs his car this morning."

Grinning, Lily hopped in and closed the door behind her, leaning over to press a kiss to her father's cheek. "Sorry. Mama saw me on my way out."

Daddy's smile was fleeting. "I didn't think she would give you any trouble if she thought you were going to the hospital."

"Not trouble—just the usual warnings to be home on time." She wasn't even going to mention the propaganda, as she had no desire to bring it up. "Is there an assignment waiting already, or will Admiral Hall want to speak with me?"

"I believe he left you written instructions, including the time by which he needs the results. We'll be cutting it close for him to get to an appointment on time."

She didn't have to ask why her father hadn't left the admiral his car and fetched her in his own. It wouldn't do to risk Mama glancing out the window and spotting him picking Lily up. Usually it was easy to make excuses for riding together, but not on a day when Daddy had already been at the office for hours before he summoned her. Though he *could* have just let her make the twenty-minute trip on foot or the tube.

"Well." She shot him a smile. "As long as I can get it finished before the dinner party this evening. Mama was rather insistent that I not be late again."

Her father chuckled and turned at the corner. "I'm certain you'll find our guests riveting tonight, Lily White. Who knows but that one of them will sweep you off your feet and steal you away from us."

He always said that. Twice a week. Each and every time they entertained more of the young men he brought home. Most of them were navy men, of course, because what captain didn't want his daughter to marry a fine, upstanding officer? But occasionally he invited veterans from the army, home to recuperate from trench fever, or an academic who'd been refused service for one reason or another, poor chap.

She had no desire to ask who it would be tonight. If she showed the slightest curiosity, he would spend the entire drive listing the virtues of Lieutenant This and Professor That. And while she knew her friends considered her lucky to have a parade of young men around in these days when so few were in London, she just wanted to get through the war. Be done with the secrets.

The two parts of her life came to mind. Charing Cross Hospital on Agar Street, where she went in the mornings. Where she did the volunteer work of which her mother approved. And along Whitehall Street, the Old Admiralty Building. Where she brought very different skills to the aid of the navy. Where she did the work of which her *father* approved.

Her parents disagreed about so little. How had she managed to get caught in the middle of one of their few arguments?

A minute later, the parade grounds were before them, and then Daddy was navigating around the building, to the rear entrance she always used. Out of sight of anyone who might recognize her. He pulled the car up to the curb, where Admiral Hall himself opened her door for her. No doubt because he needed her and Daddy out so he and his driver could get in.

Still, he greeted her with a warm smile and a few rapid blinks. "Lilian. I appreciate your coming in on such short notice."

"My pleasure, sir." She put her hand in his so he could help her out. "Daddy says there are instructions awaiting me?"

Hall nodded. "If you have any questions, just send a note up to Commander James. He's been briefed on the project."

"I will. Thank you."

"We'll see you at dinner tonight." With a tip of his cap, he slid into the seat she'd just vacated.

Daddy had gotten out too, and Hall's driver had taken the wheel. Apparently, they really had no time to waste; it was unusual for her father's friend to be so quick in his greetings. But when one was the Director of the Intelligence Division, sometimes one's time was not one's own.

She smiled and waved as they pulled away again, stepping

to her father's side. "I take it he and Mrs. Hall are among the guests tonight?"

"Mm. As well as a few young officers, of course, to entertain you and Ivy Green." He gave her an indulgent smile.

Lily put one of her own in its proper place. She knew he was trying to help, trying to see that she and Ivy were cared for. That they would have a future full of security and family. She never had the heart to tell him that she couldn't let herself think of the future quite yet. Not when it took so much effort just to navigate today.

He didn't understand how hard it was for her to keep this part of her life from Mama. When she'd mentioned it once, years ago, he'd just waved her off and insisted she would get used to it. He, after all, had been keeping secrets from her mother throughout their entire marriage. It was necessary when one had a job like his.

But it was altogether different for her. Mama never tried to be involved in Daddy's work. But she maintained that her daughters' business was very much under her jurisdiction.

Lily drew in a deep breath and turned toward the entrance. "Well, I had better get to it. I daren't be late again today."

Daddy chuckled and walked with her to the door. "If you want to drive home together, send a note up. Though I do need to stop at the bank this afternoon."

Lily took care not to react. She avoided the bank whenever she could. Stepping inside it inevitably reminded her of Johanna. Johanna, whose father had been the bank manager. Johanna, whose family had been friends with the Blackwells since they moved to the neighborhood when Lily was five. Johanna, whose family had fled home to Germany two days before war was declared.

Johanna, whom Lily had been so sure was loyal to England . . . up until she'd been proven wrong.

She smiled at the guard who held the door open for her

17

and said over her shoulder to Daddy, "With a bit of luck, this won't take that long and I'll be able to leave before you. But if not, I'll certainly let you know."

Her father nodded. "I'll wait to hear from you. Let me know if you have need of anything, dearest."

"I will." Though in general, Admiral Hall saw to it that she had absolutely anything she needed. In addition to her magnificent retouching desk, her darkroom at the OB also had drying racks, solutions, gels, frames, scalpels, brushes, paints, ink, an electric fan, and even a heater to speed up the drying process when they were really pressed for time.

Her hand rested on her camera. "Have a good day, Daddy."

He smiled, but the shadows never left his eyes these days. Not fully. "I'll have a good day once we've routed the Boche for good." He hurried up the stairs.

She watched him for a moment. The war had aged him. Four years ago, his hair had still been a rich brown, his face scarcely lined, his form robust. These days, there was more salt than pepper in his hair, he looked older than his fifty-two years, and his tall frame had gone gaunt.

Perhaps some of it could be blamed on the illness within the first six months of the war that had landed him behind a desk instead of on his ship. But she suspected it was more because of the war itself, and the responsibilities that came with that desk.

Turning to the familiar stone steps, she padded down to the rooms she had made her own. The door was closed, as always. She let herself in, turned on the lights, and smiled at the beautifully ordered chaos. Mama had her oils and watercolors and canvas. Lily had her solutions and gels and baths. But this was her art. Perhaps it wasn't art that would make her a household name, an accolade Euphemia Blackwell could claim.

But it made a difference.

And that was what kept her coming back here day after day, developing and altering photos for the admiral. Her mother wouldn't approve, not of the second part of her job. But her country needed her. Needed her skills.

She settled at her table and skimmed her eyes over what Hall had left for her—two photos to combine by three o'clock, when the field agent in need of it would pick it up before disappearing into the Continent again.

She smiled and turned for her scalpel. Getting out on time today would be no trouble at all.

2

Zivon Marin gripped his briefcase and breathed a silent prayer. It had taken him weeks of watching, waiting, and gauging to be ready to sit in this chair before Admiral Hall's desk. He had known the moment a return telegram reached him in Paris that he would work quite happily with his czar's allies against the Central Powers. But that hadn't meant he could trust them with his own country's secrets.

The admiral gave him the easy smile of a man who knew well he held this portion of Zivon's future in his hands. "How are you settling in, Marin? Any questions for me?"

Zivon splayed a hand across the flat side of his briefcase. "Yes, actually. I received my paycheck today—thank you. But I have not a bank here in London."

"Ah, of course. I'll refer you to mine. Well, many of us here use it. I'll just jot the name down, shall I? And the direction?" Even as he spoke, the admiral pulled forward a piece of paper and a pen.

Zivon waited for him to scratch a few of the words onto the paper. Let him engage his mind in something positive, something easy. Then he drew in a breath and moved to the real subject he'd wanted to broach. "There is one other thing, sir. Directly before I fled Russia, my colleagues and I were still trying to do the work we had always done, despite Russia pulling out of the war. I intercepted a message that may be of interest to you."

Hall paused, pen halfway through a word, and blinked up at him. "Oh?"

Zivon forced his hands to relax, his face to stay neutral. Still. Empty of any doubt. "Yes. From a soldier in the Prussian army, but who is apparently sympathetic to the soviet cause. He heard German officers whispering about a mutiny in the German ranks."

Hall sucked in a breath. "Mutiny. I've not heard these rumblings."

Not until that moment did Zivon realize he'd been hoping England already had the same decrypt in their archives. That would make it all so much easier. "I had not either, until then."

Hall leaned back, tossing his pen to his desk and steepling his fingers. "Implications? Why would this Prussian have alerted someone to this—the soviets, I presume, if you intercepted it?"

Zivon nodded. "Everyone knows that the White Army has been asking for assistance from Allied forces."

"Ah." Hall tapped his fingers to his lips. "Yes, of course. So the Bolsheviks would be quite interested in those allies staying busy in Europe."

"Exactly." A fleeting smile touched Zivon's lips. At least he never had to explain anything to his new superior.

Thoughts raced through the admiral's eyes. "You have a copy of this message?"

"I . . . had." Zivon couldn't quite contain the wince. "It was in my bag, lost in the train accident in France."

And just as quickly as the thoughts had raced in Hall's eyes, they stilled. The light went dark. The fingers lowered.
Dismissed.

"Well." His tone still sounded casual. Interested. Friendly. But he might as well have ordered Zivon from his office then and there. "You know my dilemma, then. Without the actual message to give credence to this information, I must classify it as rumor more than fact."

Of course he knew that. But in Russia, his word would have been enough. Not to take action, perhaps, but to look into it. To search for other evidence.

But as every single thing in this place kept hammering home, he was not in Russia anymore. No one here knew him. No one trusted him. No one . . . *He* was no one.

"We'll keep our eyes and ears open." With another easy smile, Hall sat forward again and folded the paper. Held it out. "And if this mutiny does happen, we'll be ready to strike."

"Nyet!" It came out too vehemently. Zivon knew it the moment his lips parted. Knew how it would sound. He sighed. "If the Revolution has taught me anything, Admiral, it is that when the people cry out against their leaders, rebellion cannot be put down by an outside force coming against them in strength. That will give them reason to rally and forget their complaints for another day or week or month. If we want to encourage this mutiny, we must convince them that those complaints—their own superiors—*are* the enemy, the only one worth bothering with. Turn them on themselves, not on you."

As his people had done with their own government. Their czar.

Hall just blinked at him. "Interesting theory. I'll consider that idea, of course. But I daresay I'd have a hard time convincing any of the brass to back away if such a thing happened rather than doubling their efforts."

That was the true power of the Director of Intelligence, though, wasn't it? It had been in Moscow. Hall got to decide what story to tell these generals and admirals making decisions on the ground. And at this point in the war, they'd learned to listen to him.

But Hall hadn't yet learned to listen to Zivon. Though frustration filled the blood in his veins, he understood that too. Hated it but understood it. He leaned forward and took the paper with the bank's name and address. "Thank you for allowing me to speak, at any rate. And for this."

"Of course. Have a good evening, Marin."

He nodded, though it promised to be an evening just like all the rest. Solitary. Empty of anything but his own nagging thoughts and worries. He hurried from the building, glancing at the words on the page.

Hall hadn't finished whatever he'd been writing, but he'd gotten the name and street number down, and that would suffice. Zivon had studied a map of London and recognized this street name. It wasn't far off.

A few minutes of walking, then he would hand over his first paycheck from the British Admiralty. Open an account. Take the first real step toward becoming English.

English. No, not quite. He would make his home here. He would serve with loyalty. But he would never—*could* never—be anything but Russian. He would live here and become a subject of the Crown *because* he was Russian. Because this was the best way to help his people.

Assuming he could ever convince Admiral Hall to listen to him.

He needed his album. The telegram. But he didn't have that. Just as he hadn't had the money stashed in his bag, or the clothes he'd had tailor-made in Moscow after his last promotion, or the invitation from the czar that he'd promised himself he'd never part with.

Just as he didn't have his brother.

Evgeni. Lord God, where is Evgeni? Zivon forced the fist in his chest to release, his breath to ease out, back in. Every time he thought of his brother, urgency filled him. Had been filling him ever since he'd awoken in that French hospital, dazed and so very alone, Evgeni's bag with him instead of his own, and a shadowy *something* gnawing at the edges of his mind. He'd remembered feeling irritation with his brother for being gone so long, gone during the entirety of the water stop. He remembered Evgeni waking the other passengers when he came back in. And then . . . nothing. Blackness. The twisted rails that had sent the train careening had stolen a few minutes from his memory too—or, rather, the concussion had. The French doctor had assured him this was normal.

The French doctor had also said that, no, the memories wouldn't return. That it was God's blessing, really, that the mind didn't retain those moments of trauma.

God's blessing. He'd once thought he knew the meaning of that. These days, his prayers seemed to be only hollow, echoing words. Cry as he might to the Father—morning, noon, and night—only unfamiliar silence greeted him in return. Well . . . unfamiliar silence and the continued echoing of a long-ago memorized Scripture.

Be still, and know that I am God.

Zivon turned the last corner, noting the puddle in the street up ahead. The bicyclist who would have to swerve to avoid it. The oncoming car that wouldn't allow the cyclist to swerve into the road and so make the sidewalk the better option. The woman walking a few paces ahead of him who would be directly in the cyclist's path. "Madam!"

It was probably the urgency in his voice, more than the nameless call, that got her attention. She paused, turned.

The bicycle's bell jangled, and the rider called out an apology as he barely missed the woman. She clutched a hand to her chest, eyes wide. And then smiled at Zivon. "Thank you."

He nodded but made no other attempt at conversation. The bank was there, on his right.

He'd have to find the proof, find the names, find *something* to convince his new superior that he should be believed—and then consulted on what the proper course of action would be.

Because the end to this war was paramount. Only then, when hostilities were over in Europe, could the British or French or American forces spare any help for the White Army. Only then did Russia have a chance of renewed order.

Only then could the Bolsheviks be destroyed.

He thrust a hand into his pocket, wrapped his fingers around Batya's pocket watch so that the steady *tick-a-tick* could soothe him. Remind him of the eternal march onward, despite whatever disruptions came into the pattern. He let the ever-present Scripture flood his thoughts in time to the ticking.

> *He maketh wars to cease unto the end of the earth; he breaketh the bow, and cutteth the spear in sunder; he burneth the chariot in the fire. Be still, and know that I am God: I will be exalted among the heathen, I will be exalted in the earth.*

Be still. He drew in one more breath and released his grasp on the watch in his pocket.

Still. He forced the rocking of the world, of his thoughts, of his heart to halt and then forced his legs to move him forward. Through the doors. Into the elegant interior of the bank. He took his place in the back of the queue and tried to convince his pulse to stay slow and steady. Tried to convince his heart to hold tight to what his mind knew.

Despite what the Bolsheviks claimed, God was still in His heaven. He was still holding them all in His hand. He would make this war, like all wars, to cease. Zivon's job, as it had always been, was to be still, steady. To watch. Learn the patterns. So he would know when stillness should give way to action.

"Mr. Marin! Good afternoon."

Three weeks in England, and still the English words, the English pronunciation of his name, sounded strange to his ears. But he turned and smiled at the tall captain behind him. "Good afternoon, Captain Blackwell."

As strange as English sounded to his ears, it felt stranger still on his tongue. He spoke it well enough, but it never felt quite right as it emerged, not as his German and Greek and French did. And he wasn't sure he'd ever be able to truly think in it, though he was doing his best. He'd gotten permission from Admiral Hall to spend the first hour of work reading a newspaper, to get his mind accustomed to English words.

The other cryptographers seemed baffled by this practice. He'd be happy to explain his reasoning if anyone ever asked. But they were content to stare and whisper instead.

Captain Blackwell had never looked at him as though he were a display in a museum, at least. "How fortuitous that I've run into you." The captain smiled, and it looked like a lonely shaft of sunlight through the clouds ever-present in his eyes. "I've been meaning to ask you to join my family for dinner one evening."

Zivon's brows lifted. He hadn't shared an actual meal with someone in weeks. "I would be delighted, Captain. I thank you. Name the day."

The captain chuckled. "How's this evening for you? Another of my guests just cancelled—he's a bit under the weather, it seems—and my wife does detest an empty seat at the table. But if you already have plans, next week or the week after would work just as well."

How gracious of him to even consider that Zivon had plans, when surely he'd seen that their colleagues viewed him more as an oddity than a friend. Zivon knew his own smile was self-deprecating. "Tonight would be lovely."

"Excellent." A few of the clouds in his eyes shifted, though they didn't exactly flee. "I've a car outside. I'd be happy to drive you to your flat to tidy up and then to my home. It's close, I believe?"

Zivon nodded. "That is most kind. Thank you, sir."

"Next. May I help you, sir?"

The captain nodded, directing Zivon's attention back to the queue, where his turn had come. He put on what he hoped was an easy smile and approached the clerk behind her gleaming wooden counter. "Good afternoon."

If only he could speak without an accent. The woman's smile flickered, dropping into a momentary frown before she remembered herself. "Good afternoon, sir. How may I help you?"

He opened his briefcase and withdrew the crisp paycheck. "I would like to open an account and deposit this."

Now the woman's brows winged upward. No doubt she had a hard time reconciling his speech—clearly Russian—with Admiralty pay. He knew the feeling. But she produced another smile, unconvincing as it was, and said, "Of course. I'll just need to see your references."

"I beg your pardon?" His chest went tight, holding captive the air already in his lungs and barring out any fresh influx. *References?* "It is my money. I ought to be asking *you* for references."

Laughter belted out behind him, and he felt someone drawing near. Captain Blackwell, he soon realized, who leaned in and said, "I'm his reference, Miss Knight. And Admiral Hall. Let the man give you his money."

The woman's face relaxed into a smile. "Of course, Captain. My apologies, Mr. . . ." She glanced down at the check again. "Mr. Marin."

How had he become *mister* again? He had been a *kapitan* in the Imperial Navy. He'd been at the very center of the intelligence community, second in command, friends all around him, respected by his every colleague. He'd dined with Czar Nicholas, who had promised to make him chief cryptographer when Popov retired at the end of the year—a position that would have come with the honorary title of Admiral-General. Admiral-General at thirty! A far cry from the humble beginnings of a schoolteacher's son. A far cry from *this*.

Well, Matushka had always warned him against the dangers of pride. Now he couldn't even open a bank account without the mercy of strangers.

But he was alive. He'd found a new home. He wouldn't resent the demotion. He would thank God for it. Embrace it. Follow the advice of his Lord and take the lowest place at the table. He would work for his people instead of himself. Help end the war. Help restore order.

For a moment, he was back on the train, imagining what he couldn't remember—screeching and squealing and lurching. He was calling for his brother, reaching for him, grasping nothing. For a moment, the blackness was over him, a heavy blanket that whispered of death—at the hands of the war that had damaged the tracks, if not the Bolsheviks who despised him.

Then he blinked, breathed, and saw the bank clerk again, bent over the paperwork, chattering to Captain Blackwell. To his ears it sounded like nothing but babble. The words on the paper she slid across to him could have been in cuneiform for all the sense they made.

Another blink, another breath. *Be still, and know that I am God.* He counted the air in, counted it out, and the panic edged back just a bit. Their words became *words*, as did the ones on the page. English words.

He picked through them until they began to make sense and then filled in the information they were requesting. His name. His address. His place of employment. Simple answers that felt far from simple.

With Captain Blackwell signing something, too, as his reference, Zivon finally had his money safely in the hands of the bank. After indicating that he'd await his impromptu host outside, he exited back onto the busy street and drew in a deep breath.

He leaned against the stone wall behind him, letting the world rush by for a moment. Let the patterns of speech and movement soothe him.

It couldn't soothe for long. Despite the command for stillness, his mind spun. He visualized the map he'd been studying that morning. Tracing out the path to the church he'd yet to visit, where fellow Russians and Greeks would meet together. He wanted to go. *Needed* to go. But couldn't, not yet. He didn't know which Russians were friends, which had ties to the Bolsheviks. And he couldn't risk word reaching home that he was here. He didn't think Lenin's organization was ordered enough to have sent operatives after him . . . but they might if they realized who he was. What he'd done. That he knew their plans, knew their hopes.

He had to guard himself. His identity. Take care with every introduction.

But he needed help. Needed someone with friends in France to help him search for what he'd lost. His album. His papers.

His brother.

He'd considered asking Hall for that help today—but Hall didn't yet trust Zivon. So could Zivon trust Hall? He'd nearly spoken of it, but the words wouldn't come.

No. First he would try his own people—a few, carefully chosen. He would go to the embassy, using the false papers Evgeni had gotten for him. A different name for his face. He knew well that the ambassador had no ties to the Bolsheviks—not with his ties to nobility, instead. Nabokov was an imperialist, through and through, outspoken in his admiration of how Britain ruled its empire. Vastly opposed to anything socialist. Nabokov could be trusted that far, at least. And Nabokov would know his counterparts in France. Perhaps they could help.

Perhaps.

At the sound of a door falling shut nearby, Zivon opened his eyes again and smiled over at Captain Blackwell. "Thank you," he felt the necessity to say. "For your intervention in there."

The captain laughed and motioned him toward an auto parked along the curb. "Blinker—assuming it was he who referred you to this bank—ought to have remembered to provide a reference when he did so. Standard practice when one is opening a new account, I'm afraid."

"Had I known this, I would have asked explicitly for one."

Blackwell waved that away. "Not your fault." He chuckled. "They ought to show *you* references—I say, you do have a point!"

Zivon felt his lips pull up. He hadn't had much cause to smile in the last few months, but it was good to know his mouth remembered how it was done. "Perhaps. Even so, had you not been there, I suspect my observation would have earned me an escort out the door."

"Well, we can be thankful I was. You got your account, and I got a story to tell." Blackwell opened the passenger-side door and motioned for Zivon to slide in.

A familiar fragrance, scarcely discernible, teased his nose. Lavender? No . . . lily of the valley. It must be a remnant from the captain's wife. Once his host was settled behind the steering wheel, Zivon gave him the direction to his flat and then asked, "Will you tell me of your family, sir? I am afraid I know little."

Blackwell's face creased into lines worn by smiling, smoothing out a few of the ones that must be from worry. "My wife is Euphemia Blackwell—a rather celebrated artist, I'm proud to say. You may not have heard of her work as far away as Russia, but she's gained quite a lot of acclaim here in England, and into America and the Continent as well. Oils."

Though Zivon nodded, her name didn't sound familiar. "I am afraid the world of art has never been one with which I am accustomed. Though if any of her work is in your home, I will be most honored to view it."

Blackwell laughed. "You won't be able to help but to do so. She swears the best light is in the drawing room until noon and the dining room thereafter, so she has work areas set up in both chambers and forbids anyone to move them."

They pulled out into the road, and Zivon focused on the street ahead of them. "And on what is she working now?"

"Oh, some classical scene from a myth, I believe. She's using our younger daughter, Ivy, as her model."

He made note of the name. "And you have how many children?"

"Two daughters." Affection saturated the man's voice. "Lilian—Lily, we call her—is the elder at three and twenty. She's in the VAD—Voluntary Aid Detachment. They work in the hospitals. Ivy has just turned twenty-one and keeps busy as a teacher in her former school. Her mother required a bit of convincing for that, but with the war on, it was a way she could help. She hadn't the stomach for nursing."

Zivon could well imagine Mrs. Blackwell needing to be convinced, though. Society ladies never sullied themselves with such things, in his experience. Though he had the utmost respect for it. "My mother was a teacher—a linguist. It is thanks to her that I knew four languages already when I went to university."

Blackwell glanced over at him before making a turn. "I'm afraid I know little of your family history. Did you leave anyone behind when you escaped?"

Zivon's throat closed. He had to count to five before he

could convince his muscles to relax, his lungs to keep pumping air in and out of his chest. "No. Batya—my father—was killed in action during the Lake Naroch Offensive in 1916. Matushka in February last year, during the riots on International Women's Day."

If only she'd come to stay with him in Moscow after Batya was killed, as he'd begged her to do. But St. Petersburg—he'd never been able to remember to call it Petrograd—had always been her home. *Their* home. She'd refused to leave. Her house, her students, her neighbors . . . the very people who had trampled her during the riots, when the police fired into the crowd.

If only he'd been there. At her side, there to read the mob and anticipate their movements. He could have pulled her away. Warned her, as he'd done the woman in the path of the bicyclist. If only . . .

Zivon cleared his throat. "I have a brother. Evgeni. He fled with me, but we were separated when our train derailed in France. We had set up a place to rendezvous in Paris, but he did not show up. Not yet." Zivon hadn't been able to wait there longer. With the loss of his bag, he'd had no money beyond the few bills in his pocket. And the French cryptography department had never responded. He'd had no choice but to continue to London, leaving a note for his brother at the bookshop they'd favored on their one European holiday when they were boys. It was the only place they'd known to set as a meeting spot. "He will find me when he is able. Of this I am certain."

The captain braked to a gradual halt in front of Zivon's building. "I will be praying your brother finds you soon. That he is well."

Zivon curled his fingers tightly around the handle of his briefcase. Perhaps the captain's prayers would have some effect his own hadn't. "I thank you. And I will be but a few minutes. You are welcome to come up, of course, if you like." He had nothing in his flat to allow for hospitality—no newspaper to offer him to read, no books collected with care, nothing to eat or drink aside from tap water and the few rations he'd been granted.

Blackwell's smile looked unconcerned. "If it's all the same, I think I'll take a stroll down the street while you're tidying up, old boy. I could use a stretch of my legs, and I certainly won't get it once I'm home."

With a bit of luck, his host wouldn't see the relief in his nod.

Zivon hurried inside, up the stairs, and to the spartan flat Admiral Hall had provided him. He barely spared it a glance as he let himself in. There was none of *him* here, not yet. Just borrowed furniture. Borrowed curtains. A borrowed life.

He'd forge his own, as soon as he could. For now, though, it was a change into the closest thing he had to suitable dinner attire and a quick wash of his face, and he was positioning his spectacles on his nose again, pocketing his keys, and hurrying back down.

The captain was strolling his way when he emerged. They both climbed into the car and were soon talking of normal, unimportant things for the ten-minute ride. The weather. The rations. The news.

"Here we are." Blackwell pointed to a proud-looking stone house near the end of Curzon Street. Not exactly the grandest home in Mayfair, but not exactly modest. Befitting this family's standing, Zivon supposed. A generation or two removed from nobility, but still of good society. They would have noble connections. Titled cousins, or perhaps Blackwell even had a brother with a country estate or ancestral holdings to his name.

Zivon drew in a breath as they drove a little farther, to the carriage house that would serve many of the homes on the street. This wasn't the world he'd been born to. But it was the world he'd found himself a part of with his advancement in the czar's codebreaking division. He knew how to get along in it.

Blackwell checked his watch as they walked back up the street, nodding at whatever time it told him. "We'll have arrived a bit before our other guests for the evening. Hall and his wife will be joining us, as will Lieutenant Clarke. Have you met him yet? He's on my floor, one above you OB40 lads."

Zivon shook his head. "I do not believe I have. But I look forward to making his acquaintance."

"He's a stand-up chap. I think you'll like him."

A friend would be nice, but Zivon wouldn't get his hopes up. He'd yet to make many solid connections with his new colleagues. They were all polite enough, but they no doubt held him in a bit of suspicion. He would, were he in their shoes.

He would change that, though. He'd prove himself trustworthy. Gain their esteem.

Zivon followed his host up the steps, through the door that opened for them, and into a lovely, bright entryway that carried the scent of turpentine and another whiff of lily of the valley.

The servant who had opened the door—an older fellow with a kind-looking face—offered a smile to his employer. "Mrs. Blackwell hasn't yet come down, sir. But your daughters are in the drawing room already."

Blackwell grinned. "Lily made it home in good time, then?"

The servant chuckled. "Over an hour ago."

"Excellent. Thank you, Eaton. Come along, then, Mr. Marin. I'll make the introductions to my daughters, and they can entertain you for a few minutes while I make myself presentable."

Zivon handed his hat and overcoat into Eaton's waiting hands, thanked him, and followed Blackwell into the drawing room. If not for the empty easel and case of paints by the window, it would have looked as he'd expect—pastels, cream-colored walls, furniture and appointments that were all of good quality but showing their age.

"There are my darlings, Ivy Green and Lily White. How were your days?"

Zivon pulled his attention from the room itself and directed it instead toward where Blackwell had leaned down to greet the two young women who occupied the settee by the unlit fireplace. He couldn't see much of them through their father, but their laughter and quick answers sounded cheerful. Innocent.

He couldn't remember the last time he'd spoken with girls who were cheerful and innocent. A year? Two? Life in Russia had been so tense for so long. . . .

"Allow me to make introductions." Blackwell stepped back, revealing his daughters. Zivon couldn't tell at a glance who was the elder, but both were pretty, in that Western European way. One with brown hair, the same shade as her father's, and the other with red-gold. "Girls, this is Mr. Zivon Marin, formerly a kapitan in the czar's Imperial Navy. After the Revolution, he was forced to flee and has found a home here in London, where he assists Admiral Hall in his endeavors."

Were he his brother, he could simply grin and have them as instant friends. But that had never been Zivon's way. With his back as straight as a train's rail ought to be, he bowed.

"Marin, this is my elder daughter, Miss Lilian Blackwell. And my younger, Miss Ivy Blackwell."

They both smiled at him as he straightened. Easy, welcoming smiles.

Or maybe *not* so easy. His gaze snagged on the crystal-blue eyes of the elder, Lily, and his breath snagged with it. Her eyes . . . they were much like her father's. They carried within them a knowledge of the storms always rumbling and flashing on the horizon. An understanding of these times, the good and the bad. A . . . a *seeing*. He didn't know what else to call it. Not a gathering of the facts, of the patterns that he sought. It was something different. Something he couldn't name. But something that made him think she understood things he didn't.

3

PETROGRAD, RUSSIA

Nadya Sokolova kept her back straight and her hands clasped and wished she'd been a little more generous with her hairpins that morning. A blond curl had slipped free and was tickling her cheek, presenting a picture she knew very well didn't make her look capable, much less intimidating.

To compensate, she clenched her teeth and lifted her chin another notch. She still wore her uniform from the First Russian Women's Battalion of Death. The battalion had disbanded recently, after most of them took the ill-advised stand against the Bolsheviks—defending the provisional government, true. But *she* hadn't been so stupid, and these new superiors knew it. So she still wore the uniform, as it looked fiercer than everyday clothes would. And gained her fewer leering glances.

She kept her back straight, but a finger twitched. How long did it really take to read a telegram?

Comrade Volkov cleared his throat and finally looked up from the paper in his hands. "I trust you read it?"

A brief nod. She didn't need to defend the action—the telegram had been delivered to her, after all. Two weeks late, but relief greater than she was comfortable admitting had whooshed through her when it was placed in her hands. Evgeni was alive. Injured, but alive.

Volkov took a long drag on his cigarette, staring at the words again. "This is not good news. This brother of his . . . we were told he was just a linguist."

Nadya curled her fingers into a tight fist behind her back. Of course that was what Evgeni claimed, what his brother claimed, what his whole department had claimed when the party had taken over their building in Moscow. But Nadya knew better. "He was Intelligence, Comrade. And I have reason to believe he knows about our Prussian."

Volkov studied the paper, as if those very words would appear on it. "How can you be sure?"

She'd already reported this once, to someone in Moscow. But communication wasn't yet what it needed to be. There was still far too much chaos in the party. Chaos that would only settle with time, time without outside interference. This was why they needed to know what that Prussian knew. Take action, if they could, to keep the war going in Europe. They must, at all costs, keep the White Army from getting aid.

She cleared her throat and reported it again. "The day I was sent to apprehend the Tarasova woman, she was in his house, preparing him a meal. While I was there, I went through his locked drawers, as I'd been instructed, and I found a series of telegrams sent to us—to the Bolsheviks. He had somehow intercepted them."

Volkov frowned and leaned back in his chair. "Did you take these papers?"

"No. I'd been told to leave his house looking untouched. I simply made note of which ones they were. My superiors in Moscow instructed me to go back for them the next day, but it was too late. Marin had fled, the papers with him. Along with . . ."

The man's steely brows lifted. "With?"

She moistened her lips. "Something that looked like codes. Keys, perhaps. I did not understand them and had asked whether they might be important too. This was the first hint we had that the elder Marin brother was in fact a cryptographer, not just a linguist."

She had to admire the string of curses Volkov spat out as he sat forward—colorful and varied, both. "And we let him slip away? We *aided* him?"

"A calculated risk." She'd been so certain they could use him to their advantage. Not sway him—she wasn't that optimistic. The man was clearly a czarist, through and through. But they could *use* him. Feed him a bit of false information and let him send it to the Whites he was clearly in league with.

Grinding out his cigarette, Volkov blew out a last stream of smoke and stood. "Go to France. Rendezvous with the younger Marin. We will supply you with what funds we can. Find this Prussian again, first and foremost. And then make sure the elder Marin is not a risk. We haven't the resources to hunt down *every* enemy who escapes our borders, but we must know how he got our messages. And make sure he doesn't foil our plans with the Prussian."

She snapped into a salute. "Yes, Comrade." And then she spun for the door. She would see the purser, get whatever cash they gave her. But her feet itched to run from the building, into the still-snowy street. Straight to the telegraph office.

Her words to Evgeni would be few. *Find your brother if you can. I am coming.* But he would read affection in the lines, just as he read it in her every kiss.

She'd soon have the Marins in hand.

◈ ◈ ◈

Lily tucked herself into a corner of the back garden, where she would hopefully go unnoticed while she fiddled with her camera. She didn't often bring one out at dinner parties, but when Mama had suggested they adjourn to the garden for their pudding, given the unexpected beauty of the evening, Lily had seized the chance to run up to her room and grab her newest camera—the Kodak No. 1 Autographic Special that her parents had given her for Christmas.

Because as she'd watched Zivon Marin over dinner, her fingers had itched for the device as familiar to them as a paintbrush was to her mother's. Not because he was particularly handsome, but because he was so . . . studied. Something about him struck her as photographic, as if he were already a still life captured on film. What would he look like when actually put to paper? Would the camera see the same thing her eyes did, or would it not translate into a photograph, where *everything* was caught in a moment devoid of motion?

No. She'd learned to capture motion—or its story, anyway— with her camera. She would just have to see if she could capture its opposite too. A challenge she'd never taken up before, but one she was determined to meet.

"What are you doing?"

Ivy's whisper slipped easily into Lily's concentration as her sister slid up beside her amid the green vines trailing over the garden wall. Ivy for Ivy. Lily had taken plenty of photos of *that*.

She smiled at her sister without taking her focus from her camera. "I wanted to get a snapshot of the Russian."

Ivy breathed a laugh. "Why? Just for your collection, or did something catch your eye?"

"Mm." Lily gauged the light and adjusted the shutter from the *Clear* setting to the *Gray* and then moved the knob atop the lens to the corresponding stop for exposure. She glanced up again to make sure no deep shadows had found her subject.

Lovely evening light still shone on their guests, soft and

hazy. Marin was standing near the brick wall of the house, talking to that Clarke fellow. No, listening to him, it seemed. He was acting as he'd done over dinner, focusing his entire attention on whomever he was in a conversation with. His hands were clasped behind his back.

Clarke gesticulated as he spoke, his face a work of animation. Providing the perfect contrast to the Russian, who looked as though he could have been sculpted from wax. At least until one met his gaze. The few times she'd done that over the course of the evening, she'd been struck by movement instead of stillness. A mind always at work, that was what those eyes betrayed.

Not surprising, if he was one of Admiral Hall's code-breakers—not that she would have known that's what he was, were she not a part of OB40 herself.

Perhaps she could convince him to let her take a photograph of him looking at her too. One to capture the stillness. One to capture the motion it hid.

She adjusted the diaphragm lever and then set the shutter in place.

"He's handsome, isn't he?" Ivy's whisper curled around her.

Lily looked away from the camera to direct arched brows toward her sister. Ivy's gaze was latched onto their two young guests. "The Russian?" He wasn't *un*attractive, but she was surprised at the note of wistfulness in Ivy's tone.

Her sister glanced back to her, and she laughed. "No, Silly Lily. I mean, not that he isn't. But I was talking about *him*. Lieutenant Clarke."

She blinked at Ivy—at the light in her eyes, the smile on her lips, the way she tilted her head toward their guests. Lily lifted her camera, quickly thumbed the knurled screw all the way to bring the focus in as tight as it would go, and snapped a picture.

Ivy laughed and turned to her again. "What?"

"I had to capture the moment. I do believe this is the first time my sweet baby sister has actually expressed interest in one of the chaps Daddy brought home."

They'd teased each other plenty over the years, though. About who of the endless parade was the best looking, who had looked overlong at whom. But this time, a pretty blush crept into Ivy's cheeks, and she looked toward Clarke again. "He is, though, isn't he? Handsome? And clever. And kind. The way he fussed over Mrs. Goddard when she stumbled . . ."

Lily's breath had caught when their housekeeper had nearly gone sprawling upon coming in to tell them dinner was ready. But she hadn't really noticed how Clarke reacted. She'd been more focused on how Marin had managed to move forward seconds before Mrs. Goddard entered, trying to smooth out the bunched rug with his foot, even while he steadied her stumbling form with a quick hand. All while looking as placid as a mountain lake.

How had he known she was about to trip?

A question her sister wouldn't be able to answer. Lily smiled at Ivy, trying to focus her thoughts on their other guest. "He is all those things. And he was glancing your way quite often over dinner, so I daresay if you give him a bit of encouragement—and let Daddy know of your impressions—he'll be a regular guest."

Somehow Ivy's cheeks went even pinker. "Perhaps. Let's see how the evening ends, shall we? One never knows when a prince might turn into an ogre."

With a chuckle, Lily focused on her camera again. If she wanted a shot of Clarke and Marin together, she'd better get it now, before her sister moved away from their quiet corner and stole all the male attention—or the younger men were called over by her parents and the Halls to join their conversation.

She thumbed the knurled screw again to lengthen the focus, checking through the viewfinder to verify that she had it right when she thought it nearly perfect. One more nudge and she was satisfied.

And the light was ideal. Before it—or her subjects—could shift, she trailed her fingers down the cable dangling at the camera's side and gripped the push-pin. Drew in a deep breath, held her hands steady, and pressed the pin.

The shutter clicked. The film whirred. And a moment was forever captured. It made a smile curl in the corner of her lips.

"Am I allowed to move now?" A grin saturated Ivy's voice.

Lily grinned back. "Thank you for not getting in the way of the light. Or distracting anyone."

Her sister gave a mock salute. "Between you and Mama, I have been well trained. But there's the pudding, so you'd better put the camera away, Lil."

The back door was indeed opening, a maid laden with a large tray emerging. Their dessert wouldn't be all that sweet—sugar was all but impossible to come by—but their cook could do wonders with the preserved and canned fruit that her uncle sent from his country estate. Lily folded the camera up and slid the compact rectangle into the pocket of her favorite evening dress . . . which was her favorite because it had pockets large enough to allow her to do that.

"You enjoy photography?"

Lily started at the accented voice, though she was quick to cover it with a smile. It appeared her sister had commandeered Lieutenant Clarke's attention, which must have left Mr. Marin to wander her way. "I do, yes. My mother taught me how to take good photos, develop them, and retouch them, but she's never latched on to the medium like I did."

Marin's returning smile seemed to reach only half brightness, if that. It had need of a flash pistol—something to provide that extra charge of light when circumstances didn't supply it naturally. "The photographs on the walls inside are perhaps yours?"

"They are." Lily motioned toward the table where the pudding was being set out, though she led them there at a slow pace. From across the table at dinner, she hadn't really been able to tell the color of his eyes behind his spectacles. But they were a deep brown, like the chocolate drops she hadn't tasted in four years.

How very strange that chocolate-drop eyes and a curl to his hair that was defying its pomade—characteristics that should have made him appear boyish—somehow made him seem all the more somber.

"They are stunning. I particularly am fond of the one with sun glinting off an onion dome. It reminds me of home."

And that, she had to think, was where the sorrow had its roots in him. "It's the Royal Pavilion in Brighton—it does look rather Russian, doesn't it? We went there on holiday just a few weeks before the war began." She felt her smile go crooked. "Ivy's favorite hat blew off into the sea one day, and Daddy plunged in after it, claiming no navy man would let a few waves steal from his little girl." Her gaze flicked to her father, who was whispering something to Mama. "I haven't seen him so lighthearted since."

"Memories. They are like *matryoshka* dolls, yes?"

She looked at Mr. Marin again, brows knit. "What kind of dolls?"

He cupped his hands, then brought them closer together. "They . . . nest. Nesting dolls? You know them by this name, perhaps?"

"Oh! Yes, of course." They'd been wildly popular before the war, when people could still afford to spend ridiculous amounts of money on toys. "Memories *are* like that, to be sure. As soon as you peek at one, another reveals itself, and then another."

He nodded. And his eyes churned. And the rest of him stayed so very still, even as he walked beside her.

She had a feeling *he* was like a matryoshka doll too—a placid exterior that hid layers of secrets and mysteries. And she couldn't help but wonder what lay beneath this carefully crafted shell.

Perhaps she ought to suggest that the newcomer to their city be invited more often too, along with Clarke. He could surely use the company.

And Lily hadn't yet gotten a snapshot of him on his own.

4

Zivon jerked awake, his heart hammering with such force that it felt as if his chest might crack from the pressure. The images still warred in his mind, not fading fast enough as he blinked into the darkness to clear them.

Matushka, broken in the streets of Petrograd. Alyona, crumpled and pale on his doorstep. Evgeni, bleeding and unconscious by the twisted rail that had sent them into chaos.

His eyes hadn't seen them all, but that reality didn't keep his mind from tossing its imaginings at him night after dreaded night. It didn't keep him from picturing the Red soldiers advancing on everyone who mattered, weapons raised, hatred in their eyes.

Vengeance is mine, saith the Lord.

He sat up, tossing his sweat-soaked sheet aside, and tangled his fist in the bedding. That was a promise from God that he would cling to. *Hurry, Lord. Show them the penalty for what they've done. Show them what they'll reap when they deny your very existence.*

His pulse was slowing now, finally. A bit. He dragged a

breath of cool air into his lungs and swung his legs off the bed. Just enough light came through his window to tell him that dawn wasn't far off, so he pushed to his feet and walked over to the wavy glass.

There, to the east, the sky was pearly grey instead of deepest blue-black. A new day. Another chance to find Zhenya.

It would begin at the embassy. Today. He only had to wait—he glanced at the pocket watch barely illuminated on the table under the window—ninety-two minutes.

Too much time to spend shuffling about his empty flat. He slipped out of his nightclothes and into his athletic ones. It wouldn't be the first time in his weeks here he'd resorted to a predawn jog around his neighborhood to calm the frantic beatings of his mind, and he had a feeling it wouldn't be the last either.

Once the laces on his shoes were tied, he pocketed his keys and slipped as quietly as he could from the building. His mincing steps lasted only as long as he was inside. Once on the sidewalk, he set himself at a pace that soon had sweat running down his face. His legs pumped as they always had, his muscles warmed, and the damp morning air burned his lungs just a bit. Something that *hadn't* changed, through it all.

Thank you, Lord God, for this. He sent the words heavenward, like he'd always done. Prayer had long been as intuitive as breathing. Before. Now . . . he still said the words, still remembered the motions as surely as his legs knew how to pound the pavement. But where had the certainty gone? The sure knowledge that God would hear, would answer?

Gone. Swallowed up by the Red tide. His faith as stained as the bloodied streets.

Be still, and know that I am God.

Breath heaved into his lungs, out again. "I am trying, Lord."

He ran his usual circuit, though he didn't much enjoy the views of street after street, building after building. He should find a park. Would, eventually. The sun was finally peeking over the buildings as he went back into his own. After a quick bath, he dressed for the day and, for the first time since arriving in London, reached for the passports he'd hidden away under a loose floorboard.

He opened first the one with his photograph, alongside the name *Ivan Filiminov*. He still didn't know how Evgeni had procured the false papers so quickly, but he hadn't had the luxury of questioning it at the time. It had meant salvation, so he had taken it, willing to call it a gift from God.

He slid the passport into his pocket. He only had it still because he'd done the same on the train. Unlike his brother, who had put his own papers into his bag for some reason. Why? Why had he not kept his passport on his person, as he usually did?

Zivon didn't know. But he suspected it had something to do with the photograph jammed inside it.

Lowering himself to a seat on the edge of his bed, he studied the image yet again. He didn't know the faces. No names were written on the back either, only the date—2 February 1918. All he could tell for certain was that there were two men, clearly German, given the uniforms. They were talking.

That was all. All he knew. But oh, the questions.

Not just who they were, but why did his brother have this picture? Where did he get it? When?

The water stop. Maybe. Perhaps. Zivon certainly hadn't noticed it tucked in his passport when they'd boarded the train.

But if so . . . what did that mean? What had Zhenya been up to?

He closed his eyes, closed his brother's passport. Was he an agent of some kind? It was possible. Evgeni had the charm of a good field agent—and its subsequent ability to sidestep rules. He was exactly the sort whom Intelligence would have recruited to work for them in the field. He'd never seen his brother's name on any reports, but then, Zivon was Imperial Navy. Evgeni was army. That could account for it.

He spread his fingers over the cover, felt the embossing. Were he and his brother after the same information, not realizing the other was too? Trying to restore order? If so, they would laugh over it someday. When they were reunited. When the Bolsheviks had been shown justice. When Russia was theirs again.

Well, not *theirs*. Not his. Zivon surged back to his feet and slipped Zhenya's papers back into their hiding place. He had sacrificed his right to return to Russia when he came here as he'd done. He would stay here, knowing his people wouldn't understand his decisions, knowing he would be branded a traitor, a turncoat.

He would accept that. He would accept it for *them*.

But he wouldn't accept that he'd lost his brother. Or his chance to help end this war. He slipped Batya's watch into his pocket, along with his key, and strode back out into the morning.

He'd telephoned the Russian embassy last Wednesday afternoon, near closing time, when all but the last straggler would have been gone for the day. Claiming employment that kept him busy during normal hours—true enough—he requested an early audience with Konstantin Nabokov and had been granted one today.

Nabokov had been in India and then reassigned here to London during the entirety of Zivon's career, so he'd never met the man, which was the only reason he dared to come with his false papers. There was a chance the ambassador would recognize his real name and wonder what he was about, suspect his motives, but he wouldn't recognize him by face, anyway.

A passel of schoolchildren were knotted up on the corner ahead, laughing, two of the girls singing and swinging their hands, clapping, snapping, palm to palm. His nostrils flared, faint Russian words filling his ears. How many times had Alyona crouched down beside her little sisters and taught another song with its silly claps and swings? Too many to count.

But never again. Her sisters and brothers would have no one to teach them such lighthearted songs now.

The self-accusation burned him to the quick, even as he noted the books slipping from a boy's hand. The precarious-looking buckle on their strap. The puddle under the lad's arm. Zivon burst into motion, managing to get close enough that he could send his umbrella—something he'd learned never to leave home without in London—into the space between books and water, just as the strap gave way and sent them tumbling.

The child looked down, blinked at the umbrella, and then grinned up at him. "Thanks, mister! You're *fast*."

Zivon grinned back and scooped up the books. "Anything for the sake of a book."

Something his brother had always teased him about. Zivon helped the lad secure the strap around them again and was soon on his way, lips twitching up as thoughts of books and Evgeni reminded him of their trip to Paris when they were adolescents. When Batya had forbidden them from visiting again the bookshop near their hotel, it being owned by a Jew. When he'd convinced Zhenya to sneak out with him for one more perusal of the shelves.

How his brother had scoffed! Sneaking to a *bookshop*. But, always the rebel, he'd agreed.

Zivon picked up his pace. *Remember where it is, Zhenya.* Perhaps, if he willed it with strength enough, the words would find his brother wherever he was. Inspire him to go, find the place they'd agreed to rendezvous in Paris if they were separated. Receive the envelope Zivon had left for him. *Find it. Find me. Find me even before I can find you.*

He would—he *could*. Evgeni was resourceful, capable. If he was alive, if he was well . . .

The embassy loomed before him, the familiar Russian flag flapping in the wind, breathing bittersweet peace into his spirit. That flag had been removed from all the poles in Moscow, in St. Petersburg, all over Russia. The fact that it still flew here—that only abroad did the Russia he knew still exist—convinced him this plan was a good one.

These were his people. They would help. They must.

Though the building would be bustling in an hour, it was quiet now. He presented his false passport to a man who checked the name against a list he carried and nodded him inside. A wiry young man—the secretary who had set up the appointment for him—met him moments later and showed him upstairs to Nabokov's office.

No time to be nervous. No time to second-guess. Zivon simply pasted on a smile, held out a hand to shake, and let his words happily turn to Russian. "Good morning, sir. I thank you heartily for meeting with me so early."

The ambassador smiled. He looked to be in his mid-forties, his hair perfectly groomed and his mustache neatly trimmed. "Early is better for me today anyway, as I have plans later for Good Friday."

That gave Zivon pause, made his brows draw together. It was not Orthodox Easter yet; they had another month until their celebrations.

Nabokov chuckled. "I know, I know. Surprise I get all the time. I attend Anglican services."

Odd. Especially since the embassy supported the Orthodox church in London, so far as he had been able to glean. But he hadn't time to dig into that now. "I pray you have a beautiful weekend, then, celebrating the sacrifice and resurrection of our Lord."

"Thank you. Please, sit." Nabokov motioned to a chair across from his own. "You are newly arrived in England, I'm told? Did you flee the unrest at home?"

Zivon nodded. "It became . . . necessary."

"I can imagine." His face solemn, the ambassador shook his head. "We diplomats are at a loss as to how to help from where we are, so we just keep doing our jobs, assisting our people here however we can. The unrest will settle soon, surely. Order will be restored, those soviets put back in their place."

Spoken like a man who hadn't seen the riots, hadn't had to slink around the edges of any mobs. "I pray you're right." Zivon leaned forward, not having to fake the plea on his face. "I fled with my brother, and our train derailed in France. We were separated, taken to different hospitals. It's my hope that you can perhaps get in contact with your counterpart in Paris and help me locate him. I had no luck while I was there, and no funds to stay and search. I had to get here to accept a position, you see."

"Hmm." Frowning, Nabokov drew forward a piece of paper and a pen. "You were traveling by train through France? A bit dangerous, wasn't it? Why did you not go by sea?"

"With the U-boats?" Zivon shook his head. "All options offered danger. We took the one we could best manage."

"Well. What is your brother's name? We will certainly do what we can to find him—or any record of him."

Of his body, he meant, if he were dead. Zivon's throat went dry, and he had to swallow before he could speak. "Dmitri Filiminov." That was the name on Evgeni's passport. "But he did not have identification on him. It was in his bag, which I have."

Nabokov let out a slow breath. "That does complicate matters, to be sure. But I know Maklakov will be happy to help however he can. I'll dispatch a message to him today. Just leave your direction with my secretary, and we'll let you know whatever we discover."

A wrinkle, that. The flat Hall let for him was in his real name, not the one on this second passport. He put on a smile, though, standing as the ambassador did. "I do not know how long I will be in my current room." Also true. The Admiralty had promised him a house eventually, though he didn't imagine it would come before a response from the embassy in Paris. "I will stop back once or twice a week, though, if that will do. And perhaps find a way to repay your kindness."

"Nonsense." But Nabokov smiled. "This is our purpose. Though we are a tight-knit community here in London. I'm certain if you wish to extend the kindness to our fellow Russians, an opportunity will present itself. They can give you information on the church at the front desk, if you'd like."

"I have already found it. Thank you." Zivon nodded and held his smile in place as he hurried back out to the street. He *wanted* to meet the other Russians. Make a place for himself in the congregation, find ways to help. Let Russian and Greek spill from his tongue alongside the prayers.

He wanted it—but he couldn't risk it, not yet. First, he'd do what he could to help *all* of Russia. To end the war. Then he'd let himself indulge the need for community. Once it was safe to be Zivon Marin among them.

As he walked, he tucked the Filiminov passport deep into an inner pocket and pulled forward the identification Hall had provided for him. The one that had his real name, with that odd designation—British Admiralty. He flashed it as always at the OB, and the guards nodded him through. One even smiled. A bit.

A bit. The sigh worked its way out as he turned to the stairs. In Moscow, he'd been greeted every morning with respect and eagerness. In Moscow, people sought his opinions, his knowledge, his insight. In Moscow . . .

His fingers slipped into his pocket, where they could feel the ticking of Batya's watch. He wasn't in Moscow. Would likely never be in Moscow again. What he needed was a way to find his new place here.

"Good day to you, Marin!"

A familiar voice brought Zivon to a halt on the first step, and he turned with a smile to see Clarke. "Good morning, Lieutenant."

A crooked smile greeted him. "As I said last night, old boy, Clarke is quite sufficient—or even Theo, if you prefer."

Zivon inclined his head. "Of course. Thank you."

Clarke came up beside him and motioned him onward. "I say, I think I may have spotted you this morning outside my flat." Clarke lifted golden brows. "Assuming you run like a stallion bent on breaking a record at the tracks."

A chuckle welled up in his throat. Unexpected, and all the sweeter for it. "I would not say *that*. But I do jog, yes. And I was out this morning. It could have been me you saw."

Clarke laughed too and clapped a hand to Zivon's shoulder. "That wasn't a *jog*, Marin, at least not by my definition. Have you been a runner long?"

Though Zivon lifted his shoulders in a shrug, he wasn't quite sure why. He knew the answer and had no problem giving it . . . except, perhaps, because it meant revealing a piece of himself, and he'd been in a mindset this morning to protect rather than reveal. He shook that off. "Ever since I was a boy, yes. My brother, he was the true sportsman, like our father. A fist-fighter."

Clarke let out a little breath that bespoke surprise. "You mean, a boxer?"

Zivon tilted his head from side to side. "Similar, but in Russia we do not use gloves. Just fists."

"Well. I'm much keener on running, personally. Or at least I used to be, before that nasty bout of pneumonia landed me behind a desk."

Though he had no particular trouble keeping up with the English words this morning, Zivon couldn't help but note tone more than syllables, the accompanying gestures more than sounds. Running was not just something this man preferred over fighting. Zivon smiled. "You are a runner too?"

Clarke's blue gaze went a bit distant. "I'd hoped to make the Olympics in 1912. Nearly did. Lost the qualifier by this much." He stretched out his hands and sighed out a laugh. He shrugged—though not the same sort of shrug Zivon had just given. This one said, *Some things we can never change.*

"I am impressed. I never competed."

"Those days are certainly over for me." Clarke thumped a fist to his chest. "I haven't the fortitude anymore, since I fell ill. Though I have been trying to get back to it a bit."

They reached the first landing, and Zivon cast a look over at his companion. Clarke was probably younger than he was by a few years. Not by much, but he'd guess him to be closer to Evgeni's age than his own, perhaps twenty-six or twenty-seven. And though their stories weren't exactly the same, they had enough in common that last night had been quite pleasant, even without the added bonus of two lovely young ladies to admire and hosts who were experts at setting them at ease.

He was also grateful for an opportunity to get to know his new superior a bit better. He didn't think one shared dinner would make Hall trust him, take his advice. But it couldn't hurt.

Right this moment, though, even more than those grand goals, he just wanted—no, *needed*—a friend. "I would like my routine to be more regular as well. Perhaps we could run together certain mornings each week?"

Clarke's eyes lit up. "That would be just the thing. Accountability, you know. Perhaps we could work out the details over lunch today? If the weather's fine, I'll be up on the roof at one o'clock."

Zivon nodded. "Perfect. I will look forward to it."

"Ah, good. Just the chaps I was hoping to catch."

They both looked up, spotting Captain Blackwell coming

down the stairs, a smile on his face. Zivon had a feeling he wasn't alone in the question of *why* the captain was looking for them both, though of course they merely said their respective good mornings and waited for the older man to explain himself.

"I've come with another invitation for each of you. I just received word that my brother and his wife won't make it to Town as planned today, so we've two seats open for Easter dinner on Sunday. I thought, given that neither of you have people in London, you might like to join us. It's a shame to spend a holiday alone."

Zivon exchanged a glance with Clarke—who had told him on their shared tube ride home last night that Blackwell *never* invited the same young men to dinner more than once. What did this mean, that he was doing so now? For both of them, no less?

Perhaps it was simple Christian charity, not wanting them to be alone for the holiday, as he said. And if so, Zivon hadn't the heart to tell him that he hadn't been planning on celebrating until next month. What harm could there possibly be in observing his Lord's resurrection now too? He nodded. "It would be my honor."

"And pleasure," Clarke added. "How good of you to think of us, Captain. I would certainly be delighted to join you."

"And I."

"Excellent." Blackwell clapped them each on a shoulder and continued down the stairs. "I'll let you both know of the time after I've verified it with Effie."

For a long moment after he'd gone, Zivon and Clarke just stared at each other. Then they smiled, chuckled, and Zivon peeled off toward his door. "I will see you at lunch."

His heart had never been quite so light as he passed into the corridor that housed the intelligence hub. Perhaps that was why he found himself following the voices toward Room 40 instead of his own desk across the hall.

"I think it must be another alphabet entirely." It was De Wilde's voice. He hadn't yet learned them all, but it was certainly no trouble to recognize that of the sole female cryptographer.

And the words *another alphabet* drew him like a moth to flame.

He recognized the grumble too—Phillip Camden, one of the few of his new colleagues who always greeted him with an easy smile instead of polite distrust. "How in blazes am I supposed to decode something in a whole different alphabet? And how the devil can I know which one?"

"If it's too much for you, you can put it aside for someone else, you know." The note in De Wilde's voice said she knew well that by phrasing it like that, she was making it an issue of pride.

Much like his colleagues had done in Russia, this group greatly enjoyed poking fun at one another. He stepped into the room and cleared his throat. "Pardon me. I heard mention of alphabets. I could perhaps be of service?"

Not everyone was in for the day yet, but those who were all came to a sudden halt, five sets of eyes upon him.

His fingers curled into his palm. Why did he feel as though he ought to apologize? This was, after all, why Hall had hired him, wasn't it? He pulled out a smile. "I do not mean to be forward. But I studied linguistics at university. I am fluent in nine languages and able to translate several more with the aid of a lexicon. I am likely to know any alphabets we have intercepted."

That use of *we* was calculated. It would, with a bit of luck, remind them that even before he came here, he'd been an ally. Doing this same work, on the same side.

Camden stood with a grin. "And the Lord provides. Here, sit. See if you can make sense of it, Ziv."

Ziv. He blinked at the nickname but moved toward the

chair. On Camden's desk a few papers rested, including a hastily drawn Vigenère table with the Latin alphabet filled in. It had, apparently, produced nothing but gibberish when applied to the message also sitting there.

He sat, looking first at the encrypted message. The length of the words, the frequency of certain repetitions of letters, the patterns of language. Borrowing Camden's slide rule, he flipped over the paper with the table on it and drew his own. One with thirty-three letters instead of English's twenty-six. Into this he put the Cyrillic alphabet and then applied to the message the new pattern it created.

It required only a few minutes to realize he'd selected the correct alphabet. Words definitely began appearing, though they weren't the most familiar. "Not Russian—but Bulgarian, without doubt. Shall I . . . ?"

"You had better." This from one of the other codebreakers—Adcock, who smiled at him genuinely for the first time in Zivon's three weeks here. "If you leave it to Camden, he'll make a mess of it."

A ball of paper sailed through the air, striking Adcock in the shoulder. "You aren't exactly fluent in Bulgarian yourself, there, Ad. And I make no pretense of being the best code-breaker. I'm a pilot. That is why, if you'll recall, I'm useful to you."

Adcock snorted and sent the missile back to Camden. "Well, from what I hear, Old Ziv goes beyond most of us. You were the czar's best, weren't you?"

Zivon shook his head and stood again, gathering the papers. "That was Popov—my superior, head of the division." But Popov had trained him. And then trained him to take over, though the Revolution put a halt to all those plans.

Camden took his chair again, brows arched with challenge. "That's not the story the admiral tells. For that matter, it's not the story that giant hunk of ruby on your finger tells."

Of its own accord, Zivon's gaze flicked to the ring he was inadvertently flashing as he clutched the papers.

"I've been meaning to ask you for the story about that, Marin." Adcock leaned back in his chair, clearly not minding a bit of distraction so early in the day. "Family heirloom? Gift? It must be of sentimental value for you to have kept it during your escape rather than pawning it."

The very thought of pawning it made something hot boil up in his veins. The anger wasn't aimed at the codebreaker, who he knew was only teasing, but at the situation that had forced him into a position where it could even be an option. "I could never."

Camden's grin was every bit as teasing and mocking as Adcock's had been. "Because . . . ?"

Zivon sighed. He hadn't intentionally decided to keep his past a secret from these new colleagues—he'd simply fallen into it. But just as he'd shared his running with Clarke that morning, perhaps it was time to offer more of himself here too. "It was a gift from Czar Nicholas. Before the Revolution. Popov had told him of my work. To show his appreciation for my service, the czar invited me to dine at the palace and presented this to me as a token of his esteem."

"There, see? I knew it had to be something like that." Leaning an elbow onto his desk, Camden let his smile relax into something purely friendly. Or mostly, anyway. "As Adcock said—the best. Unless he gave *every* cryptographer a ring in thanks?"

How long had it been since he'd had the leisure of bantering like this with colleagues who understood him? Too long. He grinned back. "No. Or if he did, they did not wear them to the office."

Adcock laughed. "If the king gave *me* a ring, you can bet I'd never take it off either. And you know, now that you mention it, perhaps DID can put a bug in his ear, what do you say?

Royal-issued rings for all of us! That would shut up all those old biddies who berate us for having desk jobs."

"I doubt it." De Wilde stood as she spoke, crossing to the secretary's desk where they put their handwritten decrypts in a basket to be typed up.

"Speaking of rings." Adcock narrowed his eyes at her. "When's this wedding of yours, De Wilde? We're all invited, aren't we?"

Never in his life had Zivon met a young woman like this one, who looked downright irritated at mention of her upcoming nuptials. "The nineteenth of May. Yes, everyone will be invited. And now can we get back to work, or would you like to help me pick out the pattern for my gown too?"

"Careful, De Wilde. You'll have everyone thinking you're reluctant to wed Elton if you keep up that attitude." Camden reached over to snag another encoded piece of paper from the waiting stack of them.

"Don't be an idiot." De Wilde fetched a new message, too, and returned to her desk. "If you want to talk weddings, talk about your own."

"Can't. We can't set anything in stone until Ara's father gets back from Mexico."

Zivon moved toward the door, rather eager to get to work himself. Though he didn't mind when Adcock shot him a parting smile, along with, "I heard what you said to that bank clerk yesterday. Good one, old boy!"

Apparently Blackwell had already made good on his promise to share the story. Zivon smiled back and slipped across the corridor without another word.

He would always be Russian. Never really be English. But for the first time, the thought of staying here didn't feel entirely like a sacrifice. Not if he could find a place like this one.

5

Evgeni sank onto a bench across the street from the church, not sure he could move another step if he had to. Every muscle and joint ached. Well, no. Some screamed, especially his ribs. *Ache* was far too benign a word for his ribs.

From somewhere in the distance, a *boom* sounded, making Evgeni wince. It seemed he'd arrived in Paris just in time for the Germans to unveil a new siege gun, one so massive that it had put the whole city into a panic. Every twenty-odd minutes, a new shell crashed down, and they could never tell where it would strike. It made for a restlessness, a slick of fear always under everyone's feet.

How well Evgeni knew that feeling, even without the added threat. When he blinked, darkness bombarded him. A darkness filled with all he should be doing, all he'd failed to do. The man cloaked in shadow in France. The train, twisted and prone. The hospital, where he'd realized he'd lost everything.

Everything.

Zivon. Gone. Where had he gone? Was he alive? He had to be. *He'd* had his passport in his pocket, as always, so if he'd been killed, the queries Evgeni had put out would have yielded an answer.

He winced at another dark image—the expression on the face of his host. Paul was a fellow Russian, but he'd made it clear from the start that he wasn't helping Evgeni from any real feeling of camaraderie. He was helping solely because their mutual friends expected it.

Or mutual *friend*, anyway. He pressed a hand to his pocket, where the telegram rested. Nadya. Just thinking of her name called to mind the riot of gold curls, the deadly flash of her dark eyes. The way her arms wrapped around him when they kissed. He ought to be sorry she was coming—that she needed to. That he'd managed to fail so spectacularly. But he couldn't ever be sorry to see her.

He'd only known her a year, but it was enough to admire every single thing about her. She was not one of those girls who thought her sole purpose in the world was to marry and have enough babies to guarantee a few would survive the harsh Russian life. Who waited at home in a village of dirt and snow while her man fought and died on the front.

No. Nadya had been on the front too, a rifle in her hand and a look on her face that had no doubt terrified any Central Power soldier who got in the way of the First Russian Women's Battalion of Death. They'd served alongside each other during the Kerensky Offensive near Smorgon. He'd seen firsthand her ferocity. Her strength. And yes, the beauty that peeked out beneath the mud and gunpowder.

He could think of no one in the world he'd rather fight beside.

Matushka wouldn't have liked her. His mother had been a staunch believer in tradition, in the old ways, in the certainty that faith and family were the only things worthwhile. Zivon had gotten that from her. But Evgeni was more like Batya. He'd seen enough to know that sometimes the old ways only led to death, starvation, and the obliteration of the very way of life they were supposed to be upholding. Sometimes the czar who was supposed to be leading them went into hiding instead of trying to help his people. Sometimes the war that was supposed to end an atrocity just made a dozen new ones.

Sometimes tradition led to death—and so tradition had to die.

He settled back on the bench, eyes tracing the sidewalks. It wasn't their Good Friday, but knowing his brother, Zivon would attend a Mass today anyway. If he was in Paris, as he surely was, then he'd be in this neighborhood, the one they'd agreed to meet up in. He'd have found a cheap little room, and a neighbor would have invited him to join him at the local parish. Zivon, always happy for a little more religious activity, would have accepted.

Evgeni had never understood it. How could his brother not see how archaic religion was? How it tried to force outdated traditions onto a humanity that had outgrown it? He'd never understood it, but he appreciated it now. It made Zivon predictable, and that was exactly what he needed in order to find him.

His eyes passed over the parishioners aimed for the church to the street corner beyond. His next stop—if he didn't find Zivon here at the Church of St-Gervais-et-St-Protais—would be the bookshop a few streets over. It would have been Evgeni's first stop, had it not been farther from the métro. But he'd come upon the church first, and the bench had beckoned, and his ribs had been screaming, so . . . If Zivon had left him a note there, then another half hour would not change its presence. And if he could just find his brother directly, that would be better.

Find your brother. He hadn't needed the instruction from Nadya to know that was the most important thing he could do, now that he was out of hospital. Find Zivon. Hope he had possession of Evgeni's belongings, including the photograph the Prussian had pressed to his hand at the water stop. Keep his brother from doing anything stupid.

Why hadn't Zivon just left on his own? Why had he stopped first to locate Evgeni and convince him to flee as well? A breeze blew, and he turned his face into it, but it couldn't wipe away the frustration. Zivon could never just trust him, leave him to his own devices. He always had to play the big brother, telling Evgeni where to go, what to do, how to *think*.

Never listening. Never entertaining the notion that he could be wrong.

But it didn't matter, did it?

The church door swung outward, a black-frocked priest pushing the massive wooden slab wide in invitation. It was a lovely spring day; it seemed he'd decided to prop it open. And just in time too. When the father looked up, it was with a hand lifted in greeting to a couple walking his way.

Parishioners, obviously, as they turned up the stairs and soon vanished into the building. A moment later, more people joined them. Evgeni sat up straighter, casting his glance down the street first one way, then the other. Watching for that familiar stride—the one Zivon would never call *graceful*, but which was. It came of all the running he did, or at least that was Evgeni's theory. When one loped mile after mile like an animal of the steppe, one's walk was even, smooth, and strong.

What hat had he been wearing on the train? Would he still have it, or would he have gotten another here in Paris? What of his coat? It had been his heavy one—too heavy for a Paris springtime, but it had still been cold in Russia when they left. Would he have exchanged that too?

Evgeni leaned forward, resting his forearms on his legs to provide a bit of reprieve to his ribs. It didn't matter whether he'd recognize his brother's clothes. He'd recognize his *brother*. Anywhere, in any crowd, from any distance.

And his brother was not among the hundreds of people who filed into the church. Evgeni let out a huff of defeat as a woman trotted briskly up the steps with a toddler in her arms, clearly thinking she was late—as she probably was.

But Zivon was never late. Never. Not to anything, but especially not to a church service. All of Matushka's teachings over the years about showing the Lord the reverence and respect He was due guaranteed that.

Well. To the bookshop, then. It ought to be open still, since the owner was Jewish. He wouldn't close for the Christian holiday, though it *was* a Friday, so Evgeni had better get back on his feet to be sure he made it there before sundown.

He pushed himself up, his mind racing ahead. He would find Zivon. See what of Evgeni's possessions he had—hopefully the entirety of the bag he'd been clutching when the train derailed. And then he'd have to find anything that was missing. Preferably before Nadya arrived.

Mentally cursing the weeks he'd lost to the injuries, Evgeni took a deep breath. A strange noise made his every muscle freeze, tense. He was only vaguely aware of the shadow that passed him overhead. He hadn't time to think about what it might be—too large for a bird, moving far too quickly to be an airplane—before it blasted into the church across the street.

Instinct had him diving for cover under the bench, though it did little to shield him from the dust and debris. The ground shook under him, and a blast of something swept over him, making his injured bones feel like they might rip apart. But worse—far worse—was the *sound*. An earsplitting pounding of noise and then a moment of utter silence that stretched into eternity.

Slowly, ringing replaced the silence. And then came the noise of falling pieces of rock and stone and slate and glass.

And screams. So many screams.

He couldn't move. He tried, or might have tried, but the pain was a blinding white fire that blended with the screams and the shouts and the sirens and the continued crash of falling debris. Time shattered. And then the world went utterly black again.

◈ ◈ ◈

SATURDAY, 30 MARCH 1918

Lily placed the last of the rolled bandages in the cupboard where they belonged, checked the clock on the wall, and reached a hand down to her pocket. Her camera was there, as always. She'd used it this morning to take a few snapshots of patients who would soon be released and a few more of soldiers bound to call Charing Cross Hospital home for weeks yet, but who were eager to send something home to wives or mothers.

It was a little thing. But it brought a smile to their faces. It brought one to hers, too, as she turned toward the office at the end of the fourth-floor ward, where she'd just seen Arabelle go. Lily followed with a loud enough step to warn her friend that she wasn't alone.

Ara turned at her desk, which was stacked so high with papers that they looked about to topple, and grinned. "Come to do all my paperwork for me?"

Lily laughed and leaned into the doorframe. "Not a chance. You're the one who agreed to take your old position back."

Though she made a show of grumpiness—hands on hips and an admirable scowl—there was no covering the pleasure in Arabelle's eyes. She loved her job here in the same way that Lily loved her work at the retouching desk at the OB. It must have broken her heart to resign a few weeks ago in the face of her fiancé's supposed legal trouble, but the board of directors had been quick to offer her position back to her after his name had been cleared. And praise the Lord, she'd accepted. Lily enjoyed working under Ara the most.

"Had I realized no one was keeping up with it while I

was gone, I may have reconsidered their apology." Arabelle shrugged and pulled out her chair. "I imagine your shift is over?"

Lily nodded. "But I wanted to catch you before I left. Mama asked me to invite you and your fiancé to dinner at your earliest convenience. Perhaps next Saturday?"

The light in Ara's eyes was bright as a flash now, and her smile pure joy. Not at the prospect of dinner, but at the words *your fiancé*. Ara had been engaged before, and it hadn't ever made her glow like this. It had just been the status quo. But Major Phillip Camden had made something altogether new come to life in her. "That sounds lovely. I'll ask Cam if the date is convenient."

Lily darted a glance toward the framed photograph of Arabelle and Camden that proudly hung on Ara's wall. It had been the first thing Ara had brought back in with her. Hanging the picture was more statement to the administrators than anything, Lily knew. A clear declaration that people were more important than any position.

She was glad to have provided Ara with the symbol. She'd taken it without Ara and Cam knowing it, weeks before their engagement. She'd wanted to do something to congratulate her friend on the promotion from nurse to ward matron, so she'd taken the snapshot of them smiling at each other and put them on a prettier background—London still, but in the springtime, with trees in bloom all around them and the sunlight at the perfect angle.

Mama never minded *that* sort of change to a photograph, one meant to better display the subjects. It was much like what she did in her paintings. It was, she would say, the *use* of art that she took issue with. Pleasing a friend—that was lovely. But deceiving someone, even if that someone was the enemy . . .

Lily shook off that thought and refocused on the framed

picture. It made her heart happy to see it so boldly on display, no matter Arabelle's purpose in hanging it. "If Saturday doesn't work, just let us know when will. My mother is always happy to have dinner guests."

Arabelle smiled and leaned against her desk. Her gaze, however, she kept leveled on Lily. "Lil . . . I haven't had a chance yet to thank you. For what you did to help Cam."

Lily glanced over her shoulder. There was no one about to overhear, as far as she could tell. Even so, it wouldn't do to mix her two worlds. She slipped fully into the office and clicked the door shut. Her answering smile felt weak and shaky around the edges. "It was nothing, Ara. A simple task from the admiral. It took me but an hour."

"Even so." Arabelle was nothing if not discreet. She pitched her voice to a whisper. "Without your help—without everyone at the OB acting as you did—Cam could well be standing before a firing squad even now."

Lily shook her head. "They'd never let that happen. They're a family, and he's one of them."

"*They* are?" Ara had the most annoying habit of seeing the slightest hurts in a glance. And knowing just how to call someone on them. "You're one of them too, are you not?"

Lily sighed and sank into one of the chairs in front of Ara's desk. "I don't know what I am. I'm there nearly every day, but only in the basement, where the admiral has set up my workroom. Once in a while I'll have to run something up to his office, but no one really knows me. Usually all my communications are with Admiral Hall himself or Barclay Pearce. I believe you met him the other week?"

Her friend nodded. Tilted her head. "So you *want* to be more among them? You seemed a bit panicked when you saw me there. Or when I saw *you* there, perhaps."

Yes, Ara was always far too adept at seeing the heart of a matter. Lily let her attention wander over the clutter of papers. "I love what I do there. And I'm so happy to do it—to *get* to do it. But if Mama found out . . ." She shook her head. "At the start of the war, Daddy approached her about creating propaganda—rather excited, I might add, about this new work he was helping to spearhead—and expecting her to be equally excited to take part with her talents. You'd have thought he'd asked her to sacrifice her pug to the war effort."

"Your work with photographs isn't exactly propaganda, though, is it?" Ara turned to study the photograph on her wall. "It isn't meant to convince the masses of something the government wants them to believe."

"Sometimes it is. It's just that the masses aren't usually English." She paused. "I think Mama would say it's even worse. Because at least with the posters and adverts, everyone *knows* it's just an artist's rendering. With photography, I'm rewriting the facts. Deliberately lying."

Arabelle's lips turned up. "It's war, Lily. A nation *must* lie and spread disinformation to protect its secrets. I daresay your mother understands that."

When it was a matter of mere intelligence—where troops were located, when an advance was planned—then yes, of course. But her mother had very strong opinions on the role of art in the world. And *deception* was not an approved use.

"Well, I can see I've not convinced you. And I promise I won't say anything to your mother when we join you for dinner." Arabelle smiled. "Your secrets are your own to guard, my friend."

"Thank you." She'd expected nothing less, really. As a nurse, Ara was well versed in discretion. But a bit of anxiety must have been clinging to her at the thought of having Arabelle and Camden, two of the only people who knew of her work for the Admiralty, at her table. Well, aside from Daddy and Admiral Hall, but *they* would certainly never let the truth slip out.

She pushed herself to her feet again. Daddy said he'd asked

both Mr. Marin and Lieutenant Clarke to share Easter dinner with them, which was lovely. But she'd have to be careful to remain unseen at the office. She could always explain her presence in the building easily enough, saying she was there to see her father. She'd done so, in fact, other times when acquaintances Daddy had invited to their table had later spotted her and said hello. But on Room 40's floor? That would be a bit trickier to excuse.

She'd have to have a story ready to tell if it happened. That Daddy had asked her to run something down to Admiral Hall for him on her way out, perhaps.

Or perhaps it would be wiser to simply let someone else deliver her finished photographs to the admiral. Keep to the basement entirely.

Lily's shoulders sagged. If Room 40 was a family, then she was naught but a Cinderella of her own making—hard at work but self-banished to the fringes where no one could see her. A situation she had crafted rather carefully. Why was it only now beginning to chafe?

"Lily?"

She paused midway to the door and looked back at her friend, who had straightened as well. Ara's tall form had angled toward the framed photograph on the wall, and her lips had turned again into a smile. She nodded to the photo. "I've been meaning to ask you if I could get another print of that. I'd like to send one to my father in Mexico."

That, at least, was easy. Lily grinned. "Of course. I can have it for you when I come in on Monday."

"You're a gem. Now go, enjoy your Easter. I'll tackle Mount Paperwork."

With a laugh, Lily opened the door and slipped out, closing it again behind her. It wouldn't stop the other nurses and VADs from interrupting Ara for serious matters, but perhaps it would deter those who wanted an idle chat. Because it was going to take a rather large swath of uninterrupted time for Arabelle to turn that mountain into a reasonable molehill.

A few minutes later, Lily was striding down Agar Street, aiming herself toward Mayfair. It was a lovely day, all sunshine and soft breezes and the glories of spring, so she decided to forgo the tube and walk home. Actually, she'd go the long way round and call at the school first and see if Ivy was still there. There were no classes today, of course, but her sister had said something about rearranging her classroom before the students returned from their holiday.

A smile pulled at Lily's lips. Ivy was all the time rearranging the furnishings. Even back when they were both in the nursery, Lily could remember awaking from a nap to find that three-year-old Ivy had pulled her bed over to the window, or half into the closet, or piled every pillow in the house on top of it to make it look "pretty and new." A habit that had increased with age . . . and perhaps with strength. At least once a month, Ivy would enlist the help of their shared maid in scooting this piece of furniture over there or that other one into the corner or whatever suited her fancy at a given time.

After leaving St. James's Park, she crossed Piccadilly and aimed toward Hyde Park and the school perched near its westernmost edge. She slipped easily through the familiar wrought-iron gate and climbed the steps as she'd done nearly every day for the last decade. First when she attended the girls' school, and then to walk home with Ivy when she was a student, and now to walk her home when she was a teacher. The walk along parts of the park to Curzon Street was one they'd always enjoyed taking together. Whenever possible, they still did.

The corridors of the school were empty of all but that silent echo that signaled the absence of life usually filling a place. She knew Ivy loved that unnatural quiet. It had always felt a bit spooky to Lily. But after she'd trotted up the stairs inside, the corridor did magnify the few noises, assuring her Ivy was in her classroom.

Lily leaned into the doorway with a smile. "You know, most teachers enjoy their holiday *away* from school." It was still odd sometimes to come and see her baby sister about her work. Teaching—something she never imagined her sister taking on before war changed the landscape of their lives. All grown up.

Ivy looked up with a warm smile that said she was right where she belonged. "What do you think?" She motioned toward the room.

Last week, when Lily had stopped in, the desks and benches—wide enough to fit two students at each, though occasionally three were squeezed in—had been arranged in a circle, with Ivy's tall chair and blackboard in the middle. Today they were back in neat rows, but angled toward one another in a V, giving them a view not only of Ivy and her board by the window, but also of each other.

Lily tilted her head. "Do you *really* think it a good idea to give them such a clear view of the window?"

"Given that we're charting the blooming of the tree and keeping an eye on the newly built nest in that limb, yes. Yes, I do." Ivy grinned and picked up a slate pencil that must have rolled from someone's desk when she was moving it. "Only for a week or two, though, or I daresay there will be a lot more of *this* required."

Lily followed the motion of Ivy's hand to the blackboard, where a student had written *I will not chatter in class* twenty or so times. She chuckled. Chattering had never been her particular problem, but there had been a time or two over the years when she'd had to write *I will not daydream during lessons* or *I will not draw in my copybook* on the board. "Diana Oglesby again?"

"Who else?" Ivy shook her head, but amusement lit her eyes.

"Perhaps she needs a ruler to her knuckles." Lily said it solely because she knew well her little sister could never bring herself to resort to the typical punishments. She'd instead devised a merit and demerit system that seemed to keep the girls in remarkably good order, what with the promise of rewards for those who had accumulated a surplus of merits and some rather interesting punishments for anyone with a deficit, like picking slugs off the school garden's plants in the mornings before class.

Ivy rolled her eyes. And then they flashed bright, and she motioned Lily to join her at the window. "Come here. They ought to be coming by again any moment."

"Who? Diana Oglesby?"

"No, Silly Lily." The window was open to let in the spring air, and Ivy poked her head out, bracing her palms against the sill. "There. I can just see them emerging from that copse of trees."

Curious now, Lily slid into place beside her sister, her hand reaching by habit for the camera in her pocket. She didn't know who had caught Ivy's attention, but if it was so notable, perhaps it called for a snapshot. She squinted into the distance, her brows drawing tight together when she saw Ivy was pointing at two figures far too tall to belong to her eleven-year-old pupils. No, they were clearly men. Men moving at quite a quick pace along the path inside the park.

One of whom had a stride so smooth and graceful that she had a feeling she knew exactly who it was long before she could make out any features. "Is that . . . ?"

"Clarke and the Russian." Ivy leaned her elbows into the sill and rested her chin in her hands, looking more the school-girl than the teacher. "This will be their fourth lap of the mile circuit, if you can believe it. And their pace doesn't seem to have lagged."

She wouldn't have thought Zivon a runner. And yet, perhaps it explained that way he moved—almost without friction, it seemed. Lily quickly adjusted the focus and light settings on her camera and had it in position by the time the men drew near enough. Her fingers trailed the cord, found the push-pin.

Her eyes gauged the world. The way the sunlight streamed down, fresh and bright, dappling shadows on the ground as it played hide-and-seek with the leaves. She waited for the men to lope into a patch of pure sunshine, smiling when she saw they were laughing together over something. Perfect. She pressed the pin, her heart whirring along with the film. The perfect moment. She always knew when she'd found one. Nothing quickened her spirit quite like a well-timed photograph.

And not a moment too soon. The men slowed to a walk now. Clarke motioned toward the park entrance, and Marin seemed to be fishing around in his pocket for something. A watch, she saw a moment later.

"What was their pace?" Lily asked her sister, since she'd apparently known when to expect them by again.

Ivy's cheeks were that pretty rose color that meant she knew well she'd been paying more attention than a casual acquaintance really needed to do. "If they were running the mile, as I assume, then just over six minutes." She straightened quickly, all but slamming the window back down. "Come on. If we hurry, we can happen by the entrance as they're leaving, and they can offer to walk us home."

6

Lily's chest went oddly tight. She laughed to cover it up. "Ivy, really. They're coming for dinner tomorrow."

"So?"

"So . . ." Her sister was already grabbing her bag and hat and hurrying toward the door. Lily leapt to keep up. "Did it not occur to you that they may not *want* to walk us home after running four miles? They probably want nothing more than to get home themselves and bathe."

"Oh, bah." Ivy shot a grin over her shoulder. "I say we'll learn a bit more about their mettle if we surprise them in such a moment. And wouldn't you rather discover now whether they react well to the unexpected, rather than months into courtships?"

"There are no courtships." But the words were more a mumble than an insistence. Because there no doubt *would* be a courtship if Ivy made it clear—which she was obviously doing—that she wanted one. Clarke would be an amusingly besotted fool by the end of Easter dinner, if he wasn't already.

What lit a spark of unease in her chest was that Ivy seemed to think that *one* courtship meant *two* courtships.

"Ivy . . ."

"Hurry up, Lil." Ivy was already dashing down the stairs.

Lily picked up her pace, tugging her kerchief off her head as she went. It was easy for Ivy to run into an impromptu meeting, as she was dressed in a pretty white day dress, her hair arranged in waves that led to a stylish chignon. Then there was Lily, in a dowdy VAD uniform, hair pinned back for purely utilitarian purposes.

Not that she really cared about impressing the Russian. He may be intriguing, but that didn't mean she wanted a romance. Certainly not one that was mere happenstance, as his new friend called on her sister.

And why was she even thinking this way? It was ridiculous. She'd only met the man once. Besides, far more likely was that *both* of the men outside would be taken with Ivy. It was the usual way—and Lily could hardly blame them. She herself might not be bad to look at, but beside her sister's vivacious charm, Lily might as well be one of their mother's paintings. Flat, two-dimensional. Interesting for a moment's glance, but not much beyond it.

Oh, she had no doubt that in a different world, where the men weren't so outnumbered, she may have been able to find one who preferred a quiet wife. She just wasn't sure that world still existed. And wasn't all that upset at the notion.

So she really didn't mind that Ivy would unquestionably steal the hearts of both their guests. She could think of no more deserving a recipient of affection, and it was only fitting that Ivy have her choice. Her little sister's happiness was crucial to Lily's own.

And the beaming smile Ivy gave her over her shoulder as she stepped outside said that she was anticipating plenty of happiness. Lily, camera still in hand, spun the knurled screw and lifted it to snap another quick photo. It probably wouldn't turn out, given that she had only guessed at the focus, but sometimes those unplanned ones surprised her.

Ivy laughed. "Put that away and come along. They're leaving the park."

They were. And they were coming in their direction—no doubt the quickest route to their flats or a tube station—so they'd have to pass them. Lily folded her camera and slid it into her pocket even as she hurried to Ivy's side and linked their arms together, as much to restrain as to proclaim solidarity. "Remember what Mama always says, Ivy. Don't appear overeager."

Ivy's smile was the perfect complement to her rosy cheeks. "And remember what Daddy says—be yourself and any young man worth his salt will take notice."

A laugh tickled Lily's throat. "Well, in your case at least, I can't argue."

"And I do believe we've been spotted." Ivy's pace may have been reasonable, but Lily could feel the energy vibrating through her. It coursed through her arm like electricity and gave Lily a zing too.

They stepped out of the school's wrought-iron fencing, onto the sidewalk, and turned toward home, which put them facing the two men.

Lieutenant Clarke was grinning, already lifting a hand in greeting. Mr. Marin, rather than looking at them, was glancing down at himself, probably keenly aware of the sweat soaking his shirt and dripping down his face—or at least she would have been. Not that she as the observer found any reason to wrinkle her nose at a man showing evidence of remarkable athleticism.

He looked up, over the rims of his spectacles. A curl of hair had broken free of its pomade and fell across his forehead, and she had a feeling the flush in his cheeks wasn't solely from exertion.

But he didn't look at Ivy. He looked at *her*.

Another zing, though she couldn't entirely attribute this

one to Ivy's energy. She glanced down, but demureness had never really been one of her virtues. She'd always been too curious. And Zivon Marin made that curiosity spark to life every time she looked at him. Which she did again after only one second of reprieve.

She found him smiling, and it looked a bit bashful. Rather endearing, that.

Clarke murmured something to him, though they were too far away yet for Lily to hear. It made uncertainty flash over Mr. Marin's face for a moment, though, before his expression cleared back into his usual stillness and he nodded.

"Gracious but he's handsome. Even when in desperate need of a bath." Ivy's whisper was certainly too quiet to go beyond Lily's ears.

Even so, she felt a bit guilty for her chuckle. At least this time she knew which of the two her sister meant.

They were soon close enough that she had no trouble hearing Clarke's pleasant hello. He motioned toward the school behind them. "Is this where you teach, Miss Ivy?"

"It is indeed." Ivy somehow produced the perfect smile without any effort—warm and sweet, encouraging without being *too* inviting. She turned to view the building too, swinging Lily around and then pulling free of her arm so she could point upward. "That's my classroom there. The one with blue curtains."

Lily wasn't quite sure how Ivy and Clarke managed it, but a second later, the two of them were side by side looking up at the cheerful window, and Lily had been nudged back. She'd tease Ivy later about shoving her out of the way. Though since she also had no need to hear all about the latest reordering of the room, she didn't entirely mind stepping back and turning to find Mr. Marin with her gaze.

He'd followed the pointing fingers with his attention for a moment, of course, but now brought his eyes back down to her. He smiled, but there was nothing carefree about it. Nothing glad.

She wasn't so selfish a creature to think it had anything to do with her. The sort of sorrow that infected that smile had roots far deeper than a two-day acquaintance. Her fingers were already reaching for her camera, but she curled them into her palm instead. "I didn't realize the two of you were runners." There, a nice benign conversation topic.

Marin ducked his head. "We did not realize we both are until yesterday. It seems Clarke nearly qualified for your team in the 1912 Olympics, though."

"Really?" Ivy must have been listening with half an ear as she chattered about her merit and demerit system. She interrupted herself to turn wide, awestruck eyes on Clarke. "How very impressive!"

Lily pressed her lips against a grin. Another something for Ivy to swoon over later, it seemed. For her own part, she kept her attention on the Russian. How odd it was to hear someone say *your team* and not be part of it themselves. "And do you compete?"

He looked genuinely taken aback by the question. "No. That is not my purpose." Before she could ask what his purpose was, he extended an arm toward the sidewalk. "May we see you and your sister home, Miss Blackwell?"

That had probably been what Clarke had suggested to him, the thing that had made him so uncertain. But apparently he was no keener to disappoint his new friend than she was her sister. Lily smiled. "You may, of course. But if it's too much trouble—"

"This is pleasure. Not trouble." The words sounded certain, and his returning smile had no new notes of regret in it, so she decided to believe him. Though he cast another look down at his clothes. "Forgive my appearance, if you would. And I hesitate to offer an arm. . . ."

She laughed and turned toward home. "There is nothing to forgive, I assure you. How far did you run? Were you on the mile circuit?"

He nodded and fell into step beside her, though he kept generous distance between them. "Five miles today." Ivy must have missed one. "We are both, it seems, runners of long distances. Though neither of us has been able to train as much in recent times."

Yes, war had a way of interrupting such things.

"Do you enjoy any sport?" he asked, hesitating a bit, as if he wasn't quite sure what he ought to ask her.

Lily grinned up at him. "Not like that. But I play croquet."

Something flickered in his eyes. A smile whispered over the corners of his lips that seemed absent at least a bit of the sorrow. "I am largely unfamiliar with this game, I confess. You . . . hit a ball, I believe? With a hammer?"

"A mallet, through a wicket." Her own grin was probably a bit mischievous. She and Ivy had played their guests more than once—and often tromped them soundly. "Weather permitting, we always have a little Easter match. We can teach you how to play—and no doubt Mama will regale you at dinner with the story of our game twelve years ago, when an overexuberant Ivy broke a window."

She'd thought a hint of a story would bring another easy smile. After all, who didn't laugh at the thought of a nine-year-old smacking a ball through a window? But instead of amusement, that stillness descended over his countenance again. A complete absence of reaction.

What had she said? She shifted just a bit closer, so that he would look down at her. "I'm sorry. Have I opened a matryoshka doll?"

The reference to their earlier conversation at least earned another fleeting smile. "Forgive me. Talk of Easter brought to mind an article I read in the newspaper this morning. It seems the Germans' new gun hit a church in Paris yesterday, during Good Friday services. Many were killed. Many more wounded."

She gasped. Her shift at Charing Cross Hospital had begun early this morning, and she hadn't had a chance to so much as glance at the headlines yet. "That's horrible!"

"It was a church I visited once, when my family took a European holiday. Our one grand adventure." His voice was so perfectly even. Modulated. Careful. "We stayed in that neighborhood, you see. We toured the church. Visited a bookshop." He swallowed hard. "That was the neighborhood where my brother and I were to meet if we were separated during our escape. He could be there, somewhere near that devastation."

Her stomach knotted up. "Oh no. I can't even imagine." She glanced behind them, to where Ivy and Clarke trailed them by at least ten paces, laughing over something or another. She and her sister had never been apart, not really. Not by more than a few miles, a few days at a time. Never had either of them had to wonder if the other was caught in the midst of a tragedy. "Do you think it likely he was nearby?"

He didn't shrug. Didn't glance over at her. Just kept walking at the same measured pace, his movements fluid. Kept his eyes straight ahead. Kept his face clear. "If he is alive, he is there, or trying to get there. But I have heard nothing from him for weeks. Not since our train derailed."

"I'm so sorry. Such uncertainty must be tormenting." Her hand settled over her camera. Anchoring her, even though there was nothing she could do with it to make this better for him. "Are you the elder or the younger?"

"Elder." Now he looked her way, a knowing in his eyes. "Like you, yes?"

She glanced over her shoulder again. But where his brother was missing and perhaps injured, her sister was happy, laughing, and so very present. "I would do anything to protect her. Even though she seldom needs it."

"Evgeni is arguably the one of us better able to survive an attack. He is a soldier like our father, even before the war. Very strong. Capable. Charming. He will make a way."

Lily heard the words he didn't say. *He must.*

He reached for her elbow then, tugged her a step to the left. Which she found utterly confusing until she became aware of quick steps coming from a path that joined theirs. A dog came bounding along, his leash trailing behind him, followed by a child panting just as hard as the canine. They would have bowled Lily over had Zivon not pulled her out of the way.

Clearly, he'd been paying more attention to their surroundings than she had.

She smiled her thanks. And then returned her mind to the conversation. "Evgeni." She echoed the name softly, its syllables feeling strange on her tongue. As would *Zivon*, she knew, if she ever said it aloud. She'd try it later just to see. When she was alone, in her darkroom, film and plates and negatives before her. "I will pray for him. And for you."

He swallowed hard. "Thank you. He would say he does not need prayers, but he needs them all the more for thinking so."

"Mama always said something similar about her father. *'The more you tell me not to pray, the more I know you need me to.'*"

He didn't quite smile in reply. But he looked as though he could at any moment. "You have a lovely family. It is good to see."

She certainly couldn't argue with that. She couldn't quite imagine a world where her sister wasn't on the other side of her bedroom wall, tapping out secret messages to her; where her mother wasn't teaching her how to bring beauty to life with pen and paint and pictures; where her father wasn't prepared to move heaven and earth to see them happy and well.

Maybe that, too, was why she'd never been interested in a courtship with any of the young men Daddy brought home. None of them had ever made her think they were worth the change from what she knew and loved. "Family is the most important thing," she said quietly.

"It is." Something moved over his face, so fleeting she barely caught it. Something a bit sad, a bit angry, a bit resigned. "My people—at least the ones in control now—are trying to make us forget this. There are groups of women saying it is time to liberate them from the confines of family and children. They wish to make child-rearing a matter for the state instead of the family. To abolish marriage. To outlaw elements of faith. They say these are archaic."

They paused to wait for a rattletrap motorcar to clatter by, which gave her time enough to find the words for the reaction that had gripped her stomach. "Isn't that a bit like saying we don't need stone anymore, now that we have concrete and steel, and so let's dig out the bedrock? New structures are all well and good, but we must take care not to destroy our very foundations."

"Exactly so." For the first time, a bit of fervor entered his voice. "This is what I have tried to say to my people. That yes, it is important women have chance to chase dreams. It is important peasants in villages do not starve. But care must be taken not to throw out good with bad." He paused, sucked in a breath. "Apologies. I have forgotten my articles in my excitement."

She chuckled. "I knew perfectly well what you meant. And I do agree."

The glance he sent her said he appreciated that. But then it sobered. "My reward for such talk in Moscow, and for the work I did for my country during the war, was to be hunted. Flee or die—these were the options the Bolsheviks left me."

He said *Bolsheviks* like it was a curse word. She wanted

to reach over, to touch his arm, but she didn't know if he'd appreciate such a gesture. So she settled for a small smile. "I'm glad you chose the option you did, Mr. Marin."

He faced forward again. Seeing, she suspected, something far beyond the row of houses so familiar to her. "Many will think I chose the coward's way. That I have abandoned my post, my country. That I have defected."

"And being killed for your beliefs would have been better?" She shook her head and then lifted a hand to smooth back a strand of hair the wind tossed into her eyes. "I can't think so. Denying who you are for the sake of safety would have been cowardly. And dying for it would have been a bigger abandonment, don't you think? Now you live to fight another day. To pray for those you've left behind. For Russia. To do what you can for them from here."

They drifted to a halt a few feet from her front steps, and he gave her the most interesting smile. Small, still tinged with sorrow, but somehow all the deeper and more meaningful for it. A man's smile had never made her pulse increase before, but her heart took a strange little tumble now.

He bowed a bit at the waist, somehow making it look elegant and formal despite being dressed in athletic wear. "Thank you, Miss Blackwell, for seeing that perspective. And thank you, also, for the pleasure of walking you home."

She suddenly wished she was in a pretty dress, her hair done up properly. Such a bow deserved something more appealing as its recipient. But she had only her uniform, and tendrils pulling free of her chignon, and a camera in her pocket weighing heavily, begging for a chance to capture him just so.

What an intriguing mass of contradictions he was. The still and the active. The formal and the informal. The studied and the earnest.

Her fingers slid into her pocket and extracted the camera as a grin stole over her lips. "May I?"

He blinked, first at her face and then at her camera. "I . . . why?"

"Because I like to keep a visual record of my days. And I don't want to forget this conversation."

She saw the softening in his eyes and responded to it before he nodded. Already had the camera up, open, and was adjusting the focus. Perhaps it was the quickness of her actions that made him laugh. She couldn't be sure, but she didn't let it slip by her. She managed to get the pin pushed while light still danced in his eyes and the smile had full possession of his lips.

Ivy and Clarke soon caught up with them, and the men said their farewells amid promises to see them tomorrow.

"See there? Aren't you glad I insisted?" Ivy chuckled as they made their way inside.

Lily granted her a grin. But then, rather than trail her sister up the stairs to their rooms, she aimed for the small chamber—once a room for a live-in maid—that Mama had let her turn into her darkroom.

Once inside, she pulled out a box of photographs she kept for repurposing—many of which she had taken, others donated by Admiral Hall—and sorted through them until she found the one she was looking for, with Moscow's magnificent onion-domed horizon. Smiling, she reached for her camera and the film inside it.

She couldn't give Zivon Marin his home back or find his brother for him. But she could give him a souvenir, anyway. A matryoshka doll. Not a memory itself, but something to open them up.

As she worked, she prayed. That the memories would be good ones. That he would find a way to hold tight to that which he couldn't afford to lose of his past and easily relinquish that which would catch him in a snare.

And that somehow, somewhere, he'd find his brother.

7

Easter Sunday, 31 March 1918

Outside, the voices of a million raindrops sang upon cobbles and pavement and brick. Zivon had the window cracked open enough to hear them, to let the symphony of splashes and patters serenade him. Once upon a time, such music would have soothed.

He wasn't sure soothing was even possible these days.

On the table before him, he'd spread a newspaper that contained a thorough article about the Paris church shelling on Friday. Ninety-one dead. Sixty-eight injured. Was Evgeni one of those? If he had even survived the train derailment, could he have been in the neighborhood? Zivon didn't know, but that urgency that hovered always at the cloudy edges of his memory felt suspiciously like guilt when he considered the possibility. If Evgeni had been there, it was because of him. Because *he* had chosen that neighborhood as their rendezvous. Why hadn't he simply chosen something like the Eiffel Tower?

He pinched the bridge of his nose where his eyeglasses rested, then repositioned them with a sigh and sent his gaze to the other paper on his table. A sheet with his own handwriting upon it—his best recollection of what that telegram about the Prussian had said. But even as he reviewed the words, trying to remember if each phrase was right, he knew it didn't matter.

Hall wouldn't be able to do anything with this. Zivon certainly wouldn't have put any stock in a page created solely from the memory of a man he wasn't even certain he could trust. Only a fool would take this as anything but a rumor.

His new superior was no fool.

But logic aside, the telegram was *real*. Or the original had been. It was the last thing he'd decrypted before they got word that Lenin and his troops were coming and they'd better clear everything out of their offices that gave away what they were doing.

Was that the only reason he thought it so important?

No. No, he'd known the moment he decrypted it, before he knew it would be his last, that this was vital. That the war could hinge on what happened with the common German soldiers.

How, though, to make Hall take note? To make him believe without seeing it himself? Or, better still, intercepting it himself?

Zivon let the thought settle. That could be the answer, couldn't it? If Room 40 intercepted a message, decrypted it . . . that would be half the battle, anyway. Hall would at least believe the message itself. Then Zivon would only have to convince him of how the Allies ought to react to it.

He lifted his pen, thoughts swirling like a *barynya*. Round and round, faster and faster. He could almost hear the music that accompanied the dance. Only, instead of notes plucked from a string, they were words. Possibilities. Plans. Patterns.

He scribbled down a few options. He could try to re-create the message itself and send it. . . . But no, how would he send it as if it were from the Germans? That would be difficult. He could take a different tack, though. He could present the same basic information but from a different perspective.

His gaze drifted to the newspaper article. A French perspective, perhaps. As if from a French officer who had heard the rumors of mutiny among the Germans and feared his own troops might soon do the same. That if one group or another caught wind of such unrest among their counterparts on the other side, everyone would simply lay down their weapons and refuse to fight.

Yes, that could work. He scratched out his first lines of notes and jotted those down instead, in French. If only he'd thought of this sooner, while still in France. He could have encrypted it and sent it himself.

Now it was a bit trickier. It had to originate in France—the codebreakers would know if it didn't. But perhaps those embassy connections could be convinced to help. He could send it first to Maklakov from the embassy here, in a code that he knew for a fact Room 40 hadn't cracked yet. And request that he then send it back in a code they *could* break.

It may take some effort to convince Nabokov to trust him to that degree, especially as Ivan Filiminov. But it was his best option, unless he could somehow get his hands on their wireless himself.

The alarm clock he'd set on the table trilled. Zivon reached to turn it off, sighing at the half-finished state of his work. He would finish the encryption tomorrow. Heaven knew he'd have plenty of time between when the nightmares woke him and it was time to report to the OB. Perhaps he'd have time enough to visit the embassy again.

He stood and shuffled his papers back together. The newspaper could stay out, but the others would go under the floorboard with the fake passports. After that was secured, he had just enough time to tidy up before Clarke was due.

His new friend knocked exactly when he'd said he would.

Zivon opened the door with a smile. "Hello. Come in. I need only one moment more."

Clarke stepped inside with a grin that turned into lifted brows. "I say, old boy. Rather stark place you've got here, isn't it?"

Zivon hurried to the window and jammed it closed. "The admiral let it for me, with what furnishings you see. I have not yet had the opportunity to make it my own."

With a chuckle, Clarke leaned against the wall. "To be honest, my place isn't much better. Just more cluttered with what my mother would deem rubbish if she saw it."

After locking the window, Zivon grabbed his hat and shrugged into his jacket, then met Clarke with a smile. "Ready."

"Excellent."

They said nothing more until they were on the street, walking to the tube station. But given the smile that seemed to have taken up permanent residence in the corners of Clarke's lips, Zivon could guess about what his friend was thinking. Or rather, about whom. "You and the younger Miss Blackwell seemed to enjoy your walk yesterday."

Clarke shot him a look not dissimilar from the one Evgeni had sent him twelve years ago, when Zivon had teased him about having a crush on Tatiana from across the street. "I might say the same about you and the elder Miss Blackwell. Or at least . . ." The smile flipped into a frown. "I didn't force you to give attention to her against your will, did I? I didn't mean to monopolize Miss Ivy's attention. Not that Miss Blackwell isn't a lovely young lady too, of course, but if I've—"

Zivon's laugh cut him off. "You worry needlessly, my friend."

Relief as obvious as the rain clouds washed over Clarke's face. "Oh good. That's neat and tidy, then, isn't it? If you prefer her and I her sister?"

From Clarke's point of view, it certainly would be. If he

intended to court Miss Ivy, then no doubt it would be most convenient if Zivon were simultaneously occupying the attentions of her sister. But Zivon knew well his hesitation showed in his every movement, not to mention on his face.

Clarke sighed. "I thought you liked her."

"I do. Very much. It is not that at all." He focused his gaze on the sidewalk ahead, trying to rid his mind of her shining hair, that sunshine-and-clouds knowledge in her eyes. The utter sincerity in her voice as she promised to pray for Evgeni.

How to explain to this new friend all the reasons that now was not a good time to seek an involvement with a young woman? A young *English* woman?

For a long moment, the only sounds were those of the city. Then Zivon sighed. "I would not have any idea how to go about such a thing."

"Oh, come now." Chuckling, Clarke gave his shoulder a little shove. "It can't be *that* different here than it was in Russia, can it? You like a girl, you spend time with her, maybe write her a note now and then or bring her a small gift. Before the war, I'd have said chocolates, but these days . . ."

Zivon slid his hand into his pocket, where his watch ticked steadily on. Time, ever moving. Ever escaping him. Running out. "You make it sound simple."

"It *is* simple. At least in theory, as long as the girl likes you too and her parents approve. Surely you had a sweetheart at some point in Russia."

Shooting his friend a quick glance, Zivon shrugged. "That was different."

"Aha!" Laughing as if he'd just won a victory, Clarke leapt a step ahead and then half turned to face him, pointing his finger. "I knew it. Why else would you hesitate? You've still got a girl in Russia. What's her name? Is she pretty? I bet you're saving up to send for her."

Zivon's fingers tightened around the watch, until he could

feel not only the ticks but also the continual movement of the gears. "No, Alyona is not waiting for me." He should say why—and would have, had it not been a day to focus on joy instead of sorrow. But that could wait for another day, another conversation. "And it was quite different with her. We had known each other forever." Since she was born, anyway, and he was seven. His thoughts hiccupped a bit. Lily Blackwell was the same age Alyona had been. He hadn't paused to realize it before.

"Ah. That does rather eliminate the necessity for the getting-to-know-you stage. What happened? Opposite sides of the Revolution?"

"Her family had no reason to take sides. They simply kept their heads down, as I imagine they will continue to do." *He* was the one who'd had a target on his back. Because of his job, because of the favor of the czar . . . and because he'd foolishly tried to speak reason to people who had no desire to hear it. Who'd claimed *he* was the unreasonable one.

Maybe they were right. Maybe it had been madness to think he could prevail against such a maelstrom.

Clarke seemed to accept his evasion of an answer. "I suppose sometimes it just doesn't work out. Sorry, old boy. But then, that leaves you free to pursue a lady here, doesn't it?"

"Someday." He gave the watch a final squeeze and then let it go, slipped his hand out of his pocket. Someday, when he was certain the Bolsheviks had given up on tracking him down. Someday, when he didn't fear being the cause of anyone else's death. Someday, when he'd done all he could to restore order in Russia and had resigned himself to some sort of quiet life here in London.

Someday, when he had something other than uncertainty and secrecy to offer a woman.

"No time like the present, I say. We never know how much time we have left. We oughtn't to waste it." For the first time in their short acquaintance, Clarke's tone was devoid of optimism. Now he was the one looking straight ahead, the one whose fingers curled into his palm.

Zivon nodded. "You have lost friends in the war."

"There were five of us in school. Inseparable. Besides me, only one is left. And he's still on the front lines." Clarke's jaw ticked, then eased. "Pneumonia was probably the best thing that could have happened to me. Everyone on the ground prays for trench fever—one of the only ways to get safely back to England for a while."

"It was no better on the Eastern Front. I feared every day that we would receive word of death. My father's. My brother's." One had hit. One had not. Not during the war, anyway.

Clarke gusted out a breath. "Cheery thoughts for this holiest of days. We'd better change the subject so we don't arrive all dour-faced and gloomy."

Zivon breathed a laugh of agreement and cast his mind about, searching for something, anything, that was brighter as they neared the tube station. "What do you know of croquet?"

Clarke explained the game to him on the train ride, and their moods improved considerably by the time they knocked upon the Blackwell door. Though even if their moods hadn't, Zivon suspected that merely arriving here would have brought the grin back to Clarke's face.

How nice it must be to be able to give oneself over so fully and completely to fresh hope.

Eaton opened the door with a welcoming smile, ushering them in and informing them that the family and guests were gathered in the drawing room. They were soon shown to the bright chamber, filled today with laughter and chatter.

And with shaking heads. "Turn and run, lads," a middle-aged man said upon their entrance. He was smiling, though, and bouncing a toddler upon his knee. Given the man's coloring,

Zivon would have guessed him to be a close relation of Mrs. Blackwell. "Before you get pulled into the melee too."

Mrs. Blackwell swatted playfully at the man's arm. "Don't warn them off, Geoffrey. They may well take my side—which would be a novelty." Her grin covering the flash in her eyes, Mrs. Blackwell motioned to a poster resting upon an easel in the corner of the room. "Tell me, gentlemen. What do you think of the latest masterpiece my husband has commissioned from one of my esteemed colleagues?"

Of its own volition, Zivon's gaze drifted over the room until he spotted what he'd apparently been looking for—Lily, reading a book to a little girl who appeared about four years old. She glanced up with a smile that Zivon couldn't help but return.

Clarke cleared his throat. "Given that I had a hand in the commissioning, madam, I think it would be wise for me to abstain from offering my opinion. Though I take it you do not approve?"

"Should I?" Mrs. Blackwell chuckled, softening her words. "I grant you can hardly be unbiased. But what of you, Mr. Marin? What do you think of the poster?"

"Oh, Effie." Captain Blackwell moved to the easel and took the poster down. "Don't feel obligated to answer her, Marin. She's forever looking for an ally in her stand against propaganda."

The captain's wife waggled her brows. "And one of these days I shall find one."

Well, this was certainly an interesting introduction to the collection of strangers. Zivon took a moment to let their movements solidify in his mind. So far as he could tell, there was no real tension in the room. The guests wore the small, amused smiles that said they'd all heard this argument many times before. Even Captain Blackwell's posture bespoke ease. Confidence, even. Why else would he have brought out the poster to show his guests, knowing his wife's opinion?

Only Mrs. Blackwell herself displayed an undertone of . . . not distemper, not anger. But disappointment. A shadow beneath the brightness of her jesting.

How many times had he seen that same expression on his matushka's face when she tried for the thousandth time to convince Batya and Evgeni to give up their love of fighting? To pick up a book? To take an interest in the church?

He couldn't help but want to soothe her a bit, as he'd always endeavored to do for his own mother. So he stepped closer to the poster Blackwell held and studied it. The bottom of the image showed people at work on the home front—a blacksmith at his anvil, a woman loading ammunition. Behind them, a nurse on the battlefield. In the back, up higher, were two uniformed men, one beside a cannon and the other holding a rifle. A Union Jack flapped in the breeze above it all.

Tacked to the bottom on a rectangle of paper was the proposed caption: GLORY AWAITS, AT HOME OR IN THE FIELD.

Zivon pursed his lips. "Is it the artwork you find fault with, Mrs. Blackwell, or perhaps the caption?"

He stepped to the left, knowing the question would spur her to rise from her seat and come to join him, which she did, a few seconds later. "Well, aside from the fact that the art isn't my preferred style, I take no issue with it. It's an accurate enough representation of the war effort. But *glory*? Come, now, Thomas, everyone at this point knows that war isn't glorious." She sent a pointed look to her husband.

The captain sighed. "What about *honor* in place of glory? Would you find that less offensive?"

"That's my sister," the ginger-haired man said from the couch. "Insisting the efforts of the Crown be edited to suit her."

Mrs. Blackwell laughed. "Oh, quiet, Geoff."

Zivon studied the image for another long moment. But more, he studied the people around him. The teasing, the ripples of other conversation going on, the way Lily closed the book she'd been reading to the little girl. "Perhaps . . . perhaps this image should not be offering a statement at all. But maybe, instead, asking a question? A *Where do you serve?* sort. Reminding the viewers that it is their duty to find a way—some way, somewhere—to help."

Blackwell looked impressed. "Not bad, Marin. What do you think, Clarke? Something along the lines of *Where Are You?* or *Are You in This?*"

Clarke, however, had managed to slide to Miss Ivy's side, and the two of them were laughing over something apparently unrelated to propaganda posters. The captain's lips twitched into a smile.

The lady sighed. "I suppose that's better. But even so, I . . . well, I maintain it isn't good of us to manipulate our own people. Oughtn't we to be able to trust our neighbors to do what's right?"

A question that punched him in the gut as forcefully as Evgeni could do. He'd used to think the same. Until his neighbors had broken that trust.

"*Inspiring* them, darling. Inspiring them to be the best versions of themselves."

"Shaming them, you mean."

"Appealing to the inborn sense of duty that every good Englishman has anyway." Blackwell gave Zivon's shoulder a friendly thump. "I daresay the same is true in Russia, right, old boy? Though it may take painting a certain picture, the people are always ready to stand up and fight for king and country."

The room didn't go silent. But Zivon's thoughts did, for a moment. His king, his czar, was currently under house arrest, on soldier's rations. For every soldier left fighting for him, another had turned against him. And Russia itself . . .

He cleared his throat. "I am afraid that just now the Russian people cannot agree about what they ought to fight for.

But I have always found it fascinating that, historically, there has been an understanding that Russia herself would do the fighting for us. We need only to lure the enemy into the interior and wait for winter."

As he'd planned, the last observation served to soften the first, and the captain made an observation about Napoleon that soon redirected the conversation entirely. Good. That allowed him to take a step back, to smile through the belated introductions Mrs. Blackwell made to the other guests, and to revert to his favorite pastime—reading the room, finding the patterns to the people.

Heaven help him, though, he found himself mostly concerned with tracking Lily, who'd stood during her father's joke about Napoleon, edged closer during the introductions, and now stood a step away, holding a paper-wrapped rectangle in her hands.

He turned to her, not needing to make any special effort to keep his smile bright this time. "Happy Easter to you, Miss Blackwell."

Her returning smile was simple and complicated, confident and unsure. He wasn't sure how she managed to contain such contradictions within those winter-sky eyes of hers, but they were there as she held out the parcel. "Happy Easter," she said quietly. "I wanted to give you a small something. To welcome you to England."

Was this common here? He didn't know, but he took the proffered package with a slight bow. A warm smile. "How kind of you. Should I . . . ?"

"Oh, yes. Go right ahead." She clasped each hand on the opposite elbow, the glimpse of shyness telling him that whatever lay beneath the paper was something whose value was personal rather than monetary.

He peeled away the wrapping, noting first the wooden frame, the cardboard backing. When he flipped it over, his breath caught in his throat. It was him, somehow. Laughing, looking bright . . . and at home. Moscow stretched behind him, its familiar skyline pristine and impossible. Only after a moment of staring did he realize the image of him was from yesterday afternoon. But how . . . ? He looked up, met her eyes, sure his marvel shone in his. "This is astounding. How did you do it? It looks flawless."

The smile she gave him was bright. "I physically combined prints—one of you, carefully trimmed and positioned on a print of the city, then rephotographed. I had to touch up some edges manually at the retouching desk, of course, but most of the work was done with a scalpel."

His gaze fell to the image again. He'd never had—nor wanted—a portrait of himself. But this was entirely different. This was a story she'd told for him. A reminder of a life once lived. "I do not have words enough in either English or Russian to thank you." A flash of something light stole through him, as unexpected as yesterday's laughter. "Perhaps French will do. *Merci beaucoup, mon amie.*"

He was rewarded with her laugh and with a waft of the same scent he'd first noted in the captain's car. Lily of the valley. Not, apparently, the choice of her mother, but rather of her. So fitting for the sweet Lily.

"You're very welcome, in any language. Literally, in fact. Welcome to England, Mr. Marin. I hope London will eventually bring you as much joy as Moscow did."

His fingers tightened around the frame.

"You have no idea how perfect a gift that is, Miss Blackwell." Clarke had come to investigate, his grin audible in his voice. "This will be the first thing he hangs on the walls of his flat."

"You can't be serious." Mrs. Blackwell spun on him. "You have no other decorations?"

He lowered his head. "I am afraid I have not had time to

furnish the space beyond that which was already there." Nor
had he had the funds, but that was hardly polite conversation.

"Well, that won't do at all!" Mrs. Blackwell held out a hand
toward her elder daughter, even while motioning to him with
the other. "Come with us, Mr. Marin. You must choose a few
more pieces."

"Oh, I—"

"Don't bother arguing, Marin." Captain Blackwell clapped
a friendly hand to Zivon's shoulder. "There's no putting her
off when she's determined to foist her work on someone—
especially someone who championed her cause." He said it
with a wink toward his wife, who laughed with exuberance.

Lily took her mother's hand, her smile every bit as bright.
"I bet he'd like that study in blue you did a few years ago,
Mama. The one of clouds and sea."

"Perhaps so." Mrs. Blackwell looked him over much like a
tailor would, as if she could read his artistic preferences as
easily as old Vasily did his shoulders' width. Doubly amusing
since, as far as he knew, he didn't have much by way of artistic
preferences. "And that beautiful photograph you took of the
Eiffel Tower in Paris before the war."

The elder lady tucked her hand into the crook of his elbow
and used it to steer him out of the room and toward the stairs.
The Blackwell ladies continued to chat as they led him up the
stairs, and up again, and up still more. The final flight was
more utilitarian than luxurious, narrow enough that they
had to go single file, but he got the impression it was a trek
these two made quite often.

When finally they pushed through the door, Zivon drew
in a breath. He wasn't sure what he'd been expecting but
certainly not what met his eyes. The entire attic was stacked
with canvases, frames, glass, and mats. He saw cases of what
he assumed were paints, others of chemicals that he suspected were for developing photographs. Shelves had been

built with openings of various sizes that held framed paintings and photos. Other canvases were unframed, the paintings on them unfinished. Stacks of paper seemed to indicate similar amounts of unframed photographs.

If left to himself, he probably would have just stood and stared at the stacks, waiting for order to emerge from the chaos. But his hostesses clearly didn't view it as chaos. They turned directly toward two different shelves—Mrs. Blackwell pulling out a photograph, her daughter going to a painting.

His lips curved into a smile. So quick they were to sing each other's praises.

"Here, Mr. Marin. Sit." Lily motioned him to a single wooden chair, a rung missing from its back. "We'll show you some options, and you can tell us yes or no or maybe."

"And don't feel bad about saying no to anything," her mother chimed in, her smile saying she'd read his mind. Or perhaps the shift of his feet. "Art is subjective, and some pieces just don't suit a particular style. You'll want to be a bit choosy for your foundation pieces."

He pressed his lips against another smile. "Forgive me. I never imagined having foundational pieces. I confess that while I appreciate art, I have never given it much thought."

Lily grinned. "Don't worry. We'll remedy that in minutes."

"Beginning with this photograph from Paris that Lily took." Mrs. Blackwell presented a large framed print of a view from the base of the Eiffel Tower, looking up to its tip. The perspective was intriguing, the lighting extraordinary. But what made his brows knit was the fact that it had color to it. "How did you manage to capture the hue?"

On that trip to Paris with his family, he thought he'd been prepared for the sight of the tower—but what had surprised him hadn't been the magnitude or the vertigo he experienced by looking up at it. It had been that he'd been expecting it to be iron grey and instead it was a warm bronze shade.

Lily motioned to the photograph. "I actually painted with watercolor on the photograph."

"Remarkable. And beautiful."

"Perhaps when you look at it, it will be a reminder of that holiday. And a prayer." Her voice as soft as a Parisian spring, Lily gripped whatever framed painting she had chosen without turning it around.

He ran a hand down the frame of the photograph and nodded. "I would be honored to display this in my flat."

A grin bloomed over her lips. "I don't know how much honor is involved. Now, *this* one, on the other hand." She made a show of flipping the large frame around to reveal a stunning oil painting in shades of blue. Sky, flowers, water, even the grass had a blue tint, as did the silhouette of two children in the distance. "Fit for a museum, I say."

Mrs. Blackwell laughed. "But apparently not for the marquis who had commissioned it. And then failed to come and pick it up some five years ago."

"His loss. And your gain, Mr. Marin, if you choose to accept it."

He had no idea why some other lucky friend or family member hadn't claimed it already, but he had to admit that the blues were appealing. It was enormous, big enough to fill the space between the two windows in his sitting room. "I certainly could not refuse the loan of such a work of art."

Mrs. Blackwell scooted something along the floor, not so much as looking over her shoulder as she said, "What you take with you tonight will be our gift to you." Now she sent him a glance. Confident and yet weighted. "Unless you mean you expect to move again and not take with you what we have gathered here? Certainly I don't want our work left to the next tenant of your flat."

From the end of the garret, a shaft of sunlight burst through the clouds, catching the dust motes in the air and spinning them to gold. Capturing them there in a frozen, drifting moment. He could hear the familiar words echoing in his ears. *Be still and know . . .*

He could sense the future, shivering and shaking ahead of him. Elusive as fog. Yet as determined as the wood beneath his feet.

He drew in a deep breath. "I will not stay in this flat forever. But I do not expect to move from London. This will be my home for the rest of my days."

Both of the ladies went still. Matching blue eyes turned on him. "You are certain of that? Despite how you love Russia?" Lily asked in a voice as quiet as the sunlight.

He traced a finger down the edge of the picture frame. "It is because I love Russia that I will stay here. This is where God has led me. This is where I can do the most good." He forced his gaze back up to his hostesses. Though it was Lily his eyes seemed to find of their own will. "I have cast my lot with England. With England will I stay."

8

There were a thousand reasons for a telegram to go unanswered these days. Nadya shouldered her bag, schooled her face, and wished she could school her stomach so easily. A thousand reasons or more that she'd gotten no response to the short messages she'd sent to Evgeni. The lines could be down. Non-military telegrams could be given low priority. Paul could have simply not given them to him.

All possible. But none calmed her stomach any. Especially not given the news she brought with her. She needed Evgeni to have found his brother. She needed him to have the information from the Prussian informant.

She needed him to be well.

She strode away from the train platform as if she had some idea where she was going, though she'd never stepped foot out of Russia until this trip. She spoke French, anyway. She could read the signs, with a bit of effort. She'd find a map. Find her way to Paul's flat and demand to know where Evgeni was.

He'd be here. Somewhere. He *would*.

"It is about time you showed up."

The Russian words made her pause. But the tone was wrong. Too raspy from cigarettes, too deep, too smoothed around the edges by years of speaking French. Still, she put on a smile and turned her head to greet the man she remembered as a lanky teen who worked the farm next to her parents'. "Paul. It is good to see you."

Half truth. Half lie. She'd never had any particular affection for him, and the decade since he'd last been in Russia didn't look as though it had been especially kind to him. She knew he was only thirty, but he looked far older.

He was a familiar face, though. And more, the leader of the Bolsheviks in Paris. She intended to remain firmly on his good side, so she fastened on a smile and held out a hand.

He took it, but he didn't shake as she'd intended. Just held it for a moment, his gaze steady on her face. She didn't much like the way the glow at the end of the cigarette dangling from his lips mirrored the gleam in his eyes when he looked at her. But then, she'd long ago grown accustomed to such looks—and had learned how to dissuade them.

Stay on his good side, she reminded herself. And so she merely lifted her chin and reclaimed her hand rather than punching him in the nose with it. "Where is Evgeni? He hasn't replied to any of my messages since I left Petrograd."

The glow turned to a smolder. A temper-heated one. "The first time you see me in a decade, and you greet me with 'Where's Evgeni?' You don't ask after my parents? My life here?"

She lifted her brows. "I said it was good to see you, didn't I? And I've seen your parents since *you* have. Not to mention that you greeted *me* with 'It's about time you showed up.' My question is at least relevant."

He grunted. And actually reached for her. No, for her bag.

Tired as she was from the travel, she wasn't about to get off on such a foot. And she made a point of it by stepping back.

"Don't be a caveman, Paul. I am a soldier. A comrade in arms. I will carry my own bags."

"Have it your—"

Something whistled overhead, drowning out the obvious ending to the phrase. She looked up, but by the time she did, there was nothing to see. A boom sounded from somewhere in the not-far-enough distance, and a plume of dust and smoke shot into the sky. "What is *that*?"

Paul took the cigarette from his lips, waved it in the air, and blew out a puff of smoke. "The Germans' new siege gun. We will have time to get home without fear of another."

That ball of anxiety in her stomach wanted to quake, to quiver. She swallowed against it and indulged only in gripping her bag's strap tighter as Paul struck out down the street. "Evgeni?"

He muttered something she didn't quite catch. Or perhaps her French just wasn't as thorough as his when it came to colorful phrases. But he pointed ahead. "Resting in his room. He was too near a shell the other day, when he was out looking for his brother. Reinjured his ribs. Sprained an arm." He shrugged and ran his tongue over his teeth. "He won't die from it. Probably."

He took another long drag of his cigarette, then held it out to her. When she shook her head, he put it between his lips again with another shrug. "I hope you intend to explain to me what is so important that you have both come here."

She kept her gaze straight ahead. "It is a military matter."

"Military." He laughed. Until he saw she didn't. "But you are—"

"I am *what*?" She wasn't wearing her uniform now. It hadn't seemed like a good idea when traveling across lines that had once been enemy. "A comrade in the new Red Army? Yes. I am. A senior *unterofitser* in the First Russian Women's Battalion of Death? Why, yes. Yes, I was, when such a ranking mattered."

"Easy, Nadezhda." He looked about ready to pat her on the head. If he tried it, she'd bite his hand.

Good side. She forced another smile. "I am not authorized to tell anyone the details of what Evgeni had been about. But I *can* say that the party deems his brother a threat."

"I would think the party has threats enough in Russia to worry about, without traveling so far in search of one that has gone astray."

All too true. She'd welcome the day when they could hunt down all their enemies. But that day couldn't possibly come until they'd gotten their newly built house in better order. "He is an exceptional case."

Paul led her toward a métro station. "Why? What makes him so special?"

"He has knowledge that could put us all at risk if he shares it with the wrong parties."

Paul said no more about it as they approached the ticket counter, just exchanged a few quick French words with the attendant, handed over coins, and nodded Nadya down a tunnel.

She looked up at the low ceiling. "Are you certain another shell won't strike while we're in here?"

"Perfectly."

Keenly aware of the bodies packed around her, both on the platform and on the train, Nadya made no attempt at further conversation during the ten-minute ride. She was far too busy counting the minutes since the last shell. It was one thing to die for a cause that mattered, but not in a train tunnel from a random German shell, thank you.

Once they were back out in the sunshine, in a section of the city that looked nearly as run-down as her neighborhood in Petrograd, Paul turned to her again. "I have put out a few queries about a room for you. I have no doubt that someone will offer something by nightfall."

She looked behind her at the name of the métro station,

then forward again to note the street signs, the buildings. "You needn't bother."

"It is no bother. We are soviets, we look out for one another. Besides, you are an old friend."

A stretch, but she wasn't going to contradict him. "I will stay with Evgeni. We have much to plan."

Silence pounded her for three steps. Five. Ten. Paul cleared his throat. "I . . . respect that you have much to plan. But you will still need to sleep."

Nadya shifted her bag to the other shoulder. "Must I spell this out for you, Paul? I will stay with Evgeni."

His scoff sounded disgusted. Or jealous. Something, anyway, that made her hackles rise even before he opened his mouth again. "I'm sure your mother would be thrilled to know th—"

"My mother died a slave to the old ways. Giving birth to her tenth child, though she was too old for it. Too weak. A babe that couldn't last more than a day anyway." Like six of the others. Nadya shook her head, clenched her jaw. That had been the very day she'd stomped from her father's house. From the farm. The day she'd hitched a ride all the way to the city and sought out the women's battalion she'd heard about.

If she was going to die, it would be for something bigger than herself. Fighting an enemy she could see.

"I am sorry. About your mother. I hadn't heard."

Nadya didn't look at him. "I won't be enslaved to the same outdated institution. I won't accept the archaic idea that a man can do what he wills, but it is a woman's duty to stay at home and give him baby after baby in the hopes that one will survive. I will live the life I please." She shot him a glare. "And I will sleep wherever I please."

And in the new Russia, they could all do the same. Those women who actually liked tending squalling children could do so for them all, when they turned the children over to the state to be raised. *This* was a cause, a goal worth fighting for. Freedom.

Paul pointed to the right at the next intersection. "How very . . . forward-thinking of you."

His shin may yet taste the bite of her boot. "Are you judging me, Paul?"

"Your ideals? No. Your particular choice?" He made a face. And despite her frustration with him, she relaxed. Jealousy and male petulance were easier to swallow than judgment. "I cannot approve of that smooth-faced boy. Why have you chosen *him*?"

That jumpy place in her stomach made itself known again. She certainly hadn't *intended* to get involved with the too-handsome soldier she'd found herself serving beside in the trenches last year. It was cliché. And ill-advised.

But there was something about Evgeni she hadn't been able to resist forever. Not the charm in his smile. No . . . it was something in his eyes when he looked at her. Something that went beyond desire. When he looked at her, he saw what she wanted. What she stood for. He saw all she railed against. He saw it, and he respected it, and he liked her all the more for it.

She wasn't about to explain any of that to Paul, though. Instead, she tried on one of his shrugs. "Perhaps I like smooth-faced boys right now. And when I decide I do not any longer, then I'll simply move on."

She made no attempt to interpret his grunt. Especially not when he pointed at a particular door. "Well, he's in there. I'll leave you to your reunion. My lunch break is over, and I must get back to work. I'll be back this evening."

It was much easier to like Paul when he was leaving. Her smile was unforced this time. "Thank you for meeting my train, comrade."

He waved that off and hurried toward the corner, where he turned to the left and out of sight.

Nadya strode up to the door, paused only long enough to drag in a deep breath, and then knocked. Through the cheap wood she could hear the sounds of a scraping chair and shuffling feet. She tried to brace herself for the feeling sure to punch her in the stomach when she saw him again—that strange weaving of want with need and the wishing that she didn't want or need it.

The door opened, and for a moment she saw the expression on Evgeni's pale face that she had to think he prepared for Paul. Because the second his gaze dropped to her, it shifted to something far different. The only word she had for it was something she'd had little enough experience with in her life.

Joy.

"Nadya! How did you get here so soon?"

Were she a romantic like her little sister, she would say love for him had given her wings. Had she been the family-oriented woman her mother tried to make her, she'd have said he needed her, and so here she was.

But she was a soldier, so she stepped inside and said, "Surprisingly, I ran into no obstacles."

Still. Even soldiers had passions beyond the battlefield. So she nudged the door shut and leaned into him, stretching up on her toes and capturing his lips with hers.

He moved slowly, stiffly, but she knew it was only his injuries. He slid one arm gingerly around her waist, but the hand he pressed to her cheek was as urgent as ever. "Nadezhda," he murmured against her lips.

She sighed, closed her eyes, and only now, when they'd been proven false, let the fears gnaw at her. She'd thought he was dead. Feared it. Dreaded it. "I have bad news." It wasn't her fault, but still she kept her eyes closed to keep from seeing the frustration that would enter his eyes. Her bag slipped from her shoulder, and she let it fall to the floor. It made it easier to grip his shirtfront in her fingers. "He is dead. Our Prussian."

With her eyes closed, she could feel the hitch in his breath, hear it. "How?"

"The war, so far as I could gather. I claimed to be his sister, traveling to escape the unrest at home. They showed me his body. Bayonet through the chest."

"Then there is no option," Evgeni said. "We must find my bag. I have not yet been able to make it back to the site of the wreck."

"Clearly." She opened her eyes again so that she could visually trace each scrape, each bruise, each shadow visible. "How you survived so long on the front lines with barely a scratch and then managed to nearly die twice in France when you're out of uniform, I will never understand."

He breathed a laugh that was only an echo of his usual good humor. "I am a man above men."

He was. And yet when he said it, he was joking. She shook her head and touched a finger to a cut on his cheek that had mostly healed over. It must have been from the train accident, rather than the shelling. "We will find your bag. And we must also find your brother."

His expression shifted, shuttered. He pulled away. Didn't let go of her completely, but angled himself toward the table, where she could see a white rectangle with *Zhenya* scrawled across it. "That is going to prove a challenge too. He's gone to London." His voice said it was bad, even before his words did.

She braced herself. But even so, it didn't prepare her for the blow.

"He's working for the British Admiralty."

WEDNESDAY, 10 APRIL 1918

Lily licked the tip of her pencil and leaned closer to the sturdy paper secured to her easel to trace a darker line around the eye of the bird on the page. The real creature had flown away twenty minutes ago, but not before posing just long enough for her to put a rough sketch down. It had stood there on the tree branch, mostly obscured by leaves, peeking out at her. Curious but hesitant.

She'd snapped a photo first, and no doubt that would turn out better than this. But she did like to work on her other media too.

"You have such an eye for composition, Lily Love." A smile lit Mama's voice as she turned from her own easel to take in Lily's. "It never ceases to amaze me. That's always my biggest struggle in a painting."

Lily looked over at her mother's work in progress—a watercolor today, since it was easier to transport and would dry quickly. Not what Euphemia Blackwell was famous for, but she often used them as practice for her commissions. Lily could sit for hours and watch her work, try to pick up her methods. Or she had once, when she had the time to spare. This leisurely morning in the park with her mother had become more the rarity than the norm. "If you struggle with composition, no one would ever know."

Mama laughed. "*Because* I struggle with it, I put much time and effort into it. Not like you—you make it look so easy. Just lift your camera at the perfect moment, click, and there you have it. A perfectly composed piece of art."

"Oh, absolutely. It's just that simple. Much like you lift your pencil, scratch a few lines on the page, and have a masterpiece."

They shared a chuckle and both turned back to their easels. "I've missed this," Mama said on an exhale, dipping her brush into her water jar. "We haven't had nearly enough time to draw and paint together since the war began."

"I was just thinking the same thing." She tilted her head a bit, debating whether the markings on the wing needed darkening. No . . . she'd darken it with pigment later.

"I suppose this has been good preparation for me, though."
Her mother's voice had a note of sorrow in it . . . but more
loudly, a note of probing. "Soon enough you'll be married and
off on your own, both of you. I'll need to learn how to get used
to a quiet house."

Lily looked over again, a burst of laugher escaping. "Subtle,
Mama."

Her mother shot her a grin, only seconds long before she
turned back to put a masterful stroke of purple onto her paper.
"I still can't quite believe your father finally found gentlemen
you both like, and that they happened to come together. Quite
convenient, to my way of thinking."

"Don't go marrying us off in your thoughts just yet. We've
only seen them half a dozen times." Six times in the two weeks
of their acquaintance. They'd come to dinner twice more since
Easter and had dropped by to take them for a walk in Hyde
Park too.

Pleasant, each and every visit. Pleasant and . . . strange.
Zivon Marin liked her—she felt sure of that. But she wasn't so
sure he ever would have spoken to her again if it weren't for
Clarke and Ivy. It made her wish she didn't like him quite as
much as she did. But there was something about him. A depth.
A layering. And that awareness . . . Never was there a time
that he didn't react to something before she'd even noticed it.

She turned her pencil on the leaf partially obscuring the
bird.

Before Mama could do more than open her mouth in reply,
a rumble from the sky invaded the day. They both looked up,
years of habit making them hold their breath, waiting to see
what mechanical beast might appear. One of theirs, doing a
routine patrol? Or one of Germany's, ready to drop bombs
on them?

Lily, like probably every other resident of London, had
learned to identify the silhouettes of each British aircraft,

and she let out a loud breath when she recognized the Camels. "I hate never knowing when we're safe," she murmured as the engine noises faded again. "First they were only at night, then only during the day. . . . Now, unless it's raining, we just never know."

Mama's silence drew Lily's gaze back to her. She found her mother looking at her, her eyes so very serious. "That, my love, is why your father and I have been trying to secure your futures. Because we *never* know. Whether we're at war or not, we never know. We never have forever."

Lily gripped her pencil, not knowing what to say to that.

Mama sighed. "You don't seem quite as lovesick as your sister, I've noticed. Though I couldn't be sure if it was that you actually like Mr. Marin less than she does Lieutenant Clarke, or if you just hide it better."

For a moment, Lily simply studied her drawing. "There is a third option. That *he* doesn't like *me* as much as Clarke does Ivy. I'd be a fool to pin my heart to my sleeve for him to steal and then toss aside."

"He'd be the fool if he did that."

He certainly didn't strike her as such. Not in terms of intelligence, anyway. But what did she really know about him? He shared tidbits here and there, spoke of his brother and his parents, but never of his work. Never of the Revolution. Never of anything that determined why he'd decided to come here.

"Do you think . . . ?" Afraid even to put words to the nebulous fear that had been plaguing her, she had to start over. "Do Daddy and the admiral really trust him? Or is it, perhaps, that Daddy's trying to keep an eye on him for Blinker?"

Mama's brush paused mid-stroke. "Why would you ask such a thing?"

"Because . . ." Because her father had slung an arm around her shoulders last Sunday after the gentlemen had left and said how glad he was that she wasn't quite so eager to leave them as Ivy. Maybe it was just Daddy teasing her. Or maybe it was a warning not to give her affection—or her trust—to the Russian too quickly.

A lesson she'd learned the hard way four years ago. Sunday night she'd gone up to her room and dug out the letter her old friend Johanna had posted to her as her family left England. *Don't take it personally*, it had said at the end.

She wouldn't even have considered it, if not for those words. Then she couldn't *help* but do so. Couldn't help but remember anew that, all that time, her supposed friend had been someone other than who Lily had thought. She'd knowingly used her. Deceived her.

Not a mistake Lily cared to repeat—especially with a man who intrigued her in a way simple friends had never done.

Mama patted her hand and then motioned toward the path they'd followed into the park. "There's Jamie. I suppose that means we ought to pack up, if I mean to make my aid meeting on time. Are you certain you don't want to join me today?"

Her eyes darted to the path where Eaton's grandson was strolling, ready to help them carry their supplies home again, then back to her mother. "I promised Daddy I'd have lunch with him."

Mama's smile was warm. Indulgent. Unsuspecting. "That sounds far lovelier for you. And while your father has certainly not told me of any suspicions he has of Mr. Marin, if they exist, I'll say quite readily that *I* like him. And not just because he saw my point with the propaganda poster either." She paused. Grinned. "At least, not entirely."

Chuckling, Lily stood, hands moving toward the easel and their art supplies. Doing by rote the familiar while the forbidden danced on her tongue. She didn't *want* to ask the question that had settled there, ready to spring. But she had to. "Do you ever regret not helping Daddy when he asked? With the propaganda?"

Mama's hands didn't pause, just gathered her brushes. "I do not. Perhaps my stance is unpopular in our crowd, but . . . art is a powerful thing. It can inspire us, move us, create feeling in us. I cannot justify its use in deception."

Lily unclipped her paper. "But what if it could help end the war?"

"Even so. One must always ask if the ends justify the means. After working all these years in the hospital, you've seen first-hand the damage wrought by mustard gas. I'm sure the inventor of that was told that he could help end the war faster. Do you think that makes it right for him to have done so?"

Lily tossed her pencil case into the basket with Mama's paints and brushes, knowing her frustrations were mirroring her mother's growing agitation. "You cannot possibly be likening propaganda to poison gas!"

"No." A ghost of a smile settled on Mama's lips. "It's worse, I think. Poison gas destroys only a man's body. But propaganda, Lily . . . it tells them a story, invites them to believe in something it cannot back up. It lures our men into supposedly glorious battle and then crushes their spirits—their very faith in God and country—when it instead delivers an inglorious hell on earth."

Lily wanted to deny it. Wanted to provide the arguments Daddy always did—that men had always told of the glories of battle to inspire one another to take it up. That they'd always found one cause to champion and another to put down to rouse the hearts of their neighbors toward action. The ideas were nothing new. Just the methods.

But at the same time, like her mother pointed out, Lily had seen those men in hospital. The ones scarred not by gas on the outside but by horror on the inside. This war, she'd heard her father and his friends say quietly behind closed doors, was not like any that came before. The weapons were so much more deadly. The offensives so long and pointless.

The death tolls so high. The boys who signed up with glee, determined to do their bit for king and country, came home broken, disillusioned, and . . . empty. Unable to believe any longer in patriotism.

Unable, all too often, to even believe in God.

Mama may have a point when it came to propaganda that made promises so blatantly false. But that wasn't what Lily's work was used for. Would her mother see the difference? "But what if . . . what if you could do something that would *help* the men in the field?"

Leaning over to pour out her rinse water, Mama shook her head. "I've tried to think of a way to do that, my love. To help them see God still at work in the trenches." She straightened, her face lined with failure. "My imagination isn't so good. I know He *is* there. But I don't know how to show Him."

Lily slid her drawing into her portfolio. "I can imagine a situation where your art *could* be used to directly help, though. What if Admiral Hall came to you and said he wanted to convince the German High Command that we were trying to achieve a particular aim here at home and needed *false* propaganda posters to supposedly leak to them? Wouldn't that be different?"

Her mother looked amused. "Perhaps *you* ought to try to find a way to show God to the lads in the trenches, Lily. Your imagination is apparently better than mine. I cannot fathom Blinker ever coming to me with such a plan."

"But if he did?"

Mama laughed, but it wasn't her usual bright, full-hearted one. Just a dry echo blowing in the wind. "I don't know. Then I suppose I'd have to wrestle with whether using the gift God has given me in order to lie is excusable if it's lying to one's enemies instead of one's friends. From all I know of my Lord, He does not make such distinctions. And yet . . ." she said, snapping the case of paints closed, "it isn't a question your

father wrestles with at all, and he is a man of solid faith."
She shrugged, not looking exactly happy with the disparity.

Perhaps Lily's answering sigh gave away more of her own
torment than she intended.

Mama reached over to cup her cheek. "I know it bothers
you, this disagreement your father and I have over this. I'm
sorry. I shouldn't be so vocal about my opinions."

Lily shook her head. What else could she do? And conjured
up a smile. "I think Ivy finds it amusing."

"You don't, though. I suppose because you're an artist too,
so the questions hit closer to home."

Closer than she knew. She looked at the watercolor her
mother had created. Two hours of her time, nothing she ever
meant to sell, and yet it stole Lily's breath. The way she used
color was simply astounding. Lily herself hadn't even noticed
that tinge of blue in the sidewalk. The hint of yellow in the sky.
Not until Mama put it to paper. "I'm not an artist like you."

"Nor am I one like you." Her mother dabbed at the paper,
testing its dryness, and nodded. "Photography can do what a
painting can't, in some ways. Because people think it above
denial, they are willing to accept the story it tells with far
more faith." She handed Lily the painting, a spark of teasing
in her eyes. "I don't envy you having to wrestle with the questions of how God would have you use *that* power."

"Thanks for that cheery thought." She slid Mama's work
into the portfolio and then turned to dismantle her easel as
her mother did the same with hers.

Mama laughed, brighter this time. "Have a bit of faith in
yourself, Lilian. You use your gift to edify your friends, not
tear anything down. That is surely a godly purpose. Did you
not see the look on Mr. Marin's face when he saw himself
smiling in front of the Moscow skyline?"

She had. And it had made the hour of work so very worthwhile. The photograph itself may not have been genuine, but it

told a true story nonetheless. A story of his love for the home that he might never see again.

But it was a different question entirely when, after handing over the supplies to Jamie and bidding her mother farewell, she turned toward Whitehall.

She went in the back, as always, but she wished she hadn't when she heard Zivon's and Clarke's voices coming down the stairs. Had she gone in the front, she could simply say she was meeting Daddy for lunch—but no visitors ever came in this way. She had little choice but to dash down the stairs and pray they didn't spot her.

She gave them ample time to clear out before finding her father. They shared a quick lunch, though twenty minutes later she was back in her workroom. A basket of film was awaiting processing, a note from the admiral asking if he could have the pictures developed by tomorrow morning.

As she got to work, her mood lightened a bit. This was the largest part of her work, and it was strictly routine. Developing photographs. Filing the original film, along with a copy of each. Pinning to the back wall any pictures of familiar faces, next to the other pictures they already had of them. It was something she'd begun doing of her own volition at the start of the war and which Hall had called invaluable on more than one occasion. There was nothing debatable about most of what she did. It was just work.

Maybe she shouldn't, but she let the darkroom soothe all the questions away. All that mattered at the moment were the negatives, the solutions, the baths, the drying racks, the wall and pins.

The simple elements of her world.

9

THURSDAY, 18 APRIL 1918

The warm breeze blowing through Hyde Park should have made Zivon thrill with this arrival of spring, far earlier than he was used to. Instead, it made him keenly aware of the ticking of time. Of the fact that he'd heard nothing from Evgeni. That the ambassadors had had no better luck in finding him. That every day that marched onward took him further and further from the evidence he needed to collect.

He turned onto the familiar path that wove along the Serpentine. He'd gone four times already to the embassy, as Filiminov, to check in. While there, he'd paid close attention to the layout of the offices, where each secretary and assistant went, what they were carrying. He'd tried each time to make friends, gain trust.

But never had he felt secure enough to either sneak toward their telegraph machine or ask a favor of anyone else.

Coward. That's what Evgeni would have called him. And maybe he was right. Maybe he should take the risk. Ignore all the signals that told him it would be a mistake. Maybe—

Be still, and know that I am God.

Zivon sighed and slipped his hands into his pockets. Maybe that thought wasn't from God at all. Maybe it was his own cowardly subconscious trying to get him to do nothing instead of something.

But he hadn't been doing nothing. He'd been sending out a few benign messages to his former colleagues, hoping that someone somewhere was still at work. If so, they would intercept the telegrams. They'd decode them. They'd reply. And then he could ask them if they could obtain a new copy of that lost message.

But he'd had no response. Of course. He'd known it was a long shot. Still, it was possible that one or two had sworn allegiance to the Bolsheviks just to survive. That they were secretly working for the White Army. It was possible.

Just not reality.

A mist too fine to be called rain had been drifting over the city for the last hour; the chaps in the office assured one another that it meant a quiet evening on the aerial front. He would take solace in that, but still he wished for a slice of sunshine to color his upcoming promenade with Lily. Or, failing that, a lovely snow would be good.

His lips curved at what his companions would think of snow in April. It would surely be better than this, though. He never quite knew what to do with these silly mists. They were too light to require an umbrella, yet a fedora and overcoat didn't keep his face from receiving the wet breeze.

Up ahead, he spotted what his eyes had been seeking—that streak of red-gold that meant Lily. She wore a hat too, one whose brim wasn't wide enough to help protect her either, but it didn't quite eclipse her hair.

He'd taken to watching for that hair, even when he shouldn't be. It's why he had spotted her no fewer than four times at or near the OB. Curious, that. What was she doing? Meeting her father? Running errands? He didn't know. And since she'd clearly been trying *not* to be seen by them last week, he hadn't brought it up.

But he'd been paying attention.

Clarke had gotten out ahead of him tonight and was already standing with the girls, his posture that enviable one of ease and expectation, all fluid motion as he gestured about something or another. He couldn't seem to talk without using his hands.

Lily spotted Zivon before Clarke and Miss Ivy did, her smile taking the place of the sunshine that had hidden behind the mist. That was the usual way—the other two were always so busy gazing at each other that they never seemed to notice him or Lily, which they both found amusing. She greeted him now with a lifted hand, shifting away from her companions in expectation of his arrival.

A smile settled on his mouth. She always lured it out. There was something about the way she looked at him—the way she looked at everything—that warmed that place inside that usually felt as frozen as a Siberian winter.

"Lovely day, isn't it?" she said once he'd drawn near, her eyes sparkling.

He laughed and wiped at his face. "Were I a duck, I would heartily agree."

Grinning, she tucked her hand into the crook of his arm as had become her habit, and they began to walk. Her sister and Clarke would no doubt fall in behind them when they realized they'd been abandoned. "I do actually like this weather. The way the light plays on it is astounding. Just look." With her free hand, she motioned toward the lake.

Though there was no direct sun, evening light still permeated the clouds. There were patches dark as pewter, others glowing silver, some nearly white. And the mist, annoying as it was on his face, *did* add a gilding to it all, catching that soft light and spreading it around.

His breath eased out. "I have never noticed that before." But that was Lily.

He paused on the path before she could press on his arm. Three weeks had been sufficient to train him in her patterns. "Here?"

She laughed even as she drew her camera out of its home in her pocket. "I think here will do quite nicely. To start."

Always to start. Walking with her was an exploration of angles and light, things he'd never before paused to appreciate. He stayed close to her side as she took her shots, bending down when she did to see the world from the same angle, at least momentarily. But even so, he knew she'd surprise him when she showed him the prints. She always did.

She fiddled now with the light and focus mechanisms. Then her fingers found the cord that led to the push-pin, trailed down it in that way they always did. A moment later, the shutter snapped closed, opened again. She shifted just a bit, fiddled for a single second with something, and then pushed it again. Another shift. Another push.

She could be at it for several minutes if she stayed true to pattern.

Zivon glanced over his shoulder, verifying that Clarke and Miss Ivy were meandering past them on the path, their pace so slow that anyone could see it wasn't the exercise they were after, just the company. They smiled at him but didn't interrupt their conversation otherwise.

He smiled back, let his hands fall into that comfortable position behind his back, and closed his eyes against the mist. Listened.

Birdsong. Children playing. Nurses scolding.

Russian syllables, muttering about war and support and desperation.

Zivon's eyes flew open. He knew those voices. *Both* of them, which made dread slink down his spine. One was Nabokov—

not surprisingly, Zivon supposed, given how close Hyde Park was to the embassy.

But the other—to whom did that belong? He'd heard it before, he knew he had. But not from the embassy.

They were coming from beyond that line of bushes, no doubt from the bench positioned there. Zivon cast a glance at Lily—she was focused now upon the ducks enjoying a puddle—and then slid one step closer to the voices.

"Perhaps we could appeal the decision." Nabokov, he was sure of it. He spoke quietly, though not exactly in a whisper. "Ask for more."

"And risk having what was granted taken away? Be reasonable, Konstantin. The king was quite generous in allotting us enough to keep *ourselves* running. It was too much to hope that he would agree to support the other embassies as well. That will have to fall to their host nations or to generous patrons. You know as well as I that some of the other ambassadors can fund themselves."

"Assuming they can access their funds, yes." A sigh blustered out.

Zivon closed his eyes again to better focus on the unknown voice's cadence, rhythm, accent. Upper class, that much he could identify without thought. Educated. Which did little to narrow down the list of his acquaintances from recent years.

"I pray this aid we secured will be sufficient to support our people who are here in England, anyway. Surely the Bolsheviks will be brought under control soon. Have we heard any more from Maklakov? About whether the United States will intervene?"

"No. Though I know he continues to speak the logic of it to them. If Germany takes advantage of the chaos and moves into our territory, it will spell disaster for all the Allies."

"I want to trust they'll see this wisdom, Fyodor, but . . ."

Fyodor. Zivon's eyes flew open again. Not—but yes. It had

to be. Fyodor Suvorov. *Of course* it was Fyodor Suvorov. He and Nabokov were cousins or some such, a fact that had completely escaped Zivon's memory until now. *Oh, Lord, why?*

He stepped back to Lily's side, his fingers curled into his palm.

She stood. Glanced at him at first, then frowned. "Are you all right?"

He could have kissed her for not saying his name. He didn't look over his shoulder, but still, he heard the hitch in the conversation behind the bushes. They wouldn't be alarmed at hearing an English miss, but they could well react if they heard *his* voice, with its Russian accent.

In that moment, he envisioned no fewer than five different scenarios. He let them play out and deemed all but one of them unacceptable.

So he touched a soft hand to Lily's elbow and leaned close enough to whisper in her ear. "I am not. Can we walk a bit away from here? I will explain."

For five long seconds, she simply held his gaze, thoughts ricocheting through her winter blue eyes. But then she smiled, tucked her hand into the crook of his elbow, and said, at a normal volume, "I'd like to get a few photographs of the ducks from another angle now if that's all right, dearest. Over by that tree, perhaps?"

Far enough away to be out of earshot, and the tree would provide him cover if Suvorov and Nabokov emerged onto the path. That should have been all that concerned him.

So why did his heart stutter over that *dearest*? She'd said it only to preserve the anonymity he was clearly striving for. He knew that. Even so. No one had ever called him by such an endearment, other than his own mother. Alyona certainly hadn't.

It made a bit of the tundra thaw.

They ambled toward the tree as if they were just two carefree Londoners out for a stroll. But Zivon was careful to keep his back to the other Russians.

Once at the tree, Lily raised her camera again, but she didn't look through the viewfinder. She looked at him. "Talk."

First, he took in a long breath. "Apologies. It is probably nothing. It is only . . . there were men speaking Russian over there. And one of them is an old acquaintance. We served together in the Foreign Ministry before the war."

Which meant that had the two spotted him, Fyodor would have called out an enthusiastic *Marin!* while his cousin was calling *Filiminov!*

Disaster.

Lily blinked. "I'm afraid I don't understand."

He exhaled. "Of course. Apologies again. I have not announced to anyone in Russia that I am here. Given the target I painted on my back, it seemed wisest to remain incognito for a while."

She glanced past him, though only for a second, then she looked at her camera. That, as much as the soft padding of feet over grass and the voices, now speaking in French, talking of the theater and children and Kira, told him that the men had emerged. "Do you fear they're Bolsheviks?"

"No. But that does not mean I can trust them. They could say something careless in the hearing of someone with soviet ties. They could mention me in a report that makes its way back to Russia. They could . . ." They could ruin his every plan. His whole purpose.

"Zivon." She breathed his name so softly he barely heard it. Yet it zapped him like a live wire, pulling his gaze to hers from where it had drifted to the pattern in the tree bark.

No one had said his first name in weeks, other than when it was attached to his surname in an introduction. No one had *called* him by it. The closest anyone had gotten was Camden using "Ziv." But that had never been his nickname. That wasn't *him*.

She offered no apology for the liberty either. No, eyes steady in that way she usually reserved for whatever she saw through her camera's lens, she reached up and touched her fingertips lightly to his coat. Over his heart.

Over the encrypted message, ready to send, and the photograph of two German officers, where the papers were hidden away in his pocket.

She shook her head. "You cannot trust your enemies. And if you do not trust your friends, then who *do* you trust?"

Perhaps she meant it to be a rhetorical question. But the answer resounded like a gong. "No one."

She didn't shake her head or pull away or do any other logical thing. No, she sighed. And she rested her whole hand there, over all his worst secrets that she didn't even know existed. "Not even God?"

"Of course I . . ." He couldn't finish the sentence. It would be a lie, much as he wished it weren't. He let his eyes fall shut, to close out the image of her earnest face. "I want to. I try to. But He has taken everything, Lily. *Everything*. My parents. My brother. My career, my home, my future."

She didn't react to his liberty-taking with her name. Except that when she spoke, her voice seemed a few degrees warmer. "No. Not that. As long as you have breath, you have a future. One only He can see."

Zivon could catch glimpses of it too. Logical conclusions to the patterns in play. Cause and effect. Actions and reactions. He just couldn't foresee the surprises. Evgeni vanishing, likely dead. The introduction to a friend like Clarke, who shared so many interests.

Lily Blackwell, who could see beauty in a world he swore had been emptied of it.

The footsteps of the Russians had faded away, the ambassador and his cousin clearly not wanting to be overheard either. But new ones approached from the opposite direction— familiar ones. Ivy and Clarke would double back to join them soon.

He covered Lily's hand with his. "Thank you. For reminding me of that. And . . . and for calling me by name. Your parents may not approve, but it has the sound of music to my ears."

Her smile had the look of sunshine. "Then I shall continue to use it—as you may use mine. If you like."

He let her pull her hand away, given the approaching steps. But he smiled in return. "I like this very much."

Ivy and Clarke's laughter intruded then, and they rejoined them for the walk back to Curzon Street. He and Clarke parted ways soon after. Usually they kept each other company on the tube ride home, but he knew Clarke was meeting a cousin who was in London on leave tonight.

Which was why Zivon had that encrypted message and the photograph in his pocket. He'd been planning on dropping by the embassy again as they were closing. And because it was his plan, his feet took that familiar path.

But as twilight spread its wings over the city and he looked up at the building's proud façade, he paused. *If you don't trust your friends . . .*

He sighed. This game he was playing had seemed the wisest course. The only course. The only way to move the pieces on the board. This was what his division in Moscow had always done. Decide what information to give, what to retain, what to do with it.

But this wasn't Moscow. He was no longer the second in command of the codebreaking division, a man of vital importance to the entire intelligence operation.

Be still, and know that I am God.

If Zivon sent this message to Maklakov, deliberately

undermining the allies he'd decided to join, the ones he hoped to serve out the war beside . . . If he deceived them, even though it was for the greater good, then how could he possibly expect their trust in return?

The ruby ring rested heavily against his knuckle. He wanted to help his people. His country. His czar. But the *how* surely mattered. And was this the kind of man he wanted to be? The kind who would look only at the ends and not question the means?

He pivoted on his heel and strode away from the embassy. He didn't know how to untangle the web he'd already created there. But he could make different decisions moving forward. Better ones. He set his course for the Old Building, somehow not surprised when he spotted Admiral Hall just exiting as Zivon drew near.

"Admiral! Could I be spared one moment of your time?"

Though his driver already had the rear door open for him, Hall steered himself away from the car. He wore, as always, an easy smile. "Marin. What can I do for you?"

"It is, I think, the other way round." *Who do you trust?* The answer *couldn't* be no one. He'd chosen this ally. This life. It was time to act accordingly. He reached into his pocket and pulled out the photograph. "My brother had this in his passport. I have been trying these weeks to determine why. Who the men are. But I have not the resources—or, perhaps, the ability—to answer those questions. Perhaps you will have better luck."

Hall took the photo, studying it with that blinking gaze of his. When he looked up, Zivon could read nothing in his eyes. "Curious indeed. What do you know of your brother's alliances? His role in the war?"

They were questions Zivon would have asked anyone else. Still, they made his shoulders edge back. "He was a lieutenant in the army. Well respected. Certainly not the sort to collaborate with Germans, if that is what you mean. But . . ." He deflated a bit. "To be truthful, I do not know much about his activities in recent years. We have scarcely seen each other since the war. It had crossed my mind that perhaps he had been an intelligence officer for the army."

"Perhaps." Hall flipped it over, frowning at writing on the back. "What does this say?"

"Second day of February of this year. That is all."

The admiral's gaze went distant for a moment. "Hmm. You all were out of the war by then."

"This is true. But many of us still saw the Germans as a threat. I know my colleagues and I continued to do our work as we had always done. We were surely not the only ones."

"Hmm." Hall tapped the photograph against his gloved palm. "I'll see what I can discover. Have my photography expert take a look. If I learn anything of interest, I'll certainly let you know."

That was more than he likely deserved, after keeping it hidden so long. Zivon gave a short bow. "Forgive me for not turning it over more quickly."

"Heaven knows you've had enough else to worry over. Have you heard anything yet from your brother?"

How could it ache each and every time he thought of his brother's silence? Zivon shook his head. "I have posted several letters to our rendezvous. And I have asked the ambassador to have his Parisian counterpart look for him. Nothing."

Hall slid the photo into his jacket pocket. "I'll have my people look too. No offense to Maklakov and Nabokov"—he flashed a smile—"but I daresay my agents will be able to turn him up far more quickly than they can."

Zivon shouldn't have been surprised that Hall knew the ambassadors. It seemed he knew everyone. Which was no reason to be nervous . . . not when they were allies. "Thank you, Admiral. I cannot adequately express my gratitude."

"If you have a photo of him, that would help."

Zivon nodded. It would require destroying Evgeni's false passport, but that was the only picture he had, now that his album was gone. "I will bring one tomorrow."

And pray he'd just done the right thing.

10

L ily jumped at the knock on the door, looking up from her retouching desk at the OB for the first time in . . . she didn't even know. The crick in her neck said it had been quite a while. Sometimes it took a ridiculous amount of time to get her changes to look natural. *Real*.

"Come in." She had nothing light-sensitive out at the moment, just her scalpel and a slew of photographs she'd pulled as possibilities for her latest creation. The admiral had asked her to take an image of an officer on a horse, alone in a field, and put a crowd of Austrian soldiers around him. She had no idea why, but it had proven quite a challenge to integrate so many new figures without making it look clearly fake.

The door opened, and Barclay Pearce stepped in with his usual grin. "Have you got that U-boat picture ready?"

"Of course." She motioned to a photograph sitting on another table. The only change the admiral had asked for on that one was to blot out the designation painted on the side and replace it with another.

Simple. Easy. It had taken only a few minutes. But ever

since that conversation with her mother . . . "Do you know why he needed it?"

Barclay's eyes sparkled with amusement. "I'm afraid the admiral doesn't always explain himself to the mere errand boy. 'Theirs not to reason why' and all that, I suppose."

Lily huffed and folded her arms over her chest. "I don't much fancy ending up like the Light Brigade, thank you."

He chuckled. "You won't. If either of us does, it'll be me. I'm the one he tasks with slipping into government offices and depositing these."

"What?" She snapped up straighter, eyes wide.

Barclay apparently thought her reaction as funny as the assignment itself, given his laugh. Sometimes she wondered what was wrong with that man. He was already halfway out the door again. "Don't fret, Lily. It's all on the up-and-up. Mostly. Oh!" He poked his head back in. "Hall, Margot, and I were chatting this morning, and it came up that she's still looking for a photographer for her wedding. We recommended you. Hope you don't mind."

And how could he shift so quickly from what sounded suspiciously like breaking and entering to wedding photography? "Margot?" Margot De Wilde, he must mean. She didn't know the young lady well . . . and frankly, found her more than a little intimidating. "I've been meaning to ask how the two of you are related."

"She's my sister."

Lily lifted her brows. She knew for a fact Miss De Wilde had come here from Belgium at the start of the war—and that Barclay had been born and raised in the streets of London.

Not that such facts could ever move that grin of his. "My sister married her brother. Ergo, she's my sister."

"Ah."

"Mr. Pearce."

Barclay snapped straighter at the voice, though his salute

somehow looked more satirical than military. "DID. On my way out now."

Lily cast a panicked glance down at the note Admiral Hall had left for her with her current assignment. He hadn't mentioned a time he needed it by, but he rarely checked up on her unless there was a strict deadline.

"Sorry to interrupt you, Miss Blackwell." Hall strode into the room and closed the door behind him, a sure signal that whatever he held in his hands now was sensitive.

But she breathed a sigh of relief at seeing he carried something new and that she hadn't missed a deadline. "Not a problem, sir. It's coming along well."

"Excellent." He held out the paper in his hands. "Would you take a look at this for me?"

"Of course." She took it, not bothering to ask what she was looking for. Whenever he asked her to examine a photo, he gave no information on it. Nothing to bias her, he always said.

"Well, first off, it was clearly taken with an inexpensive camera. The whole thing is out of focus—not badly, but a bit. Enough to tell me the user was either a novice or in a hurry." She reached for her loupe and traced it over the edge of each figure—two German officers. "It's genuine, I think. No edges to indicate a scalpel has been at work. Even if it had been reshot out of focus to cover such tampering, I can usually see a slight line under magnification."

The admiral took a seat in the second wooden chair. He made no effort to look at it over her shoulder. He never did. "Very good. That covers the physical photograph."

"So now the subjects." She set down her loupe again and sat back to study the image as a whole. She saw more photographs by far than anyone else in the intelligence division, so Hall often called on her to identify objects, locations, even people. It was why that pin-studded wall behind her proved so useful. "Looks like France, based on the scenery. The Lorraine region, perhaps?"

"That was my thought. Though it could as easily be Belgium or the Rhineland."

"Mm. It could be, of course. But . . ." Setting that photo down, she spun for her filing cabinet and pulled open a drawer. It only took a minute or two of riffling through her files to come up with the one she wanted. "There." She set it down beside the new one. "If you look at those hills in the background . . ."

"They do appear to match." Hall nodded. "And we know the location of this older one without question—definitely in Lorraine. Excellent eye, Miss Blackwell, as usual."

She would have smiled at the compliment if her attention hadn't moved to the figures. "The men, though. I don't believe . . ." She hated to say she couldn't identify someone, or that they'd never appeared in film she'd developed before. With a gusty exhale, she shook her head. "I don't readily recognize them, so they're certainly not frequent players. But I'll look through the archives again."

"In your spare moments. And as you do, keep an eye out for this fellow too." He slid another image across her desk toward her.

This one was small, no bigger than two inches square. Clearly a passport photograph. Still holding the first picture, she picked up the second. And frowned. She was quite certain she'd never seen this face before; he was handsome enough that she'd have noted it. But that wasn't what made something odd and cold curl up inside her.

Despite being completely unfamiliar, the man was, well, familiar. The eyes. The mouth. But where . . . ?

She flipped it over, in case there was writing on the back. There wasn't. But she did the same to the larger photo, quickly finding the single line at the bottom. The single line written in the Cyrillic alphabet.

Cyrillic—Russian. Her gaze shot back to Hall's as the familiarity clicked into knowledge. "Is this Evgeni Marin?"

The admiral blinked at her. "Did I say it was?"

She placed both images on her desk. "This is what I do, DID."

He chuckled. And stood. "I told Mr. Marin we would try to locate him. This is simply my first step."

Looking for him in the photographs his field agents had taken over the last four years? And then adding in the larger photo . . . it didn't make the cold knot unravel any. "Should I . . . should I be careful? Around Zivon, I mean?"

Hall paused, half turned to the door. "You've never been one to open your heart too quickly, have you? Not like your sister."

It sounded like a compliment, yet landed like an insult. To Zivon as well as her, in this case. "Is that your answer?"

Something shifted in his eyes with his next blink. "Do you think I would have hired him if I didn't find him trustworthy?"

No. Or at least most people wouldn't have. But Hall could very well subscribe to the "keep one's enemies closer" philosophy. "You could answer with a statement, you know, instead of another question."

"Could I?" With a wink, he opened the door. But then he stopped, dragged in a deep breath, and turned back to face her. "Because you are the daughter of one of my dearest friends, I will say this—Zivon Marin is either the greatest asset or the greatest enemy I've ever encountered. I think he is the first. But I can't dismiss the possibility that he is simply more clever than I."

Something everyone who served under him, herself included, had always thought impossible. People may be more intelligent, like the enigmatic Margot De Wilde, for instance. But no one was more clever.

He shook his head. "There is still much about him I don't know. And you're aware of how I feel about unknowns."

She did. She spent hours upon hours each week trying to fill in the blanks for him, using the images sent from agents all over the world to do so. Her throat dry, she could only nod.

He said no more either, clicking the door shut behind him.

Leaving her with questions she didn't know how to answer. Feelings she didn't know how to sort. If Zivon wasn't a true ally, then she'd be a fool to like him.

But she *did*. And if he were all he promised, then she'd be a fool not to try to win a place by his side.

Assuming he even wanted her there.

Letting out a sigh of disgust with herself, she spun back to her desk and picked up her scalpel. Best to focus on what she knew.

The humming drew her up the stairs like a siren song. Lily's exhaustion slipped off her shoulders as she reached the landing and turned down the corridor, toward where her and Ivy's doors stood nestled together in the corner of the house. She could knock on her sister's door. Go in and sprawl under the canopy on her bed to exchange the news about their days.

Instead, she went to her own room, tossing her bag aside and turning on the lights after checking to make sure the blackout curtains were in place. Then she settled in the corner, onto the pillows she kept here just for this purpose. After getting comfortable and pulling a blanket over her legs, she tapped on the wall. *Tap, tap-a-tap.*

From the other side came a scurry. A laugh. And the distinct sound of an enthusiastic someone throwing herself to the floor in the next room. An answering knock. *Tap-a-tap, tap.* And a muted "You're home late! Did you just get in?"

Lily let her eyes drift closed as she rested her forehead against the wall. She'd worn a shiny spot in the paper just there—and Ivy had a matching one on her side. "I did. Daddy and I had dinner together."

"So said the note he sent home. Mama and I seized the excuse to go out too. We haven't had much time together, just the two of us, since the school term began."

"A good evening, then?" Without looking, Lily visualized the pattern of her wallpaper. Where the stripes should be, where the flowers. Lifted a finger and traced her imagined line. A peek to check her accuracy brought a smile. "Did a certain someone find you today?"

"A certain someone may have walked me home from school." The wall between them didn't stand a chance of dampening the grin in Ivy's tone. "We couldn't linger. He was only out running an errand and had to report back to the office yet. But I think Daddy gave him the errand to run just then because he knew it was when I'd be walking home."

And he'd known too that Lily hadn't been anywhere near finished enough to meet her sister herself. "That sounds like Daddy. And like your Clarke, to take the opportunity."

"Well, that's going to have to change."

Lily's eyes flew open. "What?"

"Oh!" Ivy laughed. "Sorry. I moved my dressing table today, and I just looked up and realized I can see myself in the mirror from here. That won't do at all. Just a second, let me tilt it up. I can't stand looking at myself when I'm trying to talk."

Lily chuckled and said loudly enough to still be heard as Ivy moved, "I don't know why. Your Clarke seems to quite enjoy staring at you while you talk."

"Oh, stop." Ivy's voice was more distant. But then footsteps, and the sound came of her settling in again. "And also, don't. I love how you call him that—*my* Clarke."

Lily pressed her hand to the wall where she imagined her sister to be. "He *is* your Clarke. I think he was the moment he set eyes on you. Has he proposed yet?"

She asked it solely because she knew it would send her sister into peals of laughter. The sound of it filled both their rooms and probably stretched out its fingers to find their parents too. "Silly Lily." Even the words were a chuckle. "A bit too soon for that, don't you think?"

"Oh, I don't know. It wasn't too much longer than this that Ara and her Camden knew each other before he proposed. Sometimes you know."

Emphasis on the *you*. Lily's breath hitched, and she prayed Ivy wouldn't hear it. She couldn't even be certain that the Zivon she thought she was getting to know was the *real* Zivon. Every time she turned around, she saw a new layer under the previous one. The man of faith. The man of intelligence. The man of devotion. The man afraid to trust.

Were any of those men one she should hope to make a future with?

Ivy hummed out an agreement that sounded dreamy where Lily's would have sounded tormented. "Yes. Sometimes you do. Even so—this part is so delicious. Why would I want to rush it? Every moment I'm wondering if he's going to find a way to kiss me. And to be quite honest, I wonder if the anticipation is even better than a kiss could possibly be."

Sweet Ivy. Lily leaned back against the other wall in her corner. "I certainly hope not. If you marry, you'll not have to wonder anymore *if* he's going to kiss you, but I should hope you'll enjoy it when he does."

Another laugh. Then the sound of a finger tapping on the wall. Saying, as she'd said so many times in just that way, *What about you?* "Do you think about it? With your Russian?" Walls did nothing to filter the teasing out of her sister's voice either.

Lily pursed her lips. "Maybe." She drew the word out into three syllables. She'd tried to imagine what it would be like. How she would feel. And yes, whether she could imagine looking into his chocolate-drop eyes every day, forever.

But somehow . . . somehow her every imagining always stopped with him a foot away. That was where it always seemed he was. Not physically, but in a way even more real. Whatever secrets he held tight, they kept him distant.

No. Not just his. If he stayed always a foot away, only six inches of it were his fault. The other six were *her* secrets.

"Lil?"

"Hmm?" She stirred, wondering what teasing or question she had missed.

Enough, apparently, to signal to her sister that the wall must go. A moment later her door creaked open and Ivy slipped inside. They had no reason to sneak about these days, but she still closed the door with nary a sound and padded over to her as if they were breaking curfew by talking when they ought to be in bed—a nightly occurrence ten years ago.

Lily held up the blanket so that Ivy could snuggle into the spot beside her.

"So." A word she drew out even more than Lily had her *maybe*. "What is it? With your Russian?"

Lily sighed. "It's *that*, I suppose. He doesn't feel like *my* anything." When she saw the lift of her sister's brow, she added, "All right, that's not true. He's my friend. But that doesn't make him mine. Not in the way that Clarke is—and clearly wants to be—yours."

Ivy's head came to rest against Lily's shoulder. "Do you want him to be?"

In lieu of a shrug, Lily rested her head against Ivy's. "I don't know. Maybe." If she could be sure wanting it was wise. She poked her sister in the side. "But you do."

"I do." Only Ivy could combine a giggle with a sigh to spell pure bliss. "Clarke is everything I ever dreamed of, Lil. No. Actually, he's everything I didn't even know to dream of."

"That's just too sweet for words, you know. I'm not certain I can stand it." The poke turned to a tickle.

Ivy shrieked with laughter and pulled away for a second—long enough to bat at Lily's hand—and then settled back at her side. "He said today that he'd mentioned me in a letter to his mother. She's coming to London for a visit this summer. He wants to introduce me to her."

"Oooo." Lily bumped their shoulders together. "You're as good as engaged, I think."

"In July, maybe. Maybe." She grinned, looking so perfectly radiant. Blissful.

Lily had to squash down the surge of loneliness that swelled up. She couldn't feel lonely now with her sister, her best friend, beside her.

But Ivy was in love. She'd marry. And married women didn't live forever in the room next door.

And yet . . . never in her life had she seen her sister so happy. How could she be anything but happy for her? Tomorrow's loneliness could just wait its proper turn.

"The important decisions, then." Lily made a show of folding her hands in her lap and looking intently at her sister, all rapt attention. "Hemlines have changed since our last discussion of the perfect wedding gown. Should our sketch change accordingly?"

"Now that is a fabulous question." Lunging to her knees, Ivy reached for the stack of sketchbooks that Lily had stashed on a low bookcase at the foot of their chatting nook. She was already flipping them open as she sat.

Lily let out a squeak when photos slipped and tumbled from the pages. She'd forgotten she'd stashed those in there, thinking to finish a sketch sometime.

"Oh, sorry!" Ivy gathered them up . . . and began to laugh.

Lily snatched them from her sister's hands. "What?"

"You know very well what." She pointed at the photos. Three of them, from three different days. All of Zivon as he stood in that way he did, with his hands clasped behind his back. Eyes not quite closed as they sometimes were, but distant behind his glasses. When he was listening. Picking out patterns. "You may *say* you don't know how you feel . . ."

Huffing out a breath, Lily shuffled them back into chronological order, straightening the edges. "I was doing a sketch, that's all." To prove it, she flipped open the sketchbook Ivy still held until she landed on the one she'd started a few days ago.

"Oh, I didn't doubt you were sketching him. I was pointing out that there's meaning to be found in the *fact* that you're sketching him. Just look at this." She pointed at the page where Zivon stood in rough outlines, three-quarters of his figure filling the white space.

"What about it?" Surely nothing had worked its way into the picture that she hadn't known she was putting in. And surely—surely—it wasn't some key to understanding her own feelings for the man.

Ivy bumped Lily's shoulder now. "He intrigues you. How many photographs have you taken of him?"

"A . . . few." Her brows drew together. She took *a few* every time they were together. Not exactly abnormal for her. Except, now that she thought about it, she hadn't taken quite so many of Clarke and Ivy together, though they did make the sweetest picture as they walked in the park. But, while charming, Ivy and Clarke weren't . . . well, as Ivy put it, intriguing.

Ivy lifted her brows. "So if I were to go into your workroom and look through your box of photos, I would see . . . ?"

Lily lifted her chin. "As I said. A few." *Dozen.*

Her sister laughed. "And you're sketching him. You never sketch people."

"That is not true!" In proof, she flipped back through the pages. Past Zivon, past the birds in the park, past Mama's lazy pug who never stirred from his rug when he could help it, past the last iteration of the perfect wedding dress. Eventually she landed on one of their four-year-old cousin. "There. See?"

"Mm-hmm. I certainly do." With a look of supreme indulgence, Ivy made a show of turning to the wedding gown again. "All right, I'll relent for now. But I maintain that your heart knows something your mind hasn't caught on to yet. And your camera tells the tale."

Oh heavens. She certainly hoped not. Lily sighed and tapped a finger to the page. "Gowns."

She needed a while to think of something less terrifying than the prospect of having fallen for a man who could well be an enemy.

11

Evgeni knocked on yet another door, fixed his lips in yet another smile. He'd lost track at this point of how many French farmhouses he'd visited over the last few weeks, in search of the belongings that had "mysteriously" vanished from the wreck site before officials could take them anywhere to be claimed by survivors.

Blighted scavengers. Not that he didn't understand. In German-occupied France, one had to take whatever one could find, borrow, or steal. But he wasn't searching for Zivon's ruby ring. Just their personal items.

The door swung open, and a frazzled-looking woman who didn't look more than twenty-five filled the space. Well, along with the toddler on her hip and an older boy half hidden behind her skirts.

"*Bonjour*." His French, at least, had improved with these visits. Matushka would be proud. He directed his attention fully onto the toddler, a little girl, probably three or four. "You must be the lady of the house."

The girl giggled and buried her face in her mother's shoulder.

141

The woman released a breath that sounded a little bit amused, anyway. "Can I help you, *monsieur*?"

"I hope so." He had his hat clasped in his hands and made it a point not to crowd her. Much like he'd made it a point to wear the shabbier of his shirts. "Two months ago, I was involved in a train accident about a mile from here. It has taken me many weeks to recover and now . . . well, to be perfectly honest, I'm hoping someone in the area came across a few of my personal items. I had no money." Not true, but he knew better than to hope any of *that* would be returned. "But I was hoping to reclaim my photographs. They are all I have left of my family. Have you, by chance, picked up anything blowing about the countryside?"

"Photographs, you say?" She eased back a step, though it looked more like uncertainty than an invitation. "I may have found a few, though I don't recall when it was. We . . . we make a habit of picking up any papers we find blowing about."

"As any good steward of the land would do." He inclined his head, having discovered many knocks ago that he gained far more knowledge through this humble show than by simply stating he was looking for his belongings and asking if anyone had stolen them.

No one wanted to admit to being a scavenger. But they all were. They couldn't afford not to be.

The woman pursed her lips, looked over her shoulder at the boy, and then gripped the door. "Would you wait here for one moment? I will bring out what I found."

"Of course. *Merci beaucoup*." He backed up and turned half away, so that she wouldn't feel he thought her rude when she shut the door on him.

His fingers toyed with the frayed edge of his cap. He knew better than to get his hopes up. He'd been shown dozens of photographs over the last fortnight. No one cared enough about such frivolity to hide them from him. But none had been his. He'd seen not so much as a thread of anything in his bag. The clothes he expected had been worn already, the money used or stowed away, the food long ago put into empty bellies.

But all that could be replaced. The photograph the Prussian had taken could not.

His eyes scanned the lane, hunting for curls turned gold in the sun. He grinned at the mere thought of Nadya trying to act nice and sweet, as he'd told her she must do when knocking on doors. She was many things, his Nadezhda. But *nice* and *sweet* weren't on the list.

His mother would have hated her. Hated her determination to buck tradition, hated the way she spat out the statement that there was no God, no need for family, nothing worth fighting for but the State. And Zivon . . .

The grin faded, gathered, twisted into a frown. Zivon wouldn't like her either, but that was no surprise. He and Zivon could never agree about anything. Not their books, not their friends, not their beliefs, not their politics.

Definitely not their politics.

But even so. They were brothers. And Evgeni should have tried harder to stop him from making such an enormous mistake. He should have tried harder to learn his plan. To read a few of those thoughts ever flying through Zivon's mind. He should have actually spoken to him last Christmas of the dangers his czarist leanings would pose, rather than spending their few hours together teasing him about Alyona.

The door opened again behind him, and the woman stepped out, absent the children but holding more than a single photograph, that was for certain. Evgeni's eyes went wide when he saw she had a whole album.

Not just *a* whole album. *Zivon's* album. "All of them!"

The woman's smile was tight with guilt. "The children looked through them, pretending it was a magazine. You are in here. It must be yours, then, *oui*?"

"Oui." Or close enough, anyway, that his hand shook with awe as he reached out. "May I?"

"Of course. It is yours." She handed the album over.

He flipped open the cover, sucking in a breath at the image that stared at him. Him and Zivon, from their last Christmas with both Batya and Matushka. They were both in uniform—a contrast of army and navy, field officer and intelligencer. Both grinning, showcasing the two traits they actually shared. Batya's eyes. Matushka's smile.

So different, they had always been. Differences so clear in this frozen moment. Zivon, with the spectacles that bespoke too many hours of reading. Evgeni, with the scrapes on his knuckles from his last fistfight.

Yet this was the first photograph in his brother's album. Not Alyona or Matushka or Batya or any of his colleagues. Them. Together.

The woman folded her arms across her middle. "Your brother?"

He could only nod.

"Did he . . . not survive the crash?"

"He did. But we were separated. I have not seen him since."

She muttered something too low or too quick for him to catch and leaned into the doorway. "I found a bag. This was in it. There were clothes, nice ones. Shoes. Money." She shrugged. "All that is left are the photos. I am sorry."

He shook his head. "These are hard times. I do not blame you. Only . . ." He looked up at her again, brows knit. She didn't have to volunteer that information. But if she was feeling generous, he would push just a bit. "This is actually my brother's. And I am grateful to you for it. But I wonder—I have been unable to find my passport, and I cannot easily travel without it, to find him again. Did you see this? Or a friend of yours, perhaps? It was in a bag like the one this was in."

ROSEANNA M. WHITE

The shake of the woman's head was quick enough that it announced her certainty, without being *so* quick that it hinted at deception. "I am sorry. There were a few passports collected from the site, I know, but none for a man your age. And—Russian?"

He nodded. His French might be greatly improved, but he'd never been able to speak it without an accent.

She folded her arms over her stomach. "That is the sort of thing that would have been whispered about, though not exactly valued. Not to insult you, but no one around here would be interested in running away to Russia just now. And I saw no other bag like the one this was in."

His fingers tightened around the leather binding of the album. *He* would be happy to return. As soon as he could. "I assure you, I am not insulted." He gave her another smile, though this one was sure to look sorrowful around the edges. "Well, this is more than I had really hoped to find. I thank you, *madame*, for taking such good care of it. Would that I had something to offer you as a token of my gratitude."

For the first time, her lips quirked up. "That money helped feed my children through the last of winter. That is token enough."

He inclined his head, thanked her again, and then moved off, putting his cap back on his head. Someday, no one would have to steal just to feed their children. Not in Russia, at least. They would all be equal, everyone given a fair portion—as soon as they'd wrestled the last of the wealth from the tyrants who had been hoarding it. That was why they'd had to get out of this war. Too many people had already died for it. Too many resources spent. And why? So that Czar Nicholas could keep on squabbling with his cousins. So all the princes and lords could gain new holdings, expand their empires, grow their power.

He turned right when he reached the lane, and a smile

bloomed on his lips, pushing aside those thoughts. Nadya was just coming around the bend, and she lifted a hand in greeting.

He lifted the album in response.

She kicked up into a run, her skirt flapping. Another thing to make him grin. He hadn't seen her in anything but soldier's breeches since he met her, until she showed up in Paris. He didn't much care what she wore, but it was nevertheless amusing to see her looking so much like a normal girl when he knew she was anything but.

"You found it!" Her eyes gleamed as she drew near.

Evgeni shook his head. "Not exactly. It is Zivon's photo album, that is all. But the woman was quite helpful. She admitted to finding his whole bag and using or selling everything else. She also assured me *my* bag had not been found."

Nadya lifted one dubious brow. "Do you believe her?"

Evgeni lifted one shoulder to match her brow. "We certainly haven't found it elsewhere." He motioned toward a low stone wall that separated one of the farms from the road and eased himself down, granting reprieve to his aching ribs and sore ankle. "And . . . it's possible it's with Zivon, I suppose."

"What?" It came out as a hiss as she planted herself on the stones beside him.

He rubbed at his midsection. "I've been trying to piece together those last moments. So much is a blur. But I think—I think he had ahold of my bag. It could have remained with him. He could have it still."

Her next hiss sounded like a locomotive running out of steam. "You mean to tell me that your czarist brother has the information our contact gave you? And that he has taken it with him to England?"

"I'm telling you he *may* have." Mostly for a distraction, he flipped open the album again. Past the photo of him and Zivon. Matushka. Batya. Alyona with her passel of younger siblings. A few of the Moscow skyline. Newspaper clippings. A few older images.

Nadya rested her elbows on her knees. "Evgeni."

Time and again he'd tried to get her to use his nickname. But *Zhenya* never passed her lips, nor did any endearment. He had half a mind to call her *milaya* sometime just to see what she'd do. "Nadya."

She tilted her face to look at him. "We both know he was not just an interpreter. He was Intelligence. He . . . he could have information he shouldn't have."

"Could . . . or *did*? Do you know something I don't?"

Instead of answering, she reached over to turn another page in the album.

So then. There was information she—or their superiors— didn't want him to know. They were willing to trust him far enough to have him discover what he could, but not so much that they'd lay all their cards on the table, lest he decide to take his brother's side.

He eased out a breath. "I could well have known what he knows by now, if not for the train accident." Assuming Zivon would have listened to him. Talked to him. Actually told him what he was planning, instead of barreling ahead, thinking he alone knew how to plan their future.

Blast him. No one in the world could infuriate him quite like Zivon.

And he never missed anyone quite like him either. He shook his head. "I tried to tell them that killing Alyona was a mistake. Why did no one listen? Do I not know better than any how my brother will react?"

Her chin lifted, her spine straightened. "He had to be shown how steep the cost is for his allegiances. He had to be taught what pain feels like—what the rest of us suffered under the old Russia, that made us envision the new."

He wondered, not for the first time, which of his comrades

had pulled the trigger that day in Moscow. Had it been her? Another of their friends? He dug his fingers into the stone. "We killed his betrothed, Nadya. We'd have been better to poke a nest of hornets."

"From what you've told me of him, I wouldn't have thought him the type to lash out." Her voice was modulated. Cool. The voice of a soldier on a mission, not of the woman who wrapped her arms around him and kissed him until the world fell away.

Sometimes he wished he didn't love the hard side of her as much as the soft. He could hear Matushka's voice in his head. *"Why can't you find a nice girl, Evgeni? One who will be content to tend your home and give me grandchildren?"*

It had been her argument each and every time he'd rejected the suggestions she and Batya made about potential wives for him. *"I'll find my own wife,"* he'd said then. His gaze cut again to Nadya. Or not. She'd made it quite clear she'd never marry, that she considered it a prison to which she wouldn't submit.

Still, they had plans. They would find an apartment together when they made it back to Petrograd. They'd do what the party told them to do, advance in the ranks. They'd make a difference, build a new Russia. And if ever they felt called away from each other, they'd simply part ways.

But Zivon . . . Zivon had always been traditional. Evgeni shook his head. "Perhaps his rage is quiet. But that makes it all the more deadly. He will take everything he knows now and try to destroy the Bolsheviks with it."

Her face was hard. "We won't let him. We'll go to London, we'll find him, find what he knows, get the information the Prussian gave you—and we'll silence him."

It was a wonder the rock didn't crumble under his fingers. "You will not kill my brother." He'd been careful to say *we* before, when speaking of Alyona, even though he'd been kept out of the loop once they'd made a decision. But there was no *we* here. He would do many things for the party, for the new

Russia, for this woman he loved, despite all logic telling him she'd walk away at the first sign of trouble.

But that wasn't one of them.

Her hand landed on the photo album, tugged it from his lap to hers. "If you have a better suggestion—"

"I do. We convince him to live quietly, to retire from any military affiliation. He could have a career teaching at any major university, or translating again. He could just disappear, as so many of the nobility have done."

Her gaze didn't budge from the photo she'd opened to. "So what then? We go to London so you can convince him?"

"Hardly." It came out a snort as much as a word. "He likely thinks I'm dead, and it's best that way. I've never been able to convince him of anything—and he can see when I'm lying in half a second."

With one of those disarming, lightning smiles of hers, she bumped their shoulders together. "So can I. And don't forget it."

And *this* was why he'd fallen for her so fast. He'd never met anyone else who could be so fierce and yet so teasing all at once. He leaned into her shoulder a bit. "He would never give up his career for me. We have to make him want to."

She grunted and flipped a few more pages. Then a few more, but more slowly. Her shoulders relaxed. Her face went from hard to satisfied. "I think . . ."

He knew that tone. It was the one that had convinced him to make a risky charge at her side in the heat of battle. The one that had dared him to meet her later in an abandoned barn. The one that had insisted to their superiors that they could handle the meeting with the Prussian, and that Zivon's determination to flee Russia would be the perfect ruse.

That tone meant trouble. And possible glory. And feeling more alive than he ever had before. "You think . . . ?"

She stared for another long moment at the photos and then sent him a sultry smile. "I think I know how to do this. We convince his new allies that they'd better not believe a word he says." Slapping the album shut, she shot to her feet. "Come on. We have work to do, and if it goes as planned, you'll have your way and his life will be spared."

She didn't add a *But if not* . . . She didn't have to.

❖ ❖ ❖

MONDAY, 29 APRIL 1918

Zivon moved to the edge of the roof, tilting his face up to receive the sunshine. He'd already finished his lunch, but there were a few minutes yet before he had to return to his desk.

Behind him, Clarke gave an exaggerated groan and stretched out his legs. "I don't like the sprinting days. Give me the six-mile run over the sprinting any time."

Zivon chuckled and cast his gaze out over the city. "I do agree. But the short bursts, they help build strength."

"I *know* it. I just don't *like* it. But at least I'm feeling fitter again. And I'm keeping up with you more easily—unless you're holding back."

Zivon shot his friend a half smile. "Do you really want me to tell you if I am?" In truth, he was putting in far more hours than Clarke each week, given that he ran even on their off days just to clear his mind.

Clarke laughed. "No. Let me luxuriate in my ignorance, thank you."

A few of Clarke's colleagues moved their way, balling up their paper sandwich wrappers, and asked him something about their afternoon's assignment. Zivon took that as an excuse to move a step away and draw in a breath of crisp air. He'd woken up in a dark mood again today, thoughts of Evgeni plaguing him.

It had been two months. Two long, excruciating months since the train accident. Since he'd lost his brother. Since all the pieces he'd put together so carefully for his escape had been dashed off the game board.

Evgeni was likely dead. Zhenya dead, the information so carefully concealed in Zivon's album burned up or blown away. All because of the Bolsheviks.

His gaze moved as far as it could over the city, toward the embassy. He hadn't dared to visit again, not now that he knew Fyodor Suvorov could be around. But the conversation he'd overheard in the park eleven days ago kept coming back to him. The diplomats were still working for Russia too. Were trying to convince the Americans to join the White Army's fight.

But he knew they weren't having luck yet. Much as the Europeans considered the United States to have limitless resources, it wasn't true. Especially when one considered that their greatest resource—their people—weren't terribly sympathetic to the czarist cause, what with their love of democracy. Perhaps they viewed the soviets as morally superior.

They shouldn't, though. They *wouldn't*, if they realized that socialist "freedom" involved killing anyone who held a different view. That was no freedom. That was the worst form of tyranny—the kind that lied about what it was.

Could he help them see that, somehow?

Be still, and know that I am God.

The familiar echo made him huff out a breath, curl his fingers into his palm around his ring. *Why did you create this mind in me, Lord, if you don't mean me to use it?*

Vengeance is mine, saith the Lord.

Yes—and he prayed the Lord would hurry. Because he was mighty eager to see what it would look like. Maybe He would use the Americans or the British. Maybe He would simply smite the socialists with His fist. Maybe—

A flash of red-gold caught his eye. Someone moving toward the OB. Someone he recognized even from up here on the roof. She was in her nursing uniform but with her kerchief removed from her head, allowing that flash. As he watched, Lily rounded the building, aimed for the back.

Curious. Visitors never went to the back. And what would she be doing here? Her father was out of the office all day, hence why Clarke was fielding the questions from his colleagues. Zivon meandered around the roof's raised edge, slowly enough that he'd look casual. But quickly enough that he could verify if she did indeed go inside.

He could just barely see her from up here. But he did. He saw her pause to speak to Hall. Saw Hall hand her something. Saw her nod. Then the admiral climbed into his automobile, and Lily disappeared into the OB's back door.

Zivon eased back a step, mind clicking through it all. All the times he'd seen her here or near here when she had no reason to be. All the times Hall had mentioned having a photography expert.

The conclusion was logical. Undeniable. The only surprise, really, was that he hadn't put it together sooner. Because having seen for himself her skill with retouching and developing photos, how could he think anyone *but* Lily Blackwell would be Admiral Hall's unnamed expert?

His lips turned up. She, then, was the one Hall had shown that photograph to. And if anyone the world over could divine its purposes, it was Lily. She could see the beauty, the purpose in anything.

Lunchtime was over. Zivon turned toward the stairwell along with the others, touching a hand to his pocket as he went. Margot De Wilde had given him an invitation to her wedding that morning and mentioned that Lily had agreed to photograph the event for her. Camden had raised those sardonic brows of his and asked him if he intended to ask to escort her officially.

Three hours ago, he hadn't really had an answer. Much as

he liked Lily, courting an English girl seemed no wiser now than it had a month ago. But somehow, realizing her role here . . . well, she wasn't *just* an English girl. She was an intelligence worker, as surely as he was. Maybe it shouldn't, but that fact changed something. Made him realize they had more in common than he'd dared to think.

When next he saw Captain Blackwell, he would indeed ask for permission to escort her to the wedding. And from there . . .

Well, there were still too many variables for him to know for sure what would happen. But it was worth exploring, without doubt.

12

The sigh seemed to build in Lily's very toes before it worked its way up and out of her mouth. She'd snuck away after church and let herself into her workroom at the OB so she could go through another drawer in her filing cabinet. She still hadn't found any other instances of those two German officers' faces. But she'd awoken that morning convinced she *had* seen them before, somewhere.

Or maybe she'd dreamed it up in her desperation to prove to the admiral that Zivon was trustworthy.

She glanced at her watch and winced. She'd promised Ivy she'd be home by three o'clock to start getting ready for the wedding. Already four minutes late, and she hadn't even left yet. But really, how long could it possibly take to slip into her gown and put up her hair?

Then again, she wanted to look her best. Today would mark the first time any gentleman had taken her to something without a parent or sister tagging along. That surely deserved some extra time spent primping.

Especially given that it wasn't just any man. It was Zivon. He would notice the extra care, just as he noticed everything

154

else. And maybe . . . maybe he would show her another layer to the matryoshka doll tonight. One in which he'd look at her as something more than just *friend*.

Well, regardless of his reaction, she needed to be on her way. Since it was likely to be a late night and she couldn't exactly bow out early if she meant to photograph the entire De Wilde-Elton wedding, she'd already alerted both Ara at Charing Cross and the admiral here that she wouldn't be in tomorrow.

But she wouldn't want to laze away the whole day, would she? After a moment of pursed-lipped staring at the fresh pile of film that had apparently been delivered for her yesterday, she scooped half the stack into her bag to process at home. Mama might be suspicious if she disappeared out of the house for hours, but she'd think nothing of her vanishing into her own darkroom at home.

Satisfied, she opened the door—and squealed.

The admiral jumped a bit too and chuckled as he lowered the hand he'd apparently just lifted to knock. "So you really are here. Mr. Pearce said he thought he'd seen you, but I didn't quite believe it. Oughtn't you to be getting ready for the wedding?"

She slid the strap of her bag over her shoulder. "I ought, yes. I was just on my way home—and am already later than I meant to be. Ivy will be champing at the bit, eager as she is to help me get ready." She smiled, though it faded back to neutral when she saw he had a manila envelope in his hands. "Did you need something?"

He blinked. Regarded her for a long moment. And then backed up to let her out of the doorway, shaking his head. "Nothing that can't wait until Tuesday, I'm certain. Let's just enjoy the evening, shall we? After all, it isn't every day that we get to witness the nuptials of two of our own."

Another day, she might have pressed him. Today, however,

she tended to agree. They fell into step beside each other and set a quick pace down the corridor, toward the stairs. "Was the photograph I sent up on Friday all right?" She'd spent painstaking hours working on taking an aerial photograph of one of their new Royal Air Force aerodromes and making it look a great deal busier—and fuller of planes—than it really was. Major Camden had even spent several hours at her side, advising her on where to insert tiny, blurred people, how to arrange the fictional planes, and so forth. She'd been rather proud of the result, which she had to think was being leaked even now to the German Luftstreitkräfte.

Hall chuckled. "It was perfect, of course. But that is hardly what you should be thinking about just now."

Maybe not, but she wasn't exactly going to gush about her hopes and dreams concerning Zivon with DID. "I grabbed some of the new film to process at home tomorrow, if that's all right." She'd taken work home with her before, though on rare occasions. She had to assume he wouldn't have a problem with it now when he hadn't then, but she'd rather be certain than face his anger.

Thankfully, he waved that away. "Of course. But feel no obligation to give up your day off. Tuesday is soon enough, unless you grow bored."

Entirely possible, since Ivy would be teaching and Mama had an aid meeting. Although perhaps she would see if Ara would like to have tea or something. They rarely had the chance to socialize outside of Charing Cross, but her friend had taken the day off tomorrow too.

"See you soon," Hall said by way of farewell as they mounted the stairs. He continued up them when she peeled off at the first landing and aimed herself out the back door.

The weather was beautiful, a perfect afternoon that would lead to a perfect evening for a wedding. The warmth in the air put a bounce in her step as she hurried home.

Eaton opened the door for her the moment her foot touched the first stair, his eyes gleaming. "You had better hurry. Miss Ivy is in a state."

Lily chuckled and turned toward her darkroom rather than toward where her sister waited. "I'll be up as soon as I drop this off."

She did hurry, though, depositing the film in a bin, her old bag with it, and then picking up a new bag Ivy had given her to match her gown. This she'd already packed with her two favorite cameras and more blank film than she could possibly use in a single night.

"There you are! I swear, Silly Lily." Ivy charged into the corridor, her eyes wide, as Lily closed the door on her darkroom. "You're going to be late! You aren't even dressed yet."

"I have plenty of time."

The exasperated huff of breath Ivy gave her disagreed. Her sister grabbed her by the wrist and pulled her toward the stairs. "Up to your room, young lady. Now. I won't have you looking anything less than perfect for this occasion, thank you very much. It's far too exciting."

"Ivy." How was it that seeing Ivy's enthusiasm put a check upon her own? Made anxiety overtake the hope she'd been dwelling on all day? "It isn't that exciting. I'll be taking photos—"

"You'll be breathing too." Ivy sent an amused look over her shoulder. "No point in listing what you *always* do as a reason for the night not being special."

Well, she couldn't exactly say to her sister, *"I don't mean to get any more attached to my date until I know the government has decided he's on the up-and-up."* She opted instead for the most convincing argument for temperance in this situation that she'd been able to land upon. "Well, how about this as a bit of cold water on the excitement? It's been two months and he doesn't trust me any more now than he did at day two of our acquaintance."

"I find that infinitely hard to believe." If anything, Ivy quickened their pace on the stairs, rather than slowing in thought.

"It's the truth. He hasn't told me anything about what drove him here. He'll talk a bit of childhood memories, but that's it."

Her sister sent her a strange look over her shoulder. One that, instead of being commiserating, seemed confused. "What else do you expect, Lil? Clarke hasn't talked to me of battles and fears and close scrapes either."

Not uncommon for a soldier who'd been in the thick of things, she knew. It was too hard to process the dichotomy— the trenches, where they became mere animals, and then London again, where the world had kept on spinning. Where people had dinner parties and went to the theater and planned house parties for the weekends. "It's different."

"I really don't think it is." Ivy's words themselves might not have made Lily take any particular notice, but the tone demanded it. "Whatever Clarke saw at Jutland, whatever led to the pneumonia that brought him here to London, that shaped him. But it's painful. And if I've learned anything from Daddy, it's that men don't often like to speak of what happened. Not to us, anyway. Whatever your Russian went through, it's no doubt the same. His country is embroiled in a civil war, Lily, and he was obviously caught up in it enough that he had to escape or be killed. You think that caused him no pain?"

"Of course it did. It separated him from his brother, for one thing." And she knew that the silence from Paris weighed more heavily on him every day.

"*After* he fled, yes. But what led up to it?"

"I don't know! That's my point!" And it was *that*, wasn't it, that made Hall view him with caution?

Ivy sighed, tugging her around the landing and to the next

flight of stairs. "No, you're *missing* the point. He may never tell you—or maybe not for years. Not because he doesn't trust you, but because he *can't* talk about it. Did you know that Daddy never told Mama about his role in the Sudan until we were in school? Ten years of marriage before he could talk about it with her. And I certainly hope you're not going to say that Daddy didn't trust her."

Lily's breath abandoned her. "How did you learn that?"

Ivy pulled Lily onto the same step and wove their arms together. "I had the same fears as you, you know. With Clarke. He never mentions the war, the battles, the . . . *anything* from when he was on a ship. Sometimes he'll mention a friend or relate a funny story. But nothing *real*. Nothing ugly. So I asked Mama."

What a simple way to get a bit of advice—one she'd never thought of when it came to this. "So I'm just being unreasonable?"

"Impatient, anyway." Ivy beamed a smile of pure sunshine at her. "We must grant them time. And give them the certainty that whatever nightmares haunt them, we're willing to stand by their sides. Willing to be silent about it, if that's what they need. Willing to listen if and when they're ready to talk."

Lily bumped her shoulder into Ivy's. "When did you get to be so grown-up, anyway?"

"Gracious if I know. Probably when I had to learn how to wrangle a classroom full of eleven-year-olds on my own." She bumped Lily's shoulder back. "May I say one more thing?"

Lily chuckled. "Could I keep you from it?"

Her sister studied her for a moment as they turned in unison toward their bedrooms. "I don't think it's just a matter of whether you think he trusts you. I think it's a matter of whether you trust him."

"And she's grown wise too," Lily said to the portrait of Great-Aunt Matilda on the wall.

Great-Aunt Matilda clearly found it a marvel as well. The arch of her brows said so.

Ivy laughed. "I have to think it's that his previous world was so far removed from what's familiar to us. I can convince myself that I don't *need* to know what happened aboard the ship because it's nothing every other wife and sweetheart of a sailor isn't wondering too. It's not unusual—whatever he lived through, and his silence. But Mr. Marin . . . his experiences are surely quite different from the average English lad's. So, can you live with that, or is it cause to break things off?"

The words sent a jolt through Lily, making her pause with her hand outstretched toward her door. "Who said anything about breaking things off?" She couldn't imagine doing that. Or wanting to do that. Her questions, and Hall's doubt, weren't loud enough to drown out the allure of another hour in Zivon's company. Of hearing the beautiful way he shaped his vowels, of watching him take in the world around him. Of seeing his thoughts go deeper and deeper the longer they talked. Of cajoling him into teaching her a common phrase in a language she didn't know.

What would a week be without learning how to say "pass the salt" in Slovakian or Bulgarian or Portuguese?

Ivy opened her door for her, presenting the chamber with a flourish of her hand. "Things can't go on as they are forever, you know. You either move forward or you give him leave to pursue someone else. He isn't exactly fresh from university. He'll want a wife sooner or later."

At least she didn't go on to point out that Lily wasn't exactly in her first season anymore either. She set her bag on a padded chair and moved toward her dressing screen, where tonight's evening gown was already hanging, ready for her. "Aren't you the one who was waxing poetical about enjoying the 'now' of a courtship?" She paused at the screen, wiggling her shoulders upon remembering the day dress she was currently wearing had buttons down the back.

Her sister obligingly slipped the buttons free. "But if he does share more, as you clearly wish he would, that would change things. The truth of his past will either push you away or draw you closer. But it will, without a doubt, change things."

A miniature circus sprang to life in her stomach, and she wasn't sure if it was from fear or anticipation. "I hadn't thought of that. You're probably right."

"Of course I am. I'm wise, you know." The last button must have been free, because Ivy gave her a little nudge. "You may, in fact, refer to me as O Glorious Sage. Or perhaps—"

"Enough!" Laughing, Lily slithered out of her day dress and reached for the evening gown. It was a few years old, but she'd only worn it a handful of times, so it still looked practically new.

She emerged from the screen a minute later, smoothing the fabric into place. "I still wish we'd had pockets put in this."

She couldn't help but grin because she knew Ivy would roll her eyes. "It would have ruined the lines. You can't always weigh your skirt down with a camera, you know. That's why you're carrying a bag."

One that Ivy had presented her with a proud smile two weeks before. It was sturdy enough to hold her equipment, but it was also made of a beautiful brocade that perfectly complemented her dress. "It is indeed." She sat at her dressing table and reached for her hairbrush. "All right. I suppose I'm ready for you to call Caroline in to do my hair."

"I have an idea." The words were whispered directly into Lily's ear, still barely audible over the orchestra, even as fingers closed over hers. Her heart skipped, tripped. Zivon, of course—she'd know the voice anywhere.

But somehow the touch, unexpected as it was, felt far different than when he usually took her hand. "Why do you not put the camera down just for a few minutes, and we can dance?"

She didn't dare turn her head much, given how close his face must be to hers. But she couldn't resist a bit of a tilt so she could see his eyes. They glowed with a smile, brighter than she usually saw from him. That alone would have had her lowering her camera. Or, more accurately, swinging it around to snap a quick picture of him instead of the bride and groom.

He laughed and lowered the Kodak. "You surely have enough of those by now."

"Never." She smiled at the man who hovered a few inches away. He'd been more than patient with her duties this evening, never saying a word when she slipped away for a different angle of something, other than to ask her if he could help.

If he wanted to dance, she owed it to him. And didn't at all mind the intrusion upon her assigned task, to be perfectly honest. She put the Kodak into her bag, tucked it out of the way, and put her hand in his so he could lead her onto the dance floor.

When he swung her around to face him with more flair than she'd expected, she laughed. "Why am I surprised that you like to dance?"

His brows lifted, better to showcase the glimmer in his eyes. "I do not know. My mother always said every good Russian should know how to dance. She taught us from the time we were boys."

That she could imagine—a miniature Zivon, with that curl falling stubbornly onto his forehead, dancing with his mother. He'd have approached it seriously, almost mathematically. And she'd bet he hadn't stepped on his matushka's feet more than once. That grace of his was already making itself known within their first few revolutions of the waltz. "So can you do the Cossack dance?"

His laugh was quick, deep. "Do I look like a Cossack?"

"Hmm." She made a show of looking him over. "Not to my way of thinking, but I've never met one. Perhaps they all have a charming curl to their hair that they try to deny and all move with the grace of a . . . a . . ." She lifted her brows. "What's an animal of the Russian plains known for its graceful running?"

His lips twitched. "Reindeer?"

Another laugh bubbled up. "No. Not at all what I was thinking. Don't you have leopards or something in Russia? Tigers, even?"

"We have. And I like this image much better." He puffed out his chest, lifted his chin. "Zivon, the mighty tiger."

At this rate, she'd giggle herself into tomorrow. "Zivon, the mighty dancing tiger."

He widened his eyes in mock horror. "No, no. Tigers do not dance. If we are looking for a Russian dancing animal, it must be the bear."

The image sent her into another peal. "Dancing bears are not graceful!"

"Shh. Do not say that." He leaned close, as if imparting a great secret. "Their feelings are very sensitive. Everyone knows not to insult a dancing bear."

He spun her around, his hand landing on her back again with unerring precision. She shook her head, smiling. "And did your mother hope to give you all the skills of a bear when she taught you to dance?"

Another twitch of his lips. This time a grin broke its way into the corners. "She was more set on the French dances, I confess."

"As I suspected. Now." She tilted her head closer to his. "We shall truly test your mettle when the orchestra takes a break. I overheard the bride's sister-in-law saying that a few of them are forming a small ragtime band that will entertain us for about half an hour, and I happen to be an expert ragtime dancer."

"I do not even know what this is. Ragtime?" He didn't look intimidated at the thought of something new, though. His mother really must have taught him well.

She grinned. "You'll see. The Americans brought it over with them. Apparently it's all the rage across the pond."

"Ah. Well, if it involves me dancing with you, I am certain to like it."

Heavens. She couldn't blame her rocketing pulse on the dance, not when he looked at her as he was doing now. "I have no doubt you'll be king of the dance floor, Zivon the Mighty Tiger."

His chuckle filled the space between them, warmed her, held her. His gaze caressed her face. "I like this Lily."

She bit back a grin. She was certainly more flirtatious than her usual self. "Hopefully not too much. I'm not certain where she usually hides."

But that only made him laugh more. "Perhaps what I should have said is that I like that both Lilys are within you." He pulled her closer. Not much, not enough that anyone would look at them and think anything of it. Just enough that she noticed. "To be honest, I have yet to see a Lily I do not like."

She'd probably ruin the effect of This Lily if she were to squeak out an uncertain *Oh?* like she wanted to do. So she smiled instead. "I'm glad to hear it. Because I'm rather fond of Zivon the tiger, Zivon the dancing bear, and Zivon the loping reindeer."

The thrumming of her heart wasn't because of the music. Or the next fraction closer he pulled her. It was because, for the first time, his smile went all the way to his eyes, through them, and lit something behind them.

She'd never tasted a victory so sweet.

His fingers moved just a bit against her back. Enough to make her aware of them anew. His shadowless gaze moved likewise across her face. "Did I mention how beautiful you are tonight? Like the lilies of the field, whose splendor eclipses that of a king."

Biblical flattery. It made her grin. "You did, but not so eloquently before. I won't object to the poeticism, even if it is blatant exaggeration." She nodded toward the bride and groom, who had taken to the dance floor as well. "Only one of us is allowed to eclipse Solomon in his splendor tonight, and it is without a doubt Margot."

His smile when he looked at his colleague, however, was more amused than charmed. "She does not look as though her mother insisted she have a dance lesson twice a week, does she?"

She directed her gaze there too. Margot definitely didn't take up her position on the dance floor opposite her new husband with obvious joy. She held herself stiffly, precisely, and Lily could all but hear her reciting the proper angles and planes and lines to herself.

But then Drake pulled her closer than he needed to, leaned down, whispered something into her ear, and her whole demeanor changed. Precision melted into . . . trust, she saw as she watched them move. Margot kept her gaze fixed on his eyes, kept her limbs where he'd positioned them, and let him whisk her around the floor.

"Sorry." Lily tugged Zivon back toward her bag. "That demands a photo. Quickly, before their expressions change."

Zivon laughed and moved with her. "Of course it does. Do you know what you need, Lily of the fields? A strap on your camera, so you can loop it around your neck."

"Now, that is a good idea." She rushed to her satchel and pulled the Kodak back out, taking a moment to model how it would look. "A necklace to put the jewels to shame, I should think."

"It can flash brighter than any diamond."

She laughed and opened it up. Whatever had gotten into her had clearly infected him too. She had a feeling this was a night she'd not soon forget.

13

For the first time in more years than he cared to count, Zivon found himself plotting how he might convince a girl to slip away from the crowds with him long enough to steal a kiss. He could probably achieve it by wondering what the dance, in full swing, would look like from outside the French doors, looking into the ballroom. Or suggest that they position themselves by an exit to get an unhindered shot of the bridal couple when they left for the night, which surely they would do soon.

Or, if she kept giving him those looks that said she was having every bit as good a time as he was, he might just forget himself and kiss her in the middle of the crowd.

If he didn't know better, he'd think someone had slipped something intoxicating into the lemonade. But no, this heady feeling had begun well before dinner. When Lily had come down the staircase, smiling at him and looking like a princess. When he'd escorted her into the church and helped her find the perfect position from which to take photos of the ceremony. When he'd stood in the back after the guests had gone and watched her pose the bride and groom and wedding party.

For tonight, at least, she was his. And he found he liked the feeling.

"Thank you." She handed him the camera again, that smile she'd reserved for him on her lips.

He took it and slid it into his pocket—the fifth time he'd done so in the hour since he offered to hold it for her. A not altogether selfless offer, as he'd been sure to tell her. The less time spent rushing to pick it up or put it down, the more time spent on the dance floor with her in his arms or her hand in his. She probably had no idea how pretty her blush was when he said such things.

He smiled and patted the camera. "Safe until next time."

The orchestra closed out the current set, the moment of silence from them allowing other sounds to swell. Chatter, mostly in English, but some French reaching his ears too, no doubt thanks to the bride's Belgian connections. Thunder rumbled in the distance. Had a storm moved in? The skies had been clear earlier. He strained to hear how long it might rumble, but the musicians launched into their next song.

"I beg your pardon."

At the familiar voice, Zivon and Lily both turned to where Admiral Hall had joined them. Smiling, he gave a short bow and held out a hand to Lily. "I believe I claimed this next dance, Miss Blackwell, and photography duties shan't get you out of it."

Lily laughed and tucked her hand into the admiral's. "I wouldn't dare try to escape it." But she sent a warm glance over her shoulder to Zivon. A promise, that look.

Zivon couldn't have kept the smile from his lips had he tried. "You will find her the finest partner on the floor, Admiral."

"After Mrs. Hall, perhaps." He grinned and led her away.

Zivon watched them for a moment, though his attention shifted when Major Camden cut through the crowd and landed at his side. "Admiral steal your girl?"

Zivon chuckled. "Momentarily, anyway. Where has yours gone?"

"Talking to the duchess." Camden pointed to a corner of the room, where the tall young lady Zivon had already been introduced to as a friend of Lily's from the hospital stood talking to a blond woman with bobbed hair.

His brows hiked up before he could check his surprise. "I was unaware that there was such high society among us tonight."

"She and De Wilde apparently like to talk physics and mathematics." Camden shook his head as if bemoaning two adolescents obsessing over fashion. "And Ara has been friends with her for ages. The duchess, I mean. That's actually how we met, at one of their dinner parties. I served with the duke in the Royal Flying Corps." He indicated a gentleman now, who was talking to the bride's brother.

Zivon nodded. Given the crowd, he didn't imagine there would be any call for him to be introduced to the couple, which suited him fine. He'd just as soon steer clear of anyone likely to have foreign contacts.

"So I hear you're a runner. What sort? Long distance? Sprinting?"

An easy conversation to fall into, and one that didn't require so much attention that he couldn't indulge in a search now and then for Lily and Hall on the dance floor. He told Camden about his preferences, even mentioned that he and Clarke had been running together in the mornings.

"The chap you eat lunch with most days?"

Zivon nodded.

Camden lifted a brow. "You know, I often pass Miss Blackwell leaving Charing Cross Hospital when I go to meet Ara for lunch. You could always come with me and invite her to join us. They being friends and all."

A thought that hadn't occurred to him. But then, he hadn't

realized until this evening that Camden's betrothed was Lily's friend. Whitehall, he supposed, wasn't so large a place. The web of relationships was just as tangled as the neighborhood he'd grown up in. He just hadn't paused to realize that he was now part of *this* web. "That sounds pleasant. We should work out a date with the ladies before the night ends."

Camden said something that sounded agreeable, but Zivon's gaze had been pulled away. Not, this time, by Lily. Rather, by the speed of a servant who darted into the room. No, two servants. One moved straight for Hall, the other for the man Camden had just identified as the duke.

"This is not good, I think." Panic had a very particular pattern to it—shaky movements, wide eyes, abrupt changes in direction as one sought the quickest path to one's destination. And those two men were in full panic.

The music came to another natural halt, and Zivon angled himself toward the window, listening to more thunder.

But there was no rain on the glass of the French doors he'd been musing about luring Lily through. Only the reflection of the moon.

Beside him, Camden muttered a word he didn't know and tossed the door open. With the glass removed from between them and the night, the sounds from outside were clearer.

Deadlier.

Airplanes. Many of them. Distant roars. A *boom* from somewhere far enough away that it couldn't rattle the glass.

Just his soul.

"God, help us." Camden had stepped through the door, his head back. Eyes on the skies.

Zivon had only to shift a bit to see what the pilot was looking at. Never in his life had he seen so many airplanes. None seemed to be on a course for them, but he knew that could change in an instant as the English gave the Germans chase.

And from every direction, sirens wailed. Some in warning. Others in reaction.

The musicians didn't launch into another piece this time.

Camden spun, his eyes seeking and finding someone. "Pearce! Where's the nearest shelter?"

Zivon turned too, in time to see a stranger nod toward the south. "Underground station not far off. We'll get all the guests to it. Lina! You know the drill, luv. Ellie, Rosie, Retta, do your magic."

Zivon barely caught a glimpse of a quartet of women before they disappeared into the crowd, touching elbows here and smiling there and somehow turning the cluster of anxious people into neat and orderly queues aimed for the door. But they weren't his concern. He strained onto his toes, wishing he were a few inches taller, looking for a flash of red-gold.

She appeared a second later, her camera bag on her shoulder. She was still with Hall, who led her his way, both of them grim-faced.

He caught the tail end of Hall's mutter. ". . . don't be ridiculous. If anyone is to blame, it's me. You were but doing what I asked."

Asked? What had Hall asked of her? Something to do with a photograph, obviously. Something perhaps linked to the planes now flying overhead? Lily's pale face made him think so.

He hadn't time to ask, though. Hall all but shoved Lily at him, his look fierce. "Get her to the underground *now*. If anything happens to her, her father will have *both* our heads."

With a swift nod, Zivon took her hand and pulled her into the queue.

She didn't seem very happy about it. "Arabelle said she was going to try to get to the sites that were hit already. I should go with her—help people. There will be injuries, and I have some training, after all."

He held tight to her fingers. "I was given a direct order from my superior. Do not try to make me disobey, Lily." Because the thought of her out there in the thick of it, in danger—no.

"But surely it's safe where the planes have already struck—"

"Nyet." He had to swallow down the Russian. "No. There are scores of them up there. They will strike in waves. They could well hit the same areas multiple times if they're following the river. Please." He wove their fingers together, anchoring her there beside him. "Do not ask me to put you in danger. I cannot."

The way she met his gaze and held it made the crowd around them seem like nothing but a distant roar. At last, she nodded. "All right. To the shelter."

He couldn't exactly be relieved, not given the rumble of engines overhead. But he was grateful. For the first time since that terrible day when he'd found Alyona on his doorstep, his soul whispered a prayer of gratitude rather than just a plea.

The crowd moved with remarkable order out of the building and into the street. Sirens wailed, people shouted, but it wasn't nearly as chaotic as Zivon had expected. Not like the mobs at home when the soviets had stormed their way to power. This was entirely different. Even so, he held Lily close to his side as the wedding guests merged into the street with theatergoers from nearby, all aimed at the same tube station. A few times he pulled her this way or that to avoid a run-in with another well-dressed Londoner but not as often as he would have expected.

Within a few minutes, they had hurried down the steps, where most people shuffled about looking for a bench, as if they'd all done this before. Not surprising, he supposed, since London had been facing air raids since the war began. It was not something he had encountered in Russia. And, frankly, not something he had been anxious to experience here.

"Here. Sit." He led her farther down than the masses had

gone, to where a bench still sat empty, though given the numbers surging in behind him, it wouldn't stay that way for long.

Surprisingly, she obeyed. Her eyes looked a bit dazed again, distant. Zivon crouched down before her and held both her hands between his. "Lily. It will be all right."

As if to belie his promise, a *boom* sounded from somewhere in the distance. Just close enough to hear it, to feel the slightest tremor beneath them. Another followed on its heels.

She shuddered and closed her eyes, shaking her head. "So many. Surely it wouldn't have been so many if . . ."

"If?"

She shook her head again, folding her arms over the camera bag.

He would have pressed, but another couple was joining them on the bench, the woman babbling about not getting to see the ending of the opera now. Of all the things to worry about. He stood and moved to stand at Lily's side, more out of the way of bodies still pushing in. The din was soon too great to really allow for conversation with the height difference, so he made no attempt to say anything. Just kept one of her hands in his.

The slight tremors continued, along with the muffled booms. Based on the mutterings of their new neighbors, a raid had never gone on more than a few minutes. Many consisted only of a single bomb, perhaps as many as half a dozen. But they had far surpassed that already.

They had been there half an hour when a new note among the voices snagged his attention. An older woman, well dressed, was pushing through the crowd, calling for an Estevan. She paused about ten paces away to ask a cluster of people if they had seen her husband, but she asked it in Greek. They all shook their heads in confusion more than in answer.

Zivon squeezed Lily's hand. "I should—"

"Of course you should." Color had returned to her cheeks, and she looked up with a muted smile. She returned the squeeze of his hand and then released it. "Go and help her."

With a collection of pardon-mes, he squeezed through the crowd and intercepted the woman. "Perhaps I can help you," he said in Greek. "You are looking for your husband?"

Pure relief washed over her face. "Oh, bless you! I know so little English, even after all these years. Estevan has always translated for me. He said he would be right behind me, but these crowds!"

And when one couldn't communicate with them . . . Zivon nodded and offered his arm. "Come, we will search for him together. What does he look like?"

She described him down to the color of his waistcoat. Zivon didn't recall seeing anyone of his look pass by, so he aimed her back toward the entrance and then past it. He spotted many of the wedding guests among the crowd, but his colleagues from the OB merely grinned and shook their heads when they heard him carrying on a conversation in Greek about the woman's grandchildren.

"Estevan! *There* you are!" With a thanks to Zivon, the matron hurried to her husband's side.

Zivon turned with a smile, glad that the search, at least, had a quick and happy resolution. He nearly ran headlong into another smiling man—the last one in all of London he'd hoped to see.

"Zivon! Zivon Marin, of all the surprises!"

Blast. Fyodor Suvorov was dressed for the opera or theater, as was the beautiful woman on his arm—Kira, he recalled absently. A former ballerina. He'd been invited to their wedding just before the war broke out. Zivon had no choice but to smile and reach to shake the hand held out to him. He answered in French, which was what Suvorov had spoken in. "Fyodor. You are in London?"

He laughed. "We came for our honeymoon—and then were stranded here. Though there are worse places to be stuck, given that Kira has friends in England, and my cousin is here. Kira, do you recall Zivon Marin? The most brilliant linguist we had in the Foreign Ministry."

She smiled in the very way she'd been pictured on the poster Evgeni had once had tacked to his wall. "Of course. How good to see you again, Mr. Marin. Though I wish the circumstances were different." She glanced around her with a concerned frown when a bigger tremor made itself felt. "Will it never stop? Ilya will be so frightened if she wakes up. And you know how Tionna fears these raids too. She'll do little to calm her."

"Konstantin will surely discover something. He should be back any—ah, there he is now."

No. No, no, no. Zivon took a quick scan of the crowd, the escape routes, whom he could duck behind. But the people were packed too tightly in all directions but the one from which Nabokov came. There was no help for it. He'd done nothing to untangle the mess he'd made.

And now it had caught him up.

The ambassador was before him even now, drawing even with Fyodor. Eyes lighting in recognition. Reaching out a hand with "Filiminov, good evening!" even as his cousin said, "Are you familiar with . . . who?"

Zivon sighed and granted himself a single moment of closed eyes. When he opened them, the confusion had already shifted to suspicion on both of their faces. There was nothing for it but to straighten his spine. Lift his chin. And say in Russian, "Forgive me. I didn't know whom I could trust." He executed a quick military bow to the ambassador. "Kapitan Zivon Marin of the Imperial Navy, Intelligence Division. At your service, sir."

14

Lily leaned her head against the seat, grateful for the silence in the cab of the embassy car. Exhaustion had settled on her limbs as heavily as the guilt, but at least the sirens had finally ceased. The fires had been put out. If only she could silence the barrage of accusations in her mind so easily.

This was her fault. Yes, she had been obeying Hall's orders, but even so. Instead of convincing the Germans not to attack a superior force, they had only convinced them to *send* a superior force. If Londoners lay dead tonight, she was partially to blame.

The streets had been choked with people trying to return home. And the drive, graciously offered by the Russian diplomats Zivon had introduced her to, had been interrupted with enough necessary stops that she had to think it would have been faster to walk home.

They'd gotten out the first time the car stopped, when it became clear a bomb had struck the neighborhood through which they were driving. Or perhaps multiple bombs. The streets had been covered in glass from the windows, like a million crystals of snow. A terrible, heartbreaking beauty. Zivon had rushed to help a family push their way back into their battered home, but after making certain no one needed her help, Lily had drawn out her camera.

To remind herself. So she'd never forget the cost of this work she'd thought was so good. So noble. So worthwhile.

She'd gotten a few shots she couldn't shake from her mind's eye. One of a broken roof silhouetted against the moon. One of a passel of children, some awake enough to be playing and some succumbed to exhaustion on the pavement. One of Kira Suvorova embracing her toddler daughter upon gaining their thankfully spared home.

And one of Zivon with an expression on his face she'd never seen before. He'd looked . . . haunted as he hurried to a doorstep to check on an adolescent girl who had slumped there in fatigue. She'd been well, but Zivon had seemed shaken to the core. They'd climbed back in the car after that, and neither had suggested getting out the next time the driver was forced to halt.

They were alone in the cab now, the Suvorovs and Nabokov all safe in their respective homes. Zivon's fingers had found hers again, and they still sat as close as they had when the diplomat's wife was squeezed onto the seat with them.

"This is not exactly how I envisioned the night going." His voice was little more than a breath at her ear, slipping easily into the silent car. Quieting the thoughts pelting her heart. "I had grand plans for a moonlit promenade through the garden. Hopes that perhaps I could convince you to accept a kiss."

She levered her eyes open, though she could see nothing but his outline against the window. He'd wanted to kiss her? Had been planning it?

Her fingers were keenly aware of his. Her bare arm—she had no idea where her wrap was, though she'd likely left it in the ballroom somewhere—was warm against his jacket.

Those twelve inches she'd always felt between them were nowhere to be seen.

Tears pricked her eyes, but she blinked them away. They should have had that. They should have had *that* instead of this broken, shattered version of a night. She should have been coming home in a rapture over her first kiss instead of struggling to swim through the waves of guilt. Her voice, no louder than his, was stained with that yearning. "I may have been convinced to accept."

The fingers of his other hand skimmed her cheek. He'd taken off his gloves at some point. She'd scarcely worn hers all evening, as she found it difficult to operate her camera with them on, and the feel of his fingertips on her skin sent a frisson of unexpected wanting through her. That touch bade her turn her face toward his. Her breath lost to her, she obeyed.

He was so close already, to whisper in her ear as he'd done. Just that small turn had his nose brushing her cheek, and somehow he made it feel like an intentional caress rather than an accident. Though she couldn't see much of anything, she could sense his lips all but touching hers. Almost, nearly. But hovering there just out of reach.

How could that moment of him *not* kissing her be so delicious? Something about the closeness, the near touch, the feel of his breath feathering over her lips . . . She pulled air slowly into her lungs, relishing it. Aware of his every heartbeat in the darkness. Or perhaps it was just her own. Maybe they'd synchronized.

Then . . . then it seemed the air warmed between them, and it took her a moment to realize it was because his lips had taken the place of oxygen. They swept slowly over hers, as gently as his fingers had swept over her cheek. Stilled. Savored. And then the air was back, barely squeezing between them.

Her breath shuddered out. She wanted to lean over, invite another perfect touch of his lips. And she might have, had the car not been slowing to a halt. She blinked into the darkness, vaguely aware that the roofline visible in the moonlight outside the window was the familiar one of Curzon Street.

The hand on her cheek eased away with one last caress, the hand holding hers tightened around her fingers. She felt the space between them grow, returning to what was proper as the chauffeur exited the front of the car and came around to open their door. "Shall I carry your cameras?"

Hearing his voice at a normal level made her blink. Pulled her forcibly back into the real world, the one with other people's weddings and air raids and families slumped on sidewalks because of her.

She handed him the bag that had been resting at her feet. "Thank you." It was a strange exhaustion she felt, edged as it was with a relentless barrage of thoughts. She knew she'd have no rest as long as those images were burned into her mind. But maybe once she'd put them to paper, they would release her. "I think I'll develop that last roll of film now."

"Lily." Zivon chuckled as he climbed out, helping her to do the same with the hand he still held. "You have to be exhausted. You should sleep."

"I don't think I can. Not yet." And even if her mind eventually ceased tormenting her, it would then just begin replaying that perfect kiss. A far happier wakefulness, but even so.

Zivon shook his head and led her toward her front door. "I have never met anyone quite like you, Lilian Blackwell."

Coming from anyone else, she might not have been sure that was a compliment. But coming from the man who'd just filled her veins with magic with a featherlight brush of his lips on hers, she decided it was the sweetest thing anyone could possibly say. "Thank you."

As they approached the door, it opened before them, Daddy barely giving them time to enter before he folded her into his arms. "Thank God. Blinker stopped by and told us you were safe, had taken shelter with the other guests, but even so. Reports kept pouring in of new strikes. There were over forty airplanes to reach England this time, I'm told—and nearly half made it all the way to London."

Her chest went tight at the numbers as Mama nudged Daddy aside enough that she could embrace Lily as well. Never had so many aircraft made it past their defenses. Lily shook her head. "Did you hear how many bombs fell?"

"Not yet. Some failed to detonate, some did nothing but shatter glass, but many did serious damage." Daddy looked past her, toward Zivon. He nodded at him but didn't reach out a hand. "Thank you for seeing her safely home, Marin."

Zivon must have heard the strange, stiff note in Daddy's voice as clearly as Lily did, given the way he straightened, then bowed a bit. "Of course, sir. I would do anything within my power to protect her."

Mama shot Daddy a look and then moved toward Zivon, hand outstretched and soon squeezing his fingers. "Of course you would. But unfortunately, there isn't much in these situations within our control."

Lily's brows drew together as she looked up at Daddy's face. A bit of anxiety was to be expected on a night such as this, but why was he directing it all toward Zivon? "Is Ivy asleep?"

That brought a bit of softening to her father's face, anyway. Even the edges of a smile. "Yes. She was already in bed when the commotion began. And you know her."

Capable of sleeping through the apocalypse itself, they always joked. She grinned and shook her head. "I'll have quite a story to tell her tomorrow. For now, I think I may develop the last of my film, taken at the sites we saw on our way home. I'm a bit too keyed up to sleep yet."

Zivon had reclaimed his hand from Mama and rested it on Lily's bag. "May I deposit this in your darkroom for you?"

Daddy's mouth opened—and given the dark expression back on his face, he looked ready to refuse. But Mama spoke first. "Of course you may. Lily, show him where to put everything. And perhaps show him that lovely shot you developed yesterday, hmm? Your father and I will lock up. We sent poor Eaton to bed after Blinker assured us you were well."

Lily nodded and led Zivon toward her workroom, deciding that later—or even tomorrow—would be soon enough to decipher Daddy's mood. For now, she was grateful to have even three minutes of privacy with Zivon. Even gladder when, as soon as they turned a corner, his fingers found hers.

What a strange amalgam of emotions pulsed through her veins. The light of the first half of the evening swirling through the dark of the second. The starlight of that kiss against the endless black of night.

But through all the wrong, this felt right. His fingers in hers. Long and strong and secure.

"I have never seen your darkroom." His voice was quiet as a prayer. "I look forward to it."

She breathed a soft laugh. "I'm afraid there won't be all that much to show you."

"I shall be the judge of this. And the photographs you are so eager to develop, of what are these?"

Would he think it strange that she'd found anything to record in that broken neighborhood? No. He would understand. "The glass on the road—so much of it, it looked like ice or snow."

"Yes. This I noticed."

"And some of the people we saw. Kira with her daughter. And . . ." She almost didn't want to mention the other. The one that had shaken him so badly. But that was part of the reason she'd pressed the push-pin and why she wanted to develop the film now. "And that young woman on the doorstep that you helped up."

His fingers spasmed in hers. "You took a photograph of her?"

"I wanted to remember—needed to remember the price of war, even here at home." She reached for the latch of her darkroom's door. Maybe that was why his touch fell away. Maybe.

"Some things, Alyona, are best forgotten."

Her blood slowed as she pushed open the door. "Who?"

"Pardon?" He edged into the room behind her, taking the strap of the bag from his shoulder and craning his head around to take in the space.

Lily watched her arm reach for the bag without quite feeling herself make the move. "Who is Alyona?" Her voice sounded strange in her ears. Cracked and dry.

"Why would you—" But he cut off the inane question with a Russian something or another. His eyes slammed shut. His hand went to his pocket in that way it always did, and he drew in a long breath. When he opened his eyes again, the stillness from their first weeks together had seized him again. "I apologize. It was the memory of that girl on the doorstep that brought it back."

"Brought *what* back?" She slid the bag to the floor, under the table.

"The way she looked when I found her." His face twisted. Smoothed back out. His nostrils flared, and he clasped his hands behind his back. "She was my . . ."

Sister. Cousin. Neighbor. Any of those would be logical. Any discovery of the sort this sounded like would be traumatic.

"She was my fiancée."

"Fiancée." She ought to focus on the *was*. But how, when all she could imagine was some other woman he'd never seen fit to mention?

Some of her feeling must have saturated her voice, given Zivon's raised hand. "It is not what you think. It was arranged marriage. Our parents—she was still child when it was agreed. I, still at university. We were betrothed for decade, but I—it was never like . . ."

He motioned between them, something desperate edging out the stillness.

Lily shook her head. He'd lost his articles again, which told her as much as the words themselves. Whatever relationship he had with this Alyona may not have been quite like this, but it was clearly something whose loss had fractured him. Had it been just twelve hours ago that she was wishing he'd open up and tell her more of his past? The coward in her now wished she could shy away from it. "A *decade*? You were engaged for a decade."

She had no hope of following the thoughts that rampaged through his eyes, across his face, before he slammed them down again. "Her mother was ill. She needed take care of siblings. But health had improved, so—wedding date was set. Alyona came to Moscow to prepare our house."

Lily pressed her palm to the tabletop. "Set for when?"

"Twenty-second of June."

"Of?"

The thoughts all went silent. "This year."

She pressed with all her might against the table, but the world still spun. He was supposed to be getting married in a month, to this Alyona. "What happened?"

It seemed for a long moment that he wouldn't answer. Perhaps he intended simply to pivot on his heel and march away rather than relive whatever it was. But no. Instead, that careful mask cracked. Another layer of the matryoshka doll parted.

And dark, roiling hatred peeked out. "They killed her. The Bolsheviks." He said the name as if it were the vilest of curses. "Murdered her to teach me a lesson. This is when I left."

She lifted a hand to her mouth, but the gasp slipped out before she could cover it. The rest of the pieces slid into place.

"And they left her on your doorstep. Like that girl tonight." And it couldn't have been more than a few months ago. January or February. The memories would still be so fresh. A wound still bleeding—all the more so because he clearly hadn't been grieving it in the normal way. "Oh, Zivon."

His hand fisted, his gaze went clouded. "They killed her, and they will bear no consequences for it, not from the law. But they will pay. I will see this war ends, and I will do everything in my power to show the world the truth of them. I will await the day that the Lord visits His vengeance upon them."

A chill pricked its way up her spine. The bitterness in his voice—she'd never expected to hear that coming from him. Never expected to learn that what he'd suffered had been so recent, so devastating, so consuming. She didn't know how she was to compete with that. Even if he'd never loved this Alyona in a romantic way, the way she'd been ripped from him would guarantee that he thought of her every day. All hours. That her image would haunt him in death as it may not have done in life.

And he'd been letting it fester, given his reactions tonight. "Have you . . . perhaps spoken to Clarke about this? Or a clergyman?"

Rage sparked its way through the stillness in his eyes. "There is no one I could trust with this."

Was it a compliment, then, that he was trusting her with it now? It felt more like a burden. One she would gladly shoulder if it would help him, but how? She had no idea. She was willing but utterly ignorant. "I can't think such pain is meant to be kept secret. How are you to heal from it?"

The breath that escaped his mouth was half laugh, entirely scoffing. He turned, motioned to the room. "You ought to know, I suppose, about secrets."

The anger in his tone sent her back a step, and she bumped into her chair. "I beg your pardon?"

"I have seen you almost daily entering the OB, Lily. It takes no genius to realize that when Hall speaks of his photography expert, he means you. You alter photos for him, *da*? Develop them? You do not tell people this, yet you expect me to bare my soul?"

"She does *what*?"

No. No, no, no. Mama rounded the corner, appearing behind Zivon and making Lily's insistence that the two secrets were nothing alike freeze on her tongue.

Her mother's face was a portrait of outrage. "Lilian! Is this true?"

"I . . ." She couldn't very well deny it. But she didn't want to admit it either. Before, whenever she imagined having this conversation with her mother, she'd planned to list all the reasons why it was necessary and helpful and good.

Just now, with the images from the night still burned into her mind's eye and on the film she'd yet to develop, she had no justifications.

And Mama didn't wait for one anyway. She spun away. No, not *away*, just toward Daddy, who appeared behind her. "Thomas! You knew about this, didn't you? I'd wager it was your idea. The two of you lying to me—for how long? Months? Years?"

Daddy's countenance shifted too, the warmth he always showed his family frozen over. The kind eyes gone hard. She had a feeling she wasn't seeing *Daddy* at all, but Captain Blackwell. "There are bigger issues at stake here than your high morals about art, Euphemia. Which we will discuss in private. Marin—I'll show you out. Now."

Not so much as a hint of good manners or even goodwill colored his tone. Just cold, hard authority. Lily flinched.

Zivon shifted closer to her rather than away, showing another emotion she'd never thought to see on his face. Panicked apology. "I am sorry. I did not realize—"

"Marin—*now*."

Lily tried to give him a smile, but it shook around the edges as Daddy laid hold of his arm. "It's all right. I'll see you tomorrow."

Why did the look on her father's face go even harder? "That remains to be seen. Don't make me warn you again, young man."

For one pulse, Zivon held still but for his eyes, which flashed this way and that, taking it all in. Then, in the next heartbeat, he nodded and strode through the doorway without so much as slowing down to murmur something to Mama that Lily didn't catch.

Daddy followed him. And the moment they vanished, she wished even angry, official Captain Blackwell back. That was somehow better than angry, quiet Mama.

Lily's eyes slid shut. "I'm sorry, Mama. I—"

"How long?"

She was twenty-three. A woman grown. Old enough to be married, to have children, to manage a household of her own. But it took only that intonation from her mother to feel ten again, caught eating pilfered sweets with Ivy when they ought to have been in bed. She sighed. "Since Blinker was appointed DID. But it's mostly just developing photos, I rarely—"

"Don't!" Mama sliced a hand through the air. "Don't make excuses. I don't care *what* you do or rarely do at the OB. What I *care* about is the fact that you and your father have willfully deceived me!"

Lily dropped her gaze. What answer could she really give to that?

She looked up again, though, when Mama made a sound she wasn't sure how to classify. Gasp? Sob? Hard to say, given that she'd turned her back on her. "I thought we were close. That you and I were . . . Clearly I was wrong."

"Mama—"

It wasn't the hand held up that stopped her words. It was the slump to her shoulders. "Go to bed, Lilian."

She cast a glance toward her camera bag, the film she'd hoped to develop. But she wasn't about to argue. She nudged the bag a little more out of the way and then stepped from the room, pulling the door shut behind her. Drawing even with her mother, she reached to touch a hand to her arm.

Mama pulled back. Folded her arms over her chest. Stared straight ahead, though there was nothing for her gaze to rest on save a bare wall.

Lily sagged and slunk by her.

She intercepted a grim-faced Daddy at the base of the central staircase. He looked past her, but apparently Mama hadn't followed her out, because his glance returned quickly to her face. "I will take care of this with your mother. You go on up to your room."

She nodded but didn't move away. "Why were you behaving as you were with Mr. Marin?"

Thunder rolled through his eyes anew. "I'll not go into details. Suffice it to say Hall received information today that sheds a suspicious light. You'll discontinue your association with him until further notice."

"What? But, Daddy—"

"I'll not tolerate you questioning me on this, Lilian. You will obey. Now *go*."

Given that he stalked off, she didn't have much choice. She mounted the steps slowly, eyes stinging. How could a night that began so very well go so very wrong?

15

Someone was following him.

Zivon kept walking at his normal pace, his gaze on the Old Admiralty Building, just visible when he rounded the corner. Correction. *Two* someones were following him. The newer addition was so obvious it was nearly laughable— scurrying behind other pedestrians or darting into a doorway if Zivon happened to turn a bit. Obviously never considering that he could sense him, hear him, and see him in reflections.

Irritating. Alarming, in a way. But also surely not much of a threat if he was so unskilled.

It was the other man that had Zivon's every nerve buzzing. That one he'd nearly missed. Nearly. But once he'd picked up on him, he had the unsettling suspicion that the fellow had been shadowing him ever since he stepped foot out of his flat.

Had he not been so exhausted, perhaps he would have noticed the accomplished one sooner. But he'd only slept about an hour. He kept reliving the raid. The confrontation with Fyodor and Nabokov—who had ordered him to report to the embassy at eight this morning. The kiss. The look on Lily's face when he told her about Alyona.

The look on her father's when he told him in no uncertain terms that his attentions were no longer welcome and he was to desist calling on her.

That, combined with these sudden tails, painted a rather dreadful picture. He had fallen out of favor with the Admiralty. The question was *why*. What had happened in the last day or two to change everything?

He'd reported as ordered to the embassy, ready to lay all of his cards, metaphorical and physical, on the table. He'd brought both of the fake passports, his own and Evgeni's, now without his brother's photo; the English identification papers Admiral Hall had supplied to him; and an abbreviated but truthful version of the events that had led him here.

Nabokov hadn't looked particularly impressed. If anything, he looked more dubious when Zivon finished than when he took his seat.

"You are clearly overreacting," he had said only ten minutes ago. "The soviets, they will be dealt with soon enough, I am certain. I am sorry, of course, for their violence against your betrothed, but to flee here, to work for the British?" A doleful shake of the head. "I fear you will regret that hasty decision when order is restored in Russia and you are no longer welcome home. You know well everyone will view you as a turncoat."

Zivon had bristled at the word *hasty*. He had stayed in Russia as long as he could. So long that Alyona had paid the price. He had weighed every possible decision and each path before he decided on this one, and he'd made the decision not for himself but for his people. His country. His czar.

Who was Nabokov, who hadn't even stepped foot on Russian soil in a decade, to judge him? To tell him whether he had overreacted? He hadn't been there. He hadn't seen the fighting, the mobs, the chaos. Hadn't had to wonder whether the Bolsheviks would be better or worse than the Trudoviks who had first seized power from the czar.

Worse. So much worse.

But Zivon oughtn't to have let his frustration with the ambassador cloud his perception. He should have noted *both* of the men following him immediately, not just the obvious one.

His hand tightened around the handle of his briefcase. He didn't like carrying all this with him to the OB, but he hadn't the time to go home first. But what if his new shadows meant to mug him? The thought of being without all his identification, without the few remaining scraps of his former life, didn't bear thinking about.

Perhaps he should have spent less time running as a lad and more time learning how to fight, like Evgeni. Though in this particular situation, the one could serve him as well as the other, he supposed.

Something bubbled up in his veins, spilled over.

No. He wasn't going to run. Not from anyone. He'd had enough of that. And so, rather than continuing toward the OB, he seized the cover that a passing band of secretaries offered and ducked into an alley. It had been a tight knot of women, and their distance between him and his pursuers was such that they would have completely blocked their view of him for three and a half seconds. All he needed to vanish.

Though there'd be no question where he vanished to, so he sprinted to the end of the alley, zigged this way and zagged that until, five minutes later, he smirked upon emerging back onto the main street and spotting the less skilled of the followers striding down a cross street, shaking his head. And the more skilled standing with hands on his hips, staring at the OB.

It wouldn't look odd to anyone, given the Naval Reserves uniform he wore. Zivon switched his briefcase to his left hand—just in case the fellow got wily and he did need to put to use his years of scrapping with Evgeni—and moved up behind him. Not slowly, not stealthily. At the pace of every other pedestrian out here, so that his footfalls wouldn't sound abnormal.

When he'd drawn even with him, he said, "I do not believe we have been properly introduced. Though I saw you at the wedding yesterday."

The fellow jumped, spun. And grinned. "Well, this is a first." At Zivon's lifted brow, he added, "No one's ever outfoxed me when I'm tailing them. If you ever tire of the codebreaking nonsense, tell Hall to refer you to V. We could use you."

Zivon had no idea who V was and what use they could have for him. But he had to admit that the fellow's demeanor eased a bit of his uncertainty. "Hall told you to follow me, I presume?"

"Might have done." The fellow held out a hand. "Barclay Pearce. That was clever, using that passel of girls as a cover. But where'd you go in the alley? I didn't see anywhere to hide, but you couldn't have reached the end before I got there."

Later, he would probably find it odd that his tail wanted to have a conversation on his failed pursuit. At the moment, that was the least shocking of the events that had transpired in the last twenty-four hours. "I could, actually. Sprinting is not my preferred pace, but I practice it to increase my endurance for long distances."

"Runner. That's right. Well." Pearce motioned him onward, toward the OB. "Hall's going to be livid with me, but at least I have a good excuse." He nodded toward where the other man had gone. "I trust you noticed that bloke too, then."

"In seconds."

"Quite sloppy. Definitely not one of ours. Tell you what—you go and let Hall know you caught on to me, and I'll pick up his trail and see who *else* had the same idea. Deal?"

As if it were his call? But given the choice, that was exactly what Zivon would have recommended. "Deal."

A few minutes later, he was past the guards and jogging up

the stairs toward his floor. Given the time, he ought to hurry to his desk and get to work.

Given the circumstances, he hurried instead to Hall's office. The door was closed, but voices came from within, so the admiral hadn't taken the morning off, despite the late night. Zivon settled in a chair outside the room to wait.

He could see the threads unraveling. But until he knew what had tugged at them, he couldn't plan how to stop it. Not when another tug could simply loosen another thread while he was at work on the first. He must discover the source, the root.

After a minute, he opened his briefcase, pulled out Evgeni's passport. His brother was gone. He must accept that. Were he alive, even if injured, he would have found a way to get in touch by now. Silence in this case must mean the worst. Evgeni was gone, and someone was still at work against him. He was alone. Utterly alone.

His fingers traced the familiar contours of the passport, opened it even though Evgeni's face was no longer there to stare back at him. If Hall dismissed him, would he at least return that? It was the only image he had of him.

He hadn't bothered flipping through the rest of the pages before. There were no stamps to remind him of places they'd gone together, not in this one. Other than taking out the too-large photo of the German officers, he'd not examined the pages too closely.

Which meant he hadn't noticed before how two at the back were stuck together. Now he pried them apart. And his breath caught when another piece of paper slipped into his hands.

Another photograph. This one he knew—he had a matching one in the missing album. Him and Evgeni, on that one trip to Paris. Standing together, the Eiffel Tower stretching out of the frame behind them. They looked so young. So happy, with their arms slung about each other's shoulders. *Oh, Zhenya . . . I am so sorry. So sorry I failed you.*

Hall's office door opened. Zivon slid the passport back into the case and snapped it closed. The picture he slipped instead into his pocket. It helped, somehow, to feel his brother there.

Hall stepped out with another navy man, who quickly saluted and went on his way. When the admiral's gaze flicked to Zivon, his brows knit. "Marin. What can I do for you?"

Zivon stood. "Maybe I come in?"

"Of course."

They entered, the door clicking shut. But though Zivon put his briefcase on a chair, he couldn't bring himself to sit. "I met Barclay Pearce this morning—much to his surprise."

Hall halted halfway to his desk and spun on him. "I beg your pardon?"

Zivon kept himself calm. Still. "Have I done something to make you question me, sir?"

The admiral leaned against the edge of his desk. "And why would you think that?"

"Because you have someone following me. Captain Blackwell has suddenly forbidden me from seeing his daughter again. And even at the wedding last night, your gait hitched each time you approached me. All very odd, since nothing I have done has changed." He unclasped his hands from their habitual resting place behind him, spread them wide, palms up. "I have given you all the information I have. All that I know, even what I cannot prove. What has happened to make you doubt me?"

DID folded his arms over his chest. "I never said I doubted you."

"You did, Admiral." But he could see from the look on the man's face that he wasn't going to talk about why. Not with him, anyway. He gathered a breath, held it for a long moment. "There was another man following me too. Your Mr. Pearce said he intended to find out who he is, as he is not one of yours.

I imagine he will report to you. I would greatly appreciate it if I could be informed as well. If it is the Bolsheviks . . ."

That, at least, brought him bolt upright. "Someone *else*?"

"Someone who had, I think, not much practice at tailing people." Though Zivon wanted to raise his chin, he lowered it instead. "What would you have me do, sir? Work as usual? Or has your faith in me shrunk such that I am not trusted to do that?"

"For heaven's sake, man. If I decide to sack you, you won't have to *ask*. In the meantime, get to work." He strode to the door, yanked the door open, and barked at the secretary, "The moment Pearce shows up, I want to see him. No joking with anyone, no dillydallying outside with V, nothing. Am I clear?"

Zivon vacated the office and hurried to his desk. But he didn't find the admiral's reaction encouraging. Hall was alarmed at the news that someone else had been about the task he'd assigned Mr. Pearce.

Which meant that Zivon had more enemies in London than his superior had thought.

Lily stared at the photo on the drying rack, not quite able to believe what her eyes told her. The roll of film—one of the ones she'd brought home yesterday—had come from an agent on the Continent, she knew. Strictly routine work, which was why she'd decided to do it this morning after Mama had refused to so much as look at her over the breakfast table.

She couldn't decide which was worse: the silence she was being greeted with, or the shouting that she'd heard between her parents for an hour after she'd gone to bed. She couldn't ever recall her parents arguing like that. And because of *her*.

She'd thought this familiar, thoughtless work would soothe her. Help her forget all the questions the night had raised, all the uncertainty. All the wondering about whether this job of hers that had caused such strife between her parents was really worthwhile.

Oh, how wrong she'd been.

Though it had been over five years since she'd seen her childhood friend, she had no difficulty recognizing Johanna's lovely face. Her blond hair was coiffed to perfection, her blue eyes—grey in the photo, of course—smiling.

Smiling at a man in a German uniform, whose arm her hand was tucked into.

They were one of half a dozen couples caught in the image, at some sort of event in Berlin. Lily had no idea what it was. She didn't need to. All she needed to know was that it was Johanna, in Germany, looking happy on the arm of a soldier. Proving even from hundreds of miles away that nothing was simple, and that Lily's judgment couldn't be trusted.

She gathered the photos from the two rolls she'd finished and slid them into her bag, along with the undeveloped film. It would be lunchtime at the OB, which meant she wouldn't likely run into anyone she knew.

Just as she wanted it. She couldn't bear to look at any of them right now. Not given the note she'd written upon rising that morning, telling the admiral of her intent to resign.

The house was quiet. Ivy was at the school, the maid must be upstairs somewhere, Eaton was polishing the silver. She could have just slipped out. Would have, a week ago. Today she slid to the drawing room door and peeked in.

Mama sat at her easel, moving her brush over a canvas with furious strokes. The light was all wrong in the room. Clouds had rolled in sometime while Lily was in her dark-room. Usually, that's when Euphemia Blackwell would pack up her paints and shift to another task—a preliminary sketch, perhaps, or a composition study in pastels or watercolors, while she sorted through how best to achieve what she wanted in her actual oil painting.

"Mama?"

No response.

Taking a deep breath, she edged into the room. "Mama, I'm sorry. I never meant to hurt you. I . . . I couldn't bear the thought of disappointing you—which is, of course, exactly what I did by trying to spare you. I see that now. But I want you to know . . ." She gripped her bag and wished her mother would just turn around and look at her. Scold her. Yell at her. "I'm going to the OB now. I had some film I brought home that is theirs. I'm returning it, along with my resignation."

"Why?"

Lily blinked. Mama's voice was so flat. Lifeless. "Why what?"

Still she didn't turn, just continued to lay down angry strokes of red on the canvas. "Why are you resigning? If it's because I'm upset, then don't. I won't have the entire Intelligence Division blaming *that* on me too."

"It isn't. It's—you were right, I think. This isn't what my art should be used for." Her throat went tight, stopping any other words.

Usually, Mama would have lured more out of her with a well-placed question. Usually, she would have come over and wrapped her arms around her.

Now she didn't even slow in her work. Lily swallowed down the emotion and turned. "I shouldn't be gone long."

Silence followed her out, through the familiar neighborhoods, all the way to the Old Building. Because it was her habit, she went in the back. But up the stairs, not down. It wouldn't matter if anyone recognized her. Zivon had apparently seen her anyway, had put it all together.

Zivon. Daddy had forbidden her from seeking him out, made her promise she would report directly home and not meet him and Clarke and Ivy in the park. That no more invitations would be issued. That she wouldn't try to find him here.

She'd never considered herself particularly rebellious. But the more she thought of his new list of rules, the more she found herself looking for Zivon's familiar smooth stride in the corridors and hoping, praying she'd run into him now. When she'd have every legitimate excuse for doing so. When Daddy could say nothing in argument.

She had to see him again, tell him she didn't hold his inadvertent secret-spilling against him. It hadn't been his fault. He hadn't realized Mama didn't know. And more, she *should* have. Lily never should have kept such a secret in the first place. But even more, she had to tell him how sorry she was for all the pain he was suffering. She had to tell him . . .

But he was nowhere in sight as she made her way to the admiral's office. The secretary wasn't at her desk outside it, so she tapped on the door, expecting silence in reply. He surely had a lunch meeting with some lord of this or that. She would just slip in and leave the film for him, along with her note.

"Enter."

Her hand, already halfway to the door, paused. Hung suspended for a long moment. This hadn't been her plan at all.

Don't be a coward, Lily. Rolling back her shoulders, she opened the door and stepped inside.

Hall glanced up. Gave her the barest echo of a smile, and then looked back down at whatever papers were on his desk. "I thought you meant to take the day off."

Lily cleared her throat. "I needed to bring these back to you. The film I developed this morning. And what I didn't get a chance to do."

When she set the bag down on the corner of his massive desk, DID regarded her solemnly, taking in everything with one of his blinks, it seemed. "And why, pray tell, are you giving the undeveloped rolls to me? Do them tomorrow if you haven't the time today."

A shake of the head was all she could manage for a moment.

It was tempting to just reach into her bag, pull out the letter, and hand it over. But he deserved more than that. "I won't be coming in tomorrow, sir. My mother was quite upset to learn about my involvement here, and—no. It isn't her fault." She squeezed her eyes shut to block out that knowing face of his. "The truth is, Admiral, I can't keep doing this. Not knowing the cost. I can't live with the idea that my work was the cause of death last night. Death of my neighbors, innocent women and children. And so I've come today to offer my resignation."

There. She'd said it. She opened her eyes again, not sure what to expect.

Hall rose halfway out of his chair, leaning forward onto his desk. "I decline to accept it."

He—what? "But—"

"There are no buts, Lilian Blackwell. You may not wear a uniform, but you are an employee of His Majesty's Royal Navy, and as such, your comings and goings are not yours to decide. You will not resign just because you had a bad night. You will keep fighting this war in the way God and king have asked of you. Do I make myself clear?"

Digging her hands into the back of the chair across from his desk, she shook her head. "But I *can't*, sir. I can't live with myself, knowing—"

"Knowing what?" He straightened the rest of the way, eyes flashing. "That you obeyed the command of your superior officer? Or do you think I too ought to be so guilt-ridden that I should resign?"

Lily opened her mouth, though she wasn't certain how to reply. Of course she didn't think *he* should resign, but that was different. Wasn't it?

He lifted a brow. "Or perhaps you think you know better than I how to run this division? Do you know all the inner workings of the High Command? Are you fit to decide how and when to use the intelligence that comes across this desk?"

She tried to swallow, though it did nothing to ease her throat. She could only shake her head again.

"I thought not." He rounded the desk, and though he wasn't more than a few inches taller than she was, it felt as though he towered over her. "We make difficult choices here every day. What information we can act on, what we cannot. And yes, people die, Lilian. People die because of the information we act on or file away. *This* is the burden of intelligence, but it is *not* a burden that you have the right to feel guilty over."

The last thing she wanted to do was cry in front of the admiral, but it took everything within her to hold it back. "How? How can I not?"

"Because that is grossly unfair to all the lives you *save* with your work. All the bombs that have *not* fallen because you helped me dissuade the enemy or redirect them. All the soldiers and agents whose identities you protect." He lifted her bag, shoved it back into her arms. "You will not resign."

Her arms closed around the bag. But she couldn't convince her brows to stop frowning. "Sir—"

"You *will*, however, upon your father's request, work from home rather than here."

At least the sudden fury burned away the threat of tears. "He didn't!"

Hall blinked at her. "You may feel free, of course, to take home any and all supplies from your darkroom here. After which, your father will act as courier for you."

Too many thoughts and feelings swamped her for her to make sense of them all right now. Hall's argument against guilt, his directive, would all have to wait until later to be processed. "This is because of Zivon Marin, isn't it? And you don't think that a bit of an overreaction?"

He moved back to his chair. "You're his daughter, Lily. Of course he's being cautious."

The way he sat was a dismissal. One she would have obeyed

without a squeak on any other day. Today, she moved forward and leaned on the edge of his desk, much as he had done. "What exactly is it that has suddenly appeared to make you suspect him?"

He didn't look as though he meant to answer her. But after a moment, he sighed and pulled a manila envelope from a stack of other papers. "This is what I came down to show you yesterday." He opened the flap, pulled out a photograph, and handed it to her.

She looked at it. But had no idea what it meant. It was Zivon, that much she could clearly see. In dress uniform, bowing over the hand of someone in full military regalia. "I have no idea why this would cast a poor light on him."

"Because the other man, my dear, is Lenin. Leader of the Bolsheviks."

That didn't make sense. The expression on Zivon's face in the photo was one of respect, even adoration. But he'd never felt that for Lenin. He'd spoken against him—that's why Alyona had been killed. "No." She pulled the photo closer to her nose, traced her gaze over Zivon's outline. She couldn't see any lines, but that only meant it was well done. If she had magnification, she could no doubt spot them. "That can't be right. He hates the Bolsheviks."

"He *says* he does." The photo was plucked from her fingers. "And being a socialist is certainly no crime here. But if the truth of his loyalty is so diametrically opposed to what he *says* of his loyalty—well, then, one must ask why."

She reached for the image again, though Hall held it back, eyes flashing. Hers no doubt flashed right back. "Let me fetch my loupe, Admiral, and look at it more closely. That's why you wanted to show it to me yesterday, isn't it? To check its authenticity? Because you know as well as I that photographs can be falsified."

He set it on his desk and rested his hand atop it. "I also

know that when one's heart is involved, one is far from unbiased in any examination. I'm sorry, Lily. But I saw how you looked at him last night."

Her cheeks went hot. "That doesn't mean I can't do my job."

"No, but for now, at least, I'm going to respect Captain Blackwell's wishes and keep you out of this inquiry. Rest assured that if my other photographer contacts don't prove as skilled as I require, I will overrule your father's request."

Huffing out a breath, she slung her bag's strap over her shoulder and straightened. "Zivon Marin is a good man, Admiral."

Hall sighed. "The problem is that *good* is a bit too relative when it comes to matters of national trust. My agents are good men too—good *Englishmen*. That certainly doesn't mean the governments in whose domain they're operating would agree."

She didn't know how to argue without sounding like Zivon's love-blinded sweetheart. And, frankly, she was all too aware of the photo in her bag with Johanna's face in it. Proof of her past mistakes in matters of affection.

Maybe Hall and Daddy were right to keep her out of it.

A battle for another day, at any rate. She took out the stack of photos—she'd nearly forgotten them when he gave her bag back to her—and slid them onto his desk. "I understand you have to be cautious. Just please assure me you'll find someone skilled to look at that. And that you'll remember the lessons you've learned to use so well against your enemies when it comes to this—that the same facts can be used to tell multiple stories, depending on how one tells them."

He smiled and slid the image of Zivon back into its envelope. "And you tried to say you're not suited for this work."

He probably meant the chiding as a sort of compliment. But it weighed heavy as guilt on her chest as she turned away.

Rain had begun to fall by the time she regained the street—and she hadn't thought to grab an umbrella. She could make a run for the tube, but by the time she got to the nearest station, she'd already be soaked. She could go back and wait it out. Or duck into a café, perhaps. But neither of those options suited her mood. She wanted to go home. Think things over.

A large black umbrella appeared over her head. And the man holding it made her heart patter as fast as the rain in the puddles. Zivon had deep shadows underscoring his eyes that his glasses did little to hide, and his cheeks were pale.

He cast a glance over his shoulder. "I should not be speaking to you, I know. But if you will grant me one last walk, Lily, I will be obedient hereafter."

She didn't see her father or Blinker anywhere. And if anyone saw them from a window, it would be impossible to identify them under the umbrella. In answer, she wrapped her hand around the arm holding the brolly. "I'll walk with you anytime you ask. I don't care what he says."

"Of course you care. You should respect his wishes—after this time, I mean." He grinned, but it looked sad and was too soon gone.

They hurried away from the OB, silent. But she made no argument when he steered them toward Hyde Park rather than going directly to Curzon Street. Their feet found their familiar path, and as they neared the tree beside which they'd talked before, he drew them to a halt.

"Lily." He shifted so he faced her, the umbrella's rod between them. "I have caused you trouble, and I never meant to. Your mother is very angry?"

"She is. But that isn't your fault. I should have told her long ago." She tried to smile, but she suspected it didn't look very convincing. "We'll work it out."

"I pray you do. But even so. I am so sorry for how last night ended. I am sorry for the anger I directed at you when it belongs to anyone but. And I am sorry for not telling you before of Alyona."

She wrapped her fingers around his. "I'm glad you told me at all. I can't even imagine the grief you must feel."

"It is as much guilt as grief." His face twisted. "She was killed because of me. A bullet put through her head because of my opinions, my words, my actions."

"But not your hand." Her heart twisted to match his countenance. "The guilt rests on the perpetrator, not on you." But she understood the shake of his head. How could she not? She'd been struggling with the same feelings just minutes ago.

He leaned forward until his forehead touched hers. "I will not have the same happen to you. I will not put you in danger by associating with me. You mean too much to me."

She lifted her hand, touched her fingers to his cool cheek. "I am not in danger, Zivon."

"You could be. I have enemies, and they seem to have found me. Whatever it is that has put the admiral on his guard, it is their work, I am certain."

The Bolsheviks? Here, in London? That didn't seem possible. From what she'd read—and the little he or her father had told her—the political situation in Russia was far too chaotic for them to spare precious resources for hunting down one stray naval officer.

She brushed her fingertips along his jaw. "I obviously can't speak to that. But I can promise you that whatever this trouble is, we'll sort it out. Solve it."

His lips turned up. "You cannot promise. I wish you could. But *I* will promise *you* something, milaya. I will never put you in the position of wondering if I am using you. Tell me nothing that the admiral or your father says. Tell me nothing you see in your work for them. Never disobey him."

"After this."

"After this." He leaned in just a bit more, touched his lips to her cheek in a move too soft, too lingering to be classified as a simple kiss. "My one request—not a direct disobedience, though likely only because he did not yet think of it. Letters—may I write to you? Send them with Clarke? I am told this is how one courts a girl here in England."

With all that had gone wrong in the last day, such words shouldn't be able to make a thrill course through her. But they did. "I would like that."

He kissed her then. Not an invisible touch, like in the car. There was heat in this one, and the urgency that came of not even knowing when next they'd see each other. She could taste his grief and his determination and his wish that it could be different. No doubt because they mirrored her own.

When he pulled away, his breath was ragged. "I never . . . I never thought I was the sort of man who would feel this way. Certainly not now."

That thrill coursed again. "I wish This Lily were here. She would have something clever to say."

He chuckled. "I do not need clever flirtations. Just these precious moments in your company. They will see me through the long days ahead."

Days, perhaps even weeks or months, without seeing him. Without snapping his picture. Without trying to reveal one more layer.

Days, perhaps weeks or months, when he would have no one to believe in him.

"The last time we were standing by this tree, I told you I trusted no one. But I have found that this is untrue." He pressed one more kiss to her lips and then pulled away a few inches, his gaze tangled with hers. "I trust you, Lilian Blackwell. I have from the first."

A sweeter declaration than one of love at this moment. She rested her hand over his heart, as she had daringly done that day. "Zivon, I need you to promise me one thing more."

"Anything."

"Last night, when you spoke of what the Bolsheviks did . . ."

There, his eyes darkened again. She pressed a bit more against his heart. "Guard yourself against those feelings. It's understandable that you hate them. But—"

"I do not hate them." Yet even as he said it, vitriol filled his words. "We are told to love our enemies."

Her smile no doubt looked sad. "We are. But you do not. If you trust me, then hear me in this. They have already stolen so much from you. Don't let them steal your heart. They'll ruin it."

He frowned, but he didn't argue. He wanted to, she could tell. But instead, he reached into his pocket, coming out with a small piece of paper. A photograph. He pressed it into her hands. "This is all I have left of my family. They were always my heart. Will you keep it for me?"

She glanced down, saw the image of two lads, the familiar Parisian landmark behind them. She slid it into her bag. "You know I will."

16

Nadya disappeared behind one of the shelves in the grocer's, scowling at the largely empty space while Evgeni, blast him, smiled at the girl behind the counter, leaning into it as if he had all the time in the world. According to him, he could wheedle supplies from the shopkeeper's daughter.

He probably could. The question was, how did he achieve this miracle? She'd come along to find out. Though when he gave the girl the grin Nadya clearly remembered from the first time they'd met, she began to regret her decision.

"*Bonsoir,* Claire."

The girl grinned back, of course. And darted a glance around the store. According to Evgeni, her father didn't much care for him.

Smart man. If ever a fellow was a danger to a daughter, it was Evgeni Marin. Nadya peeked between the shelves so she could see without being seen.

"I was beginning to think you wouldn't come to see me this evening, Zhenya." The chit twirled a dark curl around her finger.

"And miss out on some of the only joy to find in a day?" He

winked and made a show of peering over the counter to see what might be behind it. "The shelves are a bit bare. Have I waited too long?"

Her laugh was low and soft. "You know I put something back for you." She said it with a smile . . . but unless Nadya had gotten worse at reading silly girls, she also said it lightly. As if it were a game, nothing more.

Nadya's muscles relaxed a bit. She could handle a harmless flirtation if it meant food.

Claire pulled out a parcel from under the counter. "You know the deal, Zhenya."

He laughed and made himself comfortable, apparently not prickling any over the nickname. Why should he? Most people used it—all but Nadya. Still, it sounded odd to hear it spill from a French girl's lips.

"All right." He tapped a finger to his chin in a caricature of thought. "Have I told you the story of the Crystal Mountain yet?"

"Last week."

"Ah yes. What about Princess Never-a-Smile?"

"That was the first tale you told me." Her bottom lip came out in an inane little pout she probably thought was attractive. "As well you know."

"Hmm." He stroked his chin, though no doubt he already knew what tale he planned to tell. "I know! The Snake Princess."

"I do love the ones with a princess." The girl sat on the stool behind the counter, grinning. "Let us see what odd turns *this* one takes."

Nadya rolled her eyes at the shelf. A pretty girl who liked princess stories. Could she be any more cliché? Evgeni didn't actually *like* such girls, did he? If so, then he must be miserable with Nadya.

"It begins with a Cossack—a young man, well worn from

travel and fighting. He ventured off the road for a rest and found a haystack in the middle of a grove of trees. That seemed like a perfect bed, so he made himself comfortable and even enjoyed a pipe."

Claire's brows lifted. "Always wise around hay." So perhaps the girl wasn't utterly senseless.

Evgeni narrowed his eyes and pointed a finger. "Do not get ahead of the story."

"Sorry, sorry."

"As I was saying. He enjoyed his repose and soon got back to his feet, not noticing that a spark fell from his pipe and landed on the hay until the whole thing went up."

"I am all surprise."

"Hush." He grinned and pulled forward the parcel, un-wrapped it. No doubt his ever-growling stomach was curious as to what mysteries it held. "Here is the surprising part—in the middle of the hay stood a beautiful young maiden, and she was crying out for help. 'Save me, good sir,' she called to him. But the heat was so great that he couldn't get near enough. So she bade him to stretch out his lance so that she might use it to pull herself to safety. He obeyed. But when the fair maiden laid hold of the lance, she turned instantly to a snake and slithered up it."

"Oh!" Claire shuddered. "I suppose I should have known from the title there would be a snake, but still."

What was in the package? From what Nadya could see, it looked like a good-sized chunk of cheese, a jar of olives, a few eggs. Was the smaller package flour? She could hope. She hadn't had bread in weeks.

"Luckily for our hero, he did not react so, though no doubt he was alarmed as the snake slithered up the lance, up his arm, and wound herself three times around his neck, biting her own tail to hold herself in place. 'Do not be frightened,' she said to him."

Claire huffed out a breath. "And how is she talking if she's biting her own tail?"

Evgeni laughed. "A maiden in a fire who turns into a snake, and *that* is the part you take issue with?"

"Well, obviously she was enchanted. But I don't know why that would allow her to talk around her tail."

"Can you not talk with your mouth full?" Evgeni bit his finger and said around it, "Do not be frightened." Garbled, but understandable.

Nadya rested her forearms against the shelf and looked around the rest of the dismal little shop.

Claire sighed. "Very well. Rude but not utterly incomprehensible. Go on."

The sound of rustling paper indicated Evgeni was rewrapping the food. "She went on to say that if he carried her around his neck for seven years and looked for the tin kingdom, and then stayed in that kingdom for seven more years, he would find true happiness."

"Ah! *Her* kingdom, I suppose?"

"No, actually. I am not sure whose kingdom it was." His frown was audible in his voice.

Claire's laugh was a bit too loud this time, and a board creaked above them. No doubt the father would be coming down to see what she found so amusing. "Why tin, then?" she asked.

Nadya peeked through the shelves again and watched him shrug. "Let us call it a mystery. But when finally he reached it after seven long years of travel, the snake unwound from his neck, leapt to the ground as the beautiful maiden again, and then promptly disappeared. He went inside the walls of the castle, saw to his horse, and took a tour. It was a beautiful place—everything was silver and ivory, shades of white and grey. In the banquet hall, a feast was laid out on the table. But nowhere was a soul to be seen."

"A feast." Claire sighed and sagged onto her elbows on

the counter. "I can scarcely remember what that would have been like."

Now, with *that* Nadya could commiserate.

The creaking was moving. Evgeni fished a hand into the pocket where he'd stashed some money. "Well, he feasted every day for years. Each day, new food would appear. In the stable, there were always oats for his horse. But there were no people to be found, and the solitude began to wear on him."

"I can imagine." Claire wrinkled her nose.

The footsteps above them had halted. Evgeni held out his money, brows raised. "How much today?"

Instead of answering, she reached and plucked a bill and two coins from his palm.

"Claire, that is not enough."

Idiot—why was he arguing?

"The olives are a gift, from my personal stash." Claire grinned and put the money in the register. "Finish the story, Zhenya. Could he go a whole seven years without any human contact?"

"Well, he lost track of the days. Eventually, it drove him mad. He drank until he was drunk and decided he could take it no more. He stormed toward the nearest door—but a wall flew up in front of him."

Claire turned back to him with a frown. "Wait. The castle stopped him from leaving?"

"At every turn. He fetched his faithful horse and tried riding out, but the gates slammed closed. He tried every door, every window, but walls rose in the place of the openings." Evgeni was grinning, his arms swinging to demonstrate how the walls would have moved. "Our Cossack lashed out, smashing all the dishes, breaking all the decorations, shattering the mirrors. And then the next day when he came down, he found the banquet table empty. 'It is my own fault,' he said. 'If I hadn't behaved as I did yesterday, then I wouldn't be hungry today.' Only after he'd admitted this did food reappear."

Another creak overhead, and this time it was quickly followed by a footfall on the wooden stairs in the back of the store. Nadya shifted, ready to slip out the open door just beside her.

The girl's frown didn't ease. "A fine moral, I suppose, but . . ."

"But?" Evgeni pocketed the change. "There is no but. Three days later, the fair maiden appeared to him, and all the gates were opened. She told him he had served out his time, and that he had freed her from the enchantment put upon her by an evil sorcerer who had been in love with her. She had scorned him, and he had turned her into a snake. But her parents would be so overjoyed at her freedom that her father, a king, would surely grant the Cossack anything he asked for."

"No, that isn't right at all." Claire slapped a hand to the counter. "He *didn't* serve out his time. Not willingly. The castle took the choice from him. Had it been left to him, he'd have lost it all less than a week from completion!"

Her father was at the bottom of the stairs. He'd be coming around the shelves any moment. Nadya coiled, ready to spring. Evgeni chuckled at Claire's frustration and took a step away from the counter. "Perhaps the castle was on his side. Or perhaps it was the princess, helping him."

"Not good enough." Claire lifted her pretty little chin. "A man doesn't deserve to be the hero of the tale unless he can make sound decisions on his own."

"Well. Perhaps you will prefer his decisions in the second half of the story. Next time?"

She glanced toward the back of the shop, where her father was coming into view. Nadya took her cue and darted out the door. Though still she heard the girl say, "Next time. Bonsoir, Zhenya."

"Bonsoir, fair maiden." With a wink, he hurried out of the store.

He nearly collided with Nadya on the sidewalk, where she'd

stopped to wait for him, arms crossed and eyes narrowed. He held up the parcel of food and switched his speech back to Russian. "Success."

She pivoted on her heel. "I ought to have known you'd get it by flirting."

He chuckled and put a hand to the small of her back—a move she'd balked at when first they met. But she'd grown used to it. Liked it, even though she'd never admit it to him. "Oh, come now. It's not so bad, and you know it. A story for the food. A fine trade."

It was. It was one she'd have made readily enough if the situation were reversed. And she didn't mind *too* much, given how lightly the girl seemed to take it. Still. "Oh yes, I'm certain it's the *story* she's interested in."

He slid half a step behind her. "At any rate, we'll be adding olives to our feast tonight."

She rolled her eyes. "I can *hear* you smiling, you know."

Another laugh slipped out. "Over olives, no doubt. I haven't had any in years."

Olives. Right. Certainly all it was. She shoved aside the image of pretty Claire DuBois and rolled her shoulders. "We'd better pick up the pace. Paul will be waiting for us."

Now he went stiff, and Nadya looked up at him with raised brows. "You need to get over whatever it is you don't like about him. He is the head of the Bolsheviks in Paris. Without him—"

"I have no problem with him as the head of the party in Paris." But he scowled. "My problem is with the way he follows you with his gaze every time you move."

She didn't care for that either, but it was her problem to deal with, not his. And she dealt with it just fine. She planted an elbow in his side.

Though the hit hadn't been that hard, he let out an exaggerated grunt. "What was that for?"

"For acting like a caveman, ready to fight with another

caveman over a woman. It's degrading to us all. I'll make my own decisions on who I choose to be with, thank you, and your little manly displays of possession aren't going to impress me." The same words, more or less, that she'd given Paul.

His brows hiked up. "Hold on just a moment. My getting irritated with Paul for failing to respect our relationship has nothing at all to do with my opinion of you."

"Ha! In some ways, Evgeni, you're like every other man. Those old-fashioned instincts are still there, ready to flare up and name me yours. Try to own me. Dictate to me. Convince me my only value is as your woman."

She'd expressed similar sentiments before, and he never disagreed with her. Not out loud. But he always looked amused. Which irritated her even as she admitted silently that perhaps she repeated herself too often. Who, after all, was she trying to convince?

This time he interrupted her with a quick tickle to her side and leaned a bit closer when she squealed. "And what of *your* old-fashioned instincts, Nadya?"

She pulled away enough to glare at him. "I beg your pardon?"

He jerked his head backward, toward the shop. "That reaction to Claire DuBois? How is that any different than my reaction to Paul? Should I accuse you of degrading us all with the feelings? Of being possessive of me? Of being ready to start a fight with the girl?"

She cocked her head to the side. This was why she'd yet to grow tired of Evgeni Marin. He had a way of calling her out—and yet making it clear he liked even her faults. "I could make mincemeat of her."

He laughed. "In half a second. It's one of the things I most admire about you. But if you do not like *my* fighting spirit so much . . ."

She drew her lip between her teeth. She'd spent so much

of the last few years trying to prove to the men around her that she could fight every bit as well as they could. But that was another reason she'd found herself drawn to this man beside her—he never doubted her abilities. He just fought right alongside her. "All right, you caught me. Jealousy is, perhaps, a natural reaction when you have invested time and . . . and heart into someone. Maybe it does not necessarily make us cavemen."

It was the first time she'd even mentioned such sentiments. It had seemed dangerous. She didn't want to be one of those girls who fell in love with a fellow and threw her whole life away.

But at the same time, when she'd thought he was dead, the world hadn't looked quite right.

He grinned at her. "As long as we share the same standards, correct? The injustice you balk at is if I were allowed to indulge my jealousy but still dally with other women. You would be right, then, to be angry. That said . . . Is it such a bad thing to want a bit of security with the one we've chosen to be with?"

She tilted her head to the side. Investing so much in another person was a risk. And yet, wasn't it more of one *not* to invest anything? "I suppose I wouldn't mind a bit of assurance that you're not inclined toward dark curls and full lips, even when they offer you free olives."

He chuckled. "You have nothing to worry about there. I have always preferred hair of spun gold. . . . At least until the brunette can offer chocolate. Or, better still, baklava. Now, if she had baklava—"

This time she interrupted him with a merciless tickle in his side, making him laugh and pull away, hands up in surrender. "All right, all right. I prefer you even to dessert. And that, milaya *moya*, is saying something indeed."

Her smile probably looked a bit like the one a cat would wear when it got into the cream. But it was rather nice to know he didn't plan to run off with a pretty Frenchwoman in the middle of their mission. "Good. And, for the record, I much prefer smiling, teasing army men to dour-faced party officials. Don't waste a minute of jealousy on Paul." They rounded the corner as she spoke, and they both caught sight of his figure leaning against their wall. Nadya huffed out a breath and added quietly, "All the same, don't antagonize him, Evgeni. We need him."

Which was probably why he kept smiling as they approached. "Bonsoir, Paul," he called out, fishing the key to their room from his pocket.

Paul kept right on glowering. "I suppose it is, when one has the leisure to while away the day laughing and visiting the shops. Unlike some of us, who work for a living."

Nadya rolled her eyes. "As do we. And we've been doing our job. Now stop your bellyaching and tell us if you've managed what we asked."

Paul grunted and held out a hand indicating Nadya should enter first. She did, though she shot Evgeni an amused look as she stepped past him into the dim interior. Paul then stomped through the doorway, and Evgeni brought up the rear, closing the door behind him.

"I still do not understand why so many resources are being expended over your brother." Paul tossed his hat on the table.

The muscle in Evgeni's jaw ticked for a moment before he forced a smile. "He is of interest to the party, as I've said before."

Nadya took the parcel of food from him and set to putting it all away before he squished the cheese.

"I don't know why. The man does nothing but jog, go to work, and go straight home."

Evgeni froze in a way she'd seen a few times before. The way a tiger froze before it pounced. Muttering a curse, she shoved the food onto the table and lunged.

Too late. Evgeni had already lunged too, right for Paul. By the time she grabbed his arm, it was already on the recoil, having socked the older man firmly in the nose.

Yes, part of her wanted to smirk—she'd dreamed of punching Paul a few times over the last weeks herself. But still. "Get ahold of yourself, Evgeni. What has come over you?"

Evgeni shook her off, eyes still on Paul as the man cursed in French and Russian, hand over his bleeding nose. Probably waiting for—and hoping for—a retaliation, though he wasn't likely to get it from Paul. "He could only know that if he had someone following Zivon."

Usually she could follow his train of thought fairly well. Not so now. "And?"

Evgeni finally took a deep breath and eased up. "He would have spotted a tail in half a second. Now he'll be on the alert. And no doubt will figure out who it is, that he has socialist connections, and put together that it's the party."

Paul dabbed at his nose. "You worry too much."

If he said anything else so stupid, Nadya would have to punch him too. "You do not know this man. You do not know all our purposes. Why do you assume this is anything less than life or death? And if so grave, why do you go off without our input and authorize something that could endanger the entire mission?"

A bit of fight finally sparked in Paul's eyes. "Perhaps because I don't *know* your mission!"

"It's simple. And we need to stay focused on it." She held Paul's gaze just long enough to convey her opinion of his methods. And then looked to Evgeni. "We find the names of the Germans trying to start a mutiny, and we kill them before they can. We keep this war going in Europe as long as we can, to keep the Westerners out of Russia longer. On this we can all agree. Right?"

Evgeni nodded.

Paul lowered his bloodstained hands. "That's what this is about? What does his brother have to do with it?"

A beat of silence. Then Evgeni sighed. "Because if he has my passport—which I believe he does—then he has the names."

And he had knowledge of it even before that, so he was likely to piece together what he had. Nadya wetted a towel and handed it to Paul. Perhaps they should have told him sooner, rather than just expecting his blind help. But they hadn't been given permission to read anyone else in on the mission.

A mission that he could have seriously hindered now because of his ignorance. She motioned to the bag he'd dropped when Evgeni punched him. "You have more photographs in there?"

Paul nodded and, with a wary glance at Evgeni, reached for the bag. "Are you going to tell me why *these* are necessary? Or just let me guess about that too?"

When he set the satchel on the table, Nadya flipped it open. She drew out the first of the images, smiling at seeing exactly what she'd instructed Paul's photographer friend to create. It may not be quite as incriminating as the first one they'd produced. But it would tell a story. A continuing story. "Also simple," she said.

Evgeni didn't look quite as cheerful as he pulled out a chair and sat. "That's right. We're convincing the authorities in England that Zivon is one of us. Which will mean, to their way of thinking—"

"He's not one of them." Paul smiled and pulled out the second chair. "I believe I'm beginning to understand."

17

There. Lily held the magnifying glass over the image, finally happy that everything was blended properly. For a moment, she could take satisfaction simply in a job well done. At least until the questions started tapping away at her heart again.

What would this one be used for? All she'd been asked to do was remove someone from the background—probably one of Hall's agents. This was, in all likelihood, one of those cases where she was helping preserve someone's secrecy. The photo would be slipped into a file somewhere, replacing an original, perhaps. Or fed to an enemy. Something good. Helpful.

Right?

Blustering out a sigh, Lily swung around to put the magnifying glass away and knocked her elbow, for the twelfth time in the last two and a half weeks, into the table against the wall. Her "Ouch!" turned to a growl. And maybe a frustration-relieving slap to the offending piece of furniture's top.

This was *not* working. Her home darkroom was fine for a few rolls of film at a time, or working for an hour here or

218

there. But not until she'd tried to move all of her equipment from the OB in here did she realize how small it was. She had prints in the drying rack, prints clipped to lines above, prints stacked on every possible surface. She had furniture pushed this way and that to try to accommodate the new additions.

As a result, she barely had room to turn around, much less accomplish anything.

And she meant to relay that to Daddy and Blinker this evening, when the admiral and his family came over to dine with them.

"Lilian." Mama's voice was accompanied by a light knock on the door. "Ivy is home. You had better go upstairs to prepare for dinner."

"Yes, Mama." They'd established a peace . . . of sorts. All conversations were civil. They put on smiling faces whenever anyone else was around. Mama hadn't made a peep when Daddy announced that Lily's resignation had been refused and all the supplies from the OB were carted to the house.

But never would her mother actually step foot in here. And every time she addressed her, it was *Lilian*. Never *Lily* anymore. She was still a conscientious, responsible mother.

Just no longer a friend.

Lily stood, switching off heaters and lights and what fans she no longer needed. She had to slide sideways to make her way to the door, and by the time she opened it, Mama had vanished. Another sigh slipped out.

She missed her friend.

As she neared her bedroom, her brows drew together at the scraping noises coming from Ivy's. What in the world was her sister moving around *now*? She'd just rearranged everything last week, though no doubt that meant she'd found issue with something.

Smiling, Lily slipped into her room and went straight to the spot on the floor by their shared wall. Once the noise stopped on Ivy's side, she lifted a knuckle. *Tap, tap-a-tap.*

"Oh! You're here!" Instead of an answering tap, footsteps moved toward the hall, and a moment later Ivy entered Lily's room, closing the door behind her. From the conspiratorial smile on her face, Lily knew there'd be a letter in her pocket. "Secret delivery."

Lily patted the cushion next to her. She'd known her sister would be a willing partner in this most innocent of crimes, but she'd underestimated Ivy's enthusiasm. "Did you and Clarke have a good walk?"

Ivy managed somehow to both smile dreamily and sigh sympathetically. "We did. It was a positively perfect afternoon. The only thing that could have improved it would have been had you and Zivon been there."

Lily could hardly argue with that.

"But enough of that. Here." From her pocket Ivy pulled an envelope with *Lily* written on the front in that elegant script she'd grown increasingly familiar with since the wedding. "Oh! No, wait." Rather than hand it over, she held it high, away from Lily's reaching hands. "It's my turn."

"Ivy." She tried to inject into her voice the same censure that Mama could achieve with no effort. "Just give it to me."

Apparently she failed, because her sister laughed and shook her head. "Nope. You know the cost of my cooperation. Now, settle down and let me serenade you with the sweet music of your beloved's words."

Though she rolled her eyes, it was largely for show. "Fine. But no dramatics."

"No input from the audience, please." Ivy cleared her throat, sent Lily the look that she probably used on her students to keep them in line, and said, "'My sweetest milaya . . .'"

Lily groaned at her ridiculous attempt at a Russian accent. "Stop."

"I can't. I've barely started. Ahem. 'You have no idea how dim the days have grown, without the light of your presence awaiting me at day's end.' No, wait." Ivy screwed up her face. "I can do that better. Your presence. P-resence." Her attempt to swallow the *R* in the same way that Zivon would have done made Lily giggle.

"Ivy."

"Oh, fine, I'll drop the accent." She straightened the page. "'But it has had an effect I never dreamed. The more I am without you, the more alone I feel, and the more the older grief comes upon me. You are right that it is a tragedy I have not fully grieved. To be honest, I am not certain I know how. Whenever I think of it, think of her, think of all the similar stories my colleagues in Russia no doubt have, I am overcome. I find myself crying out, as the psalmist did, for the Lord to fight against those who fight against me. I have been clinging these months to God's command to be still and trust Him. I am clinging, Lily. But I could see no beauty left in the world. Not until I met you.' Aww!" Ivy paused to slap a hand to her heart. "That is the sweetest thing in the world!"

Lily picked up one of the extra pillows and hugged it.

"Well." Ivy laughed a bit as she scanned the next section. "This is not quite as sweet as I was thinking, though you might still think so. He says, 'You have shown me the beauty in a thousand silent moments. A feather on the breeze. Sun breaking through the clouds. The way a child studies a flower. Moments I never saw before, much less appreciated, are now quiet reminders that God is there. That He has created a world of beauty, and that His will is for us to live in it. Live in this land of the living. Every time you pause to lift your camera, I know it is because you saw something beautiful that I would have walked by without a second glance. And I cannot tell you the difference that has made in my life.'"

Lily drew her lip between her teeth. Much sweeter indeed than praising her own beauty, which was probably what Ivy had assumed he was going to do. She knew her face paled in comparison to others'. But God's world—that was an endless feast of the truest beauty.

Ivy scooted to her usual place beside her and nestled in. "There are only a few lines left. Here we go. 'But I have been remembering not only the way you draw out your camera and find the beauty in the world. I remember too the way you looked at me and saw something far different. You saw an ugliness that you named hatred. That, my sweet one, has scarcely left my mind. I have tried to deny it. I have tried to excuse it. I have sworn to God and myself that I will make it right. But in all truth, I know only this: I am weak, and I am afraid. I fear what else I do not see, that you would. I fear the man I will become if you are not shining your light into my soul. How could I have come so quickly to need you so much? I do not know. But you have become for me the proof that God does indeed bring beauty from ashes.'"

Slowly, reverently it looked like, Ivy lowered the page. "Well." Her voice was a mere murmur after her reading. "We knew he was a man of depth."

"Mm." He was more than that. He was a man who deserved to have someone fighting beside him. She pushed to her feet. "Help me get ready, would you? I intend to pounce on Blinker and Daddy the moment the Halls arrive."

Ivy all but flew to the dressing table and brandished the brush as though it were Arthur's Excalibur. "At your service, lady fair! We will wage a war of smiles and curls. And we will emerge victorious."

Laughing, Lily settled on the stool. How could they possibly lose, with Ivy on her side?

◈ ◈ ◈

SATURDAY, 8 JUNE 1918

Zivon folded the newspaper and checked his watch. He still had an hour before he was due at the office for his half day. Usually he'd have gone for a run with Clarke this morning, but the rain was coming down in earnest, rumbles of thunder punctuating the deluge. Not a day for running.

Nor a day for visitors. So why was there a knock at his door?

Zivon pushed to his feet. Probably a neighbor needing to borrow something. Or lend him something. Mrs. Hamilton, the landlord's wife, often stopped by with a new armful of books from her secondhand shop. When she'd discovered that he liked to read but had none of his collection with him, she'd taken to acting as a lending library.

He swung open the door, blinking at the last person he'd expected to see. "Admiral?"

Hall lifted his brows. "May I?"

"Ah. Yes, of course. Apologies." Zivon stepped aside and held the door wide. He gave his flat a quick glance, never more glad that Batya had drilled military precision and neatness into him while Matushka had him conjugating Latin verbs. The place finally looked lived in, but tidy.

The admiral's gaze went unerringly to the walls, which boasted the Blackwell ladies' artwork still. He'd half expected the captain to demand their return, but thus far he hadn't spoken to Zivon again at all since the day after the air raid. Executing an about-face that allowed the admiral to take in the entire flat with that all-seeing gaze of his, Hall soon faced him again.

Much as Zivon wanted to ask his superior what he was doing here, he opted for holding his peace.

He didn't have long to wait. Hall wasn't one for wasting time. "Dilly told me what a help you were yesterday. We've been trying for a year to crack that code."

Ah. He had expected Hall to mention his assistance at some point, yes. He just hadn't thought it would warrant a house call. Zivon inclined his head. "It was my pleasure to assist, sir. We had, in Moscow, a codebook for that one."

"Even so. You didn't have to share your knowledge. And it is remarkable that you remember it."

Zivon smiled. It was the code he *had* considered keeping to himself, so he could use it with the diplomats in Paris. But in light of the suspicions around him, he'd decided that withholding even the slightest information was not in his best interest. Was not honorable. "I admit it took me a while to piece it together again."

The admiral's blink looked amused. "Yes, an entire day. But that is not the only reason I've come."

Zivon's muscles stiffened. Was this it, then? Had he come to boot him to the curb? *"Thanks for your help, old boy, but you're too big a risk"*?

Hall cleared his throat, turned, paced to look at the Eiffel Tower picture, as if this were just a social visit. "Mrs. Hall and I dined with the Blackwells last night. Lily—this is one of hers, correct?"

"It is, yes." Zivon had spent countless hours over the last weeks staring at it. Studying it. Imagining Lily standing there at the base, in the same place Zivon had once stood, looking up in the way she loved best—through the eye of her camera. He imagined standing there with her in a year or two, when the war was over. Her hand in his. He imagined standing there in a decade, directing a child's gaze upward and saying, "You know your mother's photo of this? It was one of the first things she ever gave me."

Sentimental fool, that's what Evgeni would call him. But he'd say it with a smile and a teasing elbow in the ribs.

Hall nodded. "You have quite a champion in that young lady. You'd have been properly impressed with the arguments she presented in your favor last night, I think. Her photography equipment is, as a matter of fact, being moved back to the OB as we speak."

Pulse kicking up as if he were halfway through a sprint, Zivon straightened. "The captain has permitted this?"

His guest chuckled. "By the time she finished explaining how her work is hindered by not having access to her archives, he was offering to transport it all back himself—with the stipulation that she promise to avoid you, of course."

His pulse skidded, thudded, slowed again. "Of course."

Hall's lips twitched. "Though *that* lasted only a few minutes. When she then launched into a detailed defense of you and why it was utterly illogical for you to come here with nefarious goals, one could practically see his resistance crumbling. Especially when Effie joined in. Partly to poke at her husband, I think—she's still a bit angry over the deception—but whatever her motivations, they had the desired effect."

Hope sprang so quickly it left him breathless. And, frankly, terrified that it would just be ripped away again. "Did it?"

"Mm." Hall moved to the painting next. "Blackwell has granted that she may speak to you—in public, so long as others are around. He didn't relent yet on the walks in the park, but I believe you will be getting another invitation to dinner sometime soon."

All of which was of the utmost interest to *him*. But he still wasn't certain why Hall had taken the time to deliver this news personally, during a downpour. "This is most welcome news indeed, sir. But I must ask—were *you* convinced by her arguments?"

For a long moment, Hall continued to study the landscape. Then he pivoted, gaze just as steady on Zivon. "My people have not been idle. Pearce did indeed follow that chap who'd been following you. Found his home, his workplace. There was nothing immediately suspicious, so he had his sisters set up a watch and dig deeper. They gave their report yesterday."

Zivon clasped his hands behind his back to keep them still. The man had been there several more times, trailing him, hiding from him—or thinking he was. He'd seen Pearce again too, clearly keeping an eye on the other fellow, not on Zivon. "If I may guess—he has socialist ties?"

Hall jerked his head in a nod. "Attended a convention for the Allied socialists in the past and even bought a ticket for the upcoming one. He was overheard in a pub the other night complaining about a fellow called Kerensky, a Trudovik—you know him, perhaps?"

"*Of* him." The ousted head of the defeated Trudovik party. As much an enemy of the Bolsheviks, in some ways, as Zivon was.

"Right. The man was complaining that Kerensky was to be allowed a seat at the convention, though Russia is no longer an ally and his party no longer in power." Hall moved three steps closer. "More, we intercepted a telegram for him some ten or so days ago, ordering him to desist following you. It came from Paris."

Zivon frowned. "But I have seen him just two days ago."

The admiral grinned. "The instructions may have been misdelivered. I plan to bring him in for questioning soon and would prefer to apprehend him while he's about this questionable business rather than at work or the pub. I will advise you on the day this is planned so you can lead him to the place where I will have people waiting."

"Of course. Thank you." It wasn't exactly a full statement of trust, but it was something, wasn't it, to be brought in on this plan?

Hall cleared his throat. "The fact that he is connected to the socialists, who are clearly concerned with you, lends credence to all you've told me. But then there's this." He reached into his overcoat and pulled out a manila envelope.

Regarding it much as he would a serpent, Zivon reached for it carefully, bracing himself for whatever strike might come upon opening it.

His breath balled up in his chest when he pulled out the photograph. Him and Evgeni, both in uniform. The one taken at Christmas, the last time they were both home. He didn't know why the image would alarm the admiral, but he *did* know what it meant for him. "This—this is from my album. The one I lost—the one I had those intercepted messages stored in."

Hall didn't seem quite so excited. "It could be another print."

"No. No, the corner has the same fold. And see, on the back is my handwriting, with the date." But when he flipped it over, his words died on his tongue. His wasn't the only handwriting. More words were scrawled in a feminine hand. In English.

. . . by the company . . .

He frowned. "What is this?"

"That would be the question. We received another photograph that had 'You will know a man . . .' on the back. Combined with this, I expect a third one to arrive finishing out the phrase. Probably 'You will know a man by the company he keeps.'"

And why would his brother be bad company? Zivon lowered the image, shaking his head. "I do not understand. Have your people in Paris had any luck searching for him yet? Evgeni?"

"We found a hospital that had treated him after the train accident." He said it so matter-of-factly, as if it were no great thing that he'd discovered this and then not mentioned it until now. "They said he was stable but not well when he left. We have found no evidence of him since. Aside from . . ."

Something about the tone of voice had Zivon reaching for a chair at his table, pulling it out. Sitting.

Hall sighed. "A police officer we spoke to recognized the photograph you gave me. He said . . . he said he thought he'd seen him at the church that was shelled on Good Friday. Being carried off. He remembered solely because he bears a resemblance to this officer's son, and it gave him quite a fright, despite the fact that the son is in the army, not in Paris."

Zivon's eyelids sank down. *Be still, and know that I am God.*

A soft hand came to rest on his shoulder. "I am sorry, Marin. He was the only family you had left?"

He could only nod. Once. It was all the movement he could summon. *Be still. Be still.*

The hand squeezed, then retreated. "I wish we'd found something more encouraging. As it is, I have my people instead looking for whoever sent that telegram to Godfrey Higgins—the chap who's been following you. It seemed a better use of my resources."

"Yes. Of course." Zivon's voice sounded as he felt—tight and gruff.

"I'll let myself out."

Zivon held his seat, kept his eyes closed. Tried to obey that voice in his spirit. But his mind wouldn't still, wouldn't stop spinning. All he could think was that his brother had only been at that church because of *him*. He'd have thought to find him there. And it was close to the rendezvous.

All his fault. Yet another death of someone dear to him that lay squarely on his shoulders.

His fault—and theirs. The whole reason they'd fled Russia. The Bolsheviks.

He leaned forward until he could rest his head in his hands. He could see it now, hear it in his own thoughts. The hatred Lily had pointed out to him.

He could see it. But for the life of him, he didn't know how to fight it.

18

I think that's it. We're ready to go."

Evgeni looked at the passport Paul had just delivered. Yet another one with his face but not his name. This time he was posing as a Frenchman. And, much to his amusement and delight, Nadya was apparently now his wife.

She'd scowled when Paul had delivered the identifications with their matching last names, but she hadn't argued. Much. How could she, when it was the only way they'd likely be able to rent a single room once they arrived in England? Not that Paul had looked particularly happy with the arrangement either, but Paul wouldn't be his problem for much longer.

A quick trip to England. They'd steal his passport back from Zivon, verify that he'd fallen out of favor with the Admiralty and so was safe, and then return to the Continent. It would take only a week or so, if all went well. They'd find the German officers. Kill them. And then be back in Russia before June had turned to July.

Nadya checked their bags for the eighth time since she'd

packed them that morning. To Evgeni's way of thinking, all
that really mattered was that the album was in there, along
with the altered photographs Paul's friend had given them,
and bits and pieces of the originals he'd cut up to create them.
Evgeni hadn't spent too much time dwelling on the mutilated
remains of Zivon's past. If he did, it soured his stomach. Because at least half of Zivon's memories were his too. And he
hated to see them used so.

But it was for Zivon's good, ultimately. And Russia's good.
Sentiment couldn't long hold up against that.

He slid the new passport into his pocket. He didn't intend
to let *this* one out of his sight for even a moment. They'd been
held up far too long, waiting for Paul to get him a new one.

His eyes went to their pantry shelves. All but empty. "Food?"

Though she sent him a narrow-eyed glance, her lips nearly
lost the battle to a smile. "Go and beg some from your pretty
little grocer's daughter, I suppose."

Evgeni grinned. He rather liked a jealous Nadya. She made
him hope that she'd actually stick around for a while. "Not
going to come keep an eye on me?"

The smile won possession of her mouth. "I daresay she has
no chocolate, so I can trust you."

He laughed and moved over to plant a sound kiss on those
lips. "I won't be long." By evening, they'd be on their way.

He grabbed his cap and stepped out into the sunshine,
reveling in the pleasant air. His gait wasn't exactly buoyant
as he considered the coming trip. It was dangerous, getting
so close to Zivon. Letting Nadya slip into his flat and search
for Evgeni's passport. She would do a fine job, that he knew,
but, well, Zivon had always been unpredictable. Stable to the
point of boring in some ways, but then he'd simply out-think
the rest of them and take everyone by surprise.

And Zivon had been in England months already. He'd know
the territory. He'd know the normal look and feel, which meant

that if Evgeni and Nadya disrupted a pattern, he would sense it and be on to them within hours. He could foil their plans yet again.

He pressed his lips together. Why couldn't his brother just have settled in France and found a position translating? Why, *why* had he sold his services to the British?

When the grocer's came into view, Evgeni slowed, trying to get a gauge on how many other customers might be inside. He could only see one through the glass, and dawdling before crossing the street gave the faded housewife enough time to exit. He watched Claire take out her broom, pass before the window. A sure sign she was now alone.

Perfect. He hurried over and pulled open the door.

She looked up with a smile that went considerably brighter as recognition dawned. "Zhenya! You're early today."

"Well." He grinned. "I'm planning for a trip. I decided I'd better have time enough to try to wheedle a bit extra from you."

"A trip?" Claire kept on sweeping. "Where could you be going? It isn't safe to travel, is it?"

He lifted his brows. "And it is safe *here*? Need I remind you of my experience the last time I tried to attend Mass in your fair city?"

She laughed. "All right, all right. Though I ought to be put out that you're abandoning me."

"Mm. I suspect you will survive without my stories."

"I suppose that depends on if you leave me in the middle of one. You never did finish 'The Snake Princess,' you know."

"I couldn't! Your father—"

"Isn't here right now." Grinning, she reached under a shelf with her broom, though she pulled out no dust that he could see. "So begin. Then I will see what extra supplies I might be able to find for you."

"All right." He leaned against the counter, arms folded over his chest. "Where did we leave off? The Cossack had just been set free from the castle and the princess was released from the enchantment, *oui*?"

Claire nodded, though she still tossed him a scowl. "Over my objections. She also explained about the sorcerer."

"Yes. And she said that her father, a king, would surely grant the Cossack anything he asked for. This is where we were, correct?"

"Oui." She swept her way down an aisle.

"Well, she went further in her explanation. She told the Cossack that her father was certain to offer him all sorts of tantalizing rewards—gold, jewels, land."

"Chocolate," Claire added on a sigh. "I would ask for a store-room full of chocolate."

A chuckle slipped from Evgeni's throat. "You and I have much in common, Claire. But the princess told the Cossack that he must refuse and instead ask for the cask stored in the king's cellar."

"A *cask*?" She looked over her shoulder. "It had better be a magical one. One that never runs dry of the finest wine, perhaps?"

"*Mais non*. Well, magical, yes. But not because of what it was filled with. If one were to roll the cask to the left, a magical castle would appear. And then it would vanish again when one rolled it to the right."

"That would do too. If there was chocolate to be found in this castle, anyway."

He laughed again. "We can hope. Anyway, the princess and the Cossack traveled together to her father's kingdom, where, as expected, the king and queen were so grateful to have their daughter back that they offered the young man anything his heart desired. As instructed, he turned down the jewels and gold paraded before him and instead requested the cask from the cellar. The king was none too pleased, but he had promised. So he delivered the cask to the Cossack, who bade them farewell and went on his way."

"Went on his way? Without the princess?" Claire rounded the end of the shelves and disappeared into the next aisle. "What kind of story *is* this?"

"Be patient. He had to see what it did, didn't he? And he couldn't very well open up a castle inside a castle. Plus, the princess would want to visit with her family, I'd think."

Claire's *hmph* sounded unconvinced, but she said no more. For the moment.

"So off went the Cossack. He hadn't gone far, however, when he came across an old beggar sitting in the road."

"Ah!" She peeked over the shelf to grin at him. "It is always an old beggar. Is he a magician? The sorcerer? Another king in disguise, to see if our hero is worthy?"

"Whatever he was, he was hungry. He asked the young man if he perchance had anything to eat. So the Cossack put down the cask and rolled it to the left, and *voilà!* A magnificent castle appeared. So he invited the old man inside. They found the dining hall, where a grand feast was laid out, awaiting them. The old man ate an entire roast ox and drank a full barrel of wine and said he could eat more but didn't want to be rude, so he thanked his kind host and said he had better take his leave."

Claire chuckled as she came into view again. "This is a tormenting story, *mon ami*. All this food . . ."

"No more feasting, I promise." He glanced out the door at the people passing by. None of whom, thankfully, seemed poised to join them. "The Cossack left with the man, rolled the cask to the right, and the castle vanished. Well, the old man was quite impressed. 'I could do with a cask like that,' he said. 'Would you be willing to make a trade?'"

Claire paused at the end of the aisle and leaned on her

broom. "What could he possibly have to trade that would be worth it to the Cossack?"

"Exactly what the Cossack asked, at which point the old man pulled out a beautiful, shining sword. 'This,' he said, 'is an enchanted sword, capable of smiting anything you command it to smite, of its own power. With this sword at your side, you can never lose a battle.' To prove it, he commanded the sword to fell the grove of trees near at hand, and off it flew, chopping down each and every one."

Claire frowned again and moved to open the door so she could sweep her little pile of dust and dirt outside. "If he had this, why was he a beggar?"

Evgeni sighed. "You ask too many questions, Claire."

"It is a reasonable one! With a sword like that, he could have taken over a kingdom of his own!"

"I suppose the old fellow wasn't that smart. But the Cossack was. He knew exactly what to do. He made the deal with the old man and gave him the cask—"

"The princess's father would probably have something to say about that." She swept the debris into the street and closed the door again.

He ignored her. "And he took the sword. Well, the moment it was in his hands, he told the sword to cut down the old man, and of course it did. So he took the sword *and* the cask and went back to claim the princess as his wife."

Claire came to a halt, her hand still on the door. "You must be joking! The hero is now not only incapable of making his own choices, but he is a cold-blooded murderer of old men?"

Evgeni straightened. "He saw the way forward to all he ever wanted, and he took it."

"What a terrible story." Looking genuinely put out, she stomped around the counter and leaned the broom into its corner. "I thought the old beggar character in a folktale was supposed to be a test to the main character. That he would prove himself a true hero by treating him nicely, or be stripped of everything if he scorned him. If *this* is instead the sort of tale your people tell, it is a wonder you do not all go around murdering each other and stealing from each other."

Evgeni sighed. He didn't have time to get into an argument with her about whether a story was a good one. Better to laugh it off. "Well, we *were* ruled by the Huns for several hundred years. Blame it on their influence, marauders as they were."

Her movements jerky, angry, Claire pulled out a few supplies she'd tucked away and then stormed back into the store proper. "Give me just a moment to gather you a bit more."

"Claire." He trailed her to the shelves of canned meats. "Why are you so upset? It is just an old story."

"An old story that you chose to tell, of all the old stories you had to pick from." She snatched a few jars and pressed them to his stomach, then grabbed a few others. "I'm not certain what that says about you, Zhenya Marin. But perhaps I should be glad you're leaving."

It shouldn't have stung. She was just a grocer's daughter. Barely more than an acquaintance. "Be fair. I don't remember many of the tales, not well enough to recite them. I've only been telling you the ones I recall clearly."

"And *that* is one you remember?"

"Perhaps because of those oddities that have you hissing like a cat."

She pierced him with a sharp gaze and strode around him, back to the counter. "I don't think so. I think you favor that one because you like the thought of just taking whatever you want from life." She smacked her jars onto the countertop. "Perhaps Papa was right about you."

"Now, wait just a moment." He followed behind her, though he kept his distance. He wasn't sure what had her so hot under the collar, but wisdom said to stay out of swinging range. "You have no idea what the Cossack did after that. For all you know, he used his newfound wealth and power to bring health and happiness to everyone in the region. Sharing equally with all."

"Until they had something he wanted, you mean?" She gathered all the food together and then her hands stilled. "No. I find it very hard to believe that men who would steal and kill innocents to get their way would ever then be so selfless." She met his gaze and told him the total for the food.

More than she usually would have charged him—though not more than she *should* have. He drew the bills and coins from his pocket. "Sometimes people have to make a hard choice, you know. For the greater good."

"And more often people trample the helpless for their *own* good and just say it is for the sake of others." She moved to put the cash into the register, leaving him to load up his basket.

"You have a dim view of humanity." He strove to keep his voice light, though it was difficult with that scowl still in the place of her usual flirtatious grin.

She paused, hand on the register, and looked at him. "I just find it sad that so many people think they can find true happiness by *taking*. They can't. We can only ever find it by *giving*."

Now she sounded like Matushka. And perhaps Zivon. Evgeni picked up his basket. "Perhaps your father should rethink leaving you in charge of the till."

Her chin lifted. "Perhaps *you* should have tried to go to Mass again after that last time."

She really *was* like Matushka and Zivon. He fastened a grin into place. "*Au revoir*, Claire. Try not to break the heart of every young man left in the neighborhood."

She slid the register drawer shut. Softly. "Au revoir, Zhenya. Try not to cut down any innocents in your path."

"Oh, I think they are all safe. I have no magical sword, after all." *He* would cling to levity, even if she had forgotten their script. He topped it with a wink and hurried out the door.

Suddenly, he was rather glad to be leaving Paris.

Lily stepped out of Charing Cross Hospital and made her way to Whitehall with a light step that went even lighter when she spotted Zivon's familiar figure striding away from the OB. She'd planned to catch him later, after her afternoon shift back in her basement darkroom, when he'd be leaving for the day too. She came armed today with an official invitation to dinner on Sunday, which meant she had a Daddy-sanctioned reason for seeking him out.

She'd hoped to see him yesterday, the first day it would have been possible since Daddy had reluctantly agreed to loosen his restrictions. But she'd missed Zivon at every turn.

The same would *not* happen today. She dashed down the street faster than Mama would have liked. She wasn't going to shout, but that meant she had to be quick if she wanted to catch up.

He was aimed for St. James's Park, it seemed, which probably meant she should stop and turn around. Daddy had still put his foot down on promenades in the parks. But this wasn't a promenade; it was simply an invitation-issuance. Completely different.

And she hadn't set eyes on him in weeks. Eagerness fueled her, sent her onward. They hadn't walked here as often as in Hyde Park, since the other was closer to Ivy's school, but often enough that it felt familiar. He didn't turn toward their usual path, though, which nearly threw her. She'd aimed that way without thought before she spotted him on another course. And he was walking at a quicker clip now too.

"Zivon! Wait!" She sucked in a breath and ran for him.

He turned. Hesitated, eyes going wide. Then he smiled, but it wasn't quite right. Wasn't the smile he usually gave her.

He wasn't happy to see her.

She stumbled on a rock, arms flailing out, but pointlessly.

237

There was nothing to grab on to, and when she stepped to the side to regain her balance, she found a puddle rather than solid ground.

"Lily!" At a speed she wouldn't have thought possible had it been anyone else, he was at her side, steadying her. And he didn't let go of her once she was back on her feet either. Which seemed a contradiction to the false smile he'd given her.

"Hello." Her own smile felt fluttery and uncertain. She searched his eyes, looking for some answer to his hesitation. Had he changed his mind about her? It certainly didn't seem so, from the letters he'd sent. But . . .

"What are you doing here?" He softened the harsh words by lifting her hand and pressing his lips to her knuckles. "Your father would not approve."

And yet she didn't think that was the cause of his reaction. "I've come with an invitation. But . . ."

Another flash of something in his eyes, partially hidden behind the glare on his eyeglasses. "Forgive me, milaya, if my joy at seeing you has been eclipsed by alarm at your finding me at this particular moment." His words were so quiet she could barely hear them. "I am out here on covert business."

She may have laughed it off, had he not looked entirely serious. And if it didn't seem entirely possible, given recent events.

Doubt flashed through her. What *sort* of covert business? Should she be concerned?

But he smiled. "Someone has been following me lately. Hall has men in place to apprehend him even now. My task is to lead him to them."

"Oh." She smiled back, though she suspected his had been more for show than because he felt happy. "I had better walk with you, then. It would look odd if I took off in the other direction, wouldn't it?"

"Lily—"

"Don't make me leave, Zivon. I have missed you so terribly."

He sighed. Kissed her hand again. And then tucked it into the crook of his arm. "Your father will not be pleased. And I doubt Hall will be either."

"If they didn't want me chasing you down today to issue the invitation for dinner they said I could give you, someone should have warned me against it. So, it's their own fault." She shouldn't feel so happy about the chance to indulge in a small rebellion, but there it was.

He chuckled. The fingers that he rested on hers were warm and caressing too, soothing the uncertainty his greeting had sparked. "You look beautiful today."

She laughed at the obvious exaggeration. She was in her VAD uniform, after all, and hadn't even taken the kerchief from her hair. "Fairer than the lilies of the field, I'm sure."

"Exactly my thinking." He let his arm brush hers. "I have missed you more than words can say, milaya."

"How fortunate, then, that we have the chance for something more than written words now. Although"—she bumped his arm back—"I admit that I do quite like your letters. I can read them over and over again when I miss you."

"I have had this same thought."

She drew in a long breath and looked about them. She didn't see anyone out of the ordinary, but she also didn't want to look obvious as she searched for them. Pitching her voice low, she asked, "Where are we going?"

"A bench. It is not much farther."

"Well, that's a shame. I was hoping it was on the opposite end of the park."

His fingers squeezed hers. "I wish the same. But you mentioned an invitation?"

"Dinner. Sunday. If the weather's fair, we'll be playing croquet beforehand, and you're welcome to join us for that too." She gave him her cheekiest grin. "Mama said so, and Daddy grows tired of disagreeing with her, I think."

"And you and your mother? You have smoothed things over?"

Her grin faded. "It isn't how it used to be. I've been missing her too."

"Sweet Lily." He nodded toward a path that forked off from theirs and the bench within sight alongside it. "Perhaps you should tell her so."

"Perhaps." Would it help? Ease some of the hurt Mama must be feeling?

"You will not regret it if—"

A loud *crack* cut him off. Before Lily could even process what it was, Zivon had pushed her to the ground, covering her body with his own. Shouts sounded, and footsteps, and another crack that she realized with horror must be gunfire. "Zivon?"

"Stay down." Somehow, he sounded both frantic and controlled. "I will not have you injured."

But he eased off her, his attention on the path behind them where the sounds of a struggle continued. She could tell from the breath he exhaled when Hall's men must have succeeded in getting their suspect under control.

"All right. He will not escape them now. Have I hurt you, milaya?"

She shook her head and got to her knees, accepting the hand he offered to rise the rest of the way. "A bit muddy, but that hardly matters." Her hands, however, were shaking. "Was it him who shot first?"

"I believe so. He must have spotted them closing in."

That did nothing to calm her. If this fellow had been following Zivon, if he had no reason to think today was out of the ordinary, did that mean he *always* carried a weapon? And was so willing to use it?

Perhaps Zivon read her thoughts. Or just had matching ones. He touched a hand to her cheek. "They have him now. All the other 'what ifs' are now moot, yes?"

240

"Yes. Of course." But she gripped his hand and was ready to argue if he tried to tug it free.

Her gaze was pulled toward the group of navy men, the prisoner still struggling—though in vain—to break free of them. The man had twisted enough that he faced them now, and he spat in their direction, though he was far too distant to even hope to reach them.

"Blighted capitalist!" he screamed. "They should have done you in when they had the chance!"

A socialist. A Bolshevik? She glanced up at Zivon's face.

It was blank. Still. But only for a moment. His nostrils flared, a million thoughts flashing through his eyes. His mouth twisted. He held her fingers so tightly it hurt, though she'd never say so.

The officers dragged the man away while he was still shouting about the evils of capitalism and imperialism. Zivon didn't relax any when he was out of sight. "How am I to do it, Lily? How am I to stop hating them?"

She leaned close to his side. "I don't know, my love. But perhaps you should start by asking that of the Lord."

19

sk that of the Lord. For a long moment, Zivon stood in the doorway of the church, waiting for his eyes to adjust to the dimmer light within. More, waiting for his spirit to adjust. The church looked nothing like the grand cathedrals where he'd attended Mass all his life in Russia, though it was set up in a familiar way, with no pews to hinder the supplicants from kneeling or pacing in their prayers.

Was that why it felt so much like home?

He stood there in the shadows, breathing in the scent of incense and prayers, and let his eyes slide shut. So many supplications he'd sent to God since he found Alyona on his steps, since he lost Evgeni in the train derailment. So many times he'd begged and pleaded and cried out for the Lord to step in. To fight his battles. To return to him a portion of what his enemies had taken away.

So many prayers he'd spoken. Tried so desperately to believe. But none of them had made him feel the peace that stepping into this unfamiliar church on Welbeck Street had. Not, he knew, because God would hear any more clearly the prayers uttered in church. What, then?

"*Zdravstvuyte.* How are you this day?"

The accented voice drew his eyes open again. And more, answered his question. It wasn't that God would hear *him* any better from here. It was that there were simply more voices to be found among the community of believers. *More* prayers lifted up in unity.

He'd denied himself this. And as he drew out a smile for the priest coming toward him down the stairs, he regretted every day he'd not come to Mass. He'd been trying to convince himself to come since the night of the bombing, but this was the first he'd summoned the courage. Perhaps he ought to thank Godfrey Higgins for reminding him that there might not be a tomorrow.

And Lily, of course. For seeing so clearly, as she always did, what the heart of the matter really was.

Zivon bowed a greeting to the priest. "Zdravstvuyte." The Russian hello felt at home on his tongue, despite the fact that he'd not spoken it for weeks. "I am well. And you?"

The man smiled, revealing white teeth nestled behind his beard. "Very well, thank you." He reached out a hand. "I do not believe we have met. Father Evgeny Smirnov."

The name made Zivon's chest go tight. *Evgeni.* Zhenya. A loss he still couldn't fully wrap his heart around. Zivon shook the father's hand, careful to keep the grief from his voice. "Zivon Marin."

"Ah!" Father Smirnov's eyes lit, and he kept ahold of Zivon's fingers. "The one Fyodor and Kira mentioned! I have been hoping you would visit us soon. It is not the hour for Mass, of course, but if you wish confession—or perhaps conversation?"

His priest had been waiting for him. Before they'd even been introduced. Somehow, knowing that made Zivon's shoulders sag. "Conversation first, I think."

The priest patted with his free hand the fingers he still held in his other, then released him entirely. "Of course. Follow me." He led him through the sanctuary with its green-painted dome and into a small chamber that looked to be part office, part reception room. "Please. Be comfortable."

Zivon smiled and chose a chair. "Mr. Suvorov mentioned me?"

"He did, yes. He was quite pleased that an old friend had made his way to London. A linguist, are you not?"

It seemed the safest thing to claim to be. And it was, after all, what he'd been before the war. He nodded. "I understand you have several among you here?"

Smirnov chuckled. "We have found it to be quite a benefit, yes. Not only because we serve a combination of Russian and Greek parishioners, but we have also then been able to create and distribute studies and booklets in English, and even in Spanish. A great need has been met around the world from our home here in London."

He'd learned as much when he first reached England and had looked up the church. But he nodded as if it were news. "I apologize that I have not come before now. It has been . . . a trying few months."

"Well can I imagine." The priest had taken a seat in a chair adjacent to Zivon's. He leaned onto the arm, eyes shining. "But you strike me as the sort of man who knows that it is in the most trying of times that we *most* need to come."

"I do. It is just . . ." He sighed and nudged his spectacles up so he could rub at the bridge of his nose. "Before I left Russia, it had got to the point that I could not tell who to trust, what friends may be ready to turn me in to the soviets. I could not be certain it would be different among the Russians here."

"Ah." Smirnov leaned back, stroking his beard. "And this is why you did not trust Fyodor's cousin. This is understandable, I think. You suffered at the hands of these political enemies?"

Zivon stilled. It still chafed against everything in him to share, but it was why he had come. He needed someone to tell him if he was as hopeless as he felt. "They killed the woman

I was to marry. Murdered her and left her on my doorstep to find."

Smirnov muttered something under his breath. It sounded sharp, Slavic, but Zivon couldn't quite make out the syllables. The priest shook his head. "This is terrible. No wonder you hesitate to trust."

"The Bolsheviks . . ." He heard the way he said it, the way Lily must have been hearing it. Felt the bite of his nails against his palm, though he didn't recall telling his hand to fist. He squeezed his eyes shut. "How do I forgive them, Father? They took everything from me. Everything. My career, my home, my bride, my brother. Everything I thought I was, they stole. I fear . . . I fear I hate them."

"All of them?"

His eyes sprang open again. "Pardon?"

Smirnov's eyes somehow managed to look both understanding and challenging. "Do you hate every Bolshevik, Mr. Marin? Man, woman, and child? That is quite a burden to take upon your shoulders."

"I . . . do not know." He forced his fingers to relax. "I do not know who is directly responsible. I suppose I have lumped them all together in my mind."

"Easy to do, on the one hand." The priest toyed with the end of his long beard. "To hate in broad strokes. To paint everyone as the same, da? Do you hate all Germans too? Bulgarians? Ottomans? They were also our enemies."

His breath eased out. "No." He'd met some who seemed to, but that had always struck him as ridiculous. Yes, they were fighting them. Yes, the Germans were responsible for the death of Batya and countless others. But war—war where nation was pitted against nation—had never felt like this to him. It was just men from each side serving their country. "That never felt personal. Even when my father fell in battle, I knew it was not that he was targeted specifically. Not like this."

"So then. Do you think every single Bolshevik has person-ally named you an enemy? Did every single one conspire to kill your bride?"

"Of course not."

"Perhaps, then, you do not hate them all. Perhaps you hate only the one or two to blame for this."

For a moment, his spirit lifted. Then his brows slammed down. "Is that really better?"

Father Smirnov chuckled. "Better? No. But easier to overcome, perhaps. When we consider the task of forgiving hundreds, thousands, tens of thousands of men, that is daunting indeed. But one or two? Think how much easier that will be."

Despite himself, a corner of Zivon's mouth turned up. "I think you are right. Even so . . . I know it is not mine to seek revenge. That belongs to the Lord. But is it wrong, Father, to work against them? Politically?"

Smirnov lifted his brows. "God does not tell us what political party to associate with or forbid us from working for them. And that means there will always be those we work against. What He *does* tell us, though, is that we must still find joy in Him, no matter who rules us. We must be obedient citizens."

"I know the passage." Zivon had to grip his knees to keep from springing up. "But Paul is supposing a government where it is not in fact illegal to do good. This is not always the case anymore in Russia, Father. For doing good, I was branded an enemy. For remaining an obedient citizen to my lawful government, my czar, my life was threatened and my fiancée's taken. I know the Lord will have His vengeance—"

"And if He doesn't?"

Zivon froze, still gripping his knees. Breath caught mid-heave in his chest, drawn in but not shoved out.

Smirnov sat forward again. "The Lord will punish, yes. He will judge—individuals. And every nation, every political party, will eventually fall. But what if, Mr. Marin, you do not live to see it? Can you accept that?"

The balled-up breath burned. In all his thoughts, it had never once occurred to him that the Lord's justice, His vengeance, might not happen in his lifetime, might not be visited on the very men who had done this to him, whoever they might be. He shuddered with his exhale. "Surely that will not be."

"I do not presume to know. But I *do* know that when we are told to leave vengeance to the Lord, it is not so that we can glory in it when it comes." Smirnov tapped a finger against the arm of his chair. "God's wrath is a mighty and terrible thing. We should not be wishing it on others—we should be trying to save them from it. To turn them back to Him. Because if you are wishing vengeance upon the Bolsheviks, my son, remember you are wishing it on each individual, whether they have committed these mortal sins or merely wanted the promise of bread in their children's bellies. And we have already established that it is not every Bolshevik you hate."

Zivon tried to swallow, but his throat wouldn't quite work. "So it is wrong, then, to want justice?"

"No. Only, I think, to want justice for ourselves above mercy for other souls. Because if God treated *us* that way, where would we be?" A warm smile settled onto the priest's face. "I can answer that one too, of course. Unforgiven—that is where we would be. For it is only when we forgive that we can receive His forgiveness."

Zivon's hands went limp against his knees, and he sagged against the back of the chair. Lily had been right. There was much he had to sort through in his own mind, his own soul.

He should have come to visit this man weeks ago.

❖ ❖ ❖

Monday, 17 June 1918

Could nothing go right? Nadya would have cursed, but she only knew the right words in Russian, and muttering those on a London train would garner attention she didn't want. "Are you certain?" she asked in French.

Evgeni lifted his brows and made himself comfortable on the uncomfortable seat. "I am certain that's what Higgins's neighbor said. I can't, of course, be certain it's the truth."

She had to settle for hissing out a breath. The travel had been grueling, and finding a cheap room to rent had been ridiculously difficult. Apparently housing was in a bit of a crisis, thanks to the refugees who had flooded England from Belgium and other occupied territories. But this turn of events—that Higgins, their sole contact here, had been arrested—was by far the worst. "Did he leave us a message or anything?"

Face grim, Evgeni shrugged. "When he was arrested, he also missed paying his rent, and the landlord disposed of most of his personal items, including any correspondence."

How, then, were they to discover where his brother lived? Higgins's knowledge of the location of Zivon's flat had been the silver lining to Paul's mistake in asking an acquaintance to follow him. But Evgeni had been right, clearly. Their contact was now in prison, and they were left with no help.

"We find him the way Higgins did, then. We start at the Admiralty building."

"Risky. He'd probably spot us before we spotted him." Evgeni traced a finger along the edge of her hand resting between them on the seat. He was always doing that. Little touches. Absent-minded ones. They'd bothered her at first. A claim, those touches. A tether.

Now they brought a bit of peace to her heart, unless she thought too hard about it. And then the fact that they'd stopped bothering her started to bother her anew.

She shook her head to clear it of such circles. "If not that, then what options do we have?"

He didn't answer right away. Instead, he knit his brow and tapped a finger to his chin, that caricature of thought he always fell back on. "Someone will know where he lives. We simply have to find the someone and convince them to help."

"A priest? Someone from the embassy? Would he have made contact with them?"

"I would think so." He nodded, a smile smoothing out the furrow in his brow. "I would think the church would be a safer place to go. They would be less suspicious of someone asking for information."

Church? Nadya screwed up her mouth. "I swore to myself I'd never step foot in one of those dungeons again. I'll try the embassy first."

He let out an amused chuckle. "As you wish. I had better not go with you there, though. If he contacted them, it could have been to see if I had. They may have seen a picture of me."

"I don't mind going alone." In fact, it gave her a fine story to tell them. She could claim she was trying to find Evgeni too, say she'd known him in Russia. Being largely the truth, it should strike them as such. And then it would be perfectly reasonable for her to ask about Zivon.

"If we're going to the embassy, we had better change trains at the next stop. Unless you want to wait for tomorrow?"

She sent him a look of rebuke. "We've lost enough time, don't you think?"

"I do. Though on the bright side . . ." He flashed that grin of his. "It has been time spent together, and that's not all bad."

No. It wasn't. And in many ways, the weeks spent helping him get back on his feet, searching the French countryside, and even waiting for Paul to get them documentation were probably akin to a holiday, compared to what they'd be faced with upon returning to Petrograd.

He probably expected a roll of her eyes or biting retort. It was her usual way. But instead she turned her hand up under his, palm to palm, and wove their fingers together. And even leaned into his side. "Not bad at all."

They disembarked, studied a map of the tube stations—of no use to her, but Evgeni could read it. Another twenty minutes and three trains, and they were finally back in the afternoon sunlight, making their way to the Russian embassy. Evgeni tucked himself onto a bench a street away, leaving Nadya to travel the final few minutes on her own.

She frowned when she saw the flag flying outside it. The white, blue, and red with the yellow canton had been removed from all the buildings in Russia. Yet here it still flew. Directly in opposition to the ruling party.

Well. Not for long. Soon enough, everyone the world over would recognize their authority.

Today, she would take comfort in the knowledge that she was working for the true Russia. She put a smile on her face as she entered and approached a man behind a desk just inside. She greeted him in Russian, borrowing a few of Claire DuBois's mannerisms as she did so.

Predictably, the man smiled back and asked quite eagerly how he could help her.

Nadya gave an extra bat of her lashes. "I am looking for a friend of mine. He was to come here, I think. I hope. Evgeni Marin? Has he perhaps come in sometime in the last several months?"

The man frowned. "*Evgeni* Marin? No, I don't believe so. But here is the ambassador now—he would know. Mr. Nabokov, do you have a moment?"

Nadya wasn't sure if it was good luck or bad when the diplomat detoured to them. But she gave him the same smile she'd given the secretary and added an introduction. Given that no one knew who she was, she didn't see the point in using a false name. When she stated her question again, Nabokov blinked in surprise.

"Evgeni Marin? No. It is my understanding, I am sorry to say, that he perished in France. But we know his brother."

"Zivon?" She hoped her tone sounded right—a bit relieved at *someone* familiar, yet taken off guard by the news of death.

In truth, she *was* taken off guard. Even when she knew it was wrong, hearing that he'd died made her chest go tight.

Zivon must have thought he'd been killed in the train accident. He must have told them as much.

Regardless, using his name so informally seemed to have the desired effect. Nabokov gave her a sympathetic look and even patted her arm. "I am sorry to be the bearer of bad news. You knew the Marins well? Neighbors, perhaps?"

She blinked furiously, as if fighting back tears. "More than that. I . . . I was to marry Evgeni. This is why I traveled here, to meet him. I don't even know if he'd told his brother, but— forgive me." She drew her handkerchief from her pocket and dabbed at her eyes.

The men exchanged a glance. "We can put you in touch with Zivon Marin if you'd like."

"Yes." She sniffed. "Thank you. Do you have his address? I have a bag of Evgeni's belongings he may want."

"Ah." Nabokov frowned. "We don't, actually. He has always just stopped in to ask for updates. But my cousin said he was at Mass. I'm certain we can get it for you. If you could stop by again later?"

Though she wanted to seethe at yet another setback, Nadya gritted her teeth and nodded, hiding her frustration behind her handkerchief. "Yes, of course. I cannot thank you enough."

Before they had time to notice that her eyes were in fact quite dry, Nadya scurried back out. They'd assume she was just distressed and craving privacy, which suited her fine. Once back on the sidewalk and well out of sight, she balled up the handkerchief, squeezed a bit of her frustration into the wad of cotton, and swore under her breath. Another delay.

No, nothing was going right at all.

20

Y ou know, dearest sister, one of these days it may be-
hoove you to actually remember your *own* umbrella."
Lily sent Ivy a narrow-eyed glare around the shaft of
the brolly they were both huddled under. Of course, she was
also fighting a grin, so it wasn't likely to terrify her sister
into responsibility.

Ivy laughed. "Why bother, when you can just supply my
need? Besides, it's cozy."

"Until you have to walk home in the rain without it later."

Her sister sent her a mischievous smirk. "Clarke is walking
me home this evening. So if it happens to still be raining and I
happen to not have my own umbrella and must share *his* . . ."

"Ah. So this was *planned* irresponsibility. I see." Lily gave
up and chuckled as they neared Ivy's school. "Are the girls
getting antsy yet, ready for their summer holiday? I remember
this last term taking forever to finish."

"They're little monsters." Though still Ivy smiled as she
said it. "This last month is always impossible. And Diana
Oglesby has been especially disruptive this week because her

brother is coming home to recover—trench fever, she tells me. And everyone else in the class. Repeatedly."

"Luckily, their teacher is in the best of moods, thanks to a certain someone."

Ivy grinned, though it only lasted a second. She sent Lily a woebegone look and said, "I miss having you and Mr. Marin out with us. It's been a month—do you think Daddy will relent soon? I mean, I know he's allowed him to come to dinner, but it just isn't the same as the four of us out for a promenade in the park."

Lily sighed. "I've been prodding him. But I'm afraid to push too hard, lest he rescind what he's granted."

She'd been plotting exactly how far she could make that "dinners are acceptable" dictate stretch, though. This Saturday marked the day Zivon should have been celebrating his wedding to Alyona, and Lily meant to support him through it. Distract him from it. And, yes, see if any emotion peeked out about it. Mama and Daddy would be dining elsewhere that evening, so she couldn't just beg for him to be invited to their table. There had to be *something* she could do, though.

Ivy sighed too and adjusted her hat. "I think it may be time for some well-placed rebellion."

"Ivy."

"What?" Her sister shot her a look that was somehow both all innocence and all mischief. "You're a grown woman. And Daddy's letting fear govern him. Wouldn't we be honoring him more if we checked him in that than if we let it govern *us* too?"

Before Lily could do more than open her mouth to reply, Ivy jumped out into the rain and ran through the school's gates, up the steps, and into the shelter of the door.

Lily could only shake her head and keep walking toward the hospital. She couldn't imagine actually bucking her father's orders, regularly and with planning. She still lived in his house. She would obey his rules.

But then again, she also couldn't imagine going on like this much longer.

A few minutes later, she shook the water off her brolly and pulled open the door to the hospital. She stepped inside, immediately enveloped by the quiet that reminded her of how loud the rain had been.

"Oh good, you're here."

Lily looked up and frowned at the white-faced specter moving toward her. Arabelle, obviously, as no other nurse here was so tall. But . . . "Why are you wearing a mask?"

Ara held out another one toward Lily. "You know how I said we had a train full of troops coming in last night, a few of whom had three-day fever? Well, it seems to be rather contagious. The three on the train has turned into seven. We're shorthanded as it is, so let's be cautious, shall we? I've quarantined them as best I can. We don't need the whole ward vomiting and delirious."

Lily's brows pulled down as she took the mask from her friend's outstretched fingers. "Is it as bad as all that?"

Ara shrugged. "It could well be that the other four had already contracted it before they were in close quarters on the train. Or that the train itself acted as an incubator—we've certainly seen that before. But regardless, no one else wants it. So wear the mask, and do take care to wash your hands regularly, especially after contact with any of the newcomers."

"Yes, nurse." She smiled and then covered it with the cloth.

Arabelle glanced at the watch pinned to her bodice. "I think you're the last of the morning VADs. But if you notice anyone else come in, direct them to me for a mask. Otherwise, the breakfast trays are ready."

Lily nodded and followed her friend up to the fourth-floor ward. She was soon delivering porridge and tea to the men, handing it off to those who could manage it on their own and settling on a chair to assist one in need of help. It was odd to smile at him from behind a mask, but aside from a few jests, none of them seemed to mind. No doubt because Arabelle was right that no one else wanted to catch three-day fever. They had problems enough.

When the breakfast shift was over, though, Lily was assigned to folding sheets, blankets, and towels fresh from the laundry, which meant her mind was free to wander straight back to where her thoughts had been when she came into the hospital. Where they wandered most of the time, if she was being honest.

At least today she had some actual problems to solve in regards to Zivon. She knew he'd be working a half day on Saturday, as usual. But what could she offer as distraction during the afternoon that Daddy wouldn't object to?

Maybe . . . maybe something with a group. He didn't seem to mind those sorts of activities so much. It was a bit short notice to gather many guests, but she could see who wasn't busy. If she got Mama on board, they might be able to get approval for a garden party—or a tea party, if the weather didn't cooperate. She would invite Ara and Cam, and Clarke, of course, some other colleagues from OB40. She'd even see if Brook was available. And perhaps some of the Russians Zivon had mentioned meeting at church—the Suvorovs, the Smirnovs. Surely Zivon would like that.

It wasn't a bad idea. Though the fact that Mama was the linchpin made her nervous. It was true that she'd championed Zivon . . . but Lily was fairly certain that was mostly to irritate Daddy.

She put the last folded sheet in the basket and glanced at her watch. An hour left in her shift here. She'd ask if she could borrow the telephone in Arabelle's office and ring up Mama. Maybe it would be easier to carry on an actual conversation with her over the telephone.

It couldn't possibly go worse than every other attempt she'd made. It seemed every time she found Mama alone and opened her mouth, prepared to bare her heart and say how much she missed their friendship, her mother would leave the room before she had a chance, or speak first about something so impersonal that Lily didn't know how to build the bridge to what she *really* wanted to say.

She hurried up the stairs, repositioning the mask that she'd taken off while in the steamy laundry facilities, and deposited the fresh sheets in the closet. Then she turned toward her friend's office.

Arabelle was coming out of it. "I was just going to come looking for you, Lily. Would you run a note to Cam for me when you go to the OB? I'm afraid I can't get away for lunch with him today."

"Of course." Though she frowned at the thought of her friend taking no time away from the ward. No doubt she'd be missing that chance for a respite by the end of her shift.

"Perfect. I've left it on my desk. Just run in and grab it before you leave."

"I will. And I was actually going to ask if I could borrow your telephone to ring my mother. It'll only take a moment."

"Of course. You know I—"

"Nurse Denler!" Another volunteer came careening from a ward. Her mask was a bit askew, her hair escaping her kerchief in frazzled strands. "One of the men with the fever—you'd better come. He's turning blue, and I don't know what to do!"

Murmuring a prayer through her mask, Arabelle took off every bit as quickly as the aide. Lily nearly followed, but she had no more idea what to do than the other VAD. The man needed Arabelle, a trained nurse, not her.

She could pray, though, and she did as she slipped into the office. For wisdom for Ara and whatever doctor she'd likely call. For healing for the soldier. For calm in the ward.

The small envelope sat on the corner of the overcrowded desk, *Camden* scrawled hastily on the front. Lily picked it up and slipped it into her pocket, then turned toward the candlestick phone that had its own stand in the corner of the office. After drawing in a fortifying breath that did little to make her feel stronger, she asked the operator to connect her to Mayfair-1003.

"Hello?"

Her mother's voice sounded . . . normal. Bright. Cheerful. Not the voice Lily had been hearing from her lately. Without warning, tears clogged her throat. How could she miss her so much, when they were still together every day?

"Hello?"

She cleared her throat. "Mama. It's Lily. I had a question for you."

A pulse of silence. "What is it?" And just like that, the sunshine had been eclipsed by clouds in her voice.

Lily's eyes slid shut. "I need your help. This Saturday marks the day Mr. Marin should have been marrying his fiancée in Russia. I have to think he'll be eaten up all day by guilt and sorrow."

"Oh. The poor man. I hadn't realized the date was so quickly upon us." Mama sounded sincere in her sympathy. "We ought to do something kind for him."

At least they could still agree on something. "That's just what I've been thinking, and I've been racking my brain trying to come up with something Daddy won't object to. Do you think he would approve an afternoon garden party? Or tea party?"

Her mother made a scoffing sound, and it sounded like hope to Lily. "Let him try and stop us. If you can create a guest list during your lunch break, I'll call at the OB and pick it up and have the invitations out before your father even gets home this evening. Be sure and put someone important on it so he won't want to risk offending them by canceling."

Perhaps her smile was a little sad, that they were resorting to clever manipulations rather than just enjoying the harmony they'd always had before. But it was a smile nonetheless. "I was thinking I'd invite Brook. Is a duchess important enough?"

Mama laughed. "That'll do. I'll go and discuss menu possibilities now with Cook. One o'clock at the front entrance of the OB, if you would."

Lily promised. "Thank you, Mama," she then said quietly into the receiver.

Was it her imagination, or was the silence a little lighter this time? "He's a good man. He deserves better than what he got—and what he's getting. Not to mention that any man who looks at you as he does is clearly sensible."

Warmth swelled up like a flood. "I'll see you at one."

She rang off and slipped out of the office, hurrying forward when she spotted Ara coming out of the ward. "How is the patient?"

Even with most of her face invisible behind the mask, the horror was plain to see in Arabelle's hazel eyes. "He's . . . dead."

"What?"

Ara shook her head. "I've never seen the like. He wasn't even one of the first to fall ill. He only began complaining of nausea this morning, but he—he suffocated. His chest was clear earlier, but it just *filled.* . . ."

Lily's stomach twisted. She reached to grip her friend's hand. "What can I do?"

"Nothing. There was nothing anyone could do." Closing her eyes, Arabelle drew in a sharp breath. "Let's call your shift over, shall we? Go ahead to the OB and deliver that note to Cam for me. I'll feel better when I know he and Margot and the others are praying."

"Are you certain?"

"Very. Go." After giving her fingers a squeeze, Ara pulled her hand free and gave Lily a little nudge.

It felt a bit like abandoning ship, but if that's what Arabelle most needed, she would get the note to Major Camden with all speed. It took her only a few minutes to leave her mask in the laundry, pull her brolly from the rack, and hurry to the Old Building. After depositing her bag in the darkroom, she climbed the stairs up to the codebreakers' lair.

It felt strange to aim not for Hall's office but for the corridor that housed the cryptographers themselves. And she had no idea which room Major Camden called home, so she had to peek into several before she spotted his telltale olive green uniform.

A vaguely familiar secretary smiled up at her. "Hello, Miss Blackwell. May I help you?"

"I have a note for Major Camden from his fiancée."

The major looked up with a frown, rising from his chair before the secretary could answer. "From Ara? Is everything all right?"

She held out the note as he approached to take it from her. "There's a nasty fever going around the ward. She said she wouldn't be able to make your lunch date."

His frown didn't lessen any. "So she intends not to eat?"

Lily shrugged. "Let us pray things relax a bit and she can steal a few minutes away. But it's a bit frantic there right now. A man just died. She and the matron have everyone wearing masks."

Camden's face went darker still. "It's that contagious?"

"I'm sure they're just being cautious."

He didn't look convinced.

"Lily?"

She spun, smiling despite the grim news when she saw Zivon emerging from the room across the hall, a piece of paper in his hands that he held out to Camden. The major took it without a word; he must have been waiting for it. "Good morning," she said to Zivon.

"You are here early."

She explained again, quickly, ending by saying, "But I had better get down to my desk. Mama will be coming by at one to get a list from me."

As she'd hoped it would do, that brought Zivon's brows up. "I will walk with you. And this is good news, yes? You and your mother are working together on something?"

"On a little garden party for this Saturday. You'll come, of course, won't you?"

He paused with his elbow extended for her. "Saturday?" His gaze searched hers. And a small, sad smile touched the corners of his mouth. "You remembered the date."

She tucked her hand into its place and gave his arm a squeeze. "Of course I did. And you shan't pass it alone."

"You are too good to me." They started down the corridor.

"Nonsense. Besides, it gives Mama and me something to work on together."

"And this is a good thing indeed." He covered her fingers with his opposite hand. "Of course I will come. To be honest, I will welcome the excuse to stay longer away from my flat." Amusement saturated his words.

"I think I'm missing some information."

He chuckled and pushed open the door at the end of the hallway. "I told you of the enthusiastic welcome I was given at the Orthodox church."

"You did, yes." He'd seemed genuinely humbled by it. And she'd felt a bit of satisfaction in realizing that her words to him in the park had been what spurred him to make that connection.

"I seem to have underestimated exactly how small and close a community the Russians in London are. All the mothers and grandmothers have descended upon me with borscht and blini—and endless talk of their eligible daughters and nieces and sisters." He shook his head, but his eyes still sparkled.

261

Lily may have exaggerated her frown, but she didn't force it. "Should I be jealous?"

"Would you be?" The sparkle only grew. "I have never had a woman jealous over me. This is an intriguing idea."

She gave in to a laugh, and they started down the stairs. "Well, I don't know how fond you are of borscht or blini. What if I lose your heart to these girls whose mothers can cook Russian foods?"

He grinned. "If I feel this is a danger, you have my word that I will deliver a few recipes to your cook. In the meantime, I would complain to my landlord about the matushkas always camped outside my door—if it weren't his fault they were there to begin with. The Hamiltons seem to think it great fun that my community has just discovered me. They provide them all with tea and biscuits and sit about with them exchanging stories. Mrs. Hamilton has unearthed every book in her shop that even mentions Russia, and Mr. Hamilton has been reminiscing with them all about his time in that part of the world during the Crimean War." He shook his head. "Poor Clarke had to run for cover yesterday evening when he walked home with me. The matushkas mistook him for another of us at first and all but had him engaged to Svetlana before he could open his mouth to prove himself an Englishman."

Lily nearly choked on another laugh. "Ivy would declare war on this Svetlana."

Zivon chuckled too. "I daresay Clarke would be fighting right by her side."

And what would all these matushkas think of *her*, she wondered? What would *his* mother have thought of her, if she were still alive? She had a feeling none of them would be terribly pleased that he was courting an English girl. And she knew so little of their culture. She didn't even know what blini was. Borscht had beets, didn't it? They had those in their vegetable garden. Perhaps she *should* talk to Cook about getting her hands on some recipes.

"Lily?"

"Hmm?" Clearly she'd missed something. They'd somehow arrived at her darkroom already, and he was looking down at her with a combination of amusement and concern.

He turned to face her. Cupped her cheek in a warm palm. And leaned down to brush his lips against hers. "Thank you."

All those questions melted away. "For what?"

"For finding me worthy of such loyalty. It was always Evgeni who made the girls frown like that over thought of others. I never imagined myself capable of inspiring someone to such feeling."

She could relate. It had always been Ivy to inspire the lads too. "You're more than worthy. You're the most remarkable man I've ever known."

He glanced at her door, and she could easily follow his thoughts this time. He was also a man with enemies. A man not quite trusted by their government. A man who wasn't certain what his future held.

He sighed. "A third photograph has arrived. Hall did not show it to me, but he mentioned it. I know they have kept you out of this too—I am not asking you to say anything about it. But if you would pray that the truth comes to light, I would be grateful."

"Of course I will."

But as she bade him farewell and let herself into her darkroom, she couldn't help the fear that seized her. Because she knew better than most that light didn't always heal, didn't always bring grace and forgiveness.

Light could destroy too, when applied in the wrong way. Turn on a light while the film was developing, and the whole batch could be ruined. The truth, when tossed into the world without explanation, viewed in the wrong way, could be just as harmful. It was as she'd reminded Hall when this all started.

The same facts could tell many stories. And the truth, when viewed from the wrong angle, didn't necessarily set one free.

21

Finally. *Finally* the crowd of nosy Russian women dispersed, following a middle-aged woman who had just arrived as if she were a piper leading them all from the city they'd been infesting. Nadya had been sitting on this same bench outside a yarn shop most of the week, knitting needles flashing while she kept an eye on Zivon Marin's building and the swarm of matchmakers whose individual demises she'd entertained herself by devising.

More time lost. Each and every day one of them had arrived before he left for the morning, and rather than leave again when he did, they instead settled in to chat. Blighted busybodies. Nadya had never much appreciated their sort in her own village, where they'd tried to arrange her marriage to no fewer than five idiot men over the years. And she certainly didn't appreciate them now, when they'd cost her five precious days.

But finally, they were gone. Even the landlord and his wife were out. She'd watched them leave ten minutes ago.

She gave a smile to the other women on the bench knitting or crocheting—socks for soldiers, she was guessing, given the

265

basket of them by their side. She'd promised Evgeni she would blend in somehow, so his brother didn't notice her, and this had seemed the safest way. She added the pair of socks she'd completed that morning to their basket and then slipped off toward the building.

She'd better act quickly before the nest of bees came back to buzz. Striding forward with a confidence that would tell passersby she belonged here, she slipped through the front door and up the stairs to the flat Nabokov had told her was Marin's. Too bad he hadn't been able to miraculously provide her with a key, but she'd spent a few coins on a set of lockpicks in anticipation of this moment, and it only took her a few anxious minutes to convince the door to give her entrance.

When she swung it open just wide enough to slide through, a silent huff slipped out at what met her eye. It was at least four times the size of the little cupboard she and Evgeni had found to rent. Sunlight poured in from generous windows, and the furniture couldn't be more than five years old. He had artwork on his walls—the kind that looked expensive—and books on his shelves, their spines a rainbow of unintelligible English words.

From all Evgeni had told her—and from the house in Moscow she'd snooped through with a far bigger sneer—she knew the elder Marin brother had bowed and flattered his way into wealth he had no right to possess in Russia. But what sort of bargain must he have struck with the English to be given such a prime flat here, now? When she knew very well that finding anything in this part of the city was all but impossible?

Well, he would get his just deserts. And she would get to work to make that possible. She slid the deadbolt to make sure no one could surprise her and started her search in his bedroom, which seemed the likeliest place for him to hide Evgeni's passport.

She looked in every drawer, every pocket of every jacket. She checked under the mattress, examined the seams to see if there was an opening he could have slid it into. Beneath rugs. In the few boxes she found. She jiggled each baseboard to see if any would pull away from the wall. She pulled off and squinted at every cushion and pillow in the flat.

Standing in the center of the living room an hour later, a few choice words were swirling about her mind. It had to be here somewhere. It *had* to be. She stared for a moment at the oil painting, a snarl curling her lip. She'd promised she'd put everything back the way she found it, but a sudden temptation to take a knife to the canvas nearly overcame her.

Nadya swallowed it down and strode over to the other piece, the photograph. The Eiffel Tower, mocking her. Reminding her of the time already wasted in Paris. Of the German officers somewhere in the French countryside whose names she *must* discover soon.

Why, why could nothing just go right? She needed this. She needed to succeed in the mission they'd given her. She needed to be able to go home with her head high, having proven to the party that she was a comrade worthy of their esteem. She needed to know that the life she and Evgeni would build together wouldn't be stripped away on a tyrant's whim if the Whites regained power.

She needed to prove to herself, her family, her whole village that she'd been right to walk away, to scorn all they'd demanded she accept. That she didn't need them, she didn't need a husband, she didn't need a heartless king or an archaic God to be what she wanted to be.

The next surge of temptation had her arm sweeping back, her gloved hand fisting. She landed it square in the middle of the glass covering the photo, relishing the crackle of every fracture. *That* was what she thought of the reminder of Paris.

Pivoting, she was ready to give up subtlety elsewhere too

and start ripping the place to shreds. But a squeak beneath her foot stayed her.

Just the floorboard. They squeaked, this was nothing abnormal. But it was the one place she hadn't checked yet.

She dropped to her knees, examining each seam. The noisy one seemed firmly in place, but she didn't let that hinder her.

She had her reward five minutes later, when she found a short piece of wood near the wall that wasn't sealed into place as the others were. Smiling, she slid the lockpick into the crack and levered it up.

And there, in the space between the board and the under-floor, was the boon she needed. A Russian passport.

"Yes!" She kept her exclamation quiet but couldn't deny its utterance, especially when she grabbed it up and saw inside it the name Evgeni had been traveling under. A quiet laugh joined the affirmation. Evgeni's photograph was gone, but that was no surprise. Zivon had probably needed it to show to the ambassador.

No matter. The rest was here. Nadya pocketed it, put the board back in place, and cast one more satisfied look at the shattered glass over the Eiffel Tower. Yes, Zivon Marin would know someone had been here.

Let him. It didn't matter. She had what she needed.

She escaped the building without anyone noticing her, hurried to the nearest underground, and forty minutes later made it back to their stifling little room. As she neared, she shot a grin up at their window.

Evgeni was lounging in it, and he smiled down at her too. He had been watching for her. Not that he'd admit as much if she asked. "You're back early, *mon amour*," he called down in French.

She rolled her eyes at the endearment. He'd been taking far too much pleasure in using them since Paul had given them their documentation identifying them as married.

And she didn't mind nearly as much as she pretended she did.

Rather than call up to him, she simply rushed up the stairs, sidestepping a cluster of babbling children, one of whom stuck her tongue out at her. In some indefinable way, the girl reminded her of her littlest sister.

A surge of affection welled but was chased quickly away by the resentment that had possessed her when she watched Anya fade away. Starving, fevered. All the food of her own Nadya had given her, all the hours she'd spent nursing her instead of pursuing her own dreams—worthless. If there was a God, He was capricious and cruel to snatch away the brightest of them and leave the rest to mourn without ceasing.

She snapped her teeth at the English brat and stormed on by.

Evgeni opened the door for her as she neared. "Is early a good thing?"

A grin stole her lips again. As soon as he closed the door behind her, she pulled out the passport. "Early is a *very* good thing."

Eyes flaming bright, he laughed, picked her up, swung her around, and set her on her feet again with an enthusiastic kiss. "I knew you could find it. What was it like? His flat?"

She tossed the passport onto the tiny table. "Too large for one man. He has fine artwork on his walls, books on his shelves, and his kitchen was overflowing with more food than he could possibly eat—probably the work of that gaggle of fools trying to match him with one of their daughters."

Evgeni had turned to the table, but he paused, turned back to her. "Do not begrudge him that, if he wants it. Especially today. It would have been his wedding day."

Was that why Evgeni had looked so muted this morning? Why hadn't he said something?

All right, she knew why. She was the one who had taken

that from his brother. Why would she be the one he spoke to about it? Even so, the realization that he'd been mourning that today and kept it to himself made her go prickly.

She sneered. "I'm sure he could replace her easily enough. If the mothers are any indication, the daughters would be happy to accept the handcuffs and bow to his patriarchal authority. None of them would dream of stepping outside expectations—just like Alyona."

His jaw ticked. She'd seen it before, but never directed at her. "You know, for someone who speaks so much about equality, you are quick to take the chance for it from those you don't agree with. Alyona was a sweet girl who did the best she could with the life she was given. Who knows what she may have done later if her life hadn't been sacrificed?"

Nadya leaned toward him. Tapped a finger to his chest. "You sound as though you . . . *liked* her. Alyona."

He didn't so much as flinch. "She was like a sister to me. Would have been a sister to me, as of today. And it isn't right what was done to her. She shouldn't have paid the price for my brother's opinions."

Had he been blaming her for that all this time? "Oh, don't start with all the morality nonsense. I thought you were above such sentiments. What's *right* is what works—"

"And it *didn't*." He spun away. "Her death was senseless and ineffectual. All it accomplished was driving my brother *here*. She should have been one of the people you fight for, Nadya. One of the women who deserves a chance at more from life. But she was denied that."

"Sacrifices have to be made sometimes." Nadya straightened her spine, planted her hands on her hips.

"I know. But how do we keep from becoming just like the tyrants, then? Isn't that the same thing they always said, when we were dying on the front lines?" He stopped at the window, staring down at the street below, as if looking out where strangers walked would make clear all the mysteries of humanity.

Didn't he remember that they'd *already* made sense of it? "The difference is that we're not serving just ourselves—we're serving *everyone*."

"Everyone but those we don't like or agree with, you mean." He leaned his shoulder against the peeling wallpaper by the window frame.

She eased up behind him, the question scorching her tongue. Fear of the answer scorching her heart. "Are you doubting the party, Evgeni? Doubting all we stand for, all we've been working for?"

"No." He turned enough to look at her. And somehow, his eyes were clear. Easy. "But Batya used to say that the difference between a wise man and a fool was not that the wise man was right and the fool wrong—but that the fool always assumed himself right, and the wise man would wonder if he *could* be wrong. We cannot learn from our mistakes and grow wiser if we never admit to the times we've chosen the wrong path."

Chosen it. She frowned, the grocer's daughter's outrage over the tin kingdom sneaking back into her mind. He'd argued against Claire's objections, but here he was, condemning those in command for taking Alyona's choices from her. But it was different, wasn't it, when you tried to protect, rather than destroy?

"Sometimes you confuse me." She tilted her head, studying him. "I think I know you, know your views, and then you defend someone whose beliefs are vastly opposed to yours."

He studied her right back. "We are more than just our views, Nadya. At least, I certainly hope so. Otherwise, if we are ever convinced of a new thing, it means our entire person changes." And maybe that was why he still loved his brother so fiercely, even knowing they'd never see eye to eye. "Disagreeing with someone shouldn't mean I think they have no right to live, to work, to be given a chance for happiness."

She lifted her chin. "Even when they would take that chance from you?"

His grin battered down a few of her blocks of anger. "Especially then. We cannot prove ourselves better than our enemies by denying them what they denied us, but only by *giving* them what they denied us."

For a long moment, she simply stared at him. These certainly weren't ideas he'd picked up in Russia. They weren't ideas she'd ever really heard offered as a reasonable way to live. They were ideas she should have scoffed at as being utterly impossible.

And yet, as she saw the light smoldering in his eyes, they didn't seem so impossible at all. "I think . . ." She leaned against the wall on the other side of the window, her gaze never leaving his. "I think I like your version of equality. It's dangerous. But then, the best things usually are."

He reached out and trailed his fingers down her arm. "Very true. And in the spirit of that, here's another truth you may find dangerous. I love you."

She jerked. She couldn't help it. But she didn't bolt for the door as she probably would have done a few months ago. "Are you trying to shackle me?"

He breathed a laugh, shook his head. "Who said love had to be shackles? I'm not trying to hold you anywhere, force you to do anything. This is a gift to you, Nadya. I give it freely. I demand nothing in return. You can love me or you can not. You can stay with me or you can go. Either way, I will love you. I will love the very spirit that may insist you run far and fast." He caressed her fingers but didn't grip them. Instead, he held his hand beside hers, palm up. "But I hope, of course. I hope you'll stay. I hope you'll accept my love—not as a prison trying to make you be something you don't want to be. But as . . . wings. To help you reach whatever heights you strive for."

She could tell by the look on his face that he wasn't sure she believed him. Or trusted him enough to take that kind of gamble. Because whatever words he might say, the fact was still that love—committing to love, anyway—*did* put demands on a person. It demanded one think of the other, not just oneself. It demanded one think of the other *above* oneself. It demanded one work through the problems instead of choosing the easy way out and leaving when life got difficult.

And life would always get difficult. Every Russian knew that.

Did she dare take that kind of gamble on anyone?

She didn't know. So, instead of answering with words, she eased closer, stretched up, kissed him. It would have to be enough for now that she wanted to be with him. That she wanted to live at his side when they got home. That was all she could offer.

Perhaps he read her mind. When finally she pulled away, his gaze went to the table, his hand reaching out a moment later. "Where was the passport?"

"Under a floorboard. Clearly he wanted no one to find it."

Evgeni's brows pinched together as he opened it. "The photograph is missing."

She waved a hand. "That hardly matters, does it? You don't need to use this as identification anymore."

"No, not the one of me. The photo of the officers that the Prussian gave me. Zivon must have taken it out." His eyes darkened. "Would he have given it to them, do you think? The British?"

"Does it matter?" Though she admitted it gave her a prick, and any joy she'd felt over the find started leaking out. "How will they know what it is? Or find the men with just one photograph to go on? As long as they don't have the names, we are fine."

"Right. The names are written on . . ." He flipped more pages. And then hissed out a curse and slapped the passport back to the table.

Her stomach dropped all the way to her feet. "What? What is it?"

"I had a small snapshot also in there. I didn't want the Prussian writing on the photo of the officers. Seemed a bad idea to have all the information in one place." He shook his head. "The photo was the only paper I had to offer, so I let him write on it. It's gone." He paced a few steps, pivoted. "It has to be somewhere. Somewhere else in the flat."

"No." She shook her head, heart thudding. "I didn't see any photographs. I checked everything."

"Everything? Every page of every book? Every binding? Every—"

"*Everything!*" Though, of course, now she doubted herself. She'd flipped through each book, but could a photograph have been stuck between pages and escaped her notice? Could it have been under the insole of a shoe? Behind peeling wall-paper?

Not that *his* wallpaper had been peeling. She pressed her hands to her temples. "What was it a photograph of?"

He cursed again and then sighed. "The two of us as boys. From our trip to Paris."

Could it have been with that other picture from Paris? Or hidden behind the oil painting? Or—worst-case scenario— would he carry it with him? She let her hands fall. Whichever the answer, clearly her work wasn't done.

Not even close.

22

Zivon claimed to be no expert on English garden parties, but from his perspective, this one had been quite a success. He'd been amused to discover that the duchess he'd tried to avoid at the wedding had come, and that she knew Kira Suvorova from her time in Monaco. She had, in fact, been the friend the Suvorovs had come to visit when they were stranded here by the outbreak of war. He'd been touched at the arrival of Father Smirnov and his wife, who reported that she'd cleared all the matushkas and *babushkas* from his building for him that morning. And he'd been encouraged by the number of his colleagues who had made an appearance too.

Most of them had already left at this point in the afternoon, and as lovely as the day had been, he found himself ready for some quiet. On the other hand, he was also loath to leave Lily's side. So if Major Camden and Miss Denler decided to linger for another hour, he wouldn't complain.

The poor young woman had deep circles under her eyes, and she looked like a stout wind could knock her down. They'd arrived late, and Camden had just been confessing to Zivon in an undertone that he was more than a little concerned for her.

Lily moved to her friend's side and touched a hand to her

elbow. "You look exhausted. Have you slept at all in the last two days?"

"Maybe. An hour or two." Miss Denler tried to give her a smile, but it didn't last long.

"How are the men in quarantine?"

The nurse shook her head. "Three more have come down with it—and not from the same train the original chaps had been on either. Worse still, Nurse Jameson has spoken to the hospital matrons of other facilities, and this doesn't seem to be limited to Charing Cross. Others are reporting similar cases of fever and flu symptoms." She leaned closer. "Other hospitals have had men die who weren't even showing those symptoms a day beforehand. I'm worried, Lily."

"Of course you are. We all are." Lily slid a glance to Zivon.

He nodded, as did Camden. How could they not be concerned? There were always isolated examples of people dying of influenza, of course. But more often than not, that happened to the elderly or to small children. Not to men in the prime of life.

The major slipped an arm about his fiancée's waist. "And you'll be no good to any of them if you don't get some sleep, darling. Come on. I'm taking you home."

"But—"

"Don't make me call Sarah or my mother. I'll do it."

Miss Denler breathed a laugh and reached out a hand to Lily. "Thank you for inviting us, Lily. Sorry we were late."

"I'm just glad you could make it. Now go home and rest."

Zivon bade them farewell too and watched them walk away, wishing he had the right to guide Lily through the door with a hand on her back as Camden did his Arabelle. But it took only a glance at the window to Captain Blackwell's study, through which Zivon could make out her father's scowling face, to know that would be a bad idea.

The man stood. No doubt he realized that was the last of

the guests other than him and Clarke and was about to come out and thank them for coming, thereby saying without saying outright that it was time they took their leave.

Lily, hand on his arm, nudged him toward Clarke and Ivy. Zivon went along. "Thank you again for doing this for me, Lily. You have made bright a day I thought would be nothing but darkness."

The way she looked up at him, darkness couldn't long stand against the flame it lit in his spirit anyway. He'd cared for Alyona. She'd long been like family. He would have cherished her, come to love her as a man should his wife had they wed. He knew that.

But it wasn't like this.

Ivy's laughter, robust and free, drew both their gazes to where she and Clarke stood by the vegetable garden, seemingly oblivious to the fact that everyone else had gone. "I can't believe you did that! To a commander!"

Clarke grinned too. "Well, it wasn't as though he was a commander *then*. Field promotion, you know."

Lily gasped, pulling Zivon to a halt. He frowned down at her. "Are you all right?"

She spun, eyes bright. "That's it! That's where I've seen that photograph. They weren't officers in it. That's what was throwing me."

He had no idea what she was talking about, and while she might tell him simply from her current excitement, he didn't want to put her in a bad place if it was something he oughtn't to know. "Then . . . good?"

She laughed, popped up onto her toes, and planted a kiss on his cheek.

"Lilian!"

Even her father's furious bark didn't dim her expression. She just flew over to him, all but bouncing. "I've solved it, Daddy! At least, I think I have. I need to get to the OB, to my archives. Will DID still be there, do you think? Oh, it doesn't matter. Even if he isn't, I need to see if I'm right. I can send him a note if I must."

Her father's expression had shifted during her rambling speech from irritation to indulgence. "I haven't a clue what you're talking about, Lily White. But if you need to go to the office, I'll run you over in the car so you can be back before your mother and I need to leave."

"That would be lovely." She spun back to Zivon, eyes wide. "Oh, that was rude of me. What a hostess I'm being."

He chuckled and waved an arm to catch Clarke's eye. "You are the kindest of hostesses, Miss Blackwell. I thank you again, and your mother, for going to such lengths to brighten my day. But it is time we were on our way."

Always a good idea to dismiss oneself before one could be dismissed, to his way of thinking.

As soon as they entered the house again, Mrs. Blackwell was there to see them off and thank them for coming. She took Zivon's hand as he stepped back outside through the front door. "You are in my prayers, Mr. Marin."

He hadn't words enough to express how much that meant to him. Especially today. So he inclined his head in gratitude and hoped she could read in his eyes how deeply her regard touched him.

If, by some miracle, this all turned out well . . . if ever he earned the captain's respect again so he could call on Lily properly . . . if ever he dared ask her to be his wife . . . then it would be a blessing to know she came with a mother of such faith.

He was quiet on the walk to the tube station and during the ride he shared with Clarke. He'd long since confessed what the date signified, so his friend didn't push him for conversation, not until they were off the train again and standing at the corner where they would part ways.

"If you need company tonight, old boy—someone to help you eat some of those blinis—but say the word."

Zivon smiled. "Thank you. Perhaps later this evening? A few hours of solitude first would not be ill-placed, I think."

Clarke nodded. "I'll call around eight. How's that?"

"Perfect."

He breathed a sigh of relief when he entered his building and wasn't immediately swarmed by well-meaning women eager to talk about their daughters. The Smirnovs had done him a service indeed. Surrounded only by quiet, he would perhaps take a bath. Read. Pray. He'd been asking the Lord to help him forgive those who caused him such harm, but it was not a quick process, it seemed.

He turned his key in his lock, let himself in, and froze.

Something was wrong. Out of place.

Many somethings. A strange fragrance lingered in the air—soap, but not his. The tassels on the rug were flipped up, though he was always careful to put them down. The pillow on the chair wasn't in the right place.

He moved to the doorway of his bedroom, checked the drawer where he stored his petty cash—still there—then walked back out to the living room.

Sunlight from the window lit seams of fire on the photo from Lily. Seams where there shouldn't have been, in a distinct web pattern. Breath hissing out, he moved closer, until he could see the broken glass, still held in the frame but fractured to the point where the image was distorted behind it.

His gaze dropped to the floor. There was only one other thing he had in his possession that mattered. He couldn't imagine why anyone else would want it, but even so, he dropped to his knees and pried up the board.

Gone. It was gone. But why? Who could possibly want the picture-less remains of Evgeni's passport? He sank back on his haunches, board still in his hands. At least he'd taken out the photo of the two of them. It was safe with Lily. That was something. To know that the last existing image of the two of them together hadn't been taken.

But his hopes for a quiet evening evaporated. It seemed he, too, would have to pay a visit to Admiral Hall.

◈ ◈ ◈

TUESDAY, 2 JULY 1918

The empty chair at the breakfast table screamed at Lily the moment she stepped inside. Mama was always the first one up, eager to catch the morning light for her work. She was always in here, enjoying a cup of tea and some toast, when Lily came down. Always. She could count on one hand the times she hadn't been over the years.

Her gaze flew to her father even as her stomach churned. "Daddy? Where's Mama?"

Daddy looked up from his newspaper, face only a few shades grimmer than usual. "She's feeling a bit under the weather today. I'm certain it's nothing to worry over, Lily White."

No. She told herself to be calm, that not every upset stomach was a symptom of this nasty flu that seemed to be getting more serious instead of ebbing away. But she couldn't bring herself to turn to the sideboard. "I'll go and check on her, shall I?"

"Check on who, me? I'm only a minute later than usual." Ivy, apparently having just come in the room, elbowed Lily playfully aside and grabbed a plate.

She let herself be elbowed. "Mama. Daddy says she isn't feeling well."

Ivy's hands stilled mid-reach for the eggs. Her gaze, a bit wide, turned to tangle with Lily's. She didn't have to speak her fears or reiterate that a shocking number of girls at the school were out sick—and that one of them from another class had died. They'd already whispered their worries and their prayers last night.

Lily fastened on a smile. "Eat. I'll go and see her now." She fled the room without waiting for a response from her sister, running up the stairs and into her parents' bedchamber with only a cursory knock on the door.

Nothing could happen to Mama. It couldn't, not with things still awkward between them. Not with the step forward that the garden party had provided being largely undone by the hours Lily had then spent at the OB in the last week, searching every single archived photograph for those two German faces.

She'd found them. From the early days of the war, some of the first film she'd processed for Hall. They'd not been officers worth noting at the time, just soldiers who must have shown enough promise to get a promotion to something that led to a bigger promotion, and then another. She didn't much care how they climbed the ranks, only that she hadn't been imagining their familiarity.

It had taken far longer than the hour she'd expected, though. And since her regular work didn't exactly halt, and they'd been shorthanded at the hospital too, it had meant hours away from home, where she'd usually have been trying to continue the patching of her relationship with Mama.

Hours when she *should* have been here. That was so clear now. Why had she pushed her family into second place—no, third? Why hadn't she focused on Mama and let everything else slip instead?

The lights were out in her parents' room, but at least the curtains were open, allowing morning sunshine for the lazy pug to nap in. Drawing the curtains was always Mama's first move upon rising. Any comfort that gave Lily was eclipsed, however, by the sound of retching coming from the en suite bathroom. "Mama?" The connecting door was open, so she rushed through it.

Mama sat on the floor, one arm bracing herself against the toilet, the other waving Lily away. "I'll be well, Lily. Must have been that old jar of fruit last night. I knew it didn't smell quite right." Her voice was hoarse, though Lily had no way of knowing whether it had been so before or was a result of the vomiting.

But she'd called her Lily—not Lilian.

Ignoring the waving hand, Lily knelt by her mother's side and pressed a hand to her forehead. Warm, but not sizzling hot as some of the men in hospital were. "How is your breathing?"

Mama huffed out a breath that was reassuringly exasperated. "How does it sound? I'm telling you, it's nothing to be worried about. I'm just going to take it easy this morning, and I'll be right as rain by afternoon. You go about your day."

"I'm not going anywhere." Not as quickly as this flu sometimes moved. There were far too many cases of people who weren't even sick when they left for work in the morning being dead by teatime. It had all the nurses and aides at Charing Cross thoroughly shaken, never knowing with which patients the real danger lay. She fastened on a smile for Mama. "Are you ready to go back to bed, or not yet?"

"I do not need—"

"Humor me."

Mama huffed again. And then closed her eyes, as if the better to sound out the state of her own stomach. A moment later, she nodded. "Let me rinse my mouth, then I believe I'll be all right to go and lie down."

"I'll fetch you a basin once you're comfortable again so you needn't get up next time if you don't want to."

"I'm not an invalid."

No. But if this was the flu that had London in its teeth, she could be in another hour. *Please, God, no. Not Mama. Protect her, touch her, heal her. I beg you.* She didn't let herself think of the number of other prayers just like hers that must have been offered up in the last few weeks on behalf of other loved ones.

And of the number of times the Lord must have answered, *I'm sorry, my child. But no.*

She shadowed Mama on the slow walk to her bed, wanting to be reassured by the fact that she didn't need help. She made herself smile as she slipped out with the promise to return momentarily. And then she tried to hide the shaking of her hands as she poked her head into the breakfast room.

Ivy hadn't eaten more than a bite, and she stood the moment Lily appeared. "Well?"

"She says it's just that canned fruit from last night that smelled a bit questionable." She had a feeling her smile was unconvincing, though. "I'm going to stay with her. Daddy, will you drop a note by Charing Cross for me on your way in? And let Admiral Hall know?"

"Of course, my dear."

She hurried out to find paper and a pen, scribbled a note for Ara, and left it on the entryway table for Daddy to grab on his way out. A basin then in hand, she returned to Mama, who had drifted into sleep in the five minutes Lily was away. Good. Rest was always a necessary ingredient of healing. Rest and prayer.

Making herself comfortable in Mama's chair by the window, Lily picked up the Bible sitting on the side table and flipped to the page her mother had marked. Her eyes refused to focus on the words, but even feeling the weight of the book against her palms brought a measure of comfort. A small one, but a measure nonetheless. A reminder that He had been Lord long before she entered this world, and He would be Lord long after. That history would always march on, humanity living and dying, loving and losing, praising and cursing, but that He was unchanging.

Daddy slipped in a minute later, kissed Mama's forehead

and then Lily's, and promised to let everyone know she wouldn't be in today. He'd no sooner left than Ivy came in, a cup of tea and plate of toast in hand. "You still need to eat," she whispered, sliding both offerings onto the table where the Bible had been.

Lily forced a smile. "Thanks."

Her sister's gaze rested on the bed. "I should stay too. I'll send word to the school—"

"You said last night you were already down two teachers. They need you there." She reached for Ivy's hand and squeezed. "Go. I'll send word if she gets worse, I promise. I know what to watch for."

"More than I would. Even so." Ivy let out a blustery breath, but then she pulled away. "All right, I'm going. And I'll be praying all day."

"I know." Lily held her smile until Ivy left, and then she glanced again at the book in her hands. This time, familiar words came into focus for her. Psalm 56:3. A verse she had memorized ages ago. *What time I am afraid, I will trust in thee.*

Simply knowing the words couldn't stop her from fearing just now. But then, the words themselves didn't say *if I am afraid*. The psalmist feared too. It was a given. A *when*. The problem, then, wasn't in experiencing the feeling. Only in what she chose to do with it.

She could probably pass the whole morning by enumerating every time she'd been afraid and had chosen something other than trust. But that didn't seem like it would help her overmuch. Instead, she read through the next several psalms, counting each time the writer feared or cried out or complained, and how many times he turned it all over to the Lord. Though his life was in danger, though his enemies surrounded him, he chose to trust.

That required bravery as well as faith.

Mama woke from her nap after an hour, and Lily helped her sip a bit of tea . . . which sent her running back to the toilet. At least she was still strong enough to want to get up rather than use the basin, though. Upon settling again, she declared herself not tired enough for another nap, so Lily fetched a novel from the library and read aloud to her.

Her fever increased by a degree or two throughout the morning, but the thermometer didn't read a high enough number that Lily felt the necessity to alert anyone, and her mother's lungs remained clear. No blue tinge to her lips. That didn't, of course, mean that it wasn't the flu or that it might not prove itself serious later. But she didn't feel too bad for slipping out for a few minutes in the early afternoon to find a bite to eat while Mama dozed again.

Sandwich in hand, she decided to stretch her legs for another minute and wandered toward the entryway to see if the post had come.

It had. She leafed through it, chewing on her sandwich.

"Everything all right, Miss Lily? How is your mother?"

Lily turned to smile at Eaton, who stood with worry lines etched into his face. "She is resting. And her breathing is clear, which I take as a very good sign."

"Praise God for that. I shall just—"

The doorbell sang through the entryway, cutting him off and making Lily jump. And fight back a surge of irritation. Shouldn't everyone know that there was someone inside trying to sleep?

Eaton moved the three steps to the door and pulled it open. "Miss Ivy?"

Ivy? Probably stealing a few minutes to check on Mama, but why would she ring the bell? Though Lily had been reaching for her plate, she instead turned to the door.

Just in time to see her sister's pale face a moment before Ivy crumpled to the ground.

23

*Y*ou were right."

Zivon let those lovely words sink into his mind as he sat before Hall's desk, a balm on the wound he'd been trying to ignore. He didn't ask what he'd been right about, he didn't pump a fist in triumph at the mere statement, he didn't even heave a sigh of relief. He just sat there, still and calm, and waited for the admiral to go on.

DID tapped a finger to something on his desk, though Zivon couldn't see what it was from this angle, other than a photo of some sort. "These two are definitely grumbling about mutiny among the German soldiers. You may be on to something here, Marin."

Sweet vindication sang through his veins, but he did nothing more than nod. "Which two, sir?" He'd said it as if Zivon should know.

He apparently should, Zivon saw, when Hall lifted the photo he'd tapped.

The photo that had been stuffed in Evgeni's passport.

His mind whirled. Screamed.

The admiral didn't seem to notice. "Lily helped us put it together. She had another shot of them in her archives, but from the first few months of the war, when they were but *oberjägers*, both of them. It seems they've advanced in the ranks through a series of battlefield promotions, but both are from humble origins. Not gentlemen, like most of the officers."

"Their sympathies, then, are still with the common soldier." Half of Zivon's mind followed the information well enough. But the other half . . . Why would Evgeni have had a snapshot of those two? The very two who were of interest to Zivon? The two who were alluded to in the last message he'd decoded in Moscow, the one he had been wanting so desperately to recover? Had Zhenya, in fact, been an intelligence agent?

"We had their names on file, from that first photograph Lily dug up." Hall set the photo down again and leaned back in his chair. For a long moment, he regarded Zivon without speaking. Then, quietly, he said, "You were right about this. And so, I've been giving some thought to what you insisted at the start. About the proper reaction from us. You weren't born a gentleman either, were you?"

Zivon started a bit at the question, so out of the blue.

But not. Not out of the blue at all, from Hall's perspective. All this potential trouble for the Germans was coming about because two common men had risen through the ranks. Two common men saw the plight of their true comrades and wanted it to end. Two common men were ready to start a rebellion among the soldiers to force their superiors to listen.

Not so different, really, from all that had happened in Russia over the last year. Something Zivon should understand, given his similar story. "No. I was not. My mother's family had connections to the intelligentsia, but we had none at all to the nobility."

Which would make Hall question where Zivon's loyalties had really lain, even in Russia. He, like these Germans, was more common than elite, by rights.

Hall blinked at him. "Popov was going to retire at the new year. You would have taken over command of the division."

A fact he'd made it a point never to mention here, where he'd been forced to take a position at the bottom. Zivon drew in a long breath but didn't answer.

Apparently Hall didn't need one. "I knew Popov well. We set your division up together, mirroring ours here, you know. We still kept in touch—he mentioned you often. Your brilliance. Your talent with the work. He said he could imagine handing the reins over to no one else."

Zivon's throat went tight. "I admired him greatly." He had no idea, now, where his mentor even was. He'd vanished a few weeks before Zivon had fled too. Was he dead? Or safe somewhere in Allied territory? He prayed that it was the latter.

"Had you actually received that promotion, it wouldn't have come just with a military title."

Ah, so this was his point. Zivon nodded. "I realize it would have given me access to social circles to which I did not by rights belong." He ran his thumb over the ruby of his ring. "I am not like those German officers, sir. I know well to whom I owe thanks and loyalty for my advancement. And more, though I can commiserate with how my people suffer, I cannot condone the way the soviets have chosen to institute change. It is not freedom that is extended to all, only to those with whom one agrees. This is what our American allies have taught the world, is it not? True freedom means freedom to disagree."

Hall smiled and opened his mouth. But before he could say anything more, his office door burst open.

Zivon spun, frowning when he saw Clarke there, out of breath and wild-eyed. "It's Ivy—the captain just got word and took off in his car. They couldn't find me fast enough. She's ill. This flu."

Zivon pushed to his feet.

"Go." Hall had already rounded the desk, his own face lined

with worry. "If Blackwell has left, it must be bad. Keep me updated."

He needed no more permission than that. Zivon charged for the door, he and Clarke both running down the corridor, the stairs, and out into the summer sunshine. Neither paused to debate the path to take or how best to get there.

They simply ran. Heedless of the pedestrians that stared at them. Despite how constricting Zivon's suit jacket felt on his shoulders, how his shoes rubbed his heels. He ran, barely keeping up with Clarke—who usually could barely keep up with him. He ran until the Blackwell house came into view, until he heard his friend's fists pounding on wood, until the door opened and he could skid to a halt on the polished floors.

He expected Eaton. Perhaps even the captain. But it was Lily who stood in the entryway, gripping the latch. Lily, her eyes empty. Her dress stained.

Clarke's breath heaved in and out, words barely finding purchase in the air. "Ivy. They said—Ivy."

Lily's lips parted, but no sound emerged. Her fingers moved from the latch to the door itself, gripping it with white fingers. Even so, she swayed a bit.

Clarke gripped her by the shoulders, panic turning his usually smiling face into a mask Zivon scarcely would have recognized. "Where is she?"

Lily shook her head. A wisp of hair had slipped free of her chignon at some point, falling directly before her face, but she didn't even bother to move it aside.

A guttural cry tore from Clarke's throat. He dashed away from her, toward the stairs neither of them had ever dared to go up, the ones that would lead to the family's bedrooms. Someone would probably stop him—Mrs. Blackwell, the captain, a servant. But that didn't seem to occur to him.

Lily still stared at where he'd been. "She's . . ." Her voice was so faint Zivon could have convinced himself she hadn't spoken at all. She swallowed, blinked. "Gone."

"No." Zivon whispered it.

From above them, Clarke screamed it.

Lily's eyes slid shut, and he feared she was going to topple, so he did the only thing he could think to do. He pulled her to his chest with one arm and urged the door closed with the other. "Lily. My love. What happened?"

She trembled in his arms, if *tremble* was a fitting enough word for the violence of her shaking. "We sent word to Daddy as soon as we got her settled. It moved so fast, though. So fast. She must have been hours trying to get home. I don't know— she was fine this morning, but her lips were blue already when she got here." A sob overtook her, and her fingers gripped his lapels. "There was nothing I could do. She was gasping for breath, and there was *nothing* I could do!"

"Milaya." He held her tightly, far more tightly than he usually would have dared, but he couldn't fight the thought that she'd fall to pieces if he didn't.

Some part of him hadn't believed all the stories about this flu. Not until now. The keening from upstairs, the woman falling apart in his arms, demanded he admit the truth.

He buried his face in Lily's hair. "I'm so sorry." The words came out in Russian. He couldn't convince his tongue to correct itself and didn't imagine it really mattered. The words meant nothing anyway. She probably wouldn't even hear them. His arms would speak more loudly, more clearly.

Another sob tore through her, sounding as though it carried her very soul with it. Her knees buckled, though she didn't fall. She couldn't, not as firmly as he held her, as tightly as she gripped him. And he wouldn't let her. Instead, he scooped her up and carried her into the drawing room, to the familiar sofa with its faded pattern, where they'd sat together countless times. Her arms slid around his neck for the journey and showed no signs of letting go when he leaned down to try to put her on the cushions.

The last thing he wanted was to force her to release him, so he recalculated. Turned. Sat himself, letting her curl into his lap. Not exactly an appropriate posture under normal circumstances, but this was hardly normal. And it let him cradle her against his chest, run a hand up her back. Keep whispering words that would mean nothing to her. In Russian. In French. A few in English that would sound just as meaningless.

He pressed his lips to her forehead at one point, when fear overtook grief. Cool. No fever. The flu that had stolen her sister didn't have hold of her, not yet. Not ever, if he had anything to say about it.

He didn't, he knew that. All he could do was beg God to insulate her from it. For her family's sake, for her own, for his. The prayers came in every language he knew too, the words a chaotic jumble that he hoped would make more sense to the Lord than they did to him.

He held her until the sobs turned to gasps. Until the shaking slowed to more properly termed trembling. Even then, her arms didn't relax, and she didn't lift her head from the home it had found against his neck.

"This is—my fault." Her words were ragged. One of her hands moved, though not far. Only enough to shove at her hair and then fall to his chest and grip his shirt.

She'd utterly failed at getting her hair out of her face. It stuck to her cheeks, glued there by tears. He eased the strands free of the mess and smoothed them back. For a moment, he debated digging out his handkerchief to give to her, but it was in the pocket against which she was pressed, and that would require more movement than he was willing to risk. "Do not be ridiculous, milaya. You did not bring this illness to London."

"No. But I—I must have brought it—home." She squeezed

her eyes shut, and a new keening gathered in her throat. "From the—hospital."

"No, milaya. You cannot blame yourself. It is everywhere, you know this. In the train stations, on the streets—in her school. We have had a few cases even in the OB. Your father or Clarke could have come in contact with it." He shook his head and let it rest against hers. "There is no blame."

She didn't rebut his claim, not in words, but he knew his logic hadn't found a hold on her heart. Not yet. He could only pray it would eventually. Pray she wouldn't fall victim to the guilt that could eat a person whole and leave one's spirit gaping, prime fodder for bitterness.

He had no idea how long she battled the tears, sometimes letting them have their way, sometimes fighting them back. Time didn't much matter. He would send word to Hall when he could, but he had no intention of returning to the office today. He intended to stay right here until someone told him to leave. He couldn't bear to let this family, this woman suffer alone.

After a while, she did shift, though, sliding to a seat beside him—primarily, he suspected, so she could dig her handkerchief out of her pocket. Mrs. Goddard slipped in not long after with water and tea. She didn't say anything—her face looked as worn and streaked with tears as Lily's—but she met Zivon's gaze, nodded toward the tray, and then glanced at Lily. A clear command that he was to make sure she at least had a drink. He nodded his understanding.

Lily held out a hand to keep the housekeeper from leaving again. "Mama? I should go and check on her." She didn't look like she had enough energy to carry out the task.

Mrs. Goddard came closer, smoothed back Lily's hair, and dropped a kiss on her forehead. Something he suspected she hadn't done in a decade or more, as proper as she usually was. "I just came from there, luv. Your mother cried herself to sleep, so leave her to rest. The fever's no worse than it was an hour ago."

Zivon tightened his hold on Lily. Mrs. Blackwell was ill? He hadn't heard that part. But it must be why Lily had been at home already today.

Mrs. Goddard patted his cheek too. "Let your young man here take care of *you* for a bit. We can't have you getting sick now. Drink something. Eat, if you can. You've had no more than a few bites all day."

For the housekeeper, Lily nodded. But as soon as she left, she shook her head. "I can't eat."

He could understand that. But he got up and poured a tall glass of cool water. "Drink, at least. You need it."

She took the glass from him, sipped at it. Her gaze remained glazed, latched on nothing. "She can't be gone. She can't. She was well this morning. Worried for Mama but perfectly fine."

"I know. It makes no sense." No more sense than getting the news his mother had been trampled to death in a riot. Or seeing his fiancée dead on his doorstep. No more sense than realizing his brother had perished trying to find him.

He shook his head. "I wish I could take this for you, milaya. That I could carry it instead." Just as he wished he could have found a way to be here, to meet her still, without it requiring the deaths of his own family.

A moment later, heavy steps dragged their way toward the entrance. Zivon looked up, wincing when Clarke stumbled his way in like a drunkard and collapsed onto a chair. His eyes were every bit as unfocused and swollen as Lily's. Zivon had never seen his shoulders so bowed.

"The doctor is finally on his way." Clarke let out a little puff of breath that was more incredulity than laughter. "As if he can do anything now."

"He couldn't have done anything before either." Lily took another sip of water. "Not when it gets into the lungs." Her voice cracked on the last word.

Clarke scrubbed at his face and then leaned forward to

brace his elbows on his knees, his face buried in his hands. "She was in perfect health yesterday. We were to go for a walk this evening. We had plans to see a show this weekend." His fingers curled into his hair. "I was going to marry her. I have a ring. I was going to ask just before my mother arrived, so she could celebrate with us."

Lily's water glass shook until she lowered it to rest against her leg. "She would have said yes. She loved you."

Lifting his head just enough to reveal his eyes, Clarke nodded and looked over at them. "We'd said those words, at least. I'm glad of that." His gaze focused on Zivon. "How do we do this? How do we . . . keep on living?"

Something he had done such a poor job of that he really shouldn't even try to answer. Except he *did* know how. He knew the words. He'd just been executing them all wrong. "We must be still—not our hands and feet, but our minds. And know that He is God. That He has not changed. That the same Lord who loved us when all is well loves us still when all is lost. His promises are as true today as they were yesterday. He has been enough to see people through the worst since the dawn of time. We must trust that His love is enough to see *us* through now."

He didn't know if the words could mean anything yet to these two people who meant so much to him. But for the first time in six months, a trickle of peace washed over the rocks of his soul.

❖ ❖ ❖

THURSDAY, 11 JULY 1918

Lily sat on the cushions on the floor, her head resting against the shiny spot of her wallpaper. The room was dim, despite it being the middle of the day. Her curtains were drawn against the disrespectful daylight, and she'd shunned the light switches.

Brightness had no place here.

Light couldn't accomplish anything anyway. All this last week, the sun had shone, but it had done nothing to help her see. Her gaze refused to really take in anything. Not at the funeral, the church, the graveside. Not when Zivon gripped her hand so tightly it seemed he was trying to hold her in this world by force. Not when the crush of people descended, or when they left, taking their black clothes with them but leaving their shadows behind.

Nothing could ever be bright again. It wasn't possible. Ivy, her sister, her best friend, had taken all that with her when she left.

Though Lily's arm felt like it weighed five stone all on its own, she lifted it. Raised her finger to the flower she always pointed to. Tapped. *Tap, tap-a-tap*.

Waited. And waited. And waited. Some stupid, childish, foolish part of her certain that if she sat here long enough, it would all return to normal. That *tap-a-tap, tap* would sound from the other side of the wall, along with Ivy's laugh. All light. All brightness. All joy.

Tap, tap-a-tap. Her finger slid down the wall, the effort of holding it in place too great. Her eyes burned. She didn't want to cry again—didn't know how it was even possible that her tears kept replenishing every day, every hour. Shouldn't they have run dry?

Tap. It was all she could muster, not even in the right spot. The sound wouldn't carry so well from that close to the baseboard.

It didn't matter anyway.

But then a creak from Ivy's room had her head lifting, her heart racing. Were those footsteps?

Stupid. Childish. Foolish. But maybe—maybe it really had all been a dream, this whole last week. Maybe *she* was the one who'd fallen ill, and it had all been a fever-induced delirium. Maybe—

Her door cracked open, and Mama stepped inside. Even in the dimness of her room, Lily could read her expression. Sorrow, unimaginable and deep. But something else too. Something Lily couldn't name, perhaps because she couldn't bear to look at it long enough.

Mama clicked the door shut behind her, moved to the window, and pulled open the curtains. Lily winced at the onslaught but didn't object aloud. It would do no good.

A moment later, Mama sat in Ivy's spot at her side. Rested her head in Ivy's spot on Lily's shoulder. Wrapped her arm around her in a way that Ivy never did. "You need to get up, Lily Love. Out of this room. I want you to go back to work tomorrow."

The very thought made her want to scream. "No. I can't."

"They need you. The hospital needs your hands—and the OB needs your skills."

"It doesn't matter anymore." Nothing did. She couldn't care right now about the war or the injured soldiers or the rolls of film piling up. All the responsibilities that had kept her busy, kept her away from home. Time she should have been spending with her family. Time she could never get back.

"It does." Mama's voice was fervent. Her hand stroked up and down Lily's arm. "It matters. It matters enough that you lied to me for years about it. I certainly hope you wouldn't have made those choices if your work wasn't crucial to king and country."

Lily could only squeeze her eyes shut. It had *seemed* important. Then. Before.

"Darling." Mama kissed her temple, smoothed back her hair. "Blinker has come by every other day to ask after you. To ask us to encourage you to return. He's explained to me a bit of what you do—how vital it is. The people whose lives you help preserve every day. The campaigns that couldn't move forward without your work. This is bigger than us. Bigger than our grief. Bigger than my ideals about art. Look at me."

It took more effort than it should have to lift her head, turn her face.

Mama's gaze remained steady. "I'm sorry, Lily. So, so sorry that I judged you. That I let my anger at the deception cast a shadow on this house for so long. When I think of the atmosphere that I created during Ivy's last days—" She broke off, pressed her lips together, blinked frantically. Only after a swallow and a few sniffs did she continue. "The important thing is that you do what the Lord asks of *you*. Not of me. I pray you can forgive me."

"Forgive *you*?" Lily reached for her mother's hand and clung to it. "I need you to forgive *me*. I value your opinion so highly, Mama. Our camaraderie. I have missed that so, so much. I'm so very sorry I kept it from you all this time, that I—that I made it more important than our family. That I—"

"Shh." Mama wrapped her firmly in her arms, tucking Lily's head under her chin. "No more time wasted on regrets and anger. If wrongs have been done, they are forgiven. *They* do not matter. Not now, when I am so keenly aware of how much this family means to me, and how fragile it all is." She reached up and smoothed back a piece of Lily's hair. "We mustn't let such things come between us anymore. Not anger, not secrets, not fear. They will not rob us of the life God has given us."

"What about the life He's taken away?" Lily let her eyes fall again.

"Sweet girl." Mama gave her a squeeze. "Something I am realizing anew is that this life isn't ours to begin with. We don't own it as we do a shoe. It is always His—His gift to us. Our purpose ought to be in giving it back to Him moment by moment. In knowing that losing this life isn't defeat. It's victory." She pressed a kiss to Lily's temple. "If we really believe what we say we do, then we ought to know this life on earth isn't the goal. We can't cling to it. Your sister . . ."

Lily pressed a hand to her mouth to try to hold back a sob.

Mama drew in a long breath, no doubt her own attempt at the same. "We will miss her every day. But she has the reality now—this life is just a painting, a replica of what He has in store. I'm trying to focus on that. I know so well how far my art is from the beauty of God's creation. It's just a shadow, a sorry attempt to capture on canvas what He does every day in this world. So imagine what it must be like for her now, in a place of which *this* is but the imitation."

Lily shook her head. Not in denial of the truth her mother gave voice to, but because she simply couldn't think in that way right now. Perhaps Ivy had victory, but it felt like defeat to Lily. The loss was hers, even if her sister had gained. "I just don't know how to live this life without her."

"But you *do*." At the note of passion in Mama's tone, Lily lifted her gaze again and found the strangest smile on her mother's lips. "You're the one who has taught me this."

"What?"

Mama motioned to the wall behind her. No, to the framed photograph over Lily's bed. One of her earliest attempts at photography, the first she'd been really proud of. But it was only flower petals floating in a rain puddle. How did that teach her mother anything?

"That was my favorite rose, the one I'd hoped to enter into the contest at the ladies' aid meeting that week. Do you remember?"

Lily lifted a shoulder in a shrug.

"When that storm came through and destroyed it, I was angry and frustrated. It had been perfect—*perfect*. And then it was nothing. But you, my sweet Lily"—Mama laughed softly—"you brought out your camera and you got down on your knees, and you showed me that what I deemed ruin was something beautiful. You found light in the darkness. Good in the bad. Like you *always* do."

Lily's nose ached with the tears she didn't want to shed again. She shook her head. "With a camera, perhaps. But—"

"The camera can't capture what you don't first see." Mama cupped Lily's cheek in one hand. "You always see the beauty. Always. And you've taught me to find it too. That was what I woke up thinking about the day after the funeral—that the light is there, if I look for it as you always do. God is there. His promises have not changed just because my circumstances have. He is still the giver of all. The lover of our souls. No matter how bad our situation, He is still good. All we have to do is look for Him."

Like Zivon had said—they must be still and know that He was God. Which meant He was good. He was love. He was mercy. He was life.

He was light. Even amid the darkest times.

Lily couldn't see it, not fully. But if she focused, little glimmers peeked through. Glimpses of His mercies. Mama, well again—and offering forgiveness. Zivon, at her side every moment he possibly could be, and Daddy allowing it. The admiral, understanding of her need to closet herself away. Ara and all her other friends, stopping by each and every day to make sure she was all right.

And Ivy herself. All the laughter and smiles and memories she'd given her. It didn't seem fair that God had taken her, but Lily needed to thank Him for giving her Ivy to begin with. Not everyone had years of such joy to recall.

"Your father will need our help, darling." Now sorrow saturated Mama's tone, colored even darker with worry. "Do you remember that trip to Brighton before the war, when Ivy's hat blew off and he charged into the water to rescue it?"

A memory now tangled beautifully with the night she met Zivon, when she'd told him about it. Another layer to the matryoshka doll. Lily nodded. "Of course. He said no navy man would let a few waves steal from his little girl."

"That is how he's always felt about you girls—that he ought to be able to move nature itself to protect you and see to your happiness." Mama shook her head. "He thinks he's failed. And it's stolen the last bit of light from his eyes. Pray for him, Lily. Pray this doesn't devour him."

Lily's heart clenched, not just at the thought of her father's pain but at the realization that she hadn't even noticed it. She'd been too stuck on her own.

No more. She nodded, more fiercely than necessary. The world may still look dark, but if photography had taught her anything, it was that there was always more light to be found. Sometimes you just needed to change your lens. And sometimes you needed a flash. Neither ever changed what was really there . . . but they showed it in a new way.

She'd always thought of that as art. But it wasn't. That was *life*. And art was just the imitator.

24

Evgeni crossed his ankles and tried not to laugh as Nadya made another fruitless attempt to shoo a few ambitious pigeons away from the crumbs that remained of her lunch. They'd decided to eat outside today, to escape the heat in their room. Even if it *did* mean keeping their conversation to French the whole time. He'd given her another quick English lesson too, before the pigeons fully distracted her.

"Mine." She shoved the last bite of bread into her mouth and kicked at the birds. Not that they were within kicking range, of course, and they didn't look intimidated. They kept on cooing and fluttering.

Evgeni gave in to the chuckle. "Perhaps they will go away now that the food is gone."

"I doubt it," she said around her mouthful, scowling at the birds. "Filthy flying rats." She poked him in the side. "And I don't know what you're so happy about."

He certainly couldn't tell her that he found her frustration amusing. She'd gone three more times into Zivon's flat but had found nothing, *nothing* of use to them. And after each of her dejected returns, he'd been exasperated too. Then

Nadya left yesterday with most of their remaining money and had returned with a pistol. When he'd asked her where she'd gotten it, she'd merely smiled and assured him she'd been discreet.

He hadn't felt reassured. He'd felt panicked. He knew first-hand what an armed, desperate Nadya could accomplish, and it inevitably ended in death for the enemy. Which was fine when the enemy was a band of Germans. Less than fine when it was his own brother.

But he'd awoken today with the certainty that he could make it right. It would just require doing the thing he most feared. Facing Zivon.

Funny—instead of the dread the idea had instilled in him for the last months, making the decision brought peace. He smiled. "It's a lovely summer day, I'm spending it with the woman I love, and I think our next step will net us all we need it to do." He shrugged. "Why not be happy?"

She grunted and reached for the water they'd brought out with them. "I lack the faith you seem to have. Nothing has gone our way since we stepped foot on this stinking island. And if this doesn't work—if the press doesn't print the story or the Admiralty doesn't believe it or the photographs Paul gave us don't convince them—"

"Then I ask Zivon directly for what we need." He looked straight ahead as he said it, not wanting to see Nadya's face. He wouldn't put it past her to be angry instead of relieved at his decision. To say, *"You could have come to this conclusion a month ago and saved us a lot of wasted time and effort."* She'd be right to say it.

But she didn't. Instead, her small, deceptively delicate-looking fingers moved over his arm. "Do you really think he will? Come, Evgeni. This is why I haven't pushed on that point. He will not help you. Not if it means helping *us*. And I think you are right that he will see through any lie you try to tell. He will not make this decision freely." She pushed to her feet and stomped toward the birds.

They fluttered a mere few feet away. London's pigeons were obviously no more intimidated by people than Petrograd's were. She spun back to face him. "You must be prepared to force him. Or if that is something you cannot do, I will."

Somehow, the way she said it sounded like an offer, not an accusation. She'd grown in the last few months. The Nadya he'd first left behind in Russia when he fled with Zivon would have spat it out like a challenge. A threat.

He held out a hand to her. And waited the long moment until she came forward and put her fingers in his. "I will try it my way first. I think . . . I think I can convince him."

Because as he'd flipped through Zivon's now-mutilated photo album this morning, when he'd looked at the blank space where the photo of the two of them together had been, it had struck him.

That had been the image in the place of honor. Not Zivon and Alyona's engagement photo. Not their parents. Not the one of him being honored by the czar.

Them. Together.

That meant something, didn't it? It meant that brotherhood was more important to Zivon than politics.

He didn't point this out to Nadya. She would probably ask the question Evgeni didn't yet know how to answer: Was it more important to *him* too?

She sat back down beside him. "There is one more thing you should know if you plan to face him. He already knew about the mutiny. About the informant who contacted us."

So many questions stormed his mind he didn't know which to give voice to first. How could Zivon have known about that? How would she have known that he did? Why hadn't she trusted him with the information?

"What?"

She sighed. "He intercepted the telegram, it seems. I saw it in his house. The day I . . ."

His eyes squeezed shut. The day she killed Alyona. An answer to another question he'd just as soon never have asked. "What did he do with this information, do you think?"

"I don't know. He must have had the papers with him; they were gone from his house afterward. My fear? He gave them to the Admiralty."

"So if he also gave them the names . . ."

"We don't need to assume that. He wouldn't have any reason to think *you* were involved with the same thing. There is still hope, if we can convince the British to disbelieve him entirely."

Though it took some effort, he smiled. "Look at you. Being optimistic."

She breathed a laugh, but it faded to heavy solemnity. "Even I can hope sometimes. But if that hope proves vain . . . You must know, Evgeni. I will do whatever it takes. Whatever must be done to get these names, to stop this mutiny. I will do whatever must be done to earn the right to return to Russia with our heads held high. We will be honored by the party. We will advance. We will have a chance at a good life."

Her hand was squeezing his in a way she'd never done before. A way that made his heart race. "Together?"

The beat of silence felt like fear. But then she squeezed all the harder. "Together."

He lifted their joined hands, kissed the back of hers. His brother wouldn't understand, but it would all work out. This was Evgeni's chance to do something big, something that would be for the Bolsheviks what Zivon's skills had been for the imperialists. A chance to make a name for himself. And a future with the woman he loved.

All he had to do was make sure Zivon couldn't ruin it. After that, his brother would rebound. He may be angry over what was about to happen, especially if he realized Evgeni's involvement. But it wasn't the end of his life or even his career. Just a nudge to a new one. A wall thrown up to redirect him, to keep him from making a mistake that would affect them all.

Claire had it all wrong. It wasn't bad that the castle kept the hero from making a mistake. It was necessary. Because people, individuals, couldn't always be trusted to make the right decision.

Sometimes the state had to make it for them.

Nadya drew in a long breath. "Regardless of how this all goes, we must leave here soon. Get home. The White Army will be losing heart. We should rejoin the ranks to help rout them."

Evgeni nodded. The newspaper this morning had actually had news of Russia in it—or of a particular Russian, anyway. Czar Nicholas had finally been executed, along with his family.

It was over. Final. The White Army would feel the blow, and any hopes of the provisional government taking control again would surely die. The old ways were gone forever, the Romanov line at an end. The future belonged to the people now. "It will work. Zivon will have no choice but to seek a quieter life." He stood and shot her a smile as he scattered a handful of crumbs he'd been saving. "Ready to go back inside?" he asked as the pigeons flocked to the offering with loud coos.

She rolled her eyes, but she couldn't quite hide her grin. "You are such a softy."

"I have to be, to offset you, Madame Rock."

She chuckled and stood, wrapping her arm around his. "I suppose this is why we make a good pair. Balance is important."

They strolled the five minutes back to their building at a leisurely pace. Though as they neared it, a commotion at the door had Evgeni pulling up, slowing her with a hand on her arm. "Something is amiss."

A crowd had gathered outside the front door, including a

woman weeping loudly. He recognized her vaguely as an upstairs neighbor. He'd held the door for her a few times, tipping his hat and greeting her in French that she didn't understand but in which she wouldn't hear his Russian accent so keenly. She usually came and went with an adolescent boy in tow.

The same boy now being carried out toward the ambulance parked at the curb.

Nadya's fingers tightened around Evgeni's arm. Even as they watched, someone pulled a sheet up over the boy's face. Not, however, before Evgeni glimpsed his blue lips.

The curse that slipped out was Russian, but quiet enough that he doubted anyone else had heard him.

It seemed that the flu going around the city and being discussed in all the papers had found its way to their corner of London.

◈ ◈ ◈

THURSDAY, 25 JULY 1918

Over the last three weeks, Zivon had grown sadly accustomed to the new, somber Clarke. He still jogged with him in the mornings, and they still walked to and from the OB together most days. But any offers Zivon made for other outings were always met with quiet refusal. *"Not today,"* he'd always say. *"You'll want to spend the evening with Miss Blackwell."* Even when Zivon tried to tell him Lily was busy, he'd find another excuse. He was too tired or had brought work home from the office or was in the middle of a good book.

He looked over at Clarke now from only the corner of his eye and prayed. Prayed that God would show him how to be a friend to this man. He'd known him only four months, but that had been time enough that this ache in Clarke's heart pierced Zivon's too.

"I was thinking," he said as the parade grounds came within

sight, "that I may attend a lecture this evening at Kings College, given by one of the members of my church. Lily already has plans with a friend. Would you perhaps want to join me? It ought to be a good one. He will be discussing *The Brothers Karamazov*. Have you read it?"

Clarke shook his head. "Thanks all the same. I don't imagine it would be terribly interesting since I haven't."

"You may be surprised. It was hearing a talk given on *War and Peace* that made me decide to read Tolstoy as a young man."

The turn of his friend's lips looked token at best. "I find it hard to believe you weren't reading Tolstoy already at twelve."

"Well, I did not say *how* young a man. But I was thirteen, I will have you know."

The subdued chuckle wasn't much bigger than the echo of a smile had been. "Did your brother share your literary bent, or did you have friends in St. Petersburg that joined you in your lecture-going?"

Did. Zivon slid a hand into his pocket, where Batya's pocket watch resided. Would he ever get used to using past tense for the people who should still be at his side? "Evgeni . . . indulged me. But he and our father were more men of action than words. I took after my mother."

Clarke made some reply, but Zivon's attention shifted from the easy conversation. Something wasn't right. He slowed, listened.

Voices. Too many voices, all coming from ahead, near the OB. The pedestrians walking toward them, away from the building, kept looking over their shoulders. Ahead of them, a man carrying a large camera broke into a jog.

"Reporters. At the OB." Zivon drifted to a halt the moment they came within sight of the parade grounds. It wasn't unusual for men from the press to be there, but not in a crowd like that. And not outside. Usually, when more than a few gathered, it was because DID was holding a press conference.

These, though, were not the orderly collection of fellows here for promised news. These were rather a roiling, shouting group best defined by the word *mob*.

His chest constricted. He'd had enough of those to last him a lifetime. "We had probably better go the long way round and come in at the back."

"No argument from me."

They fell in with a few others in the naval reserve uniform who had apparently come to the same conclusion. When they reached the back door—the one through which Lily habitually came and went—De Wilde stood there with a newspaper in hand and a serious look on her face.

Her gaze caught his the moment he came into view, and she lifted the paper. "Have you read the news this morning?"

Zivon shook his head. Most mornings he still tried to do so before he came to work, but he'd run an extra mile today and hadn't had the time.

She thrust the newsprint at him. "DID wants to see you straightaway. Look on page three. I'd suggest still walking while you look, though."

Everything in him went cold, even before he opened the paper. This wasn't about the search for those two German officers, it wasn't about his suggestions on how to meet a mutiny if it came, it wasn't about the czar's execution.

No. This would rather be linked to whoever had been breaking into his apartment, searching for he knew not what. This would be about *him*. The shoe he'd been waiting for months to drop.

His enemies catching him up.

He waited until they were through the door before unfolding the paper and flipping to the third page, his eyes adjusting to the interior light as he walked. He skimmed over the first headings, which didn't seem to be anything of relevance. Then caught his breath when he spotted the one halfway down the page. Bolshevik Spy Infiltrates British Military.

Impossible. How? *Who?* He would know another Russian if one were here—even if their English were perfect, this was his life's work. He would recognize nuance in language, in intonation, in behavior. The patterns that would be wrong, the idioms.

His gaze ate up the words. Not *another* Russian at all. Him. This article was all about *him*, the Russian linguist hired by the Admiralty. Except the article made it sound as though he'd had the French and English bidding for his "linguistics" services and had gone wherever they offered him the most money.

His feet came to a halt halfway up the first flight of stairs. He lifted his eyes to De Wilde's. "Does he believe this rubbish? That *I* am in league with the Bolsheviks? That I conspired with them to kill my own fiancée so I would have a plausible excuse for leaving Russia and coming here?"

He could scarcely see through the haze of fury. Was it not enough that they had killed her? Must they now accuse *him* of the crime?

Because it was them. He knew it was them. It wasn't enough that the soviets had forced him from his home. Now they would seek to ruin him here, everywhere, by claiming he was the very thing he hated, the very thing that they knew he'd be working against.

The thing the British government would distrust.

De Wilde didn't nod, didn't shake her head, didn't even shrug. She just held his gaze for a long moment with that age-less look of hers. And then she said, "DID will see the truth. But that doesn't mean he can always convince others of it. You'll have to help him with that part. Give him the evidence people will demand."

Evidence? How was he to provide evidence of anything

other than the story he'd already shared? He'd come here with nothing but a ruby ring and a photograph he'd already turned over. Everything else had been lost to him. He had no proof but his word, and if that was called into question . . .

Clarke clapped a hand to his shoulder. "Chin up, old boy. It's a bunch of rot—sensationalism, nothing more. The next big offensive and everyone will forget it again."

Zivon jerked his head in a nod and skimmed the rest of the article. Whoever wrote it claimed to have an anonymous source for the information—a source that had presented "irrefutable proof" of his underhanded plot and his association with top-level Bolsheviks.

He was a bit surprised they hadn't tossed in a few accusations of being in league with the Central Powers for good measure.

Be still, and know that I am God.

Zivon pulled in a breath that did little to calm him and refolded the newspaper. He couldn't quite manage a smile, even for his friend or colleague. But he could appreciate that they still flanked him on the stairs. They hadn't abandoned him—at least not yet.

At his floor, Zivon bade Clarke a low farewell and continued into the corridor with De Wilde. It was no more abuzz than usual. No one pointed or stared. But he felt conspicuous as he aimed himself for Hall's office rather than the room in which he usually worked, De Wilde peeling off at her door with a nod that he took for support.

Camden took her place at his side. "Don't let it bother you, Ziv. They lambasted me for months, accusing me of every crime under the sun. Between the admiral and the truth, it'll all be put to rest."

"I appreciate your support." He did. But still, he couldn't shake the feeling that this was a bit different from the accusations Camden had faced. He'd been an English subject with a known record, whereas no one really knew Zivon. Not really. He could have lied about everything, and how would they know? Which meant, how could he prove he hadn't?

When he neared the admiral's office, he found Hall waiting for him at the door, face grim. He ushered him in and then clicked the door shut. "It's bad," he said without preamble. "I've contacts at the newspaper—not good enough ones, apparently, to keep them from printing this entirely, but they agreed to show me the material they received. Some of it I'd already seen, other parts I hadn't. I would show you now, but they didn't leave it with me."

Zivon stood before the desk, not taking a seat since his superior didn't. He kept his back straight and his hands clasped behind him. "May I at least know what this supposed evidence is, sir? Because I assure you, it cannot be true. Not if it is trying to prove me associated with the Bolsheviks."

Hall leaned against his desk and crossed his arms over his chest. "Photographs. Newspaper articles in Russian. All of which claim you are here under false pretenses, which then, of course, would beg the question of why." He waved a hand toward the window. "Half of the reporters out there are opposed to socialism and insist your presence here is part of a dastardly plot to undermine order. The other half are in favor of it and claim you're a disgrace to the cause, a murderer who may have started on the correct side but who has clearly been corrupted by capitalism."

"No friends either way, I see."

Hall smirked. "Enmity sells more newspapers than amity." His lips turned down again. "It's like this, Marin. I've already asked my questions, and I believe you're exactly who you say you are. But I have those I answer to who are not keen on this division receiving attention from the press, and we've had more of it lately than we should have. I've already fielded calls that demand an official investigation."

Zivon forced a swallow down his dry throat. "You will have trouble finding out anything. Communicating with Russia is difficult these days."

"And the government currently in power isn't exactly forthcoming about answering anyone's questions. But the truth can always be discovered, given time and energy enough."

He held himself still. But the world rocked around him. How could he have faith in that, when truth had played no part in what had befallen him lately? The truth hadn't saved Alyona. It hadn't saved Evgeni. The truth hadn't kept his parents alive. The truth hadn't gained him freedom from his enemies. "Until then?"

"Until then . . ." Hall sighed. "You ought to lie low for a bit. Stay at home. I'll send work for you to do via Lieutenant Clarke. But it would be best if the press doesn't see you here. For now."

What could he do but nod? Arguing would achieve nothing. No words he could give in any language could create trust where it had been broken. Even when he had not been the one to do the breaking. "Shall I leave now, sir? Or wait until the crowd has dispersed?"

"I have a feeling they'll not be going anywhere for quite some time. But they don't seem to have found the back entrance yet."

"Very well." Zivon saluted. Pivoted.

"Just a moment. I've a packet put together to take with you."

Zivon turned long enough to take the file of papers—all of which, he suspected, were already classified as unimportant. Never would Hall let it be said that Zivon had been entrusted with anything critical after his loyalties had been called into question. If he were truly here for some subversive purpose, then the best plan would be to keep him busy with trivial matters until the extent of his actions had been discovered. Or at least that's what he would have done in Hall's place.

Just as well. Trivial meant easy to decode, which meant he would be left with plenty of spare time. Something he would apparently need, since it seemed all his plans would be crumbling again. He strode from the office, down the corridor, toward the stairs. At the ground floor, his feet halted. Everything in him said he should go downstairs and see if Lily was in by chance. But she wouldn't be, not this early in the day. And even if she were, her father would no doubt reinstate his rules to keep him distant now.

Captain Blackwell would be right to do so. His sweet Lily should have no part of this.

His chest ached. He may never step foot in this building again. He may be forced even from England. Forced to say good-bye to the only woman who had ever inspired passion in his heart. But at least he had known her. Known the beauty of this love. Just as he had the satisfaction of knowing that he'd done what he came here to do. He'd convinced Hall to take seriously the threat of mutiny in the German ranks—and to be prepared to use it. He couldn't control the how, and, if the war ended, he couldn't guarantee that Western forces would come to the aid of the White Army.

But that which was within his power he had done. The rest was up to God.

He pushed out into the sunshine that felt as dark as midnight. God had done nothing to save his family. How was he to believe He would save him? Or Russia? What if it was, for some reason Zivon couldn't fathom, His will that the Bolsheviks remain in power? How was he to accept that?

He strode back along the same route he'd taken to get here, not relaxing any when he was out of earshot of the shouting reporters. Nor when he neared his building minutes later. His hands had curled into fists at his sides.

"Zivon! Wait up, my son."

Zivon paused at the familiar voice with its Russian cadence.

He turned, unable to drum up a smile for Father Smirnov, who was walking with Fyodor Suvorov. He looked from one to the other. "The two of you ought not to be seen with me just now."

His priest's bushy brows arched. "You think we will abandon our own in his time of greatest need? Rubbish."

"Especially when it may be partially my fault." Fyodor moved to his side, his expression earnest. And apologetic. "A reporter came to the embassy yesterday to ask about you. We told them very little, but he insisted he had spoken with other Russians who confirmed the story and gave him photographic proof. He described this couple to Konstantin and me, and it seems my cousin recognized the woman's description."

Zivon frowned. "A couple? Who are they?"

Fyodor shrugged. "The woman had come in several weeks ago, asking about you. She said she had been betrothed to Evgeni."

"What?" Zivon shook his head. "My brother was unattached."

"A lie, then—this did not occur to Konstantin at the time. He . . ." Fyodor winced. "He had me get your address to give to her. It was right when you began attending Mass. My cousin didn't say at the time why he needed it; I assumed he only meant to follow up with you."

Zivon traced the time back—and realization struck. That would have been near the time of the first intrusion. Quite possibly the gaggle of women swarming the place had held her off for a bit, but with the return of quiet, she had no doubt seized her chance. "What did she look like?"

"Pretty. Young—perhaps twenty or twenty-one. Blond hair, curly, but wide-set dark eyes. Very Russian-looking, they both agreed. You know what I mean. She spoke no English, so far as anyone recalled, though the reporter said she knew French."

They paused at the corner near his flat, and Zivon let his gaze wander as the words settled. He hadn't met such a woman here, he was certain. The lack of English would guarantee that he remembered her, if nothing else did.

He glanced along the row of shops across from him. Mrs. Hamilton's bookshop, which he had gone in several times. A grocer, by far the busiest of the stores. A yarn shop, outside of which young women regularly sat, knitting stockings and scarves for soldiers.

A blonde had been among them several times. A blonde with curly hair and dark eyes. She'd struck him because she'd not looked quite Western, but he'd told himself it was just his imagination, overrun as he'd been by the matushkas and babushkas at the time.

Apparently, he should have trusted his instincts.

A strong hand landed on Zivon's shoulder and squeezed. "You are not in this alone, my son."

Zivon shook his head. "I'm afraid I am, Father. You should all cease any questioning on my behalf at once. The last thing anyone needs is to be dragged into the inquiry against me."

The hand didn't move. "We do not fear this woman—or whoever she serves. The Lord will plead your cause, Zivon. Trust in Him. Be still and know that He has this, even this, in His hand."

Zivon kept his gaze straight ahead. "I feel the need to confess, Father—I do not. I do not know this. I have been reciting it day after day for months, but the truth is . . . I cannot trust. Because He lets His children taste defeat all the time. He let Israel be carried away into captivity time and again. He let them be dispersed all around the world, reviled and scorned. He let a party gain power in Russia that has stated outright its goals of eliminating the need for Him."

The priest just chuckled. "And there, my friend, is their foolishness. We can never eliminate the need for Him."

"But you yourself said He may not seek His vengeance for such arrogance in our lifetime."

"This is true. But we also know that under the cloud of persecution, His truth shines all the brighter. We know that it was in captivity that His people called on Him again. We can trust that His promises are always true, because they have always been true. He is still God. And when He leads us through the valley of shadows, we can know it is so that we are made into sons and daughters of light, capable of redeeming these evil days for Him."

Zivon's gaze fell to the ground. He wanted to both shrug away from Smirnov and cling to him. Because the days were indeed evil. But he was none too certain he had any light left in him to redeem anything for the Lord. "I thank you for your support, Father. Fyodor. But please—do not endanger yourselves or your families for my sake." He drew himself up and stepped away. "I have made my choices, and my conscience is clear. I will accept whatever consequences come, be they from friends or enemies."

He left them there on the sidewalk and strode into his building, up the stairs, to his flat. His hand hesitated on the knob, as it always did lately. But why would anyone have come in today? They'd already gotten what they wanted. They'd sown seeds of distrust and hatred against him. They'd destroyed this life he'd built here. What more could they do?

He opened the door, walked through, closed it.

A figure rose from the chair. One he'd know anywhere. And yet one who couldn't possibly be real. For a hallucination, though, he looked very solid.

"Evgeni."

25

Zivon." His brother halted in the middle of the living room, an uncharacteristic look of humility on his face. "You have something I need. And I hope you'll give it to me without too many questions."

The passport. The one that had been stolen, while nothing else had been, even after those later times he'd sensed an intruder had been in his space. The blonde. A *couple*. Evgeni's betrothed, she said.

Evidence delivered to a newspaper that painted him as a Bolshevik.

You'll know a man by the company he keeps.

Pieces. Patterns. A picture too clear to ignore, to deny.

His brother, his Zhenya.

His betrayer.

He set his satchel down on the table. Took off his hat. "The photograph is gone, Zhenya. I don't have it anymore."

Evgeni moved a few steps closer, nostrils flaring. "I'm not asking for the one with the officers. Just the small one of us. Is that so much to ask? A token."

He would risk a meeting after his betrayal to ask for a memento? No. Zivon might do such a thing, but it wasn't Evgeni's

317

way. There was something important in that photograph, or on it, that he'd missed.

Before giving it to Lily.

He kept his breath regulated. His hands steady. *Be still, and know that I am God*. Perhaps the Lord hadn't made a way for Zivon. But He would protect her, wouldn't He? He must protect her. "I am sorry. I don't know what you mean. There was another photo in there?"

His brother huffed. "Don't play ignorant. If either of them fell out in the crash, it would have been the one of the officers. Not that one."

Zivon turned. Slowly, carefully. Faced his brother. Batya's eyes. Matushka's smile. All they'd ever had in common. "I don't have it."

All they had in common, but they knew each other. Too well, perhaps. Evgeni cocked his head. "So you get it. You get it, Zivon, or I will, from whoever has it."

Lily. He'd keep her safe, keep her out of this, if it was the last thing he did. She'd not end up dead like Alyona. Not because of him.

His mind raced. The first image—soldiers. Officers fomenting rebellion, Hall had said. They knew now who they were. They had their names.

But Evgeni and the blond woman must not—and they must need them. All he had to do was keep that information from them as long as possible. Delay them until the Germans could put their plan into effect, perhaps nudged along by Hall's contacts.

He lifted his brows and prayed his brother would read disdain in his eyes instead of desperation. "You just made that rather difficult for me to do, given that I'm no longer welcome at the Admiralty. How exactly do you expect me to get it back now? Or do you think you can break into the Old Building as easily as your lady friend got into my flat?"

A corner of Evgeni's mouth quirked up. And that was why Zivon had always loved him so fiercely, even when they were at odds. Only his brother could laugh at a time like this. "I told her you would know."

"Yes. Even before I saw the glass she broke in my picture frame." He motioned to where it hung on the wall, the shards long since removed and thrown out.

Evgeni huffed, but it still sounded amused. "She didn't mention *that*."

Zivon borrowed one of Hall's mannerisms and blinked at him. "Who is she? She told the embassy you were engaged."

"Did she?" That seemed to please his brother as much as it surprised him. "Interesting."

"Would Matushka have liked her?"

Evgeni snorted a laugh. "Hardly. But as to how you are to get the photo back—you're clever, Zivon. You can come up with something."

"No doubt. But I will need time."

"I'll give you a day."

"You'll give me a week." He folded his arms. And prayed, prayed with every grain of faith left in him, that a week would be enough. "You've already ruined all I've built here. You'll let me get this in a way that won't have me kicked out of the country before I can put another plan in order. Am I clear?"

Though he sneered, Evgeni's shoulders had that line of capitulation to them. "Still the tyrant, determined to have your own way."

"Me?" Fury pounded, so consuming and quick he couldn't stop it. "You think this was my way, any of it? You think this is what I wanted to do with my life? They *killed* her, Zhenya!" The *they* echoed in his head, more than in the room. The implications, white hot, scalded his heart. He staggered back. "No. Tell me it wasn't you. Tell me you didn't kill Alyona."

"I didn't!" His eyes flashed the truth of that. "I wouldn't. You have to know that. She was a sister to me."

And Zivon a brother—in blood, not just in affection. Yet he would do this to him. His hands shook. "I don't know what I know anymore. Not about you."

For a moment, they just stared at each other. Neither speaking. Neither moving. Then Evgeni shook his head. "We will never agree. But we are still brothers. I still want you to be happy. You just have to promise to lead a quiet life somewhere, away from the military and politics. Is that so bad?"

If it meant leaving England? Leaving Lily? It was the worst thing possible. But his brother might not know about her. And if he didn't yet, he must preserve that ignorance at any cost.

Evgeni sighed and moved toward the door. "A week, brother. I will send you a note with instructions on where to meet me—and don't try anything clever. Please, just do this the easy way. You know I would never hurt you, but Nadya . . . I am not so certain she wouldn't."

And yet Zhenya seemed to love her. He bit his tongue against any retort, held his silence until his brother had drawn even with him. Then, quietly, he said, "I was only trying to save you."

Evgeni paused with his hand on the latch. "Believe it or not, Zivon, that's what I'm trying to do too. Please let me. I don't want to see any harm come to you."

And then he was gone. Again. The brother he'd risked everything to save, the brother who had been his enemy all this time, the brother he'd mourned as dead.

He'd been praying since that first conversation with Father Smirnov that the Lord would show him how to forgive. How to crave mercy for his enemies' souls above justice. He'd been praying God would show him how to love them.

He sank to a seat on the hard wooden chair at the table. This wasn't the answer he'd anticipated.

Lily stared at the newspaper, but no matter which sentence she focused her gaze upon, it still made no sense. She knew that the Zivon Marin who had captured her heart was in fact the Kapitan Marin named by the reporter. The history outlined in the article was a distorted reflection of the one he'd told her. But the man painted with words in black and white and the man who held her while she sobbed and entrusted her with his heart were entirely different.

Black and white could lie. She knew that better than anyone. It was no great thing at all to take what was there, cut it out, and put it somewhere else instead, where it meant something entirely different.

Mama pushed her tea aside with a shake of her head and tossed a second newspaper onto the table, disgust in every line of her face—and the lines had deepened in the last month. "Rot and rubbish, the lot of it. Zivon Marin is no murderer."

"No. He is most assuredly not." And that, in her opinion, was where whoever had orchestrated this had overplayed their hand. Zivon was many things, capable of many things. She'd glimpsed that soul-deep bitterness in him, yes. But it was the sort that came of being wronged, not of doing the wronging. Of feeling the guilt and shame for being unable to save someone who was his responsibility, not for taking actions against her.

And she understood that bitterness now. She hated this influenza with the same passion he'd applied to the Bolsheviks. And though her hate wasn't aimed at people, it would still eat away at her if she let it.

She tapped a finger to the second column of the story. "This here, this mention of the evidence they were shown. That sounds like photographic evidence, does it not?"

Mama moved around the table to stand beside Lily and

skimmed the paragraph in question. "It does. Do you think Blinker has copies?"

"I don't know. But there's one certain way to find out." She spun for the door.

Mama was hot on her heels. "I'm coming with you. I want to help, if I can."

They didn't waste time on conversation as they hurried onto Curzon Street. She avoided looking toward Hyde Park, toward the path she usually walked with Ivy. Instead, they turned to Mayfair, directly toward Whitehall. And as the OB came into view, she also tried not to wonder if her halfhearted hours at work were in part responsible for this wretched article.

If she'd gone in as often as she should have, would Hall have shown her whatever evidence this was? Asked her to authenticate any photographs? Had her grief and bitterness kept her from helping the man she loved?

No. Hall had kept her out of the loop long before Ivy's death. But if she'd been there, maybe she could have convinced him by now to read her in.

She shoved the useless thoughts aside as they gained the back entrance. Barely slowing on the stairs, she was soon opening the door to her darkroom.

"Oh my. Lilian. I had no idea."

Only at her mother's gasp did Lily pause to realize that Mama had never been down here. She hadn't seen the space, so many times larger than her darkroom at home. The newest equipment, the endless supply of chemicals, the photo archives, and the most frequently appearing faces tacked to the wall.

"No wonder you couldn't work so well at home. This is—this is . . . well, professional, isn't it? This is a career."

"I suppose it is." She rarely thought of it as such. A calling, yes. And she received a paycheck, but she never even saw those. Daddy always took them to the bank for her.

Mama was wandering to the photo wall. "And these?"

"I keep track of how often the same people appear. The admiral says it has proven useful innumerable times." Including the last one, with the German officers.

The photo Zivon had given them. She frowned. Hall had promised to tell her what came of that, but she'd scarcely darkened the door of the OB since then. And the mountain of film on her desk awaiting processing told the tale too.

"Lily? Ah good, it *is* you." Barclay Pearce stuck his head in with a smile. "Saw the lights as I was heading out the back. Here to help your Russian?"

Lily gave a decisive nod. "If Hall will let me."

"He just sent me to fetch you, actually. Declared all hands on deck to help clear Marin's name. I'll tell him you're here."

He vanished again. Mama was still perusing the wall, so Lily occupied herself by ordering the canisters of film while she waited for Hall.

She didn't have to wait long. And he arrived with an armload of manila envelopes, his expression grim. "I finally convinced one of my reporter friends to bring all these over. And we've the ones that were sent to us, of course. They're on top."

Seeing no need for small talk, Lily began with those while Mama and DID pulled the others from their envelopes and arranged them on one of her long tables. She switched on a lamp, grabbed her loupe, and turned to the trio of images that had made Hall and Daddy suspicious of Zivon to begin with.

The one of him with Lenin, with *You will know a man . . .* on the back.

One of him and Evgeni, with . . . *by the company . . .*

And finally, one of a group that included many men in Russian uniform. She didn't recognize most of their faces, but she spotted Evgeni in the mix, smiling at the soldier next to him. This one finished out the message with . . . *he keeps.*

She started with the first one, the one of him bowing over

Lenin's hand, that Hall hadn't let her get a good look at back when he received it. With the aid of her loupe, she looked at the outline all around Zivon, fully expecting to see a telltale white line or a too-dark one. To find his head had been put on another's body, perhaps. Or even some evidence that the image was old.

But his hair was cut in the same style. His eyeglasses the pair he was still wearing. And it was without question his lithe runner's form. One thing, however, was out of place. The ruby ring was missing from his hand. She straightened. "Admiral?"

He was still spreading papers out and had what appeared to be a newspaper clipping in hand. "Yes?"

"Did Zivon ever mention when the czar gave him his ring?"

"Shortly before he abdicated in the spring of 1917, I believe. Why?"

"He isn't wearing it in this photo—but he never takes it off. Even if he had done so before meeting Lenin, there would be a dent on his finger. But there's none. This photo must be from before he received it."

"It can't be. Lenin was in exile in Switzerland until after the Revolution began."

"Then . . ." It was clearly Zivon in the photo, and he was seamless with his background. She moved the loupe. And laughed. "Lenin was put in after the fact. Look." Once Hall had moved to her side, she held a larger magnifying glass in place for him and used the tip of a pencil to point to the faint white line around Lenin's figure. "Were I to guess, I would say this is a photograph of Zivon meeting the czar, not Lenin." That would explain the adoration on his face.

Hall breathed a laugh. "Well done, Lily. What of the others? I showed him this second one—he verified it himself. Said it was from the album that he lost in the train accident."

She reached for the third. "If his enemies found it, that explains how they created these." She used first a magnifying glass and then the loupe to study the group picture but shook her head. "This one seems to be genuine too. What does that mean? Who are these people?"

Hall's face looked grim. "Bolsheviks."

"Even—his brother?"

"So it would seem. According to some of this information, the false passport Zivon traveled under was even given to him by the Bolsheviks—though that would make sense if his brother is among them." He turned back to the table. "Take a look at these others. I need to find someone who can translate this." He tapped the article he'd been holding. "It's in Russian."

"Father Smirnov." Mama grinned. "And I just transferred his telephone number into my book this morning. I recall it, if I can use your phone, Blinker."

"Of course. I'll take you up. Lily?"

She surveyed the spread of photographs. "More than enough to keep me occupied here for a while, sir."

While they were gone, she went over each image, making notes on separate sheets of paper as to what was added into—or where something was blotted out of—each one, clipping the paper to the images. The further she got, the more confident she grew.

Nearly every one was altered in some way. The story these enemies of his had told—they were fiction, without doubt. And she could prove it, which was the important thing. There were even a few that clearly used the same original photo of him, pasted onto another image and re-photographed.

Whoever had done it had been careless, though, or in a hurry. There were places where she could see bubbles or spots that indicated a glare on the original pieces. Shadows underneath the imposed images.

Hall never would have let her get away with such sloppy work. And frankly, she was surprised that the reporters who had received these hadn't noticed the inconsistencies. Some of them were obvious.

She was nearly finished by the time she heard footsteps approaching. They'd been gone quite a while, but the number of voices told her why. Father Smirnov had joined them. And so, apparently, had Daddy.

Mama took the priest directly to the Russian newspaper clipping. He accepted it with a smile. "This will only take me a minute. Shall I write a translation?"

Lily motioned him to the paper and pen she'd been using. "Help yourself."

"The sender provided a translation," Hall added. "But I'm not much inclined to trust its accuracy."

"I should think not." Lily turned back to the photos. "Especially given how inaccurate all of these are. Shall I talk you through them, sir?"

"Please."

By the time she'd gone over everything she'd found, even Daddy looked convinced that Zivon was anything but a Bolshevik out to undermine capitalism and imperialism. And certainly there was no evidence that he'd had anything to do with Alyona's death.

"But sadly, I don't believe this alone will convince the brass." Hall sighed, bracing himself against the table. "Not with the embarrassment that the article has given them, and given that you're biased in his favor, Lily. They'll want the original photos these were made from."

"Zivon's album." How, though, were they to get that?

"This article agrees with those findings." Setting down his pen, Father Smirnov held out his handwritten page. "It mentions a Marin who is part of the Bolshevik party. But the translation they provided changed one key word—the rank of this brother. Zivon was a kapitan. This is about a lieutenant. Zivon Marin is not a Bolshevik—Evgeni Marin was."

"Not was." At the new voice, they all turned to face the door. Zivon stood there, his hat in his hands and his face emptier and darker than she'd ever seen it. "Is. It seems my brother is alive, Admiral. And that he is responsible for all of this."

Chaos erupted as questions were asked and answered, information volunteered, theories hypothesized. Lily kept her gaze, however, on Zivon. He didn't budge from his place just inside the door, didn't relax, didn't for a moment enter in to become a part of this group determined to help him.

Didn't show anyone for a moment how shattered his heart must be.

But she saw it. She saw it in every move he didn't make, every smile that didn't touch his lips. Every tone that stayed steady instead of rising or falling with emotion. "Zivon." His name was a breath, surely not even heard above Daddy and Hall's animated talk.

But Zivon heard. He looked her way, eyes shuttered.

She rounded the table to stand before him. "He wouldn't have shown up now for no reason. What does he want?"

If possible, his eyes went even blanker. "The photograph. The one I gave to you. I do not know why, but it must somehow be linked to the German officers."

Her hand slid into her pocket. Her camera was there, as always. But alongside it rested the snapshot. She'd taken to carrying it too, so that she'd always have a piece of Zivon's heart with her.

Yet, for all the times she'd carried it with her, she hadn't looked at it much. The lad in the photo wasn't quite the Zivon she knew and loved. Surely she would have noticed something odd about it, though, wouldn't she have?

But it was just two boys standing in front of the Eiffel Tower. The only thing on the back was a few age-browned words that must be the date. Nothing else. Nothing.

She flipped it back over. And the light from her lamp caught something strange on the front. Black against black, but glinting. "Hold on." She held it under the lamp and tilted it this way and that.

Words. Tiny, barely legible against the shadows in the image, certainly not without a light directly above them.

"Names." Even that didn't bring Zivon's voice out of its monotone. "But the names we already have."

"We do. But clearly they don't."

"And they will kill to get them." Zivon's hand covered the photo, pressed it to the table. "Leave it here, milaya. Do not carry it anymore. Do not—do not even act as though you know me. Do not try to defend me. Just . . . make me a copy of this, perhaps. Without the words. Blot them out, or put false ones on. I will give it to Evgeni in a week, when he has said we will meet."

He stepped away, bowing to the room at large, which quieted Hall and Daddy in time for him to address them. "That will give me time to make arrangements. I thank you all for what you are trying to do, but I will not be responsible for anyone else suffering because of me. I will leave England."

"No!" It burst from her lips. "You can't just *leave*. You can't let them win!"

"They will not win. Not at what matters most to them. These German officers will remain safe, and their rebellion will move forward. But I . . ." He shook his head. "I will reap the consequences for what my family has done. And I will apologize, Admiral, for not thinking clearly when he turned up at my flat today. I should have followed him. But I . . ."

"Don't fret about that, Marin. We'll find him. We'll stop him. *And* we'll clear your name. I'm not about to let England lose you."

The admiral's determination ought to have encouraged her. But if she'd become convinced of anything, it was that Zivon Marin was the admiral's match in nearly every way.

And Zivon Marin had absolutely no hope in his eyes. Whatever his brother had threatened, he was clearly convinced that leaving was the only recourse.

She couldn't think he was right. And yet, if so . . . did she dare to go with him?

26

The fire raged around him, above him, below him, within him. Evgeni watched the flames dance, watching for the snake that would turn into a princess. Sometimes he could glimpse her—the girl through the flames. Her hair was a brilliant gold, her eyes a startling brown. Her brows pulled always together into a frown as she reached for him.

Try as he might, he couldn't lift his lance so that she could use it to escape the flames. His arm was too weak. Too heavy. But he must try harder. He couldn't leave his princess in there to be consumed. "Nadya." He whispered the name through a scorched throat. Reaching, always reaching for her. "Nadezhda."

Her face wavered into view through the fire, and something cool touched his face. "I am here. Stay with me, *lyubov moya*. Here. Drink."

Lyubov moya—my love. How long had he waited for her to say such words to him? He felt something hard press against his lips, and then water touched them. He opened his mouth, greedy for the cool liquid. But after a few swallows, it turned from dribble to torrent, and he coughed, pushed against it.

"Sorry." A clank of glass on wood. Then she was back, his princess, dabbing at him with a washcloth. Even through the haze of smoke and fire, he could see the worry in her eyes.

Had she really called him her love? Or had it been only part of the folktale? He tried again to lift his arm, and this time he got it high enough to snag her hand. "Nadya. My princess."

Her laughter soothed away some of the heat. Strange how that just made him more keenly aware of the aching in every limb, every muscle. "Now I know you are delirious. No one would ever call *me* a princess."

The water he'd sipped reached his stomach—and set it to churning. He felt the heave working its way up from his core, and hard as he tried to subdue it, he couldn't. He could only roll onto his side, toward the edge of the bed.

She had a basin there, waiting for him. And she held it as he retched, emptying his stomach of what felt like life itself. Not food—he hadn't eaten, that he could recall. Just the water and bile.

Had he the energy, he would have been mortified. But he hadn't. And as she eased him back to his sweat-soaked pillow, he had a vague recollection of having done this many times before. This time wouldn't be any great shock to her. "Sorry."

Her fingers caressed his forehead, cool and soft and welcome. "Don't apologize. Just get well, Zhenya. Do you hear me? I won't have you dying. I won't."

She'd used his nickname. He wanted to grin. To tease. To ask if she only needed him to help her fulfill their mission, or if it was something more. If perhaps she was finally ready to admit that she loved him.

Mission. What was it? Something . . . something urgent. Something . . . What day was it? Zivon. He needed to meet Zivon. Get the photo. The names.

He meant to ask. But the words wouldn't come to his lips. Maybe because he was too tired, already drifting away.

When he blinked awake again, the light was different. Later that day? The next? The next *week?* He had no idea. But the fire had receded a bit, though the aches were as torturous as ever. The room was quiet, the rushing of flames gone from his ears. He moved his hands around, searching for a hand, a head, something. "Nadya?" He meant to speak it but wasn't sure if it came out as anything more than a croak.

He waited a few long minutes, but he couldn't sense her anywhere. No body sleeping next to his. No sounds of breathing or footsteps nearby.

Panic ate at him. Where was she? Not here or . . . or *gone?* "Nadya?" He managed to raise himself a few inches before he collapsed again with a groan. He couldn't see every corner of the flat, but he could see enough to verify that she hadn't fallen to a heap on the floor. He closed his eyes, telling himself she must be out looking for food. *She* had to eat, even if he hadn't been able to in . . . however long this fever had been feasting on him. That must be it. It must be.

He would just wait for her. That was all. Wait until the door opened and then smile over at her and let her know he was on the mend. Surely he was on the mend. He *had* to be on the mend.

He intended only to blink. But when he lifted his lids once more, the light had shifted yet again, and precious sounds of life met his ears, bringing instant relief. Even if the particular sounds *were* Russian curses from the direction of the window.

His lips curved up. "What is the matter, my princess?"

"Evgeni!" She was there in the next second, gripping his hand in hers and lifting it to her lips. "It is nothing. Nothing at all. How are you feeling?"

"Awful." He tried to swallow, but his throat was so dry. "But less awful than before." Probably. He knew where he was, at least, which seemed a vast improvement over the few recollections he had from before.

She eased a cup to his lips and helped him drink. With the water came a bit of clarity, which had him narrowing his eyes at her. "You are pale." And she'd been nursing him, and he'd obviously had this flu that had struck the city, that had left one of their upstairs neighbors dead. He gripped her hand. She couldn't get sick. She couldn't.

"I am well. Just tired." She leaned down and pressed her lips to his forehead. "Don't worry for me."

He pulled away, as much as he could. "You ought to keep your distance. I don't want you to catch this."

But she laughed. "It's a bit late for that, don't you think?"

Yes, blast it all. He let his eyes slide closed. "You need to rest. How long has it been?"

"A few days, that's all." She climbed over him, into her usual spot on the bed between him and the wall. "I thought I was going to lose you." Her hand settled on his bare chest, over his heart. "I don't want to lose you."

He covered her hand with his. "You won't. I'll beat this." Wouldn't he? He felt much better than when last he woke, which must be a good sign. He squeezed her fingers as the exhaustion crept over him again. "I love you."

I love you too. He wasn't sure if she said the words or if he only dreamed she did. Either way, he slept with the memory of them weaving into story after story in his dreams.

◈ ◈ ◈

FRIDAY, 2 AUGUST 1918

Nadya waited until the rise and fall of his chest had gone steady, telling herself she would get up as soon as he was sleeping soundly. Telling herself she would reread the telegram. Go out into the city. Do what needed to be done.

Instead, she closed her eyes and nestled deeper into his side. She'd always thought love was a weakness. And maybe it was. But even so, it was true. She loved him. Beyond all reason, beyond all sense.

And it terrified her as much as the nausea that made the room spin. Terrified her because she'd thought for sure he was really and truly lost to her this time, and she didn't know what she'd have done if it were true. Never had she wanted to be dependent on anyone else again. And yet here she was.

He murmured something in his sleep about his princess, and she surrendered a small smile. Perhaps she hadn't meant to love him, but it was no great mystery why she did. There was no one else like her Zhenya. Handsome and strong, compassionate and respectful, quick-tempered and quick-witted.

She trailed weary fingers over his jaw, rough with nearly a week's worth of beard. A week. He'd missed the rendezvous with his brother. Hadn't even set one up. And though she *should* care, she hadn't. All that had mattered was getting him well again.

But the telegram lying now on the table told her the time for such indulgence was over. Mutiny was imminent among the German ranks. If she didn't leave within the next day or two, find the men, and put matching bullets in their heads, then all was lost. The rebellion would brew. Spread. The war would end. And the interfering imperialists could well come to the aid of the White Army.

She didn't know how she was going to get Evgeni to France again in this condition. But that was a problem for tomorrow. Today's was just as big. She had to arrange the meeting with Zivon herself and get that photograph from him. And if he wouldn't give it willingly . . .

Levering her eyes open, she stared at her beloved's profile. He'd never forgive her if she hurt his brother. He would leave her. She'd be alone again, as she'd thought she wanted to be, but which now sounded like the worst punishment in the world.

So, for Evgeni's sake, she would spare Zivon. But there was another way to force his hand. When she'd been watching him before they gave the information to the press, she'd seen him with a girl. A girl he looked at in the same way that Evgeni looked at her, a smile always in the eyes they shared.

She hadn't mentioned her to Zhenya. He would object to that too, saying they couldn't take another sweetheart from Zivon, that it would destroy him. But if all went well, she wouldn't have to actually hurt the redhead. She just had to convince him she would. That should be all the incentive he needed to hand over the photo and let them slip away.

Now. She needed to get up now and go to find him. She even pushed herself all the way to her feet before her stomach rolled and the few bites she'd managed to eat for lunch heaved their way upward.

She took off for the water closet they shared with two other rooms, a hand clamped to her mouth.

Later. She'd find him later. When she could convince her stomach to stop rebelling.

◇ ◇ ◇

Saturday, 3 August 1918

Zivon stretched his legs to their full stride, modulated his breathing, and tried to memorize the way the early morning sunlight streamed over the buildings, through the trees, and into the park. Tried to see it as Lily would. To imagine the way she'd stop here, or perhaps there, and find a branch or bird or cloud to capture in her frame.

He'd not seen her since that day at the OB—by his choice. Her father had stopped by a few days ago to assure him he could come to visit, but he had informed the captain that he'd do no such thing. Being near him right now meant danger. And there was nothing in this world that could convince him to put her in such a position.

Leaving her would be like death itself, though. England he would miss now and then. The world of OB40 he would think of fondly all his days. His church he would grieve the loss of. But Lily . . . Lily had become air to him. He didn't know how to see the world anymore without her camera lens pointing the way toward beauty. He didn't know how he would smile without the love in her eyes to ignite it. He didn't know how his heart would keep beating without knowing she was near.

But it would have to be enough to know that hers still beat. That by leaving, he had saved her.

He'd booked passage on a steamer to America that was scheduled to leave next week. He'd telegrammed a handful of universities and had quickly received three offers of a teaching position. They were all shorthanded. His skills would be welcome. He didn't know yet which he would choose. He'd make his decision on the crossing.

Or maybe a U-boat would sink his ship and save him the trouble.

Forgive my morbid thoughts, Father God. He'd spent countless hours on his knees in prayer. For himself. For Lily. For England and Russia and Germany.

For Evgeni. Especially for Evgeni, and doubly so when the expected note didn't arrive and his brother didn't appear in his flat again. Worry had begun to gnaw at him, as it had done that week of the shelling in France. Something had happened to Zhenya. And, furious as he was with him, the thought had accomplished the impossible.

Don't let him die, Lord. The same begging filled his mind now as it had been doing for the past three days. *He doesn't know you. Don't take him. Not while his heart is hard to your*

*grace. Have mercy on him, Lord. If you must take one of us,
take me.*

Mercy above justice. He understood it now.

He rounded the final curve of the mile circuit, and the
sunshine glistened in a way he hadn't expected, off human
hair of spun gold. Curls. A woman, sitting on a bench. Young,
twenty or twenty-one. With distinctly Russian features.

He slowed, stopped.

She stood, looking exhausted, with pale cheeks and circles
under her eyes.

His hand curled around his ring. She too was his enemy.
But no hatred filled him at the sight of her. This woman his
brother loved. This Bolshevik. She was just a girl, too young
for the horrors she had probably seen. A girl who also needed
mercy.

"Nadya, I believe?" Remembering that she apparently
spoke no English, he opted for Russian. "Where is Evgeni?"

"Where's the photo?" Her voice had a rasp to it.

He held out his arms, displaying his athletic clothes. Lily
had created the duplicate just as he'd asked. She'd even
matched the wear of the edges. The only difference was that
the names written in the shadows were fake. Hall had delivered it days ago. "Obviously not on me. You should have come
to my flat. My brother . . . what has happened? Is he well?"

Emotions chased each other over her face. "He's fine. Let's
get it. Now."

"All right." He lowered his arms and turned toward the exit
to the park. He wasn't sure he believed her about Zhenya—or
that he could trust her even to walk beside him. He focused
his attention entirely upon her.

She wasn't holding herself with the coiled readiness of a
soldier, though. Her shoulders sagged, and her hands hung at
her sides as if they weighed more than they should have. Only
her eyes showed the alertness he'd expected of her, darting in

every direction. Rather than try to maintain an awareness of everything around him, he let her do that for him and focused instead upon her reactions to each snapping twig, each tweeting bird.

For a few steps, she kept pace at his side. Then she hissed out a breath. "Ninety minutes. I will come to your flat. If anyone else is there, the redhead will pay. Do you understand me? I know where she lives, and if you don't give me exactly what I want, I'll put a bullet in her head as I did Alyona's."

She pivoted and fled. Zivon considered going after her, a million pointless screams vying to escape from his lips. But none would undo the terrible truth of reality, of the threat, of the despicable crime she'd just claimed. Bringing down Nadya would do nothing to solve the bigger problem right this moment.

He instead opted for discovering what had scared her off. The moment he turned his head, he had his answer. Hall and Blackwell were both striding his way.

He met them with a nod. "Admiral. Captain. I have heard nothing from my brother, but the woman—Nadya—she was just here."

Two sets of eyes flew to the path, but she must have been out of sight.

"I'm not surprised," Hall said. "We intercepted a telegram to her from Petrograd that came in yesterday and just made its way to me. Orders to move immediately, that the window was almost closed. We believe it's referencing the impending mutiny."

"She's clearly used up all their patience." Blackwell's gaze was still on the path. "It'll make her desperate."

"Tell us what she said, Marin." Hall stepped closer, eyes flashing between blinks. They were knowing, those eyes. Not in the same way Lily's were. He never left Zivon with the impression that he saw his heart, but somehow he saw more.

He saw how people fit into the world, which meant he could predict what they would do in it. And he was shaking his head. "I know you well enough to know you'll try to handle this on your own, to spare us. But don't play the hero. Please. Trust us."

With his own life, he would. He'd let them come to his flat and take the risk that Nadya's exhaustion would dim her perception long enough. But this wasn't just about him. There was Evgeni, who was still out there somewhere.

And more, there was Lily. Had the blonde really been the one to kill Alyona? Would she do the same to Lily? If she saw anyone from the OB lingering around his flat, she could take off and do it before anyone could stop her. No, he had to play it safe. For Lily's sake.

Be still, and know that I am God.

Zivon let his eyes slide shut. The Lord would be exalted. He would make the wars to cease. But would He do it soon enough to save anyone Zivon loved?

Draw out also the spear, and stop the way against them that persecute me: say unto my soul, I am thy salvation.

He opened his eyes again. For months, Zivon had tried to prove who he was. He had tried to forge a new path. He had tried singlehandedly to save his brother, his people, his country. But the truth whispered now through his soul.

I am thy salvation.

27

Lily paid no attention, for once, to the way the sunlight glinted over the buildings, through the trees, onto the path in Hyde Park. She'd risen at the first breath of dawn this morning, dressed, and spent a few minutes in prayer. Then a few more studying the photographs she'd made duplicates of.

He meant to leave her. Soon. Though Zivon hadn't so much as strayed into her neighborhood, Daddy and Blinker had kept her updated on all he was doing. Putting affairs in order here. Saying his farewells to everyone else. Booking passage on an ocean liner to America.

She'd had an hours-long conversation with her parents last night, in which she looked them squarely in the eye and declared she meant to go with him, wherever he went. To America, to the Arctic, back to Russia—it didn't matter where. She'd have to convince him to marry her first, of course, but she could do it. If he'd just talk to her . . .

That was probably why he'd been avoiding her.

Her parents hadn't exactly been pleased with her determination to leave England at his side, but instead of arguing with *her*, they'd focused on devising ways to get him to stay. And oh, how she prayed one of them would work. Not for her own sake, but for his. So much of his life had been in chaos for the last year. He needed a resting place.

For that to be England, though, they had to clear his name. Which meant they needed the original photographs used to create the fakes.

Which meant, in turn, that they must find his brother and the Nadya woman. The admiral had his best people on it, so surely they'd soon be found.

In the meantime, Zivon.

She spotted him with Daddy and Hall, talking, gesturing, and she held back. Whatever they were discussing, she wasn't going to intrude. Better to wait until they'd finished. So she slipped around them, thinking to get closer to the entrance he always used when he came and went.

So many times she'd come and gone on these paths too. With Ivy. With Zivon. With her parents. Was this the last time she'd walk here?

It should have been a sad thought. But when she blinked, she saw Ivy's laughing eyes. Full of innocence. Full of mischief. Her sister would think this a grand adventure.

And she'd be right. Love always was. It would require sacrifice—but the best adventures always did.

Hurried movement caught her eye, stealing her focus from the future. She frowned when she realized it wasn't a squirrel, but rather a woman who was even now rising from a crouch, swaying a bit on her feet, and pressing a hand to her stomach. Had Ivy done the same on the way home that day? Ill and desperate, but with no one to help her?

Her feet started her forward, even before the face registered.

She'd never seen it before. Not in person. But she had in a photograph—the one with . . . *he keeps* written on the back.

The one with Evgeni in a crowd of Bolsheviks, smiling down at a smaller soldier.

Only this morning had she realized the recipient of his smile was a woman. *This* woman. Nadya.

Nadya. Here.

Lily glanced back over her shoulder. She was too far now from the men to get their attention quietly, though they might hear her if she shouted.

The woman would too, though, and would be gone before they could get here. *Lord? What do I do?*

Never in her life had she felt such clear direction in her spirit. It wasn't a word, but it was an urgency pressing down on her. One that clearly said, *Go*.

She went, keeping enough of a distance that the blonde wouldn't see her without turning around to look.

Footsteps sounded, running, a moment before Barclay Pearce appeared at her side with an exasperated look. "What in the world do you think you're doing?"

The urgency didn't relent, though it felt a bit more optimistic now. "Barclay. Perfect. Once we see where she's going, you can run back for help while I get the album from her."

He looked at her as if she were a madwoman. "No, *you* go back now and tell Hall I'm on her trail—as he told me to be if she showed up. You've not been trained for this sort of work."

"Haven't I?" She nodded ahead, to where Nadya still had a hand pressed to her stomach. "She's ill. Likely Evgeni is too, then, and that's why he's not shown up again. I can examine him. See if there's anything I can do to help them."

Barclay shook his head. But he didn't make a fuss or try to force her to turn around. "You're going to get me sacked."

"Oh, rubbish. Who else would the admiral get to run his 'errands'?"

"Shh. Here." He pushed her into an alley a second before Nadya turned partway around. They watched her from their

342

hiding place until she faced forward again and continued on her way.

Thank God He'd sent Barclay to join her. She really wasn't trained for this.

Together, though, they trailed her to a tube station. Lily wasn't sure how they'd manage to keep an eye on her on a train without being noticed, but Barclay didn't seem to recognize this was a problem. He just handed over the fourpence for two tickets and led her into the carriage behind the one Nadya had boarded. The way he kept his face glued to the window told her how he meant to know when she debarked.

Lily didn't dare say a word to distract him during the twenty-minute ride. She just spent the time praying. Thinking. Focusing. She was ready when Barclay nodded and sprang to her feet.

The blonde didn't even bother looking over her shoulder again after she got off the train. The coughs Lily heard from people waiting on the platform had her wishing for one of Arabelle's masks.

The Lord would just have to insulate her for now.

"I hadn't made it out this far yet," Barclay muttered as they walked into a tired-looking neighborhood Lily had never visited before. "Not in this direction."

"I'm sure you would have soon."

He smiled. "The next day or two. I do know some blokes from this part of the city."

They'd followed her only a few minutes when she ducked into a building of flats. Lily sucked in a breath. "What do I do? Hurry to catch up?"

"No. Oi! Quigley!"

After their whispering for the last half hour, Lily jumped at the sudden shout. But it blended into the normal noises of the neighborhood and soon had an older fellow who'd been sweeping a doorstep straighten, turn, brighten.

The chap lifted a hand. "Oi! Barclay!"

Apparently, one of the blokes he knew from here. Barclay hurried to his friend's side. "The curly-haired blonde—Russian. Know where she's staying?"

Quigley scoffed. "Everyone does, so we can steer clear of 'er. You saw the building, aye? She'll be in 5F."

Barclay turned back to Lily with a smile. "Voilà."

The urgency that had spurred her on since the park settled into peace. She returned the smile and spread it equally between Barclay and his friend. "We thank you, Mr. Quigley. Now, I'm going to say hello. Barclay, you'd better hurry back to Whitehall and tell Hall and Daddy where I am."

Barclay's face went grim. "It could be close to an hour before we get back. Thirty minutes at the least."

Lily kept her face clear. "That's all right. I can fill the time."

He didn't look appeased. "They're going to have my head."

"For keeping me safe? Hardly." She gave him a little nudge. "Go."

He grumbled something she didn't catch and lifted a brow at Quigley.

The old gent grinned. "If she's one of yours, don't worry. My sis is in that building. We'll make sure all's well."

It was all the reassurance Lily needed. Without waiting for any more arguments from Barclay, she crossed the street.

By the time she stood before the door with a tin *5F* on it, she'd had so many second thoughts that she hadn't bothered counting them. She could turn around, even now. But still that undercurrent of peace flowed through her heart. And so she raised her hand and knocked.

For Zivon.

"*Quoi?*" The French "what?" sounded irritated and raspy a second before the door was yanked open. The blonde's eyes went wide.

Lily smiled and forced her tongue to wrap around French.

Thank heavens Ivy had taught it to her pupils and so had used it a bit at home, otherwise Lily would probably have forgotten what she'd learned in her own school days. "Did someone need a nurse?"

She'd taken this Nadya by surprise, that was certain. "No." The door started to shut.

Lily stopped it with a hand and a lifted brow. Letting the smile fall, she said, "I have the photograph you want. Let me in. We can make a trade."

A war raged through Nadya's eyes. "Zivon has it."

"He did. He gave it to me weeks ago, before he knew what it signified." Moving slowly, she reached down, into her pocket.

The photo was there, with her camera, as always. Not the original, of course—that was safely pinned to her wall at the OB. But when she'd made a copy for Zivon, she'd made a second for herself.

He'd given her his heart when he gave her that photograph. She wasn't about to go anywhere without it.

When she pulled it out, Nadya snatched for it, but Lily held it back, away from her. Let her see it without touching. "A trade, I said. Now, let me in."

Her mouth set in a firm line, Nadya backed up a step. "You will regret coming here, English girl."

"Funny. I was going to say the same thing to you."

"Nadezhda?" A second voice came from within, hoarse and faint. "Who's there? What . . . ?"

Evgeni. And he sounded ill. Sliding the photo back into her pocket, Lily pushed Nadya aside and strode into the room. A sweeping glance of the place showed her a tiny kitchenette, a table for two with matching rickety chairs, a small shelf with one book on it, and a narrow bed.

That was where Evgeni was. Pushing himself even now to a sitting position, confusion on his face.

Lily rushed to the bed. "Evgeni. I have been praying for

you. The flu?" She perched on the side of the bed and pressed a hand to his forehead.

Cool, praise God.

His gaze went from her to Nadya. "Who is this?"

Lily gave him a smile. They looked nothing alike, these brothers. Not in coloring or the shape of their faces or their builds. But the eyes. The mouth. There she could see it. "Lily Blackwell. I'm going to marry your brother."

For a long moment, he studied her. Perhaps trying to ascertain whether it was true. Perhaps something else altogether. Then his gaze moved to Nadya. "You knew? About her?"

Nadya crossed her arms over her chest. "I told you, Zhenya. I will fight for *our* family. Not his."

"Your mistake, Nadya, is that they're one and the same." Lily reached for Evgeni's hand and checked the pulse in his wrist. "They're brothers. You can't ignore that. Can you, Evgeni?"

He said nothing. But his mouth turned up into a bit of a smile. Zivon's smile.

Nadya stepped closer. "Give me the photograph."

"I will. And you'll give me Zivon's album."

A beat of silence. Then a terrifying *click*. "How about this for a bargain? You give me the photo now and I won't kill you."

Lily looked over to see a pistol leveled at her head. She should have panicked. Screamed. Dove for cover. But the blanket of peace wouldn't lift. And so, somehow, she smiled. "You won't kill me. If you do, you'll never get out of England. They'll be looking for you at every port, every station."

Nadya's nostrils flared. If she knew anything about Lily, she'd know her father was a captain, that he had connections. Was it a risk she'd take?

All Lily knew was the woman didn't pull the trigger then and there, snatch the photo, and run. Which meant there was hope. She just had to stall until Barclay returned with help.

Swallowing, she turned back to Evgeni and patted his hand. "Put the gun away, Nadya. We're going to do this the easy way. The photo for the album. But we'll make that trade in a bit. First, let's take care of Evgeni. You'll need him stronger than this if you mean to leave soon. Open the window to get some fresh air in here. We need to make him some broth. It will fortify him—and you too. You look pale."

"I told you that you looked pale," Evgeni croaked.

Nadya scowled. "And I told you I'm fine." But she glanced at the tiny kitchen area, then at Evgeni's prone form. She sighed. "*You* make the broth. And make it fast. I mean to be out of this wretched place by nightfall."

Lily smiled. Formidable a soldier as Nadya may be, she was still a woman.

A woman clearly concerned about the man she loved.

That would grant Lily all the time she needed.

Zivon checked his pocket watch and grimaced. "I have only thirty minutes to get back to my flat, gentlemen."

"We'll have you on your way in just a moment." Hall scratched one more note onto the paper they'd all been poring over, then handed it to Blackwell. "How about this?"

"I think it will work." Lily's father reviewed the plan with a nod. "As long as there are no unforeseen—"

"There you are!" The office door flew open, Barclay Pearce leaping through, chest heaving. Followed by—Father Smirnov? "Whatever you're planning, shelve it. Lily and I found their flat. She's there now, with Nadya. We haven't any time to lose."

"What?" Blackwell's roar could have shaken the whole building, had it been made of flimsier material.

The roar in Zivon's ears was nearly as loud. He pushed to his feet. "You left her there?"

"She's not exactly alone. I have people keeping an ear out.

347

But . . .” Pearce’s gaze flicked to the priest. “There *was* a bit of information I wasn’t privy to at the time I agreed to Lily’s plan.”

Father Smirnov stepped into the office, lips pressed together and eyes flashing apology. “Fyodor and I have been speaking with everyone in the congregation. Describing this Nadya. Asking everyone if they’d seen her. There was someone who admitted that she’d come to him just before the article was published. He did not know who she was, of course, only that she was a fellow Russian. A pretty young girl who claimed to be alone and frightened by a refugee neighbor who’d been making overtures. He sold her a gun.”

Zivon charged toward the door. “The address.” His Lily was in their hands—*her* hands, the very woman who had killed Alyona. He had to reach her quickly. He had to save her. He shouldn’t have let Hall and Blackwell talk him into trusting them, he should have—*no*. Had he not been here, he wouldn’t have known this new information. He’d been right to trust.

He reached Barclay. Waited, half expecting *Be still* to echo through his soul. Instead, Pearce told him the address, right down to the flat number, and even some rudimentary directions.

He didn’t wait around for anyone to argue. He flew out, legs pumping as hard as they’d done the day the news of Ivy came. To the nearest tube station, onto the train just pulling in. He caught his breath during the ride. Charged upward into the sunshine again as soon as the train squealed to a halt at his destination.

He’d done his best to protect Evgeni and his girl. He’d gotten Hall to agree to let them slip from the country with false information to deliver to their superiors. They’d be as safe as Zivon could make them, but they wouldn’t be able to interfere in Europe.

All that could go up in smoke now, though. If they hurt Lily . . . He choked on the breath he dragged in. They couldn’t.

If there was one thing he must do today, it was stop that tragedy. Lily must, above all, be safe. For her sake. For her parents'. And even for Evgeni's. Because if any harm came to her, all deals would be off. Zhenya would pay the price too.

He couldn't let them hurt her. That was the thought that became clearer with every footfall. Whatever it took to save her, he would do it. *Lord, guide me. Show me how.*

Pearce's instructions had been flawless. Once he reached the right building, he slowed. It wouldn't do to pound up the steps and alert them too soon that he was coming. After pausing to catch his breath, he walked into the building and up to their floor.

For a long moment, he stared at the door with its tin *5F*. Behind that door, his past and his present and his future were all a-tangle. His brother. The Bolshevik who had killed Alyona. The woman he loved with all his soul and never would have met had circumstances not brought him here.

The unanticipated.

A year ago, even with all his watching, all his decoding, and every pattern he saw, he never could have predicted where he'd be standing now. For every detail he thought he knew, God had proven him ignorant of many more.

But He had been Lord through it all. He'd known. He'd seen. And He'd delivered Zivon to this moment, to this door. He raised his hand and knocked.

28

Zivon stepped inside with his hands held away from his body, wanting to do nothing to inspire Nadya to pull the trigger on the gun that she'd pointed at him.

His gaze, however, wasn't still. He found Evgeni with it in the first second—sitting at a small table and looking as though he might collapse onto it at any moment—and Lily in the next, spooning up a bowl of broth.

She nearly dropped it when he came through the door. "Zivon! What are you—"

"Milaya." On second thought, he'd risk the bullet to hold her again. How could he ever have thought he could leave the country without doing so one more time? He rushed in her direction, and she met him halfway, his arms closing around her. "What were you thinking? Why would you come here?"

"The album." She held him tight, then pulled away enough to catch his face between her palms. "You'd have let them leave with it, never thinking of yourself. I had to think of you for you."

"Step apart, now!" The command was in French.

"Nadezhda. Relax. Let them have a moment." Evgeni

350

sounded terrible, if one were to listen only to the quality of his voice. But if one listened to the tone, he also sounded amused.

Zivon turned his face enough to kiss Lily's hand. "The album does not matter. My reputation does not matter. All that matters is that you are safe."

"And that I'm with you. You're not leaving without me, Zivon. Where you go, I go."

How could that be possible? When it meant leaving all she'd ever known, the parents who loved her and needed her, her work here? Yet, as he looked deep into her eyes, he saw she *did* mean it. Somehow, this woman loved him that much. A blessing he'd done nothing to earn and could never deserve.

Evgeni coughed, a hard, racking sound that drew Zivon around to face him. Nadya had crouched beside him and was rubbing her free hand over his back.

Clearly, she'd been lying this morning when she said he was fine. "You are ill," Zivon said.

Zhenya waved that off. "Was. I am on the mend."

"He has no fever." Lily wrapped her arms around one of his, as if to make it clear he wouldn't walk away without her again. "I think he only needs to regain his strength."

"Which he'll do in France. In Russia." Nadya pressed a kiss to his brother's brow and then stood again, her eyes cold and hard when she turned them on him and Lily. "We are leaving today. With the photograph. Hand it over now, English girl. You have dawdled enough."

In English, so quietly he barely heard her, Lily murmured, "How far behind you are the rest of them?"

"Only a few minutes, I should think."

Evgeni narrowed his eyes at them. If he'd been able to hear, then he would understand.

Zivon stepped forward, putting himself between Lily and the pistol. Hands out again, so Nadya could see he had no weapon of his own. "Please, lower the weapon. We are family.

I have negotiated for your freedom, but you will compromise it if you use that."

"Our freedom?" Nadya barked a laugh. "You don't know the meaning of the word. You who would grow rich while others starve. Freedom comes only when the people steal the power from their oppressors and force them to do the right thing."

Zivon's chest ached. How many times had he heard that sentiment being shouted in Russia over the last year? A cry from a desperate people who had been pushed past their breaking point. He commiserated. He cried for them, with them.

But they were wrong. "No. Freedom comes only when the people realize that it cannot be stolen and forced. Freedom that is denied to anyone who disagrees is no freedom at all."

Lily had reached into her pocket, and she held out a photograph that he would have sworn was the same one from the passport, had he not seen that one tacked to her wall an hour ago. She must have made herself a duplicate too.

Of course she had.

"Here," she said. "Take the photo. Give us the album."

"And put down the weapon," Zivon added. "No one needs to get hurt."

"Nadya. My princess." Evgeni reached out for her free hand. "We can all win. Put down the gun and get the album for him. Please. We can let them live their lives. We can live ours. Let's just go." To Zivon, he offered a small smile. "Sorry so many photographs have been ruined. I wouldn't let anyone touch the one of Batya and Matushka, though."

The original telegram decrypt, then, could well be there. They didn't need it anymore. But somehow it was a comfort to realize that his parents had, in a way, protected him. His secrets.

Nadya hesitated a moment, in which Zivon could see this going many different ways. But then she nodded and reached to set the gun on the table. "For you, Zhenya. For us. For our future."

It all would have been perfect. If only the door hadn't burst open behind them at that exact moment.

One moment, Lily had been watching the descent of the gun, anticipating the reach for the lone book on the shelf. Thinking in the back of her mind that she wished she could get a photo of Evgeni and Nadya before they left.

The next moment, chaos poured in. At first she could see only the blur of fast-moving men in dark blue. Then she recognized Daddy, Hall, Barclay, and, of all people, Father Smirnov behind them.

There were shouts—from Daddy, from Evgeni, from Nadya. A single bullet fired, which must have lodged in the wall, given the plaster raining down. Zivon threw himself in front of Lily. Evgeni tried to protect Nadya. Nadya brandished the smoking gun with such clear intent that Daddy, who had probably never dreamed of raising a hand to a woman in all his life, had no choice but to go on the offensive.

He caught her wrist with one hand, struck her arm with the other. She lashed out, kicking at him, but he sidestepped. Tugged her forward with that arm. Bent his knee in what Lily assumed was meant to be a blow to the stomach to make her double over and relinquish her weapon.

Only before contact could be made, Nadya screamed. All but tossed the gun aside. Wrapped her free arm around her middle and recoiled as far as she could get from Daddy, eyes wild. "Nyet! Nyet!" she screamed over and over again.

Lily's father, still caught in the throes of adrenaline, didn't seem to hear her. Didn't seem to see the desperation in the young woman's eyes.

But Lily saw it. Just as she saw the single bed in the room.

As she'd seen the looks between Nadya and Evgeni. She saw the *our future* Nadya had really meant, and she did the only thing she could think to do.

She jumped around Zivon, between Daddy and Nadya, with her arms raised. "Stop!"

The whole room went still, other than the heaving breaths of the men who had stormed in thinking to rescue them. Her father's eyes cleared, then confusion descended. "Lily?"

She stepped into his arms, letting him crush her to his chest. "I thought I'd lost you," he muttered into her hair. "That you were gone like Ivy. I couldn't have borne it, Lily White."

She clung to him, as much because he needed her to as because she needed it as well. "I'm fine, Daddy. I promise you."

"No thanks to them." Daddy drew back, lightning flashing in the gaze that landed on Nadya.

The woman was trembling, crumpled into the second chair, hunched over, arms wrapped around her stomach.

"They weren't going to harm me." She pressed a hand to her father's arm, willing him to believe her. And then she went and knelt beside Nadya, brushing back a curl from her face. "Are you all right?" she asked in French. "The baby?"

Nadya's eyes, wide and terrified, lifted to her face. "I . . . I don't know. I think so?"

"The what?" Evgeni's voice sounded wooden with shock.

Lily spared only a quick glance toward the men. Evgeni had no color at all in his face, though whether it was from his recent illness, the exertion, or the news of a babe she didn't know. He sank onto the floor and stared at Nadya. "You don't have the flu."

Nadya's hands were trembling as she lifted them to brush aside her fallen curls. "I told you I was not ill."

Zivon's breath escaped him in a whoosh. With a glance to Lily that begged for understanding, he straightened and stood before the admiral. "I present myself for your consequences, sir. I accept the full responsibility of their actions on British soil."

Hall's blink looked suspiciously like a roll of the eyes. "It doesn't work that way, Marin. They're too late anyway. The mutiny has already begun."

"What?" Evgeni's face went paler still. At a word from Nadya, he said something in Russian, presumably a translation of the admiral's statement.

DID pulled a sheet of paper from his pocket. "De Wilde stopped me on our way out. The Germans are in revolt."

Nadya was shaking her head. "No," she said in French. "It doesn't matter. Even if the war ends, it doesn't matter. The West won't help the Whites. And even if they do, the Bolsheviks will win."

"Perhaps." Zivon looked toward Father Smirnov, then over to Nadya. "Perhaps they will. Perhaps this is what Russia wants and God will allow it. But even so, it is good for the war to end. For lives to be saved."

"As for the two of you." Hall crossed his arms over his chest. "You're going to turn over the album with the photographs you used to create those false ones. And then you're going to leave within the next forty-eight hours. I'll not tolerate any more threats against one of my men. And you can tell your superiors the same thing, if they question you. At the moment, the Crown has no quarrel with the Bolsheviks. Don't give us a reason to."

Nadya's shoulders rolled forward, and she didn't look up at any of them. Evgeni slid his hand across the table, palm up. Waiting, clearly, for her to put her hand in his. "We accept, sir. With gratitude for your generosity."

Evgeni kept his hand outstretched across the table. Kept his gaze leveled on the face he knew so well, but which he'd never seen bearing this emotion. She looked defeated. And *defeated* was the last thing in the world he wanted his warrior queen to be. "Nadezhda."

She shifted, but she didn't lift her gaze.

He did. Toward his brother, asking a silent question with a swing of his head toward the women. He didn't want anyone to overreact if he dared move over to her, but he had to be near her now. Had to touch her. Had to see her eyes.

Zivon nodded. He must be judging him, them—he *must* be—but he made no comment. Just exchanged a few gestures with the navy men still in the room, giving him space to round the table. Drop to his knees before her.

He touched a weak hand to her chin. "Look at me, my love." He'd let his words drift back into Russian. At least then Zivon would be the only one to understand them. "Please."

Slowly she lifted her lids, and he saw what he thought he never would.

Tears.

His fingers moved to cup her cheek. "Is it true?" In all their talk of women not being trapped in the home, of the state being the proper institution for a child to be raised by, he'd never anticipated *this*. This quickening inside him at the thought of a child—*their* child—growing in the womb of the woman he loved.

But what about her? Did she want a baby? With him? Now? She must, at least in part, if her first instinct had been to protect it. Right?

"*Dorogoy.*" She leaned into his hand, breath heaving. "I faced down the enemy on the battlefield without flinching. But this . . . this terrifies me."

"I know. But you're not alone. I'm with you. I'm not going anywhere. We can go home, tell our superiors how the flu interfered with the mission, but all else is well here. Yes?"

She huffed out a breath and looked ready to roll her eyes.

But she was a Russian soldier. She knew when to accept defeat. Or, at the very least, when to cut one's losses and run, leaving only burned ground behind them for the enemy. She nodded.

"And then . . ." He settled his other hand on one of her wrists, still wrapped around her middle. "Then we do as we planned. We make a life for ourselves."

"But I don't want the life we planned." She squeezed her eyes shut but only for a second. When she opened them again, her gaze held his. Too warm to be speaking a farewell. He hoped. "I want . . . I want to love our child. I don't know how to be a mother, but I have to try. I *want* to try."

"Then marry me, Nadya." He caressed her wrist with his thumb. "It will not be a prison—I promise you. If you but let me, I will be your wings."

A million thoughts warred across her face like a battlefield, and he couldn't be sure which would win. Hope . . . or fear? But at last her eyes slid shut, she drew in a breath, and she leaned toward him. "I trust you, Zhenya. I . . . I will marry you. If you'll have me."

If he weren't still so weak, he may have leapt up and danced. Instead, he grinned. "I will have you, milaya moya."

"Well. We can take care of that before you leave England, if you like."

At the unfamiliar voice, Evgeni startled. He hadn't even noticed the man hovering in the doorway, but he was without doubt a Russian. The long beard gave him away as surely as the smoothly spoken words. Evgeni looked to his brother, who was chuckling.

Zivon waved toward the older man. "Allow me to introduce Father Evgeny Smirnov."

Evgeni breathed a laugh. He'd *known* his brother would find any Orthodox church to be found. "A good name."

"I was thinking the same of yours." The priest grinned and lifted his brows. "So? A wedding before you go?"

Evgeni looked to Nadya. This certainly wasn't what they'd planned. Not in general, not when they came to England. Not when they'd plotted how to render Zivon neutral. But it also wasn't what he'd expected if the mission went wrong. He'd thought there would be death, or arrest. Fleeing in the dead of night, perhaps. Defeat.

This was no defeat, even if it wasn't the victory he'd expected. It was better. Thanks, he knew, to his brother's bargaining for them.

That was Zivon. Always needing to be the one moving the game pieces. Always anticipating the patterns and reacting to them.

Always taking care of him.

Nadya finally moved her arm. Put her fingers in his. And nodded.

A *click*. A *whir*. And his brother's laugh.

"What?" Lily grinned. "I wasn't about to let *that* moment go uncaptured."

29

D o you have it yet, milaya?"

Lily pushed away from her retouching desk, smiling over at the door. Zivon leaned into the doorframe, eyes bright behind his glasses. "You mean since you were last sent down to ask ten whole minutes ago?"

His smile sent a lovely wave of warmth flowing through her. She'd thought it would ease by now, but it seemed the opposite had happened. Every time she saw him—especially when it was unexpected—she was hit anew with how much she loved him. "The admiral is impatient. And I do not mind being his errand boy in this case, as well he knows."

No one would ever hear her complain about it. She stood, casting a look over her shoulder, where Mama still held the loupe to the photograph Lily had passed to her five minutes before. "You'll have to ask her. What do you think, Mama? Is it ready?"

She looked up with a sigh—and glinting eyes. "I don't know, Lily Love. The composition is terrible. No effort was made at all to balance foreground and background, and—"

Lily's laughter cut her off. "You'll have to blame the German

359

photographer for that. All I did was change uniforms, faces, and the ships in the background."

"Ah yes. That is *all*." Zivon had apparently moved to her side, given that his voice now came from beside her ear. And his hand slipped into its usual place on her waist.

Mama grinned at them, then at the photo, which she held up. "I see no evidence at all of your hand. It is, as usual, flawless."

It ought to be, given the number of hours she'd poured into that one. She still had the crick in her neck to prove it, too, and lifted a hand to rub at it.

Zivon's fingers brushed hers away, and his thumb dug into the knot in her shoulder. He always knew just where it hid. "Shall we take it up, then?"

"Of course." But she didn't move. In part because it would mean dislodging Zivon's hand . . . but mostly because she knew what this photograph meant. If it worked as the admiral and Zivon thought, then it could well be the last one he ever called on her to create.

If it worked, the German army would think the English were mutinying too.

If it worked, those flames of rebellion on the Continent that had been smoldering and flaring up since August would erupt into a full-out blaze.

If it worked, the war would be over before another week could pass.

She wanted that. Of course she did. It was what she and everyone else here, everyone else *everywhere*, had been striving for these four-and-a-half interminable years. But it would mean a change to everything she'd come to know.

No more reporting here every day. No more Room 40 to report *to*. All the codebreakers would go back to their lives, their real careers. Professors and scholars, linguists and music critics, bankers and students.

Mama came close, handed the picture to Zivon, and gripped Lily's hand. "You have done good work here, Lily Love. I'm proud of you."

"Thank you, Mama." Another something to be grateful for, that her mother had been working alongside her. That Zivon, his name clear, had stayed at his desk upstairs, where everyone knew they could turn to "Old Ziv" for any necessary help with languages. That the admiral had finally come to agree with his advice on how the British forces should, in fact, react to the mutiny.

She was ready for the war to be over. She just wasn't entirely sure what life would look like when it was. They wouldn't need her here, and they wouldn't need her at the hospital much longer, now that male medical personnel were returning to take over. There was no Ivy to plan and laugh with. There were just her forgotten dreams, her camera, her parents . . . and a man who had to be wondering as much as she was what the future would hold.

They'd spoken of everything else—of churches and children and whether they thought it would be a niece or a nephew to be born in Russia in the spring. Of Paris and Moscow and neighborhoods in London where they might be able to find a house for a reasonable price. But he hadn't asked yet the one question she was waiting for. He hadn't presented her with a ring, though he *had* given her a strap for her camera, so she could sling it around her neck, which she'd proclaimed far better than jewelry.

He hadn't said a word about what he meant to do professionally when the war ended. He would have a plan—Zivon always had a plan. But he'd also be listening for the Lord to direct his path. Would they stay here? Or would he instead feel the call to accept one of those teaching positions in America that were still open to him?

Wherever the Lord called, she'd be there. By his side.

She twisted her head so she could smile up at him. "Let's go."

He nodded, though his eyes were on the photograph rather than her. "This really is remarkable, milaya. The admiral will be pleased."

She tucked her hand into the crook of his arm as they walked, smiling as Mama chattered behind them over how ready she was to be able to plant flowers in the garden again instead of vegetables. "I daresay I shall have it positively gorgeous again this spring. We'll have to host another garden party, Lily Love. Or . . . some sort of reception, anyway."

"Mama." Lily laughed, even in the face of the unknowns that remained.

"Mother Effie is not subtle," Zivon said in a stage whisper. If he was trying to keep from grinning, he was utterly failing.

But then, his willingness to join her family wasn't exactly in question either.

They climbed the stairs, strode down the corridor toward the admiral's office, and her mother greeted by name every secretary and cryptographer they passed. When Euphemia Blackwell decided to join something, she did it wholeheartedly.

A lesson Lily had taken to heart. She greeted her colleagues too—and apparently quite a few of them knew what she'd been about in the basement today, because they had a rather long procession by the time Zivon knocked on Hall's door.

"Enter."

He pushed open the door with a flourish and bowed. "Ladies first."

Lily couldn't laugh now. She could only smile a bit, and then a bit more when she saw Daddy folded into a chair before the desk, clearly waiting for them. "Well, Lily White? Have you managed it?"

"Mama says I have—and you daren't argue with *her*." Her grin soon faded as she held out the photograph for Hall's perusal. "I hope it will do, sir. Though it's not a photograph I ever thought to create."

"*Create* being the key word, my dear. Not *take*. Never would you have occasion to take a photo of our boys in revolt." He sat on the edge of his desk, lifted a magnifying glass, and studied the image.

Praise God for that truth. As much despair as she'd seen in the injured soldiers she'd nursed and as she heard in the voices of men home on leave, they'd never lost their determination to see it through. Just their belief that there was a purpose to it.

She glanced over her shoulder at her mother. That would just have to be their job when this was over—showing those lads through their art that there was still something to live for. Something to believe in. There was still a God in heaven, and He still loved His children . . . even when His children had failed to love one another.

Hall looked up, and the half smile on his face told her she'd done her job—this job—well. "Excellent work as always, Miss Blackwell. You have served king and country faithfully and fully." He straightened and barked out, "Elton!"

"Yes, sir?" Margot's husband stepped into the office. Lily hadn't realized he was back in London, but she could never keep up with his comings and goings.

Hall held out the photo. "You're going back to the Continent this evening, correct? See this gets into the hands of Agent Twenty-Two."

Drake nodded and reached for it. "I'll have it to him by morning, sir."

"Good. And then report back here." Hall tugged down his jacket, lifted his chin. "This war is about to end. And I daresay your wife would like you home for the celebration."

MONDAY, 11 NOVEMBER 1918

The eleventh hour of the eleventh day of the eleventh month. Zivon drew in a long breath as he stepped out of the Old Building, knowing that was a refrain that he'd see plastered in every newspaper headline come tomorrow—some even this evening.

Finally, at long last, peace. The guns would be silent. The trenches left behind.

At least in Europe. According to both the official reports and Evgeni's letters, the White and Red Armies were still clashing. His brother never said anything about his hopes—the hopes so opposed to Zivon's—and just related the facts.

Russia remained in upheaval. The Bolsheviks' power didn't appear to be waning.

But his brother was safe. Married. With a child on the way. Perhaps they were still set on advancing in the party. Perhaps all mentions of faith still went unaddressed.

But he had hope. And that wasn't something Zivon would ever take for granted again. Hope for himself, hope for his brother. Hope for his people. The Reds might win now, might stay in control. But Father Smirnov was right—it was in persecution that faith always bloomed. And if he knew anything about the Russian spirit, it was that it could survive the longest of winters. God would see them through it. And when spring came, whether it be in a few months or a few decades, the people would cry out for His touch.

Just as Zivon had done. He strode for the park, winter's night closing in rapidly. It was cold—or so said the others at the OB, who grumbled as they tugged on gloves and hats.

Zivon thought it felt rather mild. A fine day for a stroll in the park, if the light would just grant him twenty more minutes. He lifted a hand to say farewell to a few colleagues. And then lifted it again as he entered the park and spotted Konstantin and Fyodor exiting. They shouted a greeting but didn't slow. Fyodor would be hurrying home to his family, and he and Zivon had seen each other at Mass just yesterday.

Shadows were creeping in too quickly. He picked up his pace still more, not slowing until he rounded the bend on the path and saw her there, kneeling among the brown grass, her camera raised and her attention focused entirely upon a squirrel scavenging for a forgotten nut.

A pattern as familiar to him as breathing. He waited until he heard the *click*, the *whir*. Then he knelt down beside her and whispered in her ear, "What do you see?"

Lily smiled, turned, stole a quick kiss. "Life. Going ever onward." She put her hand in the one he proffered and let him help her to her feet. "You're late. I was beginning to think the admiral had decided to keep you all for an extra shift, just for old times' sake."

He chuckled and wove her fingers through his, though he didn't immediately lead her toward Curzon Street. They had a *few* minutes of daylight left. He meant to make use of them. "On the contrary. He had several of us in a meeting to discuss the future. *Our* future—Room 40's."

She caught her breath. "Is there one? I thought . . ."

Zivon nodded, squeezed her fingers. "It will dissolve after this, yes. A secret to be kept and protected at all costs. But the work cannot stop, milaya, and the Admiralty knows this. They have decided . . ." He paused, looked about. Drew close enough that he could whisper into her ear. "They are starting a school. A cryptography school. I have been asked to join it as an instructor, along with several of the chaps. And Margot, after she finishes the schooling she desires."

"That's wonderful!" She slipped an arm around him. "Right? Isn't it? Is this what you want?"

"To stay here in London, with the people I most admire,

close to the family I call my own, doing the work I love?" He shrugged, held his lips tight. "It will suffice, I suppose."

She laughed and settled at his side with a happy sigh. "You must be so relieved to know what's next."

"Mm. But I confess it is not that *next* to which I have been giving the most thought." He lifted her hand—the left one—and dropped to a knee.

She gasped and brought her other hand to her lips. She had to have known it was coming. But he hoped he managed to surprise her in the moment, at least.

Smiling, he slipped the ruby off his finger and onto hers. It was too big, of course. But she'd forgive it. "I offer you all I am, Lilian Blackwell. All I have. All I have ever fought for or stood for or been willing to die for. You already have my heart. I offer you also my life and every most precious thing in it. Will you be my wife?"

"Yes!" She curled her hand to keep the ring in place and then dropped to her knees beside him and pressed her lips to his.

He kissed her there in the twilight, not caring who saw. And he laughed when she pulled out her camera. "I do not know how you mean to capture *this* one, milaya."

"It might require your help. But I think we can manage it." Grin in place, she fiddled with a few of her dials and levers and then held the camera out as far as her arm would allow, its lens facing them. "You do the push-pin."

He breathed a laugh. And reached for the cord that led to the pin.

A *click*. A *whir*. And a moment he never would have forgotten anyway, now captured forever on her film . . . as she was captured forever in his heart.

Author's Note

When I began the research for this series and read about all the colorful personalities that made up Room 40, I knew I couldn't let THE CODEBREAKERS end without highlighting two of the people who most intrigued me—the Russian who fled the Bolsheviks and joined the cryptographers under Admiral Hall, and the unnamed photography expert who kept DID in a supply of falsified photographs to use against the enemy. Both of these characters have their basis in fact. But, of course, I fictionalized as well.

The real Russian cryptographer was Ernst Fetterlein, who was an Admiral-General in the Imperial Navy and head of Russia's cryptography department, working under the name of Popov (because of the German sound of his actual last name). While he inspired the character of Zivon, I didn't want to use this historical figure entirely, since he was a decade older than I wanted and already had a family. Instead, I used him as Zivon's mentor, borrowed some of his stories—like the scene at the bank and the ruby ring he valued above all—and then made a hero of my own. I enjoyed creating a character with his own unique traits and imagining what it must have been like for a man to go from being the well-respected top of his department in Russia to a suspicious nobody among his English counterparts.

Lily's character is largely fictional. I could find a few mentions of the work done by these staff photographers but not information on the actual people—which meant I was free to make it all up! It was fun (and a bit intimidating) to learn about early cameras and photography and, most of all, to imagine the world through the eyes of someone who sees it best through a camera lens. The photograph used to spur on the mutiny at the end of the war is a true story, which I learned about in *Blinker Hall, Spymaster* by David Ramsay. The massive bombing in London in May 1918 was factual (though not, so far as we know, a result of false information leaked to the Germans) and is referred to by historians as the first real blitz. All other specific occurrences of photos used for the war effort were my imagination.

The Russian Revolution was a complex and long-lasting civil war that I could only scratch the surface of, but I hope through Zivon, Evgeni, and Nadya that I captured just a piece of the Russian heart. I got lost for hours, trying to determine what would have happened to the embassy staff stranded abroad after the February and October Revolutions—Konstantin Nabokov was indeed the ambassador assigned to London at the time, and he wrote a memoir called *The Ordeal of a Diplomat* that tells of his experiences during this trying time. I also found a wonderful little pamphlet about the sole Orthodox church in London and enjoyed bringing the real priest, Evgeny Smirnov, onto the page. The idea that the Bolsheviks would have had a vested interest in keeping the war going by halting the mutiny was fictionalized, but the continued attempt by White supporters to draw America and Britain into the conflict on their side is the true inspiration for my added drama.

I also found it very telling that in Hall's retirement speech not long after the war ended, he not only congratulated his countrymen on the conclusion of this war, but he also warned them to keep an eye on the soviets in Russia, from whom he anticipated a great threat. Insight he'd probably gleaned from many sources, but no doubt chief among them was the Russian on his staff, who did indeed go on to help found the cryptography school that continued to train codebreakers between the two world wars, and whose school eventually led to the founding of Bletchley Park during World War II.

Before I began this story, I'd never given much thought to the Bolshevik point of view, I confess. But in researching it for Evgeni and Nadya, I certainly came to understand the cry for a people's champion, even if I can't approve of the way they went about it. I was especially struck by the Russian women's movements of the day that demanded that institutions like marriage and family be abolished—not just that they no longer be mandatory, but that they in fact be made illegal. But though initial laws were put into effect, I found it rather telling that socialized child-rearing was never really instituted, and marriage certainly persisted too. Because when it comes down to it, ideology can never replace a parent's instinct and drive to love their child and provide a steady home.

And finally, a note on the Spanish Flu that struck the world such a devastating blow in 1918–1919. The flu reached London in June of 1918 and within months had killed more people than the war had. It's estimated that more than fifty million people around the world died from this terrible pandemic. Many more contracted it but recovered. Some languished for days or weeks; others were well in the morning but dead by afternoon. What really baffled the doctors was that it seemed to kill people in the prime of life more often than it did the very young or very old, setting it apart from other strains of the flu.

I hope you've enjoyed THE CODEBREAKERS and their adventures! Special thanks to my family for their patience with me; to Rachel for taking over all she could while I vanished into my writing world; to Elizabeth for checking for American-isms; to Kelli for answering my questions on Russian names; to Steve for pretending I'm his only client (ha!); and to Dave, Jen, Elisa, and the rest of the amazing BHP editorial team for always making my words shine! And, most of all, to the readers who greet those words with enthusiasm. You make it all worthwhile.

Discussion Questions

1. Zivon was forced to flee his homeland in order to preserve his life—and to continue to fight for what he considered the true Russia. How bad would life have to get for you to consider leaving your homeland? Would you determine to settle forever where you landed or would you hope to go home someday?

2. Lily sees the world best through the lens of a camera and finds beauty "in a thousand silent moments." When are you most aware of God's touch in the world around you? Is there anyone in your life who helps you see it when otherwise you might not?

3. Zivon went from being a man of authority to a man at the bottom of the ladder. What difficulties do you think this presented to him? Have you ever been put in a position where you were more qualified than your superiors?

4. What did you think of Lily's early decision to keep her true work a secret from her mother? And about her mother's reaction when she found out? Would you have acted differently at either point?

5. Who is your favorite character? Your least favorite? Why?

6. What did you think of Nadya and Evgeni and their mission? Did you understand their perspective or think them beyond sympathy for all they'd done to Zivon and Alyona?

7. The Russian folktale that Evgeni tells to Claire (in two parts) is my paraphrase of a real one. What were your thoughts about the story? What do you think it means?

8. Several themes about art and its purpose, and what "true" really means in some situations, are woven into this story. How do you feel about art being used to influence or even deceive? Do you think a fiction can ever tell a true story (such as the photo Lily created for Zivon in the beginning)?

9. One of my favorite quotes is that "history doesn't repeat—it rhymes." What "rhymes" did you notice between the world of 1918 and our world today?

10. With the end of this series, this world of thieves, spies, and codebreakers has reached its conclusion. I hope you've enjoyed it as much as I have! If you've read multiple books in THE CODEBREAKERS, SHADOWS OVER ENGLAND, or even LADIES OF THE MANOR series (which are all interconnected), which story most resonates with you now? Which characters do you most love? Are you satisfied with where everyone ended up?

Roseanna M. White is a bestselling, Christy Award–nominated author who has long claimed that words are the air she breathes. When not writing fiction, she's homeschooling her two kids, designing book covers, editing, and pretending her house will clean itself. Roseanna is the author of a slew of historical novels that span several continents and thousands of years. Spies and war and mayhem always seem to find their way into her books . . . to offset her real life, which is blessedly ordinary. You can learn more about her and her stories at www.roseannamwhite.com.

Sign Up for Roseanna's Newsletter

Keep up to date with Roseanna's news on book releases and events by signing up for her email list at roseannamwhite.com.

More from Roseanna M. White

In the midst of the Great War, Margot De Wilde spends her days deciphering intercepted messages. But after a sudden loss, her world is turned upside down. Lieutenant Drake Elton returns wounded from the field, followed by a destructive enemy. Immediately smitten with Margot, how can Drake convince a girl who lives entirely in her mind that sometimes life's answers lie in the heart?

The Number of Love, THE CODEBREAKERS #1

You May Also Like . . .

Rosemary Gresham has no family beyond the thieves that have helped her survive on the streets of London. Pickpockets no longer, they've learned how to blend into high society and now work as thieves for hire. But when a client assigns Rosemary to determine whether a friend of the king is loyal to Britain or Germany, she's in for the challenge of a lifetime.

A Name Unknown by Roseanna M. White
SHADOWS OVER ENGLAND #1
roseannamwhite.com

Haunted by painful memories, Olivia Rosetti is singularly focused on running her maternity home for troubled women. Darius Reed is determined to protect his daughter from the prejudice that killed his wife by marrying a society darling. But when he's suddenly drawn to Olivia, they will learn if love can prove stronger than the secrets and hurts of the past.

A Haven for Her Heart by Susan Anne Mason
REDEMPTION'S LIGHT #1
susananmason.net

When a strange man appears to be stealing horses at the neighboring estate, Bianca Snowley jumps to their rescue. And when she discovers he's the new owner, she can't help but be intrigued—but romance is unfeasible when he proposes they help secure spouses for each other. Will they see everything they've wanted has been there all along before it's too late?

Vying for the Viscount by Kristi Ann Hunter
HEARTS ON THE HEATH
kristiannhunter.com

BETHANYHOUSE

More from Bethany House

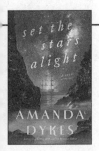

Reeling from the loss of her parents, Lucie Clairmont discovers an artifact under the floorboards of their London flat, leading her to an old seaside estate. Aided by her childhood friend Dashel, a renowned forensic astronomer, they start to unravel a history of heartbreak, sacrifice, and love begun 200 years prior—one that may offer the healing each seeks.

Set the Stars Alight by Amanda Dykes
amandadykes.com

Upon discovering an abandoned baby, Pastor Abe Merivale joins efforts with Zoe Hart, one of the newly arrived bride-ship women, to care for the infant. With mounting pressure to find the baby a home, Abe offers his hand as Zoe's groom. But after a hasty wedding, they soon realize their marriage of convenience is not so convenient after all.

A Bride of Convenience by Jody Hedlund
THE BRIDE SHIPS #3
jodyhedlund.com

Years of hard work enabled Douglas Shaw to escape a life of desperate poverty—and now he's determined to marry into high society to prevent reliving his old circumstances. But when Alice McNeil, an unconventional telegrapher at his firm, raises the ire of a vindictive co-worker, he must choose between rescuing her reputation and the future he's always planned.

Line by Line by Jennifer Delamere
LOVE ALONG THE WIRES #1
jenniferdelamere.com

BETHANYHOUSE